A Soul to Protect

Duskwalker Brides
Book Seven

Opal Reyne

<u>Author's note on language</u>

I'm from AUSTRALIA.

My English is not the same as American English.
I love my American English spoken readers to bits. You're cute, you all make me giggle, and I just wanna give you a big ol' hug. However, there are many of you who don't seem to realise that your English was born from British English, which is what I use (although a bastardised version since Australians like to take all language and strangle it until it's a ruined carcass of slang, missing letters, and randomly added o's).

We don't seem to like the letter z.

We write colour instead of color. Recognise instead of recognize. Travelling instead of traveling. Skilful instead of skillful. Mum instead of mom. Smelt is a past participle of smell. We omit the full-stop in Mr. Name, so it's Mr Name. Aussies cradle the word cunt like it's a sweet little puppy, rather than an insult to be launched at your face.

Anyway, happy reading!

<u>*Trigger Warning*</u>
Major spoiler below

Please only read further if you have triggers, otherwise you will seriously spoil the book for yourself.

Firstly, I will list what triggers **AREN'T** in the book so you can stop reading in order not to spoil it: No purposeful harm done between the characters, torture, physical abuse, cheating, suicide, abortion, incest, drug/alcohol abuse, ow drama, or child harm. No main character death.

Please consider stopping here if your trigger has been detailed above as the rest are major spoilers.

This book contains sensitive and triggering details revolving around rape and domestic violence. None of which is done by our sweet and caring Duskwalker.
I do not go into any flashbacks or on page details, so as to not disturb the reader too deeply. I've attempted to skirt around it as best and as respectfully as I can. However, this trauma is quite startling, and the healing process is hard to swallow. Linh doesn't wish to look back on it, but it is there. You will go through her healing with her, and there may be potential triggers revolving around particular, heart-wrenching details. She is depressed, but quite a sunshine despite her pain.

I also try to combat this with humour, and as much heartwarming and very naughty smut as I could shove into the book.

Nathair is suffering from a special kind of Duskwalker eating disorder. It is not like a human eating disorder. He is also suffering through a magical disorder involving voices, that sometimes lead to accidental self-harm.

There is a vorarephilia and snake phobia triggers – due to Nathair being part serpent. However, I have tried to make him very sexy, so hopefully this is a quality many are able to overlook!

Breeding kink. One anal scene. Epilogue pregnancy.

As always with my books, there is gore.

To all the serpent loving MonsterFuckers out there,

this book is for you.

Will he have one peen or two peens? Will he coil his long tail around you for some sweet, therapeutic cuddles, or will he smother you with his lust? One thing is for certain, he is big, he is long, and he is deadly.

Enjoy our danger-noodle.

I would like to give a big shoutout to the wonderful **sensitivity readers** who helped to make this book a safe place for those I am trying to positively represent. As you all know, representation is a big part of what I want to do, but I want to do so in a way that isn't harmful.

Thank you to Susan, Marcella, Emily, Sue, Charna, and Amanda for your contribution towards Asian sensitivity.

Thank you to Rosie, Jonah, Kay, and Rebecca for your contribution towards disability sensitivity.

I would also like to give a special thank you to Crystal for your contribution towards BIPOC, disability, and overall sensitivity.

I appreciate all the time and effort you put into helping me with this book. You will forever have a place in my heart.

PROLOGUE

Curled up at the bottom of his lake, Nathair attempted to ignore his creator's bellowing. *Leave me be.*

The gills on both sides of his neck opened and closed, yet he couldn't perceive the comforting flow of water easing in and out of them. His lungs, which usually expanded and compressed on land, were still as oxygen entered his bloodstream from the capillaries connected to his gills.

Then again, if he so chose it, his lungs could have remained still within Tenebris. Much like missing the comforting flow of water, he breathed on the land within the afterworld to attempt a sense of normality.

Normality he was never given – until the abnormality had become life. Until it was all he knew.

"Nathair!" Weldir yelled once more, likely standing next to Nathair's flat lazing rock.

He just rolled his head before burrowing beneath the coil of his tail even further to block him out. Hopefully Weldir didn't come to stand under the water as if it didn't exist, since he'd done that a few times with his hands on his hips to show vexation at Nathair's antics.

Why must he insist on speaking with me when it is obvious I do not wish to? Were those not the actions of a foolishly insane being? To repeatedly do something, to persist over centuries, despite the result never changing?

Nathair was tired of repeated conversations. He was exhausted of learning about the outside world beyond Weldir's soul-confining stomach. What use was there in sharing with Nathair the new thing the deity had discovered?

The world suddenly came out from under him as he was sucked to the surface against his will. Nathair clawed at the dirt to keep himself beneath the surface, only to be dumped on land seconds later. Droplets didn't stick to his scales, but rather dragged off him when he was unwillingly forced from the lake.

In a rapid strike, he orientated himself, spun to Weldir, and hissed. Two fangs, long and once deadly, fell from the roof of his maw. His lower jaw segments split in the middle, revealing the patch of flesh that kept them together.

Weldir, the little shit, bashed the bottom of his chalky fist against the top of Nathair's skull so hard he was sent hurdling to the ground.

"Don't hiss at me, you ill-mannered snake," Weldir growled.

Opening and closing his maw, Nathair mocked him by pretending to speak as he lifted himself on straightened arms. With his orbs an angry crimson, his tail slithered underneath his body until he was able to support his humanoid torso. Then Nathair threw his arms to the side, silently asking what he wanted.

All the while, Nathair ignored the chatter in the back of his mind – dozens of voices that refused to relent. The cause of his lack of voice, the screams that overshadowed his own. The mess of memories that tangled with the few he knew belonged to him.

Some moments, his will to hold them back was strong. If he went without a long rest, they broke through the metaphorical barrier of his will, and ate him alive. Which, given the fact he rarely slept, was quite often.

He'd been suffering a sleepless life for what felt like eons.

Weldir, a cloudy version of himself with a chalky centre, glared at him. Nearing Weldir's usual eight-foot height, they saw eye to orb. Staring into Weldir's black eyes, that didn't show a single bit of white nor iris, had once been daunting. They were like voids, an abyss that stared back at him, threatening to suck Nathair into their dark depths.

Now, they just irked him.

"Good," Weldir stated, nodding his head in approval. "I can see you're lucid today."

Lucid? Rarely. His mind was never stable, and even now it threatened to weakly collapse. *I wish he would hurry. I need more rest.*

After teasing Aleron, his silly sibling, he'd used up his rare lucidity to... *play* with him. He chuckled every time he remembered. Although he was sure Aleron would be rather annoyed for quite some time, it was one of the few new memories he'd obtained in Tenebris that wasn't soaked in boredom or a haze.

He'd forever cherish it.

An image flashed within Nathair's grip on his sight, and he winced at the blur of it speeding past. Once quiet, a scream bombarded his senses. He managed to swiftly wrangle it back where it belonged – in his subconscious.

Noticing some kind of tell, even though Nathair hadn't moved a muscle, Weldir sighed.

"I wish I could give you back your voice," Weldir grumbled, remaining unmoving as well. He didn't often move, as if the urge only came consciously, rather than an instinctual muscle reaction like every other living creature.

Wanting to get past the useless repetition of Weldir's wants and wishes, since he'd been saying them for centuries, Nathair spoke with his hands. He wiped two fingers on top of two on his opposing hand and then touched the tip of his claws – knowing he'd understand.

The point, Weldir, he thought.

The sign language they'd created was unique. Nathair had been here for hundreds of years, and without his voice for much of it. Weldir hadn't liked that he couldn't speak with his own child, so they made what Weldir liked to call 'Nathair speak.'

Nathair had no idea if he was speaking an actual sign language from a specific country, but doubted it, as he and Weldir created many of the gestures themselves. He also used his orb colour changes purposefully, since he didn't have skin upon his face to mimic an emotion to go with them.

This, unfortunately, meant he couldn't sign like a human.

"I want to preface this with the truth: I am unsure of what will happen, or if it will work," Weldir started, holding up a clawed finger. "I also ask that you do not take this in the worst way possible, but I am choosing you to experiment with, as you have no earthly ties."

Purposefully shifting his orbs to a dark yellow to signify his curiosity, he tilted his serpent skull.

Weldir noted it and then shook his head. "It is not that I care less about you. Aleron has Ingram, and they are not doing well apart. Should something go wrong, this gives me a chance to try again without damaging his soul. You have been here for so long that I wish the best for you as well, but..."

Nathair raised his hand to stop him.

He understood, and he also cared very little about whatever reasonings he had. He trusted in Weldir's judgement, trusted that if he put him in a dangerous situation, he had the best intentions.

He had no reason to think otherwise.

He refuses to let go of his guilt. It was not Weldir's fault that he didn't know destroying a Mavka's skull would kill them. Yet, he always tried to make amends, while never being able to, since the only way was to bring Nathair back to life.

Nathair tapped his dominant index finger on top of his left wrist, telling him to hurry up.

"Fine. Here." Weldir brought his chalky hands forward, and a skull materialised within his palms.

Cupping the lower segments of his jaw, Nathair lowered his torso to gain a closer look at his own skull. *The last time I saw this, it was in pieces.* It had once been harrowing to look upon it, but he'd gotten over it. Nearly two hundred and eighty years had passed, and he'd long ago accepted it.

He'd also forgiven Merikh, as neither had known what would happen. The truth was, Nathair could have been the one to kill Merikh had he ever grabbed his bear skull hard enough to shatter it. That journey of acceptance and forgiveness had been long, but one he made in the many years he'd been here.

Nathair pointed a claw at the multiple golden hairline cracks keeping it together, noticing it glittered in a way that was unnatural for ore.

"I asked Aleron to meet with the Gilded Maiden, and she offered me a fragment of her crown. In doing so, she has given me the ability to repair your skull. My theory is that I should be able to use her magic and my own to bond your soul back to your skull."

Nathair pointed to the ground, then his sternum, before he moved his hand in a circle just in front of his skull. Then he fisted his hand and pulled it to his abdomen before pointing down to the ground. *This is my skull. You kept it for this?*

Nathair leaned back and folded his arms in thought.

"Yes. I held onto it in hopes I could one day bring you back with it." Then Weldir peeked down at it as if inspecting it, his voice quietening as he said, "If it's successful, I can then also return Aleron to his twin."

Ughhh. Nathair dropped his head to the side in annoyance and audibly groaned. *I have little interest in being returned.*

His life here in the afterworld wasn't too bad. Sure, there was no progress, but it was also peaceful. He rested, and he rather liked being lazy. Other than hunting, he did exactly what he'd done on Earth – which was nothing but sunbake. He had no need for goals, as he never truly had one to begin with.

Much had changed in the afterworld. He'd watched it grow, change, and form with every new soul Weldir consumed and drew power from.

It had once been dark in many places where no light or

shadow could reach. Just a vast amount of nothingness. Nathair had watched it change into the bright world it currently was and had even helped partially shape it. He'd demanded lakes and waterfalls to play in, even if the water was false and felt unnatural.

If this helps the bat-skull Mavka, then I will assist. It was the only reason Nathair would agree to it. He'd feel guilty if he didn't try, and then that would gnaw on his conscience like a scale ache.

He was tired of feeling guilty for his siblings' sake, as he was quite aware of how his death had twisted Merikh into a spiteful being.

I can just be lazy in the living world as well.

"Lindiwe will be waiting for you when you come back to life," Weldir explained. Seeing Nathair had easily been won, Weldir brought his detached skull closer. "Should you need anything, she will be there for you."

As if he was putting on a hat, or perhaps a well-fitted shoe, the skull clung to his form as though it longed for its owner. There was no resistance. Although he didn't look much different to himself, he instantly noted how his claw tips turned ghostly.

Before long, an orange spectral form completely covered him, and his head felt... heavier. He lifted his hand to inspect how his soul covered his entire body and wasn't a tiny flame.

"How do you feel?" Weldir asked as he floated back.

Nathair shrugged in answer. Perhaps due to still being within Tenebris, the biggest change was that his gut twisted with hunger. *I remember it being worse before.*

However, the moment he was taken from Weldir's stomach and set upon the living world, Nathair's sense of smell bombarded him. That gut twist rotated further. Hunger, more prevalent now that he'd been without it for so long, became cruel and unrelenting within his mind.

A sharp gust of wind rustled the frosted autumn foliage around him, and it was entirely too loud compared to the muteness of Tenebris. The bright sun was somehow blinding, and the scents of the grass, the dirt, and the trees were too strong against his inexperienced senses.

And the chill... the one that surrounded him due to the oncoming winter, invaded him like blades beneath each of his scales. His lukewarm-bloodedness, the reason he instinctually sought the sun and warmth, shoved in like an ice shard lancing his sternum. It shattered and bled coolness within him.

The lucidity he'd gained a solid grip on was released, and he let out a roar when chatter instantly made him squirm.

Red infiltrated his sight as he gripped his skull, clawing at it, needing to *silence* it. He didn't care how. He bashed it against the ground, the nearest thick tree trunk. Even if it broke him once more, he wanted his skewed peace back!

He pleaded, he begged, but those words never left his thoughts. His whines of pain, of distress, all of which broke low in his throat and chest, echoed within the forest. His mind's speaking was still present, but he could no longer project it past his skull.

Had he not gorged on dozens of souls during a time in which Weldir had rested, this never would have happened. He'd hurt his creator by doing so, had prolonged his weakened rest, and hurt himself in the process.

Nathair would never have gained the humanity, intelligence, or knowledge he now possessed. A blessing yet a terrible curse that outweighed it.

He'd been hurtled into a much brighter mental state, yet it had cracked his mind. Weldir had rescued him at his worst. When the memories of all the souls he'd consumed ate away at Nathair's consciousness, his subconscious, and every part of his mind, Weldir had removed all that he could.

Unfortunately, scars had been left behind. Ruminative fragments. Memories that refused to leave him, voices that had pestered him for centuries until they blended with his own. He'd been many people, had faced many deaths. He became them, or they became him, and they never ceased, never left him be.

And, as he was thrown back into the chaos of life, they, too, demanded a chance to live it.

The Veil lay just behind him, barely a short distance away, but its existence meant little to him. The air, the pleasant forest scents, the warm sunlight he was bathed in... he couldn't enjoy any of it. All he felt was suffering in every drop of his physical and mental being.

Make it stop. Nathair bent his body forward and whined as he dug his claws into the underside of his skull from behind, trying to rip it from his shoulders. To remove it so he could have quietness, to have control. *Make it stop!*

Warmth cupped the undersides of his skull, and a face became clear in the murk of his sight.

A woman with brown skin and dark curling hair looked up at him with comforting and welcoming eyes. She spoke to him, her voice gentle, beseeching, and soothing.

Her scent was strong. Her blood pounded viciously in his ears and mind, making them throb. The pulsating of it only pushed him further into madness.

Lower jaw segments parting, he struck with the suddenness of lightning. When he shut his maw together, he clasped air.

The scent was gone, as was the sound of her inviting pulse.

"Nathair," she called.

He let out a hiss as he spun to her, finding she'd turned as intangible as air. Her mostly white cloak of feathers floated around her body, as if a tiny gust within the afterlife lifted them.

"Shhh, little one," the Witch Owl cooed as she regained her physical form.

A mistake. The moment her scent and sounds of life bombarded him, he raked his claws sideways towards her. She managed to turn her face to the side quick enough to only be slashed across the cheek.

She cupped it, as the sickly sour aroma of cloaking magic bled into the sun-filled gap they were in. It did little to help, only hiding the scent of blood and confusing him. He recoiled from her presence.

To escape the coldness, the scents, the harshness of the world, his trembling form coiled around itself. In 'S' shapes and figure-eight patterns, he attempted to hide within the sanctity of his tail while holding his aching skull. *Make it stop... please.* He felt as though it would burst at any moment, but the dozens of human voices refused to relent.

They wanted out. *He* wanted them out. Freedom from their torture, his torture.

Light pressure settled onto him from above. Hidden within himself as a barrier of scent and partial sound, the warmth provided was the only thing that became soothing. The longer it remained, bleeding heat, the more he wanted to bring the Witch Owl into his folds.

He didn't let her sink within him due to her sickly magic aroma making the hunger worse. His gut would gurgle, bubbling with an emptiness as if it wanted to punish him for being without it for centuries. His inexperience with it made him forget how clutching and cruel it had been.

"It's okay, Nathair," Lindiwe cooed, as he felt a light tap tap of a hand. "You have not been here for a long time, but I will remain by your side until you readjust. We'll find you a home before the frost of winter settles in."

Winter? Nathair let out a tiny whimper. How could they bring him, a lukewarm-blooded Mavka, back right before winter? *Fucking idiots!*

"All that matters is you've returned. Weldir told me something ails your mind. Hopefully I can aid you."

Aiding him would be to send him back to Tenebris. To serenity, calmness, and all the quietness that came with it. There would be little she could do, as her power was only a fraction of the god's she borrowed it from.

She'd be of no help. He was doomed.

I shouldn't have agreed to this. The most harrowing part of that thought: it had not been his own. A woman's voice rung within his mind. Nathair saw white, just as a scream pierced his consciousness and the face of a Demon tore out his, *her* – their – throat.

No. Please, he pleaded with dread, clawing at the sides of his skull. His orbs switched between blue and white as fear choked him. *I don't want to relive their deaths.*

The dozens of human souls he'd eaten always left the same fragment behind. Their final breaths, all of which had been filled with panic and terror, and were accompanied by the image of a Demon. Their pain became his own, and he shuddered at the woman's.

He didn't want to experience these harrowing last moments in the forefront of his consciousness again.

He wasn't given a choice.

His entire body locked up, and his mind slipped away.

ONE

Present day – 4 months later

Unlatching the lock that had been broken weeks ago, Linh quietly removed the cast-iron shackle from her ankle. She winced, her face pulling tight, when chains clanked together as she settled it upon the ground. The thin cloth below her did little to keep the chilly earth from assaulting her backside.

She checked that her captor remained asleep, his pile of travel bedding rising and falling with steadied breaths. It likely hadn't been changed in years, considering it reeked of his body odour.

Linh shuddered in disgust and crawled on her hands and knees to get away from him. *Winter is almost over. It's safe now.*

Being so far north, the area could become rather barren during the snowy season. Spring was in a few days. Although the mornings were rather cold and dewy, and the nights harsh and cruel, she refused to stay.

She could have survived another month here. It would be wiser if she did, but she also just… couldn't risk it.

My period ended. She hadn't told her 'husband' it ended a day ago. She always played that it was long and gruelling, but Linh was smart enough to not let it drag on. He would have caught on and started checking for the truth otherwise.

She had a day of peace, and to let her body fully heal: *I'm so glad it came.* She didn't know if she would have had the strength to escape had she known this bastard had gotten what he wanted from her.

Digging her bag of belongings from underneath unwashed clothes and hide armour stained with dirt and dried blood, she didn't need to check its contents. She wouldn't waste time doing so.

The satchel held another garment, her second pair of shoes, and a jacket she would throw on once she'd left this ugly grey tent. Like an animal preparing for hibernation, she'd been eating sparingly so she could tuck away what may last a few days within the bag. She stole Bragg's water sack because fuck him – she needed it.

After pushing her feet within a pair of slippers and clipping their straps firmly on, she crawled to the corner of the tent opposite the entryway flap. With his dagger, which she also intended to steal, Linh cut a section of thread and opened it.

Frozen night air instantly stung her nose, but the chill was blessed.

Once she was outside, she ducked down when she heard a few stragglers still awake. That was fine, as she'd already mapped her way to freedom and considered a few drunken idiots may still be carousing. She'd exited the tent into darkness which would shield her, rather than within torchlight.

She skulked to the closest wall of the encampment, then followed it to the northern exit. A guard came into view, and she pressed against the wall.

I just need to wait. The guard barring her freedom disappeared momentarily – who cared what the reason was, so long as he temporarily left.

The moment she was outside of the camp, she put her back against the wall. The short, criss-crossing wooden logs in front of her were a sharp reminder of what danger lingered in the night. Beyond them, the valley of many dark mountains was outlined by the twinkling navy sky.

Her lips flattened with terror, while her brows narrowed in determination. *I'd rather take my chances with a Demon.*

With her satchel secure around her torso and her jacket on, Linh bit her lips together and shifted her weight between her feet.

I can do this, Linh told herself. *I have a few hours before he wakes.* Just a few hours to put as much distance as she could between her and the bandits who had taken her.

She leapt into a sprint.

Wind rustled past her ears and pushed back the stray hairs that had fallen from her braided bun. Her feet crunched in the dirt, dust, and mountain rock. Her racing heart filled her with warmth, even as her fingers grew numb from the cold.

Eyeing the top of a mountain cliff directly to her right, Linh groaned at the deadliness of her situation.

No. Don't be afraid.

It was either face the possibility of a Demon, or go back – and she'd claw, kick, and bite before she ever went back to that hellhole of a camp. She'd put the dagger to her throat before she let Bragg drag her back by her long black hair to his bed. Or she'd sink it inside his gut – whichever method gave her freedom.

Her breaths sawed in and out, frantic and tired. Despite their quietness, they sounded so loud against the canyon of rock. They reverberated against the trees as she swiftly entered a thin forest. Her footsteps thudded against the ground, occasionally slipping due to the nightly dew settling in. Although usually rather clumsy, she managed to keep her footing.

Throughout the night, Linh only ever rested by quickly leaning against a boulder or a fallen tree to massage her aching legs. She winced at the pain in her right foot, and fixed her calf-high sock bunched around the heel of her shoe. Then she unwrapped last night's vegetables and shoved them into her hungry maw, as they would surely expire soon.

I can't return home. As much as she wanted to, longed to,

and knew she would be welcomed with open arms, she didn't wish to endanger her people.

Cupping her side, she tried to settle her seizing lungs and the stitch radiating across the left side of her torso. Limping, she blinked rapidly to fight the tears welling.

Why can't I just go south? Away from the hope of her family being closer with each step.

She knew the answer: the last time she went south, she'd been captured within minutes by Bragg's men. Going southward through the beginning of the mountain's canyon would have been suicide due to the Demons. The campsite down that way had more men patrolling it for danger.

Linh had been forced to go north, where she was more likely to escape successfully. But it'd take her weeks to go around the eastern mountain, and west was a death trap of falls and slips straight into the ocean.

She sniffled as weeks of fright, pain, and horror twisted her heart. Her chest radiated with hurt she doubted she'd ever shed, and trauma she didn't know she would ever heal from. *I just want to go home.*

At the tender age of twenty-one, crying for one's parents was usually frowned upon. Yet, all she wanted was her loving parents to bring her into the fold of a tight and much-needed cuddle.

I want my mum and dad.

She wanted the warmth of her fellow villagers, the laughter of her few friends, and the guidance of her mother. She wanted to prank her father or have him be his goofy self. She wanted to tease her younger sister. She wanted to go back to the life she'd been taken from, and knew without a doubt she couldn't return to it without endangering them.

They were already in danger.

From Bragg and his soldiers, from the Demons the men swore to protect them from while also robbing them. They starved them of much-needed trade, with every intention of abandoning them once the two villages in this part of the world had been stripped of their usefulness.

I have to go east, Linh told herself as she wiped her frozen face and settled her shuddering breaths. *I have to go to Duneside.* The town near Mount Vernant.

From there, she could explain to them who she was, and where she'd just come from. Their people were being choked just as much as her own village, and she doubted their mayor would hand her back to the cretins. They could help her go northeast around the mountain and travel down to Slater Town for aid.

It's really risky, though. And likely why they hadn't already done so. *I'll go by myself if I need to.*

A branch or stick cracking in the distance made her gasp, and she quickly bolted into action once more.

I need to keep moving. She couldn't stop for too long.

Day broke just as she was crossing empty fields, and Linh turned a longing glance towards the western peaks of this mountain range. Despite the light mist, the snowy peaks glowed in the sunlight cresting from the east. Linh turned towards the brightening horizon.

With her brows narrowed in spiteful determination, she made a vow. One that she made on each fogged breath, and in the lance of pain that jolted up her legs from each hard footfall. One that sang in each of her quick heartbeats that shunted pain throughout her chest, warning her she needed to stop running or it'd give out.

I'll come back. I promise I'll come back.

When she did, she'd bring an army to finally set them all free.

TWO

I can't, Linh thought with anguish, keeling over to breathe. Placing her hands on her knees to steady herself, her whole torso arched as she heaved. *I can't run anymore.*

She needed to rest, a break from running. Her hands shook as much as her legs from the exertion. Her feet were killing her, and she was so hot she bet her face was blotchy. At this rate, she was going to break out in hives.

Once she'd stopped hacking up a lung, she pinched the neckline of her lavender Ao Dai garment so she could pull it away from her body. She flapped the dress, moving air inside it as well as fanning her overheated face.

She licked at her dry lips; it wouldn't be long before they started to crack. There was no point in reaching for the water sack, since it'd long been empty. Instead, she limped while pulling an apple from her bag, hoping to feed and hydrate herself at the same time.

Her gaze lowered to her slippers, and she grimaced at how muddy her socks were. At least the bottoms of her grey linen pants only had a few speckles on them, likely due to the internal ribbon keeping them snug around her ankles.

Supporting herself on a nearby tree trunk, she wiped the sweat from her forehead. Although her head pounded with heat and high blood-pressure, the air was cold. The tendrils of winter were still fading, and the constant shade of the forest didn't allow the earth to truly warm.

If I keep going like this, I'm going to vomit. She'd been running on and off for at least fourteen hours. The sun was past its highest peak, and she'd barely stopped moving.

No matter how far she ran, it didn't feel like enough.

An oppressive, dark energy nipped at her heels, pushing her forward in fear. The further she got, the more she worried her newfound freedom would be ripped away. Her anxieties weren't getting better, they only worsened. She thought it may be more painful if she tasted freedom, only to be barred back in a cage of tent walls with a new shackle at her ankle.

Her face drained of heat. *If he catches me...* Her stomach churned at the fate she knew awaited her.

"Don't think about it, Linh Nguyen," she told herself, throwing her apple core to the side. "Just keep going. Duneside is half a day's walk from here."

She refused to look west, knowing that her hometown, Ashpen Village, was directly that way. She was about halfway between the two towns, despite being far more east along the cape.

Every step towards Duneside only brought on more worry.

I thought I could go there, but... Shit, she hadn't thought about the bandit soldiers situated inside both towns, which were there for their 'protection.'

Bragg's main camp was designed to keep humans from aiding them, and Demons from rushing through the middle of the two mountains. Safety at the cost of their freedom.

I'll have to forage. She could do that, since she'd been learning the trade her entire life. She could point out what was poisonous or edible just by looking or sniffing.

Why hasn't the northern Demonslayer guild sent people to help us yet? They were supposed to protect them, yet they'd been suffering for *months* at the hands of bandits.

Shaking her head once more, figuring they had good reason for abandoning them, Linh paused when she heard trickling. Her expression grew lax, then her eyes widened.

Is that...? Despite her aching body, she hobbled as she ran, chasing after the sound. *Yes! Water!* She followed the tiny stream's westerly flow.

Linh nearly wept when she came upon a small pond. Only a few metres wide, both sides of its oval mouth were collections of boulders and stone. The water dropped down as if it'd been made via a sinkhole, and she could see cracked earth through the grass surrounding it.

Linh didn't care how it was formed, only that it existed.

Rolling up her long sleeves, she dipped her hands into the water. It was clear, but she sniffed it to make sure it didn't have any pungent odours. As much as she would have preferred to boil it, she still sipped it. Refreshing and much needed, she scooped handfuls of it to her mouth.

Quenching the worst of her thirst, she opened the water sack and watched it bubble as it filled. As if she couldn't help herself, needing to gorge on it in case she didn't come across another water source in future travels, she scooped more to drink.

Her tired reflection rippled as she slurped, but she ignored the wispy strands of black hair that stuck out around her head. Her eyes shone a rich brown in the sunlight, glittering with the patterns of the water.

She washed her face, removing the grime and sweat from her skin from running. She even rinsed her neck.

Just as she scooped another handful, she hurled out a gasp and fell to her backside. *I saw a face!* Or something... *like* a face. Then again, it'd been rather pale, like a skull.

If there are dead bodies in the water, it'll make me sick. But it had smelt and tasted fine, and waterlogged bodies would generally leave a distinct taste in it. There would also be more bugs in the water, but she hadn't seen any.

With her eyes wide and stark, she leaned forward. *Oh god, please let it only be a hallucination.* Cautiously, she peeked over the rocky edge.

Nothing. She rubbed her eyes before checking once more.

With the surface unmoving, she saw nothing in the deep darkness. The walls of the pond appeared to be made of stone, rather than mud, and nothing moved beneath the surface.

A sigh of relief fluttered past her shaking lips, and she sagged to the side. *Just a hallucination.* Unsurprising, considering she hadn't slept in what must have been over thirty-six hours. She'd stayed up all night to make sure she could escape.

I need rest. As much as she didn't want to, she crawled to the boulders to her right so she could lean against them. She soaked in the warmth cascading over her. *I can't run forever. I need sleep.*

Sitting upright, she rolled her head against the boulder to glance towards the water, a little spooked by it. At least the sun would keep her safe from any Demons. A bubble popped at the surface of the water, but she thought little of it as her exhausted eyes slitted with a heaviness before they started to close.

Just a few minutes. She could hopefully afford to close her eyes for a little while. Sitting upright would ensure she didn't sleep long, as the ground beneath her arse, the rock at her back, and the position she was in were all insanely uncomfortable.

Just a few...

Linh gasped when something tapped against the side of her cheek, and her eyes flung open. At the man's face in front of her, one that had a horrible smirk across it, she let out an ear-splitting scream.

She never got the chance to jump to her feet to run from one of Bragg's underlings, nor to truly settle from her shock. A cry ripped from her when he grabbed the ball of her braided bun and dragged her across the ground as she kicked her legs. She reached up and clung to his wrist, trying to take away the pain.

The area was shaded, dusk quickly descending upon them.

Her features twisted up in anguish when she realised she'd fallen asleep for hours. Her body ached from being in a seated position, and all her exhaustion made her too weak to truly fight back.

"We knew we'd find you," Glendil stated with a chuckle, his blond ponytail shifting side to side as he shook his head. He tossed her against the ground.

Randy then lunged for her, pinning her legs to the ground as he went to bind her hands. His long, auburn beard almost tickled her nose as she struggled to get away.

"You know he's pissed, right?" Randy stated, his blue eyes cold and unfeeling. "He warned you he'd cut one of your Achilles tendons next time you ran away. He doesn't care if you limp, only that you've got a pretty face and a warm–"

Linh belted out another scream as her struggles doubled. "Get off me! Leave me alone!" Tears instantly welled in her eyes, as a fear so harrowing bled into her veins like ice. "Please!"

She just wanted to be free! She'd rather die than go back there – to *him*.

"Shut the fuck up!" Randy yelled, slamming his fist into the dirt next to her head. She refused! She kicked harder and screamed louder, knowing he couldn't hurt her unless he wanted to experience Bragg's wrath. "Fuck, Glendil. Help me get a rag in her mouth."

A beastly, inhuman, hissing roar sounded from below her feet. Water sprayed through the air like a mighty wave. Then Randy was gone from above her.

Linh gasped as a gigantic black... *something* dived above her, tackling Randy to the ground in a swipe of claws. The sheer mass of it, the length of it, was so utterly daunting, and the end of its tail landed on her stomach.

When the breath slammed out of her due to the weighty limb, she retched, crossing her arms over her torso as her knees came up. Her entire body clenched as if she'd been punched in the stomach before it slithered off and away.

When she sat up and spun on her backside, Linh kicked her feet to get away from the monster that had unwittingly saved her. Her back met the boulders she'd slept against, and she brought her knees up to make herself smaller.

Oh my god, what is it?! It didn't look like a Demon. At least, not like any she'd seen! It was also so long and big – she'd never heard of such a large monster.

Glendil, brave but undeniably stupid to think he could take it on, charged with two hands firmly on the hilt of his claymore. While the creature ripped off an arm belonging to Randy, who yelled and screamed, Glendil sunk his blade through its torso until it came out the other side. He tried to yank it out, but his tugs proved futile.

A white serpent skull splashed in blood turned to Glendil with a bone-chilling hiss. Two long fangs dropped and lengthened as it removed the blade itself and turned. The monster lunged, diving for the man with such a swiftness he only had enough time to pull out a dagger. It sunk its fangs into the crook of his neck and shoulder as Glendil stabbed it multiple times. Anywhere and everywhere he could reach, dark-purple blood splattered as its side was opened.

The attacks did little to stop it, and Glendil eventually sagged the longer its fangs remained. The dagger fell to the grass with a quiet thud.

The third and final bandit had his battle axe prepared, but his eyes were stark and wide. He was too frightened to move.

So was Linh as she took in the enormity of its serpent body.

Its long tail, spanning metres in length, supported a humanoid torso. White bones protruded from its ribcage, the knuckles of its hands, and the hundreds of vertebrae down its spine and tail. Black serpent scales glinted with a rainbow sheen. Menacing claws tipped its blood-soaked hands, and it turned them towards the last man, who went visibly pale at having a set of crimson floating orbs upon him.

He screamed as he ran, heading for the shade of the forest.

Massive fins darted from its back, appearing out of nowhere to create one giant sail, as it gave chase with a roar. The last bandit barely made it into the tree line before he needed to swiftly turn. He sunk his axe into its chest, cutting deep, but it was too late.

In a singular swipe of claws, it tore open his throat and chest. He gurgled, cupping his throat to stem the bleeding.

Linh covered her mouth to stifle her whimper, shaking her head as the creature opened its maw and bit around the bandit's head. Her fearful tears from earlier fell faster, but she knew she had to steady herself.

Her gaze darted to the gloaming sky and then back to the monster, noticing the way the light glistened against the scales covering its back. Linh absorbed its snake skull, watching as the lower segments of its jaw separated so it could easily swallow an arm. It appeared it wanted to eat the man piece by piece before it just started trying to shove his limbless torso into its mouth.

It has a skull. Demons don't have skulls. Her nails dug into her cheeks. *A Duskwalker?*

How the fuck did a Duskwalker get to the northwest cape of Austrális? They would have known about it. It couldn't have wandered through the mountain gorge without Bragg knowing of it. Or maybe he did and considered it too big of a challenge to confront.

Finally removing her hands from her mouth, she cupped them to her chest. *Breathe, Linh. Breathe.* She tried to settle, to remove her scent of fear from the air. Closing her eyes, she ignored it eating the men, especially when it doubled back to eat Randy still bleeding out. *Go numb.*

Glendil, from what she could tell by his chest moving, was alive but paralysed, as if he'd been envenomed. He bled from the puncture wounds in his shoulder.

D-Duskwalkers are considered intelligent... right? One could even bargain for a bride by offering a protection ward. *T-that means they can talk, and not kill humans if they choose it.*

She winced and then recoiled at the sound of skin tearing and bones cracking, but shuddered in another breath. She let it out, and calmed her heart rate along with it, utilising a skill she hated to suppress her fear. She peeked open a singular eye.

It's not attacking me? She warily watched it, refusing to move or make a single noise in case she caught its attention. Cringing, she watched Randy's bag slip from his limbless body and crash against the ground when the Duskwalker split open its maw to swallow that too.

Once more, she thought, *It's not attacking me.* Her fear ebbed as hope bled into her veins. *Did it hear me scream? Did it... protect me?* She wanted to believe that was true. It was better than the alternative: that Linh had accidentally led a four-course meal to it, with her being the dessert.

Glendil, still alive but unmoving, was disposed of quickly.

For a long while, it moved its blunt snout towards the three pools of blood, its clawed hands opening and closing. With its tail coiled up underneath it, and its back to her, it just sat there, *searching.*

Then it quaked while crossing its arms over its torso. It dug its own claws into its shoulder blades, and sunk into itself, coiling its meaty tail over its torso. The Duskwalker continued to shiver and shudder as it wrapped itself into a ball.

Purple blood glistened against its scales, pouring from it in rivulets, and it hissed at nothing, only to whimper moments later.

When nothing seemed to give it what it wanted, it leapt out of its coil and slithered to the water's edge. With orbs white, it dipped a hand into the pond's surface, only to yelp and back up.

Something is wrong with it.

Either it didn't know she was there, or her existence had been forgotten amidst all the blood. Maybe it didn't care, like she was too small to be good prey. Less than a foot away, it was so close to her that she could have kicked her leg out and bashed at the base of its tail.

Should she move? She darted her foot away when the tip of its serpent tail brushed over the top of her ankle.

Snapping in her direction, the Duskwalker's skull loomed

over her. One moment white, the next red, its orbs flickered between the two as it took her in. It towered ever closer, dauntingly blocking out the last of the sun.

Oh gods! She sprung to her feet when it looked like it was about to lunge and barely made it a step before she was tackled.

Her scream was instantly muffled by a writhing limb curling around her. Linh expected to be eaten. Instead, soft scales brushed over her as she was swallowed up by its body.

The quaking from earlier was far more intense now that she was in the middle of it. She felt it in the way muscles contracted, pulling and releasing in pulses. The Duskwalker tightened around her, but she never felt its head near her – not the puff of breath or the hardness of bone. Just a dense body trying its absolute hardest to envelop her.

Unable to help it, the constriction sent her heart racing. She struggled to breathe, unsure if that was due to her terror or her air being blocked.

A growl reverberated from the Duskwalker, seeming to travel down each of its protruding vertebrae to vibrate her. It squashed her until the pressure was constricting and painful.

"I can't breathe," she choked out, unsure if it would care.

The tighter the pressure surrounding her from everywhere became, the less afraid she was. Gulping uselessly for air, her heart began to slow. It was squeezing her to death, and each decompress of her chest as she gasped for life only worsened it.

I'm going to die.

THREE

Cold, Nathair whimpered, tightening around the only heat source available. *So cold.*

His warmth continued to bleed from his many wounds, hindering his ability to think clearly. Despite the rage that still simmered beneath the surface, lingering in the back of his consciousness, his pain and the shivers that invaded underneath his scales were too prevalent.

He didn't even move or uncoil himself from the living heat source he'd tucked within the folds of his tail. Even when night fell and Demons came to inspect the area, he continued to shiver around it.

The fear scent from within him had long ago subsided. He gave his prey just enough room to breathe after forcing her into unconsciousness, refusing to let her die simply for his own benefit.

With orbs white, hating how the air felt colder than usual rushing over his scales, he opened a coil just enough to check on a Demon with one orb. They ignored his presence as they licked the ground for human blood and entrails.

Nathair's own scent hid the woman within him, so they left him be. He was thankful for that, as his wounds were already rather debilitating. He didn't wish for another battle.

As much as he would have preferred to sink within his deep pond, shifting from breathing upon land to underwater came with many changes.

There would be a few seconds where his body had to adjust to the morph of breathing water, requiring a transformation into what most Mavka would consider their monstrous form. A physical change occurred, one that allowed him to adjust to the temperature of the water in some way. However, that first dive... if the liquid was too cold, it'd feel like blades against his flesh.

He hated the delay, and how it clutched him all the way to his bones. He'd scream, writhing beneath the water until his gills took over and offered him salvation.

Rather than subjecting himself to such agony, he coiled around the woman he'd... saved. He'd never intended to reveal himself to her when she'd been drinking from his pond, but he'd leapt from it at her loud screams. The high pitch of them, the utter terror in them... He'd been unable to deny their beckoning call. It didn't instil hunger within, but panic.

He groaned as he absorbed her heat, relieved when it seeped beneath his flesh.

Why did I save her? He had no reason to, nor did he care for her wellbeing whatsoever.

Creating enough space to wedge his arm forward, he clutched at the side of his skull when voices wailed within his consciousness. Women and men of all different ages pleaded for help, for mercy, for someone to save them from the Demons that tore at their flesh. They made his blood run colder. The perception of their wounds infected his own, making them ache and throb tenfold.

Make it stop. His heat source let out a quiet gasp, and he forced himself to soften around her.

"Please, stop," a woman cried within his mind. *"I'm scared."*

They were always scared at their deaths. They felt like the world had abandoned them as they suffered as prey. A man roared, twisting as he tried to crawl away, and a tanned hand became his own when nails dug at dirt to escape.

The memories twisted into something else, thankfully more pleasant.

A blanket was put over him as he stared at a fireplace, before a mug of brown steaming liquid was placed in his hands. *"Thank you. I feel much better now,"* a young teenage boy said, as he smiled up at a red-haired woman who suddenly became Nathair's parent.

Nathair huddled around his own living fireplace desperately, waiting for the chill of night to fade.

Ruminative fragments of memories slipped into the front of his mind. Some pleasant, most not. He wanted to sleep, to rest, but resting out in the open never allowed him peace.

A Demon crawled on top of him.

He ignored it, since it wasn't attacking him, and it eventually left. Many of the Demons throughout the night had eaten dirt just for a speck of human blood or flesh, but they ensured it lessened the scent for Nathair and gave him slips of lucidity.

His wounds helped, centring him in the shitty reality he found himself in.

The question remained, why did he save this human?

Perhaps a part of him thought if he protected one, it may stop the many voices that pleaded throughout his conscience. It didn't, but he was tired of hearing their call and being powerless to stop them, to save them.

Although he couldn't care less about the female he held onto, he'd watched her from his pond. He'd wondered why she'd chosen to fall asleep out in the open, alone, considering most of the humans in his memories never left their towns alone.

Why did she not want to go with those humans? Her scream had been ear piercing, even when muted through the water.

She'd kicked and fought, which had slapped a rather harrowing memory into the forefront of his mind. One in which he was a victim at the hands of human men.

Perhaps that is why he leapt to her aid. He'd suffered

through a mere fragment of terror and assault in comparison, and he'd panicked, thinking that was her fate. Just a taste of it, and he knew the action was repulsive and cruel.

If given the opportunity, he'd eradicate all such disgusting perpetrators from the world. Alas, he was a Mavka, and his justifiable desire to neuter would likely see all humans within his vicinity eaten.

I no longer desire to eat the humans. Or any creature.

He just wanted to rest, to cope with the chaos of his ill mind, so why the fuck had he gotten involved? Now he was in pain, freezing, and felt unwell from his rage and the males he'd just eaten, as if their flesh had been rotten.

Now that the Demons were gone, and it was safe, Nathair leapt forward when his gut twisted further. Keeping the female covered, he supported himself on straightened arms as he hacked. Drool flooded his mouth. When he retched for the third time, ethereal tears floated as tiny white specks around his eyeholes.

With all the flesh he'd eaten already fully absorbed, nothing physical came out, no matter how hard he tried to vomit.

Get out, he pleaded, whimpered, anything to remove what he held onto. His entire body quaked in repulsion as he hacked again, and again, until something came up his throat.

It burned on its way out, hot and painful. When it was in his maw, he spat out one of the souls he'd been carrying. The white flame, the evidence of a dead soul he couldn't fully consume, and therefore, couldn't bind to himself, was saturated in drool when it splattered against the ground.

Within seconds, it floated, before disappearing to whatever would tie it to this world. He'd once wondered if the souls he'd been expelling would later become Ghosts, unable to go over to an afterlife, as he wouldn't ferry them. As much as he wanted to carry them to Weldir's black mist like he was supposed to, as both his son and servant... he couldn't.

The idea of consuming souls had left his mind broken, and he feared he'd obtain their memories and deepen his suffering.

He was aware it was some kind of fucked-up Mavka eating disorder, but he just couldn't overcome the paranoia of potentially worsening his sickened mind. It was a mental barrier that gave him a horrifying physical reaction.

When he violently hacked up the second and third souls, he sighed in relief, despite the pointlessness of it all. In the back of his mind, he knew it didn't matter, but the irrational paranoia meant he couldn't hold them.

As much as giving him new life meant he now lived, he was no longer useful as a Mavka. His purpose, his reason for existence, was pointless if he did this.

The Witch Owl had been horrified when she'd witnessed the first time it happened, but she'd also comforted him. That only earned her a new claw strike from a confused and panicked Nathair, but she'd been lucky to evade his paralysing venom when he attempted to strike her.

His poor mother creator had been violently attacked many times by him. Yet, she never abandoned him, nor blamed him, only offering comfort and guilt-deepening pats in understanding.

Now that the souls had been violently and painfully expelled, he slunk back within the comfort of his tail. He moaned at the heat that surrounded his torso, shifting the female within it so she could warm another part of him.

He tried not to press her against his wounds.

With dawn slowly ascending, he let her soothe him. He focused on her subtle and constricted breathing, her heartbeat, the way she spread salvation through his flesh.

With a last shudder, he refused to sleep, but rested in the only way he could: orbs bright, but body lax.

With a groggy groan, Linh stirred.

When she opened her eyes, she was greeted by suffocating

darkness. *I feel so heavy.* Every breath was tight, her limbs weighed down, her mind hazy.

I can't even move my arms. She tried to rip them closer, but both had gone numb. The grainy, deadened feeling in them caused her to wince, so she wiggled her fingers to ease it, doing the same with her toes. Somehow, that made it ten times worse.

"Ah!" she gasped, recoiling from the pain.

Where am I? The walls around her were tight, unmoving, and she was so dizzy that she found it hard to feel fearful despite the spike of unease. Thank goodness she wasn't claustrophobic – otherwise, she may have screamed.

But the constriction was unsettling.

Linh tried to think of what she could last remember. *I fell asleep... Then I woke to Bragg's men...* Her eyes flung open wide. *Oh my gosh! The Duskwalker!*

Turning her head proved futile, but she managed to wiggle enough that smooth scales brushed over her cheeks. Well, at least feeling them meant she wasn't nestled within his stomach. That would have been harrowing to discover.

That settled her fear so she could get a bearing on what was going on. She needed to stay calm, to not be afraid if she didn't wish to be eaten. Although information about the Duskwalkers' existence was mostly rumour-based, she'd read all she could on them.

She needed to be smart if she wanted to survive.

Did it protect me? Why? On second thought, who cared? She was alive, and still no longer in Bragg's clutches, thanks to it.

The fact I find being trapped by a Duskwalker better than being with Bragg just proves how much of a piece of shit that man is. He was worse than a monster. *Or maybe I've just gone insane.*

She snorted a mild laugh at that, as she stared at the nothingness.

Linh could fret, or she could just accept this super-weird

cuddle. She was choosing to just let it be. It'd let her go eventually, and she could figure out what to do from there.

It's a serpent... and it does feel rather cool. Does that mean it's cold-blooded? Or, at least, had a lower body temperature than most other creatures? *I saw it shivering. Maybe it's soaking up my heat?*

Weren't most reptiles heat seekers?

Alright, you freaky big danger-noodle. Soak up as much of it as you like. She closed her eyes. *You have a little longer. If you don't let me go, then it's your own fault if I pee on you.*

Linh didn't know how long she lay there, unafraid but absolutely wary. However, now that her mind was alert, the more her bladder gave an uncomfortable throb.

Ignoring it as best she could, she pondered on her predicament. *It'll take me roughly a day to get to Duneside.* There likely wouldn't be an opportunity to sneak inside due to Bragg's soldiers, so she'd have to pass it. Then it'd take her a week or so to go around the mountain, and then another to walk down to Slater Town.

Her lips pursed and puckered forward. *Slater Town is military, but I don't know if they'd be willing to send out that many men.*

Colt's Outpost, though, was the largest village in the north, and they trained all the soldiers within the region. Many Demonslayers started their training there before moving to Hawthorne Keep further in the east.

Unfortunately, Colt's Outpost was further away. The longer she was outside of protective walls, the higher the likelihood she'd be eaten.

I miss home, though. She'd been forcibly taken over two months ago. *If Bragg doesn't catch me, will he tell my parents I'm out here by myself?*

Biting her lip, she held back tears at how much they would be suffering. The guilt they'd feel for letting her be taken, even though they tried with all their might to stop it.

She buried her face against the monster who had protected

her.

If... if only you could help. A sob broke, only for it to shake out of her as realisation dawned. *Wait... didn't it kill like three men within the span of minutes?!* Minutes! All by itself, the Duskwalker had destroyed and eaten those men like it was nothing.

Her mild pulse spiked as possibility, hope, and excitement bled into her veins.

What if... what if I ask it to save us? Then she could be home within days!

The Duskwalker could gorge itself on vile bandit meat for all she cared. She'd toss pieces at it, shove them down its bony maw herself, if it meant their freedom.

Kicking her legs, she squirmed to get free. She wanted to talk to it, and her bladder was seriously starting to throb. If she waited much longer, she'd be bursting and unable to hold it.

"Hey," she called, her lips brushing over it and muffling her voice. "Hey, let me go!"

The smooth, scaley limb wrapped around her clenched, rending a gasp from her. Then, as if woken or startled, Linh was crudely dumped against the ground as it uncoiled itself. The Duskwalker slithered to get away from her, just as she let out a cry when her head smacked against the ground.

Bringing her knees up, she cupped the back of her head with a pained groan. "Ow! You dropped me!"

Linh then remembered what she was in the presence of, and swiftly sat up and turned to it. Heat bled from her features at the sheer size of it towering over her!

Oh my gosh. It's... it's huge! She scuttled back, just to get out of its mere shadow to take it in.

The Duskwalker stared down at her with dark-orange swirling vortexes that seemed to glow brighter in the sun. Unsettled under the scrutiny of its luminous orbs, Linh drew her gaze over each of its features.

Its snake skull looked like a mix of a death adder and a viper. The black horns on top of its head almost looked ram-like as they hooked backwards, their tapered ends pointing towards the ground.

Bones protruding outside its flesh made it look undead and fierce, causing the scaled flesh around them to puff like it was trying to absorb them. With the sunlight glittering down on them, the Duskwalker's black scales glistened with subtle rainbows, the blue and purple hues being the strongest.

The back fin from yesterday is gone. The others were light grey. Almost like a ruffle of fabric that started from its humanoid sides, they trailed down to its tail tip. More fishlike fins lined the backs of its forearms.

It looked so strange.

She eyed the muscled dips of its abdomen and chest, only to frown at its navel. *It has a belly button. Does that mean it was birthed rather than hatched from an egg like a reptile?* She noted its dark-grey nipples, and something became startlingly apparent.

It's a male.

The Duskwalker's torso was masculine in shape, since it appeared to lack breasts. His waist was narrower than the rest of it, showing he was lean, yet his broad chest and thickly muscled tail stated otherwise. Her gaze darted down to what she thought may be his hips, since she could see the lightest imprint of hip bones. She found no genitalia, but could see a section of scales that appeared smoother and had a seam line down the middle.

From what I can tell, his junk must be beneath his flesh, like most snakes.

And this male Duskwalker had to be at least thirty feet, if not more, long!

"H-hey," she shakily greeted, forcing a smile upon her face. "Thank you for sav– Hey!"

Linh reached out when he spun to the side and walked on his hands towards the pond's edge. He moved so fast, and panic clutched her throat. Stupidly, foolishly, thoughtlessly, she pounced on the end of his tail.

"Wait! I want to talk to you!" she pleaded, grabbing ahold of him as tightly as she could. She squealed when she went sliding with him.

Despite using all her strength, Linh did nothing to stop him. However, he did halt and twist around to stare down at her.

The little hairs all over her body stood on end when he released a quiet growl. Throwing her hands up in surrender, she fell back to give him space.

What the hell am I doing?! her mind screamed. *I just grabbed him like an idiot!*

"Sorry," she blurted out, hiding how freaked out she was as best she could.

I've gone insane. I'm asking a Duskwalker to stay when most people would be fleeing.

She looked at the colour of his orbs, noting the red hue of them, and lowered her arms. *Oh. I didn't know their... 'eyes?' changed colour.* Didn't take a genius to figure out what this colour meant, since he was giving her a warning growl, even though it had softened now that she'd let him go.

She blew a strand of hair from her face as she thought, *hypocrite.* He'd been the one using her as a teddy bear all night against her will!

Still, she made sure her forced smile remained. "L-look, Mr Duskwalker..."

He sucked in a triple snort before letting it out as a deep, obviously annoyed, huff.

It was impossible to tell if he was actually listening. *Maybe they aren't as intelligent as we were told?* So far, this one hadn't attempted to speak with her, and she wondered if he could even understand her.

Oh, screw it.

Sucking in a deep breath, she prepared to just spit it all out quickly. "I wanted to thank you for saving me. I really appreciate you coming to my aid."

His orbs shifted to a bright orange, just as he reared his head back and his whole upper body went with it. Linh gestured to where the corpses of Bragg's men once were, thankful they were gone, as she didn't particularly want to see dead and dismembered bodies.

"I'm not sure if you understand what I'm saying, or if you noticed, but those men were bandits who have been terrorising these mountains for the past seven months."

As if he didn't care for what she was saying, he twisted towards the water.

"Wait! Please!" She reached a hand out, despite refusing to touch him. "We need help."

He halted once more, and without turning his body, the Duskwalker slowly twisted his head to the side to face her. Dark yellow lifted into his orbs, swirling inwards to eat at the orange that had been there.

Then he finally gave the first indication that he was truly capable of intelligent thought. The Duskwalker lifted an arm and pointed his index claw against the white protruding bone of his sternum. He creepily tilted his head, and she could almost *see* a question mark forming over the top of his bony head.

"Yes," she stated with a nod. "You killed those men with such strength and speed. I know if you were to aid us, they would leave."

Before he could even think about leaving or denying her request, Linh shuffled to her knees, dropped down to her chest, and crossed her arms against the ground. She laid her head down to bow to him. It was the biggest gesture she could think to give something like him, a monster, but she hoped it conveyed how desperate she was. It also likely showed trust, which was utterly false on her end – she couldn't trust him as far as she could toss him, which was not at all.

She was willing to bow to him like he was a god.

"They aren't good people. They choke our supplies, stop us from freely trading, all under the guise of protection. They are killing us, both directly and indirectly, through famine and sickness. They take our food, our medicine, and then barter with us with those supplies we desperately need when towns outside of the valley try to bring it."

Eerie silence greeted her.

When it went on for far too long, she fisted the grass stalks in front of her. Once more, she wondered what the hell she was doing. But... Linh was so desperate, she couldn't stop.

I'll die if I go around the mountain. It'd been a dream, a hope she knew didn't truly exist. It had been action, but it also would have landed her straight into a Demon's stomach. *But this Duskwalker. If it helps me, us...*

"I know you have no reason to care or help us, but I am asking you anyway. It will take me weeks to leave our valley and get to the villages south of here." She'd have to go northeast and then southwest, just to do a freaking loop. "More people will die, and the chance of me making it there is low. You saved me from them, from being eaten throughout the night, so–"

She flinched when a hand gingerly slid under her forehead, and she lifted her face. Linh tried not to recoil when his snake skull was less than a foot from her nose. She didn't resist him when he lifted her chin and forced her upright on straightened arms.

His touch was surprisingly gentle, especially with his claws.

Her long, straight eyelashes fluttered as she blinked in surprise. *Oh wow, I didn't notice the tiny streaks of gold in his skull.* They were so tiny they were only the thickness of hairs, as if someone had glued perfect pieces of his skull back together. They looked more like hairline fractures, but the way they streaked over his skull made it obvious it'd been broken.

Do their scars always appear golden?

The Duskwalker parted his maw, let his serpent fangs come down, and released a quiet, yet bone-chilling hiss! Her heart clenched so powerfully, it sparked pain all throughout her chest. Before she could even properly react, he dived into the water. A large wave washed over the grass right next to her, ripping a squeal from her as she backed away to avoid its spray.

Her heart nearly came up her throat, and she fell to the side as a delayed reaction to such a frightening and menacing warning. He nearly scared the pee out of her, which was already threatening to burst from her at any second.

But he hadn't hurt her, and that made her remarkably foolish. She was also just so frazzled from the past twenty-four hours, she let the most unhinged thoughts prevail.

A stone the size of a fist caught her eye, and she threw it into the pond.

"You big jerk! You didn't have to hiss at me!"

Heat bled from her face when he popped his head above the surface with blood-coloured orbs. Then she squealed again and threw her arms up when he squirted water at her from his mouth.

"*Ew!*" she cried, fighting the long stream of water by tossing her arms around.

Wet and now cold, the top of her completely soaked, she shot him a foul glare when he stopped.

She *swore* she heard a snicker as he creepily sunk beneath the surface, leaving behind large bubbles that popped at the top.

Inching slowly towards the edge of the pond, Linh hesitated as she peeked into it. He was gone, fading into the abyss, as if it was much deeper than she originally anticipated. She couldn't even see the bottom of it.

She stumbled away and palmed her rosy cheeks, dozens of shocking and startling emotions heating them. *Oh my fucking gods. I spoke to a Duskwalker!* Well, at him would be more accurate, but still! He only squirted her with water, further proving he wasn't as bad as his hissing and monstrous exterior seemed.

Pouting in thought, she wondered if she could convince him to change his mind – since she figured his little tantrum was a rejection.

I'm pushing my luck though, aren't I? The longer she lingered, the more likely he might turn her into a yummy snack.

Her shoulders fell as she averted her gaze to the forest surrounding the large clearing and this small pond in the middle. Her gaze landed on the western peak of their valley's mountains.

I'm out of luck, and I was out of it two months ago. If she'd been lucky, or if the cosmic universe cared about her wellbeing, it wouldn't have allowed her to be taken in the first place.

There were very few options for someone in her position, which was a horrible realisation. The reality was: her future, her next heartbeat and breath, was all uncertain. Hopelessness radiated throughout her entire being.

She could either brave the perilous journey ahead of her or remain in hopes this Duskwalker helped her.

Both could end with her dead.

FOUR

She refuses to leave, Nathair grumbled, as he crept his head high enough from the water's surface so his orbs could see the female. The rest of him, from just below his hollow eye sockets to his tail tip, was submerged.

All day, she remained.

He, at first, thought she'd leave after he warned her away with a hiss. Most humans tended to reek of delicious fear when he showed them his fangs, which is why he'd leapt into the water before that tangy scent could cascade off her supple flesh.

Retreating to his underwater cave and lake, he'd gone to do what he always did. Which was nothing but huddle around himself, trying to deal with the irritating human voices that didn't belong to him. They were quieter since his wounds took his focus, but he didn't know which was worse – his injuries or the memory fragments.

He'd prefer not to be subjected to either.

Since he always left his tail tip in the water so he could perceive movement in it, he hadn't expected to feel her drink from it again. Even with the grand distance of water stretching between them, he'd been able to feel the sensation. He'd dived under to come closer, curious about why she'd remained.

I saw her fill a drink sack yesterday. He wondered if she'd only chosen to drink from his pond to annoy him, or to preserve her stored supply in case she needed to make a quick escape.

For a long while, she sat near the edge of his pond, waiting for him with her arse and the bottoms of her feet against the ground. She hugged her knees with a remarkably disgruntled expression – which somehow made her look both saddened and annoyed.

During that time, he refused to come up, but did watch her from within the darkness. Her body wavered through the ripples.

He thought she'd given up when she disappeared, finally giving back his small territory she so rudely trespassed upon. He rose to watch her leave, discovering he was wrong.

Instead, she crouched over one of the bags he'd dropped when he ripped the limbs off his meals. She rifled through it, shoving some kind of fluffy food into her mouth – if the fragments of his memory weren't wrong, he thought it may be a bread roll.

Stuffing her face, she appeared to be starving. He could hear her *omnomnoming* from all the way over here.

After rifling through the bag, she went to the two others. With the way he ate, which was limb by limb, by the time there was nothing but a torso, anything carried tended to fall right off.

If he wanted to, he could swallow even the largest prey whole. Nathair didn't like doing that, as it often left him immobile for long periods of time. He'd need to lie there and let his internal throat muscles push the body down as he swallowed bit by bit.

It was just easier to do it in smaller bites.

Nathair ducked beneath the surface when she turned towards the pond with her arms filled with her stolen haul. She walked to her personal bag and started shoving supplies into it. Then she ran over to grab a sword that had been dropped and brought that over too.

"It's creepy to just watch someone," she shouted, without

ever looking his way.

Nathair wiggled his head under water, opening and closing his jaw mockingly. *I will observe you, since you refuse to leave my territory.*

Be thankful I have no desire to harm you.

He also had no desire to help her.

Nathair had his own problems. A warped mind, for starters. He also had to defend his home against sea Demons occasionally, who liked to enter from below this mountain's cliff.

She likely does not understand that I would do more harm than help.

If he were to chase away the bandits from her village, the scent of blood from the wounds he delivered, the pain of the injuries he gained, or the tantalising scent of people's fear, would send him violently into a rage. He would kill the bandits and then turn on her people.

He was of no help to anyone.

Now that he'd eaten the dozens of human souls within Tenebris, his humanity was higher, his intelligence well rounded, and his body had thickened a large amount. He'd also grown, as if his physical state could be altered this way in the afterlife.

It'd also grown stronger and longer since coming back to life.

He now knew that eating more humans would do nothing to aid his hunger, and would only gift him humanity. After merely those three bandits he'd eaten, he could already tell the unravelled strings of his thoughts were better connected. His mind was able to decipher itself and the world around him, and process information in a much more efficient way.

But he had no longing to better himself. He was fine with his intelligence, thought it sufficient, and he'd rather not deal with hacking up souls because his sanity was broken. He'd rather not be reminded that he was a useless servant for his father creator, especially with how much that cloudy god had helped him in Tenebris.

Without Weldir, he would have been undeniably lost. His creator had welcomed him into his realm with open arms and fed him information about the outside world. Nathair knew what the other Mavka were up to, who had brides, and that two of them had younglings.

When Weldir wasn't slumbering to recuperate his magical energy, or spending time with his mate, he could often be found by Nathair's side. That was, until Aleron, the bat-skulled Mavka, had joined them.

Weldir had switched his focus to the child who needed him most, especially since, after many years of not being able to speak, Nathair had... cast his creator away. Nathair had given up trying, and just all around became rather unhappy.

Although he'd lost the yearning for life, Nathair had been hoping his return would mean he could have a purpose again. One which he had been tasked with at birth, and now understood.

He wanted to assist Weldir, wanted to be a useful servant and soul carrier. To be a good... *son.*

The hue of his orange orbs often darkened in guilt; he felt like he was failing.

He also lacked the will to do anything selflessly, especially not for a human such as the loitering female. His return to the living world thus far had been unpleasant.

Nights were particularly hard. Due to the snowy season, he'd been rather lethargic. It cost him energy to maintain and regulate his low body temperature. And, if the surface thickened with ice, he also couldn't stay within the water, as he faced the same problem.

Before he'd died, he'd always struggled in winter.

Summer, though? He'd almost itch to move. The heat was like a form of nutrition, and he found himself going further and further from his territory to chase after scents, sounds, or even a sparkle in the distance. It made him wish to explore and frolic almost playfully.

Currently, he just sulked in his cave, grumpy about the temperature and waiting for balmier winds.

A high-pitched squeal snagged his attention and dragged him away from his musings.

Nathair unlatched his tail tip from the jutting ledge coming from the vertical channel wall of his pond, the only thing keeping him afloat. Battling how he immediately began to sink, he flapped his tail back and forth to rise through the water. He peeked above the surface.

She fell. He rolled his head in disbelief. *She is so noisy. She'll bring Demons upon her with little more than sound.*

It appeared she'd been carrying sticks she collected around the clearing, and dropped one, which caused it to either go under her foot or twist between her ankles. Regardless, she'd hurled a bunch more to the ground as she fell on her face.

Nathair chuckled, causing bubbles to come from his mouth. *She's kind of funny.* In a silly sort of way.

"Did you really just laugh at me?" She shot her head in his direction, and he ducked beneath the surface to hide. "What if I'd hurt myself?"

He would have laughed harder.

Still, he was rather perplexed about her.

She doesn't appear to be afraid of me. Wary, maybe; she did eye him cautiously whenever their gazes briefly met.

Since he was using his gills to breathe, he couldn't scent the air around him. It was partly the reason he refused to leave the pond – if she smelt of fear, he'd give her a real reason to fucking scream.

When the subtle vibrations of thumping movement brushed against his sensitive scales, he knew she was on the move again.

His tail swivelled beneath him as he rose to watch her, using it to keep himself afloat. She dumped her sticks near the boulders on one side, without glancing at him, as if she knew he would retreat if she did. Then she started searching for more.

Nathair followed her with his gaze, observing her everywhere she went.

He tilted his head as he took in her features. *She is very striking.* From what the memory fragments told him, this female would be considered quite beautiful to humans.

Her fawny-brown skin didn't appear to have a single flaw upon it. Her hair was such a dark colour of brown that in the shade it appeared black, yet in the sun, it shone with a deep chestnut hue. Her brown eyes followed the same pattern, darker in dimness but sparkling with molten hazel in the light.

Her gentle, heart-shaped face featured prominent cheekbones and a pointed chin. With a subtle plumpness of her cheeks, her countenance radiated a benevolence she couldn't lose, even when she glared sharp eyes at him. Then there was her expressive mouth. Full and pale pink, her lips pulled to the side, twisted, or curled back as she did whatever task she had decided to take on.

The arch of her nose, her brows, and her small ears made her appear even lovelier. Little red gems dangled from her lobes, and often glittered when she turned her head.

He didn't know if she was short, as his perception of everything could often change depending on where he rested his weight on the long length of his tail.

Her body had curves. Her purple dress garment was tight enough to highlight that her breasts were rather substantial for her thin frame, and her backside rounded, making the back of her garment dangle off it. With each kick of her legs, the side vees in the lavender garment revealed grey pants and black shoes that had straps crossing over the tops of them.

If it wasn't for his fragments, he wondered if he would have noted her attractiveness at all. It did little to change how he felt about her invading his space, but it did mean she was pretty to look upon from afar.

It left him wondering why she was... alone. *Humans tend to guard pretty females like this.*

He tipped his gaze into the forest. *Is that why those bandits attacked her?* He shuddered at the thought of what may have happened to her had he not intervened.

His attention was stolen when she started building some kind of fire. He internally groaned. *She plans to stay throughout the night?*

Then he would have to decide on whether he would assist her should a Demon come. If so, then she was just purposefully being bothersome. A fire may attract Demons, which would then be her own fault that she was eaten. She'd have no one to blame but herself.

If the Demon then went to the Veil and into Weldir's black mist, then her soul could feed him. He considered letting her die for such a noble reason. Sure, Weldir would have to waste energy first in cleaning it of the green Demon sickness that cracked their souls, then heal it, but he'd still gain a tiny amount of energy and strength.

Nathair pensively looked her over.

I have decided.

He would let her be eaten.

Linh let out a scream when a Demon slid into the open clearing. Shuffling back near the icy water's edge, she held up the short sword she'd found throughout the day. The fire reflected in the length of the blade, and she trembled as she pointed the tip towards it.

Its breaths came out as white condensation, but it didn't charge straight away. Instead, it stepped to the side, its red eyes zeroed in on Linh cowering upon the ground.

It seemed wary of coming closer to her, and she braved peeking behind her at the pond. The Duskwalker wasn't there; he'd disappeared long before night fell.

She was frightfully alone, and didn't actually know how to use the weapon in her shaking hands.

I thought Demons were uglier. This one looked remarkably human, even with its shark-like fangs, horns, claws, and tail. Its skin was a mixture of patchy pale flesh and the common void-like appearance of all Demons.

Crouching on its hands and feet, it snarled at her, baring its fangs as it inched closer.

"S-stay back!" she exclaimed, jabbing her sword forward.

Blonde brows narrowed in displeasure at Linh's threat.

"Don't fight, human. It will only make the end more frightening," it stated, its voice feminine and soft. Then the she-Demon reached out, beckoning Linh closer. "Come, and I will make it quick."

She didn't know they could talk, but she found that worse. Would it start threatening her, telling her she was tasty and about all the horrible ways it would start eating her? She'd rather not have something talk perversely to her like she was a succulent meal, sucking on its fingers or smacking its lips for more.

"I'm warning you," Linh pleaded, because she was too scared to actually have any bite to her tone.

She eyed the water once more, wishing she'd see a glow of colour or the peek of a skull. She saw neither, and knew without a doubt she'd been abandoned.

Tears welled in her eyes. *I'd rather drown than be eaten.* Both sounded horrible, but those were her choices.

M-maybe he wasn't helping me. Maybe he was just hungry and ate the bandits because they were there. So why did he leave her alive then?

She'd put her faith in a monster because she had no other choice. Linh had weighed her options, and death awaited her no matter which path she took. She'd run from Bragg with a fantasy that she could go around the mountain if need be, but that was just as suicidal as trusting the Duskwalker who had inexplicably saved her. Linh was truly desperate.

She wanted to live.

"Please," she begged when the Demon stepped a hand

closer. Every second longer that she remained alone, the more frightened she became.

"Come away from the water, and I can give you the mercy of a quick death," the Demon said, her voice still quiet and unthreatening despite her words. "If you hurt me, I will make it long. Nothing will change your fate, human."

Oh shit, she thought, just as it bolted towards her. Linh closed her eyes, screamed, and waited for the worst.

That was, until a large splash of water sounded right behind her. Her skin crawled with dread, and she shivered from it. When cold droplets fell on top of her, she opened her eyes and looked up to find the Duskwalker had rested his hands upon the ground on both sides of her.

She flinched inwards, shrinking, when the coldness of his body touched between her shoulder blades. He bent over her, shielding her on three sides while her front was open.

In a spray of bits of grass and dirt, the Demon skidded to a halt. Her red eyes grew stark as she gawked up at his skull and then shuffled back when he released a horrible, venomous hiss.

"Don't leave your meal out if you don't want others to try and eat it, Mavka!" the Demon shouted, before she returned his hiss with her own. She scampered away, darting into the forest to flee.

Stunned, Linh panted as the tip of her sword thunked against the ground. Her heart raced, refusing to settle when she'd been so close to facing death – and may still.

She also didn't move since her back continued to press against the Duskwalker. *I have a bad feeling.* There was a light rumbling resonating through her, vibrating into her torso, and she couldn't tell if that was his stomach or a growl.

What do I do? Should she move, stay where she was... play dead? She doubted playing dead would work in her favour.

Craning her head back slowly, she braved looking up once more. His skull was already directed downwards, bright-red orbs greeting her, and she shrunk further under the threat of them. The moment her gaze fell on them, a menacing, loud growl bubbled from him.

She finally turned, retreating, and he lowered himself. On his hands, he balanced his weight to follow her, crawling from the water and never allowing more than a foot's worth of distance between their faces. The fire forced her to stop, or she'd end up crawling through it, and he halted as well.

Why isn't he attacking? He just continued to growl at her.

Her eyes slipped to his unmoving chest before darting to his bony nose hole. No breaths fogged from him, nor could she hear him huffing. *He's... choosing not to breathe?*

She wanted to believe he was doing that for her sake.

Then, as if he couldn't hold it anymore, or didn't want to, he finally released a harsh and sharp breath. A large spray of water puffed out as two clouds. He slinked back, slithering into the water to disappear.

Linh remained where she was, her eyes never leaving where she last saw him. A bubble floated on the surface.

He saved me again. Her plan had worked.

What took him so damn long?! She hoped it wasn't to punish her by letting her think she was truly going to be eaten, just to save her at the last second. That would be rather cruel, otherwise.

Regardless, she had her answer. A small smile began to curl the corners of her lips.

The Duskwalker was protecting her. *If I stay, maybe he'll warm up to me and help us.*

FIVE

Sitting at the bottom of his pond, his tail wrapped up beneath him, Nathair yanked downward on his black hooked ram horns. *Dammit. I couldn't let her be eaten!*

He'd tried. Nathair had tried to ignore her screams, the way her cries shattered through the water to tingle his ears and vibrate against his scales. Her begging, her pleas, each one had made his orange orbs shift to a darker hue incrementally. His insides had twisted, crawling as if tiny fish sickeningly swarmed within him.

He'd reminded himself it would be for Weldir's gain, and that it would give him the peace he sought.

Yet, as guilt clutched at his throat like a set of hands, he couldn't take it. The voices in his head, the many last moments he was forced to suffer, bombarded him worse than ever. They hounded him, bashing at the inside of his skull like they wanted to crack it open from within and rush out.

They were harrowing, making him claw at his back in disgust and hate.

Despite his desire to remain impartial, he'd saved her.

And, as another Demon came hours later, beckoned by her silly fire, her human scent, maybe even her fear, Nathair had assisted then too.

The second one had been less developed than the first. It'd had goat-like features: back legs with hooves, a prey snout with fangs, jutting horns, and stood on all fours. Although its upper body was similar to a human, its skin was void-like and glistening, showing it hadn't eaten many.

Refusing to exit the water completely, he warded it back. When it wouldn't leave, he had to swipe until he clawed its face, and it only retreated due to its pain.

The female huddled against his abdomen, trustingly pressing against him, and he couldn't help thinking that foolish. Had he taken a single breath through his lungs, rather than holding his breaths through his gills, her fear scent would have enraged him. Despite not flicking his tongue forward to taste the air, it still managed to settle on his tastebuds.

His stomach had cramped, hunger eating away at him.

Before he could turn his rage upon her, making it far bloodier and mindless, he slipped back into the cold salvation of the water. Holding his breath via his gills also stopped the shift of his body, allowing him to accept the colder temperature at ease.

He currently sulked at the rocky bottom of his pond, annoyed with her and this situation.

Tomorrow, I will make her leave. He didn't care if he frightened her, so long as she gave him the peace he sought.

I will have to... speak with her. Nathair shuddered at what that meant.

His own voice was currently locked behind some barrier within his mind, but he did have another option. He just... he fucking hated it, despised it, would rather tear his own scales off than do so, but he would do it as a last resort.

Clutching at his skull, he whimpered in the water, and waited.

Only once day broke, and light reached him, did he float to the surface. He peeked out of the water and took in her limp form sitting against the boulders.

Although her eyes were open, they blinked lazily. Dark smudges had formed just below the inner creases, and her fawny-brown complexion looked sickly. Even Nathair could tell she looked utterly spent.

With the hilt of the sword in her hands, she lifted her weary gaze to the sun. Dust particles floated around her face in the beam of light, making her entire aura seem to glitter.

Something about the way she smiled up at the sky, her lips parting to flash white even teeth, twisted his chest. She looked so soft in that moment, somehow even prettier, as relief settled over her features.

Then, as if that was all she'd been waiting for – light and safety – she closed her eyes. Her head lolled to the side, her lips parting to let out quiet breaths, as her shoulders and arms sagged. The sword's hilt dropped to the ground.

With a light growl, Nathair grumbled at the fact she'd fallen asleep – even more so when he discovered he wouldn't disturb it. She looked so peaceful resting there in the sun on his very territory, and he just didn't have enough of a spiteful heart to wake her.

His tail swivelled below him to keep him afloat as he thought on what to do. *Why did it have to be a female who came here?* He thought he may have been less inclined to be benevolent towards a male.

He eyed her petite, curved form, disliking that she looked soft in all the best places. She was so small in comparison to him, so feminine and unguarded, as if she truly needed protecting. He didn't like that he was helpless to keep protecting her, and kept doing so when he'd never had the desire before.

Swimming forward, he came a little closer to the pond's edge where the boulders were. Quietly, as not to disturb the sleeping beauty, he placed his hands on the stone ledge. His claws dug into the grass just behind it as he lifted.

Water flowed from his gills, and he parted his maw to let it freely escape his lungs on a singular, hard compression. He leaned in closer. Like the day before, he took in her delicate features.

Her long, black eyelashes fanning down in her slumber

were like the wings of a dark moth. Her lips looked utterly malleable, as if they would feel like cushions against anything hard – like his skull. He let his sight roam over her smooth skin, free of imperfections, and it seemed to glow in the sunlight. Even with barely an inch of distance between them, he knew her flesh would be hot.

Then something had Nathair choking back a strangled breath.

Drool flooded his mouth, saturating it completely, when he finally took in a long and deep draw of her scent. His entire being pulsed – his mind, his biceps and pectoral muscles, his entire tail clenched and shuddered. Even a throb lanced low in his groin, making him wince in confusion.

His mental fragments immediately pieced together the peach-and-vanilla scent currently rudely clogging his nose hole. He dipped his neck beneath the water, forcing himself to breathe through his gills.

Somehow, it'd stained his essence. He struggled to rid himself of it as it clung inside his nostrils, saturated the flood of drool, and invaded his bloodstream.

Annoyed that she'd elicited such a strong and visceral reaction from him, he retreated to the side. Once his tail tip grazed the ledge of rock lower down, he rested on it to keep himself buoyant.

He averted his gaze from her, only to bring it back with his sight flaring a bright reddish pink in embarrassment, as well as shame. With just how much looking at and smelling her had pleased him so profoundly, his reaction to her made him feel guilty over what he planned to do when she woke.

I have no right to feel anything towards her. Once more, he looked away, only to let himself sink.

Nathair wouldn't change his mind and keep this little creature just because he thought her attractive and her scent called to him so intensely. He wouldn't steal her, or keep her, even though he was aware that focusing on her tended to minutely quieten the fragments within his mind. He wouldn't hunger for her presence for such a reason – he wanted to fix his brokenness on his own.

I will only... hurt her. Currently, he was lucid. Should his lucidity slip, he had a tendency to harm himself. He may claw her in confusion, in agony, and if he grew attached to her... and then *ate* her, the guilt of that may set him back.

Nathair was aware most of his Mavka siblings had brides. Weldir had kept him informed to the best of his capabilities while he'd been stuck in Tenebris. Sure, he'd suffered much envy, but he'd also just learned to accept that nothing about it could change at the time.

He knew that possibility was still unobtainable for himself. *I am not deserving of a bride.* He harmed when he did not mean to, expelled souls when he shouldn't, and could not even speak freely unless he wanted to be riddled with unpleasantness.

Even if he longed for one, the chances of him keeping a human safe while he gained their trust were low.

He wouldn't hold out on those chances changing, even if this particular female persisted in remaining. She would eventually run off scared; it was better he made it happen sooner rather than later.

His sight shifted to a deep blue as he coiled up on the ledge within his pond, waiting to feel the vibrations of movement from the surface. Such an ability had once irritated him, but he'd become reliant now that he was able to decipher it through his increased humanity. What had once itched his scales, now became a necessity for his senses.

Nathair picked at one of his scales, mulling over the last two days. *I wonder what her name is.* He'd like to know the name of the little female he'd likely remember for all time. The one he'd protected for a short while and didn't end up eating.

Is it as pretty as her face and scent? Even her voice had been lovely. When she'd spoken to him the day before, she'd managed to lull him enough into listening to her plea.

Soft, gentle, sweet – her voice had been audible heaven.

He opened his maw and stuck out his tongue with a *bleurgh*. Already she haunted his thoughts, persistently invading them.

Yes, he very much needed to get rid of this female before he became irrevocably obsessed.

Just as the nagging to rise and watch the female sleep began to itch his scales like an infection, he sensed the tiniest movement. A foot moving, perhaps even a groan, but enough of a disturbance highlighted she'd woken just as the sun was at its zenith.

Nathair immediately lifted to the surface, just in time to watch her rub the sleep from her eyes. With her face screwed up, she tilted her head to the side, and a crack sounded from her neck, which made her release a little cry. It appeared she had hurt herself by sleeping the way she did, which was upright against the boulders supporting her back.

Her eyelids fluttered open, and she stared at the grass with a docile gaze. It flicked to the water before darting to his skull.

The female gasped and recoiled to the side, falling away from him.

"You scared the hell out of me!" she exclaimed, before immediately settling. The dark circles under her eyes had eased exponentially, but they became sunken as something seemed to register. "H-have you been watching me sleep the whole time?"

Nathair rolled his head in annoyance, then flicked his tongue in her direction to taste the air. No fear had entered her scent.

Perfect. There was still plenty of day, and she had rested: time for her to leave.

Placing his hands on the pond's edge, he slipped up until he'd exited to just a foot below his hips. That gave him enough leverage to skulk onto the land, slithering the long length of tail underneath him until he was completely free.

"I keep forgetting how big you are," the female stated, giving him a weak smile that showed just how wary she truly was. "H-have you decided to finally come talk to me?"

Due to his torso not being flexible, nor having the ability to slither, he walked towards her on his hands. He did so cautiously, trying not to spook her too badly with sudden movements.

He halted his breathing when he was barely an arm's length from her, her smell finally turning tangy as he reached out. She shrunk into herself, her arms and legs curling inwards, and her eyes clenched shut. Nathair ignored her response to his closeness and reached down beside her.

Her bag clinked and clanked as he dumped it onto her lap. The breath she'd been holding fluttered out of her, and she flung open her eyes to look down. She touched at the pale-brown satchel, before pouting her lips and frowning up at his skull.

Nathair pulled back and pointed to the forest.

Her gaze darted that way, and she quickly leapt to her feet. The bag thumped to the ground. She threw her hands out, like one might do to halt another.

"Please, wait," she begged, before she dropped her head and held her elbow. Her stance appeared defeated, and almost... hopeless? "I know you want me to leave, but you saw what happened last night. That's what awaits me every night, whether it be this coming night, or the one after that, or even after that. I'll be travelling for weeks if I go around the mountain. I'll be alone, and the area is infested with Demons."

Her features tightened, and orange darkened in his sight as little droplets collected on her glittering eyelashes. *Don't cry. Don't make this harder than it needed to be.*

"If you don't help me, my only option is to pray I don't die before I make it to the villages south of here."

Steeling his heart, Nathair folded his arms. He hoped it conveyed that he wouldn't be moved from his decision.

Her lips tightened, her eyes narrowed, and she tsked as she turned her head to the forest. "You've shown that you can be merciful to someone in need. That, despite what you are, you do have a heart and compassion for another being."

Nathair's arms loosened, and he tilted his head. *I've never had a human speak so fondly of me or my kind before.* Yes, he did have a warm heart, should he so choose. He could be understanding and sympathetic. The fact she'd seen this in him already was quite startling, and quite touching.

It wasn't enough to subdue his determination.

"Y-you're probably wondering why I don't just go to the other human villages nearby, but I... can't. If I do, I'll just be taken again, or people will get hurt if it's discovered they harboured me. I'm alone, and I'm... scared. I know you have no reason to help me, or anyone else, but I'm begging you anyway."

Shaking his head, Nathair sighed. He crept forward, picked up her bag, and handed it to her.

Leave, female. There is nothing I can do for you.

Even though she took it, she only fisted it in one hand and stomped her foot. Her pretty features twisted up beseechingly towards him.

"Please don't make me leave," she yelled, before she ran her free hand over her hair, pushing down the loose strands. Nathair released a soft growl, and his orbs flared red in annoyance – weak annoyance. "If you make me leave, I'll likely die. I'm only twenty-one, for pity's sake! I want to live. My people deserve to live. I'm so desperate that I'm asking you, a *Duskwalker*, for help! Do you even understand how insane that is? But here I am, trying, because I have no other option."

I don't want to help you! Because helping her meant bloodthirst, death, and sorrow. The humans had never been kind to him. They had been cruel as they shoved him with blades and called him foul names.

Nathair shot forward and released a resounding hiss. *Why should I help such horrible creatures?!*

The female gasped, stumbled back, and fell onto her round backside. He held his breath as he slithered above her, then leaned around her on straightened arms.

He pulled a memory fragment to the surface. His sight blackened as he let it take hold, let it swim in the forefront of his conscience, while battling to keep his own mind present.

An argument between two human males played out, one in which would shortly morph into physical blows. They argued over cheated coin, one a villain and the other a victim.

But Nathair only needed one second of it, and he opened his maw just before it played out.

"Get out!" he roared, echoing the voice from within his mind. It shook out of him, quaked, and the voice in which he spoke with was not his own, but the human's he was borrowing.

He shut his mouth and tried to push back the fragment, stuffing it into the back of his mind. He shuddered, his entire body rippling in disgust. His sight came back, filled with white as agony swirled within his skull. His throat became tight at what he'd just done, accessing a memory to speak with it, never able to use his own voice.

Dread filled her features, which had turned gaunt as she gawked up at him. She had the foolish courage to say, "Y-you won't hurt me."

She didn't sound so sure.

Fuck! She refused to listen, refused to bend to his will. She was more stubborn than he was, and Nathair could be rather unmoveable.

His sight blackened as he let another memory lift to his forethoughts. A woman, begging, pleading for her life, right before it was ended. Her screams would follow him for the rest of the day, but he took what he needed from it.

Opening his maw once more, he, she, *they*, weakly said, *"Please."*

Please leave me alone. I don't want to help you, and even if I did, I cannot. He'd slaughter them all, and then she would regret asking him for help.

Even now, just holding back his ire was a strangulation he

was barely maintaining. Invisible hands attempted to mould the goo of his brain, to turn his anger and annoyance at her into fang-filled hunger.

She was at risk, and she didn't even know it.

"Oh gods," she cried, attempting to scramble out from underneath him. Her head butted into the boulder behind her, stopping her from going far. "Are... are they the voices of the people you've eaten?" she whispered.

Unfortunately, yes. At least their souls, ensuring he'd snuffed out their entire existence, even from the afterworld.

Dizziness swam as Nathair pushed down the fragment, staggering on his hands as his right elbow attempted to cave in. Lassitude and weakness softened his muscles, and his lack of breathing didn't aid the overload of pressure in his mind. His skull throbbed, a painful reminder as to why he shouldn't have done this.

He'd never be able to string together a conversation like this, as he couldn't change the fragments, but he could sometimes borrow what lingered there. So long as he opened his maw, it was as if he was able to speak from his belly, rather than his mind. Doing so brought on discombobulation, and his skin tightened as confused rage flooded his muscles.

A large stick snapping in the distance caught his attention, just as voices softly began to reach them. They were close, *too* close.

"Their footprints went this way," a male said, grunting as he fought through the brush.

"Hopefully we find them, and they weren't eaten," another added, disgruntled and obviously displeased with such a notion. "It's been two days. That's rarely a good sign."

Forest debris cracked and snapped under quickly approaching footsteps. They weren't far, only a few metres deep into the trees.

I was not paying attention to my surroundings. His fragments had dulled his senses, as did his focus on the female.

"They better have left her alone if they have her," a deep,

guttural voice bit. Another branch snapped under the power of an axe, yet their voices echoed louder and louder. "Or it'll be the chains for them. I won't have my woman be sullied by other men."

A sob broke below him. Nathair turned his wavering sight down to her.

She's crying. Why was she crying? She'd covered her face with both hands, and even turned on her side with her back towards the forest.

Warmth wrapped around his wrist – blissful, groan-inducing warmth. His focus sharpened momentarily, and he sucked in a quick breath. He regretted it when red entered his orbs at the terror-stricken scent coming from her, and he sunk his claws into the dirt to fight it.

He halted his lungs once more.

"Please," she whispered, tightening her tiny hand on him. "Please don't let him take me."

In a final bid to make the female understand, he released a quiet hiss. She flinched and brought her knees up to make herself smaller. Yet, she didn't let him go, didn't try to run. Her tears fell faster, wetting her face in streaks as they dripped onto the grass below her. Her weeping worsened.

Nathair's heart began to race.

Look at her, he told himself, watching her tremble and shake.

Not once had she been this terrified before him, nor had the Demon made her nearly paralysed with fear. She was reaching out to him, a Mavka – a skull-headed *monster* – as if he was preferable in comparison to the four human males approaching. Her own kind.

Had he taken a second breath, he could tell by her trembling that her scent would have sent him into a bloodthirsty rage.

Her delicate hand tightened on Nathair. A snap decision was made. *Fine. If she desires guarding so deeply...* Then he would guard this creature, and *only* her.

Scooping her up with his right arm, Nathair dived for his

pond. With his tail hooking around her bag, he submerged them both just before the other humans could enter his clearing.

Oxygen flooded his system, giving him acute sharpness after being without it for so long. The female released panicked air bubbles, but he covered her mouth as he let them both sink. Then he turned, pointing the end of his snout downwards as he swam deeper and deeper, swiftly gliding through the water.

Darkness surrounded them, but he could easily make out the stone walls of the tunnel he descended before ducking to the right where an entrance opened. Nathair swam fast and hard, knowing she wouldn't last long without air.

A small pocket opened, and he shoved her against it, letting her breathe what little air was there. She sputtered, gulping it down, then he pulled her back under. He swam on, his long tail wiggling up and down and propelling them with intense speed.

A little while longer, the tunnel opened into a wide and vast area. He shoved the female above him, and they broke the surface of an underwater cavern. He dragged her towards the land available; it was a large and long section of rock.

She sputtered and choked, clinging to him. That was until he dumped her onto solid ground and joined her.

"You almost drowned m—"

Before she could finish whatever silly complaint was about to fall from her lips, he slapped his hand over her face to quieten her.

Nathair listened to the bandits above them, their voices echoing as the sounds moved through the many chambers. It wasn't strong – the water muffled and diluted their noise – but the area they were in was tall, only leaving a small amount of rock between the ceiling and the land above. Even thin streaks of light glittered here and there, brightening the area through deep cracks in the rock, which could topple if the world violently shook.

He hissed at the foulness of indecipherable chatter.

Instead, releasing his grip on her face, he turned his sight on the wide-eyed female he'd just brought to his *home*. An inferno of swirling, violent heat radiated behind his sternum, and a dark, possessive green flared into his orbs.

This human... who had time and time again pleaded for his help, his protection, and had even reached out to him as if he were safe. The one who had shown little fear towards him, but quaked near males of her own kind. The one who was as powerless as tiny prey.

Hello, bunny.

SIX

In the background, trickling water echoed from everywhere. Subtle waves lapped at the rocky shore as stray droplets fell into puddles.

Linh barely listened as she leaned back on her arse with straightened arms and stared up at the Duskwalker towering over her. His orbs were such a dark green they were swallowing, and somehow menacing.

She didn't feel fear. How could she? So what if their little swim was frightful and she'd almost drowned part way through? He'd saved her from... *Bragg.*

Gosh, when she'd heard that stomping, gruesome bear of a man getting closer, she'd wanted to crawl out of her skin. To shed it, if it meant removing the memory of his touch upon it. She'd wanted to dive into the water, into this Duskwalker's maw, anything to escape him.

The serpent creature before her had done just that: given her a way out.

She barely made him out in the low light. Thin streaks of sunlight dimly illuminated the area, just enough that she could still make out parts of him, the cave, and the wide expanse of lake beside her. Much of the cavern was shadowed and dark, but that was fine since she could see.

A broken and weak smile curled her lips. "T-thank you for saving me... again," she stated, hoping he could hear her sincerity despite her shivering.

The water had been icy, and her clothing and hair were soaked. Her bun had come loose, revealing a thick braid that swung behind her.

The Duskwalker pushed back as he bundled his long tail underneath himself and sat in the middle. He folded his arms, while something swayed back and forth in the curl of his hovering tail tip.

Since he appeared displeased, she averted her gaze to the ground next to her. *I must admit, he did frighten me earlier.*

The voices which he'd spoken to her with... She shivered in repulsion at the thought of them. They had been haunting, and she couldn't help thinking they sounded far too human for something like him. Somehow, she knew they were the voices of people he'd eaten.

I can't be a hypocrite. I can't be thankful he ate those bandits for me, but horrified that he ate other humans. It'd be cruel otherwise. *So long as he doesn't hurt me...*

Unable to stop herself, her gaze slipped back to him.

She blushed when she noted how strong his flexing biceps, chest, and abdomen muscles looked. Perhaps because he'd been her saviour multiple times, she oddly thought him attractive. Even his white, viper-like skull didn't diminish his appeal, although it also did instil a deep-seated wariness within her.

When she wrapped her arms around herself, he tilted his head at her for it. He slowly brought her bag forward with his tail and let it slip into her lap.

Then he turned, slithering off into a particularly dark section of the cavern. He was gone, and since he didn't exit into the light on the other side, she guessed there was a cave tunnel opening there.

Her muscles eased, his daunting presence no longer weighing on her, and it allowed her to roam her gaze over the area. The chamber itself was oval, with noticeable edges between the ceiling, walls, and floor. Grey, maroon, and white stone streaked the walls, and she didn't know what kind of rock sediment they were.

Two-thirds of the area was made up of an inky and frightful lake – who knew what could be lingering in it, ready to gobble her up? The rest of the cavern was made of natural stone ledges in the shape of a crescent moon. Where she sat was the widest section of land.

Bryophytes such as dragon's gold moss and liverwort plants clung to rocky surfaces, especially in the ceiling where cracks of light twinkled in. It gave the area an earthy, dewy scent.

The air wasn't stale, but had a mild taste of brine to it, as if sea air was pushing in somehow. A sharp whistle of wind came from where he'd disappeared, further proving her theory that there was an exit to this cave.

That's handy to know. Should she need an easier way out, there may be one.

Scraping noises drew her wandering eye back to where he'd disappeared from, and the Duskwalker returned with a massive tree branch.

He's so quiet. If it weren't for the broken limbs scratching the wall, she wouldn't have heard him slithering closer. She didn't like that she could easily be snuck up on, but she'd make do.

The Duskwalker came near her and then rested back on his tail folded beneath his humanoid torso. He snapped the branch into many little pieces with nothing but his hands and sheer strength – even when it was as thick as his meaty arm.

Placing a thick log in the middle, rocks scraped against the ground as he put them in a circle. He threw smaller pieces of wood on top of the log.

Once he was done, his body making very little noise, he gestured to it. Her brows drew together, and she shook her head.

"I don't understand."

He snorted out a loud huff and then wrapped his arms

around his torso. He rubbed his hands up and down his biceps and mimed a shiver.

"Oh," she stated, a small flush heating her cheeks.

He made me a campfire, duh. It was rather obvious, now that she thought about it. *He must have seen me start the last fire.*

Linh put it up to being utterly freaked out. She wasn't in an optimal state of mind, still whirling from the fact this Duskwalker spoke with voices of those he'd eaten, Bragg almost finding her again, and nearly drowning. She also struggled to think past the way her toes, fingers, and nose burned with a coldness.

On her hands and knees, she crawled over to the ring of stones. She pulled out a fire-starting kit from a decently watertight ceramic jar in her bag. She cracked her flint and steel, her numb fingers and hands shaking as she worked to start it.

Her eyes grew wide when he leaned forward until he was above her. She couldn't feel his heat, but his presence was far too large to ignore.

After she dropped the flint multiple times while trying to ignore the way his dominating essence affected her, he eventually cupped his hand over the flint on the ground. He picked it up, then waved his fingers at her. She gripped the steel with uncertainty and turned to him.

His bony face was less than a foot from her own, and her skin prickled with how close he was. He waved his fingers at her again, and she looked down. Hesitating, hoping she wasn't misreading what he wanted, she placed the steel in his outreaching palm.

His claws, not particularly sharp, poked into her inner wrist. She tried not to touch him, just in case, but she noted how *tiny* her hand was in comparison to him.

Although Linh was almost five feet and five inches tall, which was average for a woman, this Duskwalker had to be six times that in length, if not more. Now that she was utterly alone with him in a confined space, their differences in size and strength became more apparent.

He was big – and frightening. He was also quiet, making it hard to gauge him. A silent predator.

Snakes usually ate prey of varying sizes, but most were small, like mice and rabbits. That was their size difference, Linh nothing more than a tiny piece of meat.

If she were to curl herself into a ball, she thought she may be able to fit completely within his torso. His head was also huge, twice the size of her own, and she'd seen his lower jaw segments split apart like a snake. He'd have no trouble swallowing a kicking and screaming Linh whole.

She flinched as he struck the flint and steel together, and she darted her gaze to the campfire. He was able to put in a lot more strength to his hits, and he not only started the fire, but also broke off a chunk of flint. Flames slowly came to life, and it eased her.

"Were you watching me to know how to do it yourself?" she asked, hoping to fill the tense silence between them.

After placing the stones upon the ground next to her, he nodded as he pulled back to rest on himself. He huddled down until all that could be seen was his chest, and he crossed his arms on a coil of his thick tail.

He nodded. Okay, that means he wasn't being creepy. She thought he'd been inspecting her, and not the task.

Since the wood was dry, it didn't take long to begin burning. Linh removed her jacket, laying it on the ground near the flames so the rest of her could dry off. She wiggled her hands out to the heat, and even removed her waterlogged shoes and socks to better soak it in.

"Where are we?" she asked, looking up at the mossy ceiling. She received no answer. "I never would have imagined there was an underwater lake here. How did you find it?"

Nothing.

Hmm. Maybe he'll only answer yes or no questions? He did respond earlier, after all.

Linh licked at her lips nervously. "Is this... your home?" He nodded. "Do you *have* a name?"

He nodded again before laying his head upon his folded arms resting on his tail. He'd made himself comfortable, and obviously had no qualms about rudely staring at her.

The fire reflected in his ebony scales, glinting with a rainbow sheen she found rather pretty. He was quite close to the fire, and he seemed to be enjoying soaking up its heat as much as she was, considering he'd never moved away from it.

"So, you have a name. Will you tell me what it is?" she asked, trying to get him to talk. When he didn't say anything, just stared without moving, she added, "I'm Linh Nguyen, by the way."

He lifted his head just enough so that he could raise his hands. Then with one palm flat and sticking upwards, he drew on it with the foreclaw of his right hand.

Shaking her head, her lips pursed and her brows drew together. "Are you asking me how to spell it?"

Bright yellow lifted into his glowing orbs, and he nodded.

"I'm sorry, but I don't understand why you didn't just say that. I heard you speak earlier."

This time, reddish pink flared into his orbs, and he patted at the front of his snout. He shook his head, and she tried to decipher what he was saying with his gestures.

"You... can speak, but you also can't?" she asked, squinting one eye when she wasn't sure.

He pointed a claw at her and nodded.

"I see..." She averted her gaze to the fire before needing to bring it back to him so she could read him. "You can only speak with the voices of those you've... eaten?"

She threw her hands up when he shook his head, as if that was incorrect.

He snickered, then slipped forward to scratch his claw against the ground. She watched him, her eyes growing wide when she realised he was writing something. He was slow and seemed to second guess what he was writing as he hesitated at each letter.

When he was done, she braved coming a little closer so she could twist her head and read the words from his perspective.

Her expression scrunched up, since it made little sense. *My voice lost?*

"So, you used to be able to speak?"

The Duskwalker nodded and scratched out more words. *Voices not mine. Hurt.*

"It pains you to speak with the voices of people you've eaten?"

His skull dipped up and down, informing her she was correct. She inwardly groaned as she rubbed her cheek. *Well, that makes communicating with him difficult.* She eyed the crudely written and shaky words, as if he wasn't confident. She figured trying to communicate through writing would prove difficult with more complex words, especially since they didn't have parchment.

He wrote again. *Nathair.*

"Nathair?" She winced, not knowing this word.

He patted his chest and then pointed at it.

"Oh!" She gave him a hopeful smile. "Your name is Nathair?"

His orbs brightened in their yellow glow, and he reached for her hand, enveloping it with both of his. He also inadvertently explained what the colour meant by doing so: joy.

She smiled at that, while trying not to rip her hand from him. Thankfully he let go swiftly.

"Well, Nathair, it's a pleasure to meet you." It really was, all things considered. She wouldn't be alive, nor free, if it wasn't for him. He attempted to write something, which only softened her gaze. "Linh has an 'h' at the end. L-i-n-h, that's how you spell my name."

He added the letter and tilted his head inquisitively at her. She couldn't help the giggle that bubbled.

"Yes, that's correct."

As he slinked back within himself, plopping his head down to rest, a soft rumbling came from him. She didn't know if that was a growl or a purr, but she was hoping for the latter.

Heat rose into her cheeks, and she cuddled towards the fire more. *Is he seriously purring? I didn't think Duskwalkers could do that.*

Then again, she knew very little about them.

Texts always said they were destructive and violent. Nathair had shown those qualities, but he'd also been protective. *Even the one who exchanges a protection ward for a human offering couldn't be trusted.* Many villages who received such news considered this to be a made-up story. Her people told this tale as a way to keep young children from doing the wrong thing: *"If you don't behave, the Duskwalker will come and take you as a sacrifice."*

They said he always wore a scent barrier cloth over his snout. Here Nathair was, not wearing one, and he seemed fine. He hadn't even tried to eat her once.

"If... you brought me here," she started, flicking her gaze to his bony face. "Does that mean you'll help us?"

He immediately shook his head, and her bottom lip stuck forward into a pout.

"Why not?"

He proved he was indeed purring when that rumbling morphed into an obvious growl. He pointed at her.

"You won't because of me?" He shook his head and poked the air to show he was pointing at her. Her brows knitted together, then she guessed, "You'll only protect me?"

He nodded, and Linh sighed. *I guess that's better than nothing.*

She looked away to stare at the flames, wondering what she was to do then. *Does that mean I could... force him to come with me?* She didn't really like the idea of tricking the Duskwalker, but if she was to go to one of the towns, would he chase after her? *That's if he intends to keep me here captive.*

If she escaped, would he save her if Bragg's men tried to

take her? He would be forced to intervene then.

Her heart twisted at being so deceiving.

He could also choose not to save me. She would need to trust that he would, and she didn't know if she was willing to risk it.

I don't know if I trust him. Not that deeply, at least.

Bragg was an unkind man. Randy had only echoed Bragg's threat that if she ran away a second time, he'd cut one of her Achilles tendons. He didn't care if she would limp for the rest of her life with a foot she could barely move, so long as she was within his grasp.

She hadn't made it far the first time she fled, which was a month ago. She barely made it a hundred metres before she was dragged back by her hair while she kicked and screamed.

There are worse monsters than Demons and Duskwalkers, she thought, as liquid bubbled in her eyes.

She wished her memories of all the abuse she'd suffered would cease existing, but they were too fresh. A week ago, she'd suffered. She'd come to accept her torture through prolonged exposure, but it also meant her mind had locked her emotions away regarding it.

At the time, she'd silently shed tears and gritted her teeth, but now that she was free... it was like she couldn't hold back the grotesque and frightening images.

Her skin didn't itch, nor did it feel dirty – especially not after her cold dip in the water – but she did feel... unclean. She didn't have the urge to scrub at her flesh until it turned raw, but her essence felt unfairly tainted. Something had been stolen from her, and she worried this would forever cling to her mind like sticky mud.

She didn't want it to. She would rather remove those memories and pretend they never happened. That, for the past few months, Linh hadn't existed. From the day she'd been walked out of her village, to when she woke up that first time sitting against the boulders next to the Duskwalker's pond, she wanted it to all fade away.

It's not fair. She clenched her eyes shut, willing herself to push all of it to the back of her mind and lock it away. She'd been so close to being trapped once more. If this Duskwalker had left her to defend herself... *Oh gods. I don't want to think about what would have happened.*

Linh sucked in a breath when a gentle pressure wrapped around the bottom of her jaw. She opened her eyes as she was forced to look upon the Duskwalker, who had silently come closer. He lifted her face with his entire hand, his orbs a dark yellow.

I thought yellow meant joy. She knew the darkness of it didn't when he tilted his head questioningly. His claws weren't sharp, but they still felt deadly as they lightly pressed into her cheeks and throat.

Linh froze when he came even closer and sniffed one of her cheeks with less than an inch of room separating them.

"A-are you wondering why I'm crying?" she asked.

Her skin prickled when a long and purple tongue flicked forward. It wasn't entirely shaped like a serpent's, since it was thicker, but it was forked at the tip. It wiggled near her skin, and she swore the very points of it just ghosted against her – precariously close to the outer corner of her eye.

She backed away while swiping where he'd... tasted the scent of her tears?

"It's nothing," she lied.

When he didn't let her chin and jaw go, instead holding her gaze, her skin flushed with shame.

She felt like a crybaby, when she'd never particularly been that way before. *How do I put all the tears I've shed back inside me?* she thought with a sniffle.

"It's fine. I just have a lot on my mind."

As if he could read the truth, a soft and quiet growl rumbled from him as his orbs turned red. He gently released her and pulled back to lie down like before. With his head on his arms, he let out a snorting huff.

Despite knowing she'd annoyed him, she didn't expand

further. Talking about it meant vocalising it was real and had happened, which took it from her innermost thoughts and gave it to the world. In doing so, it would no longer become forgettable, as it would linger in someone else's mind – even a monster's.

Maybe that was another reason she wanted Bragg, and all his men who knew what had happened to her, dead. Not for vengeance, but to erase any evidence of it beyond herself. People were witnesses, and it lingered in the subconsciousness of their minds.

Linh wanted to snuff that out permanently.

Ignoring Nathair in the periphery of her vision, the longer Linh sat by the fire, the less she shivered. Her clothes dried.

After a while of her thoughts spiralling, a soft snore stole her attention. She fully turned to the Duskwalker who had fallen asleep near the fire.

Her crinkled brow of concern settled as surprise overshadowed her musings.

One of his arms had slipped forward to dangle, while the other rested under his twisted head. *He looks like he just passed out.*

She wondered if her presence, and her constant needing to be saved, had meant he hadn't slept. She didn't dare go near him, since he was a predator who was in a vulnerable state, but it was kind of sweet that he'd suffered for her sake.

He stated that speaking with the voices of those he ate hurts. It probably wore him down.

Since he fell asleep, she figured the area must be safe then. So, she just soaked in the flames, and tried to figure out what decisions she should make. *I don't know what to do.* No matter what she did, everything was a risk. She was one woman in a world filled with fangs and claws.

For now, she could stay here until her food ran out. Here was safe while she collected herself mentally, and *finally* rested – after what felt like two months of utter hell.

If he wouldn't aid her people, she would leave to go to the

towns below the mountain range.

I can't stay here if there's no point to it, she thought, just as a small whimper made her frown.

Muscles twitched and clenched as the grip of a fragment clutched at him in the form of a nightmare. Images flashed, penetrating his mind with a confused chaos he found difficult to grasp.

Shuddering, he burrowed within the folds of his coiled tail to shelter himself. It was a useless attempt, as he couldn't escape the delusion that masked itself as his own memory.

A woman shrieked, and it seemed to come from his own lips as well. His tail had split into two limbs, and they shot excruciating pain up his legs as a boulder crushed them. Oddly enough, he sought mercy from a Demon, hoping it would eat him as it approached his trapped form lost in the darkness of a mining cave.

'Please,' he begged, wanting to escape the agony.

As soon as fangs lanced his throat, he awoke with the long length of his tail propped up over his back. Huffing breaths fell from his parted maw as his chest heaved with anxiety.

The scream continued to ring, battering around inside his skull like a creature trying to escape its cage. A moment of lucidity allowed him to fully wake from the fragment, when usually it would make him suffer for endless hours – punishing him for truly falling asleep, rather than just open-sighted resting.

Leaning upright on straightened arms, as if he'd darted up to defend himself against his fragment nightmare, he panted in fear. With his own claws embedded inside his limb all the way to his finger pads, and orbs white, he found the female still seated by the fire.

Her palms were flat as they faced towards the flames. At

first, he thought she hadn't noticed what had just occurred, but she eventually flicked her sparkling brown eyes towards him. They appeared like molten bronze with the fire reflecting in them.

"I guess I'm not the only one with memories that haunt them," she quietly mumbled. Then her cheeks reddened, as if she hadn't meant to say that aloud. "Never mind. Bad dream? You were whimpering a lot."

The reddish pink of embarrassment filled his sight. Nathair grumbled to himself as his tongue smacked inside his mouth, irritation evident.

I hate these dreams. They infrequently bombarded him, but that one in particular had come to the forefront because of her. *This is why I choose not to sleep.* A choice made from necessity, and one he couldn't always adhere to – every living creature needed sleep. Nathair's attempt at thwarting the need often saw him losing that battle after weeks.

He finally unlatched his claws, hissing in pain as he did, to scratch at the side of his neck. He shuddered, as a new fragment continued to flicker in his mind's eye, although much more faded and quieter.

It was unwise of me to bring her here. His nightmare was just a reminder.

Despite his desire to protect the small prey before him, the little bunny he'd found, she was in danger every second she sat there. He may lash out in his sleep or, worse still, while he was awake but semi-conscious. A fragment, if not contained, could drive him to momentary madness, and cause him to act irrationally and with deep confusion.

Despite his short sleep, exhaustion weighed on him due to her disturbing him. He needed to let his mind recuperate in order to hold back the barrage that constantly battered him within it.

Nathair turned his skull away to look at the wall.

I miss home. His simple rock and his false lake in Tenebris. It'd been his home for over two hundred and eighty years. His life may have been boring, but it had been easy and mostly untroubled – from environmental factors, at least. This life was too messy, too confusing.

Now, he was doing foolish things, like keeping this female as some kind of human pet.

What must I do to keep her content and safe? Feed her, give her water, a bed, and... pat her on the head? *Why was it my territory she found?*

Had she gone to another pond just a little east of his own, he wouldn't have grown curious about her.

Instead, he was finding himself oddly entranced by the beautiful female he currently had in his keeping. Worse still, he liked that her peach-and-vanilla scent was filling up his home. The desire to scoop her up and place her in his nest itched at his scales, and he was failing to control the urge.

He specifically hadn't looked towards it until he finally dropped his sight down from the wall to it. Although it would look like a lumpy rock in the darkness to a human, he could see something glinting from the recess of his walled, bird-like nest covered in animal skins.

Since Nathair was much taller than her, he doubted she'd see the way his nest gleamed in the firelight. The sparkling caught his eye, and it made his chest swell as dark green filled his sight.

He snapped his head away, averting his gaze before he was truly mesmerised by it. *No. Do not place the little human in your nest.* Because, once things were placed there, he had a tendency to become violently possessive about them.

Things in his nest, especially pretty little things, were *his*.

For now, she was still separated from it. Should she request her departure, he may more readily give it if he didn't mentally or physically place her in it. He'd already brought her to his home and was feeling rather... inclined to keep her here.

It was best that he didn't deepen his attachment until she made up her mind. Hopefully, she gave up on him. If she did, then he could wipe his hands of this female, who was in just as much danger being here with him as out in the mountain ranges.

"A-are you bleeding?" her sweet, high-pitched voice asked. It was shaken and unsure.

Nathair brought his gaze to her. Dark brows were furrowed in his direction while her teeth nibbled at her bottom lip. He looked down at the eight tracks of blood currently dripping from his own tail. He covered one of his own claw punctures with a hand, wincing as he did.

This is nothing. He'd done much worse to himself on accident since coming back to life.

"I have some medicinal herbs, if you need them," she offered.

When he lifted his skull to her, she darted her face away as if to nervously hide it. Then she dragged her bag closer and dug through it. A brown cloth pouch was pulled from it, as well as her drinking sack. She stood and tentatively came closer with her hands out.

"Do you want me to take a look at it? It wouldn't be good if they became infected." Linh licked at her lips and inched closer, bit by bit. "It's the least I can do for you."

Unable to answer, Nathair just tilted his head in puzzlement that she'd even suggested it, and that she was choosing to come closer. Although the front of her clothes had dried, her back still looked rather saturated. He thought she'd rather remain near the warmth.

She wishes to aid me? He didn't understand this female.

Not only was she not afraid of him, although wisely wary, she was showing him kindness. He'd never experienced kindness from another who wasn't one of his own creators. Even the few Mavka he'd met, Merikh and Aleron, had not shown him such care.

When she was less than a foot away from him, he clasped her hand holding the pouch. She gasped lightly and halted. A frown marred her features when he pushed her hand down and shook his head, making the tiniest sound of dry bones rattling together.

He didn't need, nor want, her help. *I will heal tomorrow. Has she not noticed my wounds from the bandit attack have faded already?* If he'd needed help at any point, it would have been then – not that he would have allowed her this close to him.

Now that she was nearer, so was the freshness of her scent as it poured straight off her skin.

"You don't want my help?" she asked, only to squeak when he lowered his head to sniff at her cheek.

The smell of her tears lingers. Nathair was rather put off by it. *At least she is no longer spilling them.*

Since she wouldn't explain why she cried, he, at the time, thought she may have done so because he'd brought her here. What right did she have to cry about the safety he provided beneath the ground, when she annoyingly pleaded for it?

He didn't like feeling guilty, and long ago realised he was rather sensitive and susceptible to such a horrid emotion. Whenever his orbs flared a darker orange, he had a tendency to berate himself – even if he didn't understand why. The emotion was one that tended to squeeze behind his sternum, as if punishing him for even the tiniest fault.

To make himself feel better, he'd chosen to believe her tears weren't due to him. Therefore, there was little he could do to make sure she didn't spill more. It's not like he could ask her, so she would have to choose whether to tell him or not.

He almost snorted a singular dark chuckle. *Doubtful. It is unlikely she will seek comfort from something like me.*

To her kind, he was a monster. Mavka were, in fact, just that. Born and bred for destruction, in order to ferry more souls.

To *cleanse* them so their father did not have to and then ferry them once they'd finished eating their real prey: Demons. Although their insatiable hunger was a nasty byproduct of the need to find a bride, take their soul, and bond it to them eternally, Weldir had wished for their creation to destroy

Demons.

Humans were just unfortunate casualties in a tiny war the untouchable god had created.

Still, the fact that this little female had offered to assist him was rather tender, and her scent under the lingering saltiness of her tears had him sniffing for more. His tongue tingled with the desire to see if she tasted how she smelt.

She lifted her shoulder and stumbled back to escape, and Nathair reared his head back. His sight shifted to reddish pink once more when he realised what he'd been doing, and he slunk back to rest upon himself. Linh covered the side of her face he'd been sniffing with the back of her hand, her palm towards him as her cheeks seemed to darken.

She is rather... meek. Even though she'd been stubborn and as unmoving as he could be, she was showing she had a softness to her.

To his dismay, he found that rather endearing.

He was rather fond of non-threatening things. And, from the memory of when he'd been in pain and shivering from the coldness of blood loss, he knew her to be remarkably soft. She was small, and wouldn't fill much space, but he already knew her to be warm and feminine to lie with.

"If you don't mind, could you show me a place that I can use to go to the toilet and bathe?" she muttered quietly, her cheeks flaring once more as she looked away. Linh rubbed at her arm. "I'm sure you don't want me to do that just anywhere, and I'd prefer privacy. I also... um, I don't feel comfortable peeing near the water, since you obviously swim and breathe in it."

He lifted his gaze to the moss-covered rock ceiling of his cave. *I forgot other creatures have these urges.* Where could she do these things in his home?

I do have a hidden area which contains a sprinkle of water that washes out to the ocean. It was dark, though, and he doubted she'd be able to see the way. It could also be dangerous if she went there without him to guard her.

Nathair had no ward in place, and there was a large beach entering into this cave system.

So long as she only does these things throughout the day, it should be fine. With a sigh, Nathair unfurled himself and slunk to the side, hoping she'd follow. *I will have to scout each morning to make sure no Demons have snuck inside and tucked themselves away.*

He didn't know how to explain this to her.

SEVEN

With a gasp, Linh jerked awake when something lifted her foot. She sat up, her jacket – which she'd been using as a blanket – falling to her legs as she backed away from the Duskwalker.

Pinstripes of sunlight peeked through the cracks of the ceiling, highlighting that it was daytime. The fire was low, but not gone, as if Nathair had thrown more wood onto it at some point.

The smell of brine, fresh and salty, wafted from him. *He smells like sea air.* Her gaze drifted to the two fish dangling in his right hand as he gently swayed them above her.

"Did you go fishing for me?" she asked, rubbing the sleep from her eyes before double-checking that he'd truly brought her food.

Lowering himself, he dangled the fish closer as if he wanted her to take them. She lifted her hands out and grabbed each one by its tail fin.

"Thank you," she stated, offering him a smile. "Good morning, by the way."

Although he couldn't respond, she preferred talking to him as though he could. And, considering his orbs shifted to that brighter yellow he'd shown her meant joy, she had a funny feeling he appreciated it.

Still discombobulated from waking, Linh held up the meal

he'd provided, wondering what she was supposed to do now. She'd gutted fish before, but...

"I have a dagger, but I don't think I trust using it on food I'll be eating." Considering it belonged to Bragg, it likely had human or Demon blood on it, and there was no way in hell she'd be willing to use it to cut food she was about to ingest. "Do you happen to have something sharp I can use? A blade perhaps?"

Turning swiftly, Nathair slithered towards an area she thought was a large, lumpy boulder. Using his hands to walk, as if he'd moved so fast his torso had dipped to the ground, he disappeared into shadow.

Chinking, clattering, and chiming rang out as he dug through unknown artefacts. When he returned, he held some kind of steak knife. She blinked at it, surprised there were barely any rust spots on it. It even reflected some of the pinstripes of sunlight spotting around them.

Just as she went to place a fish on the ground so she could take the blade, Nathair let loose a curt growl. He pointed at the fish and shook his head. Honestly, the fish were heavy, and her arms were starting to hurt from holding them up. She also didn't know what he was trying to say.

Once more, she went to place one down, and he let out another growl. Her back stiffened when his orange orbs flared red.

"I can't grow a third arm," she argued. "I need to put one down to take the knife, Nathair."

Linh felt a little self-conscious every time she stated his name, unsure if she was butchering it. Na-th-ere: that was how she pronounced it. He'd never spoken it, and she just reassured herself since he'd never corrected her.

He carefully reached forward and held the fish for her instead. She smiled at that, considering it wouldn't get dirty with his assistance.

I'm just choosing to ignore where his hands have been. If they were clean. Then again, she doubted her own were sanitary either, but she couldn't and wouldn't complain.

She wrinkled her nose as she tried to remember how to prepare fish. She hadn't eaten it often, as the river trout this far north were seasonal, and many refused risking overnight travel in the mountains to catch them.

With Nathair's help, she was able to gut it, remove its scales and fins, and tie it back together. The entire time, she was aware that the Duskwalker observed her with rapt curiosity. He even mimicked her, watching what she did so he could copy her while using his claws. Since he'd obtained plenty of firewood for her, she staked the fish and then set hers over the campfire that currently had no flames and only burned hot coals. Nathair did the same with the second one.

Even when they were done, he lingered far too close for comfort, with barely any space separating them. She could almost brush her shoulder against a thick wrap of tail, like he was trying to trap her in with his body and the fire.

Gosh, his presence was overbearing.

I thought he'd keep his distance from me, she mused, eyeing him cautiously.

Just as the sunlight faded yesterday, Nathair had slithered off to the other side of this crescent shape of land. She knew he'd stopped and seated himself there, his glowing orange orbs giving away where he went.

She thought he'd been trying to put space between them. Considering she'd kind of forced him to save her multiple times, she figured he was sulking about having her in his home.

She felt bad about that, but she also couldn't regret it. She'd needed someone, anyone, to aid her. She didn't care who or what they were, so long as they were safe.

And despite what he was, Linh was beginning to regard him as safe. Scary, and a little off-putting with his serpent skull and body, but he hadn't hurt her, hadn't tried to do anything cruel towards her.

She needed that. A presence that, although daunting, was

secure. It made a pang of tenderness spread throughout her chest as they both watched the fish cooking over the hot coals.

I was scared of falling asleep. Maybe that's why he put space between them – had he been able to sense she was uncomfortable?

She'd slept lightly at first, worried he'd finally make a snack of her or try to touch her while she was seemingly unconscious. Both were scary, both made her stomach tighten.

The fact he didn't come near her meant she'd finally... *rested.* Although her sleep was fitful and plagued with horrible nightmares, each time she woke up, she'd been alone. No one was holding her when she didn't want them to, and there wasn't an uncomfortable presence lingering.

The fire had been warm, her jacket comforting, and her bag the most amazing pillow – only because it meant she was free.

She blinked her lazy eyes. The area was quiet, and she'd forgotten how much she missed silence. There was no clattering of armour, or the banging of swords in the midst of training. No kicking of dirt from at least a dozen footsteps. Just blissful nature as it ebbed and flowed around her.

Even Nathair's breaths were quiet, although still noticeable due to his colossal size.

Her heart hadn't felt this settled and at peace for so long. Before, it felt like it was always racing, seconds from imploding from stress and anxiety. Her forehead didn't feel so weighted with depression and hopelessness. Her mind, although scarred, didn't pound behind her eyes as she constantly searched for a way to escape.

She took in the long, boring silence, and almost wanted to weep with relief.

"I like your home," Linh stated as she crossed her legs. She gave the fire a small smile, hoping that Nathair could see it and would understand it was because of him. "It's peaceful. I like how quiet it is."

The longer the silence dragged on, the more she wished they could fill it. She wanted to learn more about the person who saved her, yearning to be able to converse with him in the blissful quietness of the environment. She was eager to hear their conversation echo, as opposed to her previous flinching whenever a loud bash or sharp clang in the background put her nerves on high alert and rendered her silent with worry.

He said he lost his voice, so I wonder what it sounds like. Did he magically lose it, or was there something physical at play?

I wonder if I can help him. Or, perhaps, find a way for them to speak, even if it was without his voice. *I know sign language. Perhaps I can teach him.*

A small rumble came from him, and he lowered himself into his circling tail. It moved, slithering around and scraping loose rocks against the stone ground.

Her cheeks warmed when she realised he was releasing a quiet purr again, but he was so close, his chest right next to her, that it sounded loud. For some reason, her heart stuttered, and she found herself wanting to give more compliments to see if the sound could deepen.

She looked up. "I like how the sun streaks are really pretty. They make everything bright enough for me to see all the vegetation growth on the ceiling and walls." He blocked most of the underwater lake from view, so she brought her gaze to what she could see of it. "The water smells nice, and the trickling feels really good to listen to. It made it easy to fall asleep. You picked a wonderful home, Nathair."

The more she spoke, the deeper his purr became. Then she let out a tiny squeak and lifted her arms when the tip of his tail slipped underneath her crossed knees and circled her backside.

He did nothing more but press his tail around her, but her heart sped up. She wasn't sure if that was in bashful joy like before, or the nervousness of being touched.

Lifting her face, she found herself gazing into bright-yellow orbs and a serpent skull. His hooked ram horns glistened from a streak of light bouncing straight onto one. Both glittered from the fire, reflecting the golden hairline fractures, and she found it remarkably beautiful.

Moments before, his presence had felt imposing. Now, as she stared into the vortex of his glowing orbs, a sense of... calm washed over her. His touch no longer felt wrong or ugly, and instead made her feel lightly cradled and safe.

It helped that his hands never reached for her. They remained inside his wrappings, as if he wanted to hold her in the most informal way to show his appreciation for her compliments.

His orbs flickered with dark green, and she recoiled in surprise, which made him do so as well. His tail slid away, and she averted her gaze when she realised they'd just been staring at each other.

Licking at her lips, unsure as to why she was nervous – but not in a way that twisted her stomach with fear – she tucked a stray hair behind her ear.

"T-thank you again for getting me food." She assumed, since he'd given them to her, that he'd intended for her to eat them. "I've eaten fish, but it's rare – since people need to leave our villages to get them. I'm kind of excited, since I can tell you got them from the sea due to the smell of you. I wonder if they taste different from freshwater fish."

His tail tip slipped back underneath her thighs to circle her backside. She could almost *feel* his thoughts with the action: *'She likes the food I caught for her.'* His tail gripped even tighter than before.

He likes to be reassured. If it was that easy to keep the Duskwalker content, then Linh would happily supply him with plenty of reassurance.

Once her meal finished cooking, she placed the bottom of the sticks into a crack of rock so they would stay upright to cool. Then she rose to grab more wood.

All the hairs on her body stood on end when the Duskwalker let out a long but quiet growl as she left his side. Her stomach clenched like the strangest butterflies had taken flight. Yet he never stopped her from walking away, allowing her to do what she wanted, even if it displeased him.

She cast him a glance when she placed a log into the fire. Then she sat exactly where she'd been before.

The lingering growl evolved into his purr once more. When his tail curled around her, it slid her just a little closer to him until she was pressed completely against the folded thick limb. His entire body seemed to vibrate with the noise, tingling her senses and somehow softening her muscles.

The bass of it, how content it sounded, had her melting a little. Big and scary things shouldn't purr so easily, and it made him come across as caring in the strangest of ways. It also showed that he liked her presence, and she already surmised she didn't mind his.

The more time she spent with him, the easier it was to lower her guard. And not once, even when she began to eat the food he offered, was that trust violated. He just sat with her.

She did notice that his body would clench and ripple everywhere except for where she was pressed. His muscles against her remained lax, and she ended up letting out a small laugh.

"I thought you wanted to hold me, but you were really just stealing my warmth, weren't you?" It made what he was doing less sweet.

He answered her with a snorted huff. She peeked at him, and he shook his head.

She lifted her chin, while trying to keep her small smile of playfulness from curling her mouth. When she almost lost that war, she covered it with the tips of her fingers and tapped her lips.

"Excuse me, but I do remember a certain snake Duskwalker using me as a living heat source just the other day."

To her surprise, Nathair opened his maw. Then he closed it, only to open again, while he wiggled his head side to side.

"Are you mocking me?" she asked, her eyelids lowering in feigned annoyance.

It almost looked like he was doing what humans do when

mocking each other by opening and closing their hands like a mouth! So, she placed down her nearly eaten fish, lifted her hand, and did just that. She flapped it, then opened it in his direction while doing a hiss.

He paused before coming closer to sniff at her fingers. *I must admit, the shape is similar to his skull.* Her whole arm kind of looked snake-like.

His breath is remarkably warm. She hadn't expected to feel any heat from him, considering he was a snake. She expected him to be cold-blooded, but perhaps he was actually lukewarm-blooded instead. *I guess he's not completely reptilian, then.*

The heat drained from her horrified face when Nathair closed his maw around her entire hand. He didn't bite down, didn't hurt her, but a shiver of trepidation raced down her spine when his forked tongue licked against her palm.

My hand is in a Duskwalker's mouth! She didn't know whether to scream, grab his tongue and yank on it, or faint. She didn't dare pull away in case she ended up hurting herself.

Thankfully she couldn't feel the fangs she'd seen him sink into one of the bandits. As she trembled, her eyes wide, a chuckle radiated from his throat. He pulled back slowly until her hand popped out of his mouth.

Linh spread her fingers when she discovered copious amounts of saliva. It was clear and clung to itself, and her lips twisted in disgust.

"Yuck!" Just as she was about to wipe her hand clean on her clothes, she leaned forward and swiped it back and forth against his scales. "Here. Take back your drool."

Nathair's chuckles deepened. He pinched her wrist gently and shoved her wet hand against her face.

"Ewww!" she squealed even louder, rolling onto her back as she wiped at her face with the backs of her arms.

Her cheeks flushed in both embarrassment and annoyance, and she rolled to sit up with her features in a tight pout. She opened her mouth to yell her outrage, only to close it.

She began to laugh as well, since he continued to do so while he held the end of his snout like he wished to hide it. *I guess it was kind of funny*. She also hadn't expected Nathair to have an odd side to him like this.

"I didn't know you could be devious or playful," she teased.

Her heart was racing, but the humour-filled beats were so strong in comparison to the pacing of fear and anxiety she'd been experiencing for months. Each one pounded, but the relief of them touched her all the way to the centre of her being.

I didn't know Duskwalkers could laugh. Despite how disgusting it'd been to have his saliva all over her, and how much she'd been afraid that she was about to lose a hand, she found the aftermath rather charming.

If his voice was anything like the deep bass of the chuckle that came from his throat, she knew it would be soothing. He'd also... picked on her, and she didn't mind a bully – she could be rather conniving herself. She would find a way to get back at him.

It'd been so long since she'd felt anything nice. Tears threatened to bubble in her eyes at just being able to experience even a small amount of joy. The fact that she wanted to cry because she felt that way only brought on a crushing wave of sadness. The realisation why was rather painful.

The tears never came, although they tingled her sinuses. Instead, she focused on just this moment. A strange time where she laughed with a Duskwalker – someone who meant death, and currently felt like salvation.

Who else could say they ever experienced something as absurd as this?

Once his chuckles died, he turned and put his hands out to the flickering flames. His skull tilted in her direction before facing the fire again. He did it repeatedly, his fingers wiggling at the red glow.

Her brows drew together when she understood he was trying to explain something.

She didn't know what that was.

Little human, I have all the warmth I need right here, Nathair thought, as he nudged his head in the direction of the fire.

Her first assumption had been correct. He'd been trying to bring this captivating creature closer. To not just have any warmth, but the feeling of *her* warmth against him, her softness, her scent, until it touched him and soaked beneath his scales.

In reality, Nathair didn't know what he truly sought. Not from her, nor himself. He guessed he liked her presence, liked her, but he was deeply conflicted.

He desired she leave his home for both their safety, yet the moment she'd gotten up, an angry growl had slipped from him. When he'd gone hunting, he hadn't particularly cared if she truly ate what he caught. If she didn't want it, he'd planned to shrug. Yet, the moment she'd tried to put a single fish down, he wanted to see her eat the food he provided.

He slept on the other side of the cave to keep her safe. Demons may have tried to enter through the cave entrance had he not, that's what he told himself, but... he'd been afraid to keep her close in case he lashed out at her. He'd watched her for a long while, finding himself restless.

He didn't *want* to hurt her. Not because it'd weigh on his conscience, which it would, but because he rather liked this little creature. Already he could tell he didn't want to snuff out the flames of her life force.

Then Nathair's conscience had receded as fragments forced his consciousness back to freely play. His sight had remained open, white with anxiety, but it was the only way he could rest.

Now that he'd been returned to life, Nathair found himself to be rather volatile. Which was why, when he'd awoken, he'd left the female to sleep while he released some of his pent-up emotions.

To roar beneath the waves and make all the sea creatures scatter. To bash his skull against sand that couldn't hurt him, but felt soothing, like it abraded the inside of his mind. To claw at seaweed until all the frustration flowed out of him like a river.

He felt constricted by her presence. He was constantly wary of himself near her, which put additional strain on his mind and body, as he fought to keep himself lucid and at the forefront more than ever. Yet somehow it seemed... *easier*.

A fish had eventually glittered nearby, and he'd grown enrapt watching the pretty thing swimming so casually. He'd been envious of its ability to be so carefree. It even swam right up to him while he sat motionless beneath the subtle, rolling waves, its flipper tapping against him as it nibbled at the algae and sea debris he'd cast into the water.

It'd reminded him of the little female in his home – carefree of danger, and foolishly coming near him.

So, he'd darted his hand down and grabbed it for her. An easy prey to catch, just like her, and he intended to feed prey to prey and hope the prettier one smiled for him.

And smile she had, only to giggle at his antics.

Nathair gestured to the fire once more, trying to explain that he'd just wanted to bring her closer earlier. She was annoying, like sand caught under his scales, but he was beginning to like the way she itched.

She speaks to me as if I can respond. He appreciated that, as he wanted to feel like a presence worth speaking to. He could hear, could find a way to answer if he chose to. *I like her voice.*

Linh was soft-spoken, like she was demure and coy with her words. There was a gentleness every time she spoke, even if he could hear the drawl of sorrow. That dismal tone sounded *wrong*, as if it shouldn't exist within her melody.

Which made her laughter all the more compelling.

Of course, her compliments had made pride swell in his chest. His home, nest, and territory were important to him. Even if he'd gained much humanity, he was still a Mavka at heart.

When he found his pond, he'd only intended to go for a dip to wet his scales. Lindiwe, the Witch Owl, had sat upon the very boulders Linh had first collapsed against.

The Witch Owl left when he never resurfaced for her, figuring he'd found a place to call his own and accepted it. The only creature he'd resurfaced for was the little female beside him.

Once he'd sunk down and discovered this cavern, he knew it would become his nest. He'd fought for it and chased out the many Demons who lived here. The battle had taken days, as dozens of the foul vermin refused to relent. He'd pushed them all back, day by day, until the entire cave system was his.

All his. His nest, with many pretty things inside it.

For this *pretty* female to compliment it... he had the consuming desire to bring her near.

She would never know of his feats in acquiring it, but the fact she liked his home made all the pain even more worthwhile. It made him want to keep her here and tuck her away forever. To hiss at anything that dared to take what was his, much like his greedy, territorial need to defend his home.

"You like the fire?" she asked, one side of her face scrunching up in question at his nodding, making her left eye squint. "If you bring more wood, I'm sure I can keep it burning for us, then."

Nathair would have shaken his head, but he didn't want her to think he *didn't* like the fire; he very much did. Instead, he slid her a little closer again until she was against him.

He wiggled his fingers at the flames.

"I'm really sorry, but I don't understand."

An annoyed growl vibrated from his throat. He didn't know how else to explain it.

Giving up, he leaned back until his humanoid torso rested

against his lengthy lower half. He placed his head on the top coil to sulk while staring at her.

She gave him a weak and apologetic smile, and he huffed at her for it.

I wish I could speak to her. He likely would have scared her off his territory that first day, but now he'd like to just be able to converse with her.

Since Nathair couldn't communicate what his 'Nathair speak' gestures meant, he was aware that they would mean very little to this female. Even if she did know this country's signing language, the language of Nathair would only ever be one of Tenebris – a realm which existed within the plane of a hungry god's stomach.

Perhaps I can teach her? He'd rather she learn his, since he was the one who needed to speak it.

A rather dismal gloom crested over his forehead when he thought that may be a waste of time. *She will eventually want to leave.* He was starting to feel rather sour about that prospect, but he was merely waiting for her to state her desire to abandon him.

Her enjoyment of his home would be temporary.

Humans didn't like the darkness. She'd soon long for the warmth of the sun, and the comfort of her own people.

Nathair smacked his tongue inside his mouth in irritation. *I give her another day.* Despite the weird pang in his chest at the thought, he wouldn't get his hopes up.

She was a pretty human, and she'd soon long for the freedom to find a mate. Someone with a face of flesh who had two legs.

Dark orange flared in his sight at the thought of keeping her trapped here against her will. He shook his head, clearing himself of such a horrid idea even if it was swiftly becoming a greedy desire of his.

Which is why you will not put her in your nest. Or place her on his body to rest upon. On the outside of his wrappings should be fine, but if he placed her weight on him... and he *liked* it, he may want to keep her there and strangle the desire to leave him from her.

He already had the niggling itch to sniff all the places she'd left her peach-and-vanilla scent upon him.

His gaze slipped to the ruby earrings dangling from her lobes, watching them sparkle in the firelight. *I will be taking those from her, though.* Should she desire to leave, he would consider them a parting gift.

They would remind him of the human he'd saved. If he couldn't add her to his treasures, he'd make sure she left a mark somehow.

EIGHT

Nathair watched the human rise to her feet, even when he'd been content to sit next to her by the fire. He was a simple creature who desired very little and didn't particularly long for movement. She, however, was a fidgety little thing, constantly moving, craning her head around, and warily eyeing his closeness.

She was beginning to do the last one less and less.

"Alright, Nathair," she sang, as she walked over to the fresh lake to wash her hands of the food she'd just eaten. "Instead of sitting here and letting my mind wander, would you care to show me the rest of your home?"

She turned to him and placed her hands on her hips. Her smile was gentle, not grinning in mischief, but not small enough to show it was fake.

I don't particularly understand her. She was a human sharing such an expression with a Mavka. He also didn't understand why her shining it at him made a dull throb lance his groin; it was nothing but a smile. *She has a lovely smile.* At least, when it was genuine.

He knew other Mavka had gained brides, so it wasn't totally strange, but they could speak to them. In his opinion, he'd thought all those humans may be unsound of mind.

Linh didn't seem completely sane, considering she'd rather beg a monster for help than find her own kind. That was like a bunny asking a wolf for help, and not expecting to have its cute, fluffy body ripped in half.

With a sigh, and dipping his head to the side purposefully to show his reluctance, Nathair unfurled himself. Waving his hand to gesture that she should follow, he slithered to the side.

"Wait! I need to grab my shoes and jacket," she stated, her feet pitter-pattering against the stone as she ran to her bag.

He waited for Linh to don a pair of black flats and return to his side. Eyeing the top of her dark hair, he noted the double braids she'd twisted into two low buns that sat on the back of her head. Her hair looked thick and glossy, even in the shadows that had befallen them.

She shone a thankful expression up at him since he'd waited.

"I don't know why, but I keep forgetting you're so big," she said with an awkward laugh, that wariness rising in her features.

He tilted his head at her, then took in that she was three feet shorter than him currently. Should he choose to, he could make that much more vast, as he was able to lean upon his tail over halfway before beginning to tip over. Going lower meant he would eventually tip forward and need to walk on his hands to keep his humanoid torso up.

He was aware he was likely over thirty-three feet in total length, if not more, since that was the last measurement Weldir had taken of him, and he'd grown much since then. Nathair was also thicker than her, except for the last few feet of his tail.

She was tiny in comparison, in every sense possible.

The cave tunnel opening of his home immediately shrouded them in sightless nothingness. Linh let out a squeak and reached her hands out to feel where she was going, unable to see that she was about to walk into a wall.

Nathair reached his arm out so that she might hold on to his forearm. Since he was a Mavka, he was able to see perfectly despite the complete lack of light. He guided her down the right of the narrow tunnel, taking her east.

Once more, Nathair showed her the area in which she could bathe. Due to the constant trickling of water, her scent didn't linger here, even though she'd already used it.

With his thumb claw, he made a tiny incision in his palm and slapped his hand against the wall. An orange magic circle glowed to life, giving her just enough light to see the entire small area if she squinted hard enough. Which she did, her straight black eyelashes tipping.

She wasn't surprised by the use of magic, as he'd already done this for her last time.

He pushed her into the room while slithering away – his way of telling her to do what she needed to.

"Y-you better not be watching!" she shouted, her voice echoing down the tunnel.

Nathair answered her with a growl, highlighting his annoyance that she needed to state this once again.

I know humans consider this private. He had enough fragments to understand many human customs, despite how pointless he considered them. No female in his memories appreciated intimate moments being heard, viewed, or smelt, and many males were similar.

"I'm just double-checking!" she whined back. Then, as if she thought he wouldn't hear, she added, "Grumpypants. Not that he *can* wear pants."

I like this about her. She'd been able to surmise why he'd growled. He liked that she guessed, or asked questions for clarity, and made it seem like he'd stated his intentions verbally, even when he couldn't.

She also rambled and muttered a lot, and he hoped it was done freely and in comfort. Nathair intended her no purposeful harm, and he appreciated that she could sense this.

He let her know he heard it by opening and closing his maw as silent back-talk. Her cheeks cutely pinkened when she caught the movement upon her return, and realised she'd been heard. She entered the tunnel with her face and hands wet, as if she'd washed both.

Linh guided herself back to him by pressing against the wall, then pushed away from it when she must have seen his glowing orange orbs. Something about having her delicate fingertips searching for him in the dark made his stomach and chest clench. It sent a ripple down his spine until his tail tip flicked to the side when her hot palms touched his cool forearm.

As much as he would have liked to leave his light marking everywhere they went for her benefit, it would be wasted. He could only leave one at a time, otherwise the old one would vanish.

It was a rather nifty trick: a drop of blood for a small amount of light.

He'd discovered the ability before he'd died, as he often came across underwater tunnels. After battling aquatic Demons, he found himself in dark holes and desired additional light, as it was difficult to smell anything lurking below the surface of the water if he was up on land.

It just looked like ink, otherwise.

While he tried to rest and wait to heal, his blood often dripped into the water and brought enemies to him by the taste, which pushed him to plead for light at one point. Light had appeared, glowing as a tiny, hand-sized magical symbol right where he rested.

A peaceful and comforting additional glow.

Linh tentatively held his wrist as he slithered northwest down the tunnel, his long tail creating S patterns behind him. Tiny rocks shifted between his scales, as did a tiny layer of dirt. Her shoes pattered and echoed, the steps hesitant at first, but growing more confident the longer she walked beside him.

Nathair brought his gaze to her hand placement on him, and his sight shifted to bright yellow. *She touches me freely.* He didn't think he'd ever not be pleasantly surprised by this.

Many long minutes passed before he took her to a large alcove. He pricked his palm with his thumb again, placing it against the ground in the middle. The orange glow barely reached the walls, but it lit up everything enough to show what was here.

He held his breath the moment a tiny waft of fear came from her.

"Are..." Linh gulped as she shrunk closer to him. "Are they Demon *nests*?"

He made sure she was looking up at him before he nodded. He slid closer to a partially dismembered nest and grabbed one of the decently sized branches. He yanked it free and then brought it closer to her so she could see.

Her dark brows drew together as she inspected it. She even touched the bark, only to lift a questioning expression up at him.

Nathair broke it apart in many places, then placed the pieces together on the ground.

"Oh. Are you trying to say this is where you've been grabbing the firewood from?"

He pointed at her while nodding.

Her eyes trailed over the many nests here, and an uncertain glint reflected in them. "Well, I guess we have plenty of it then." Once more, she tilted her face up to his. "Did... you have to get rid of them all, or were they already empty?"

Nathair lifted a single finger and dipped it to the left.

"The first one?" He nodded, and her lips curled. "I should have figured. You're so strong that it's almost frightening. I bet you killed those Demons just as easily as those bandits."

His chest swelling and bowing outwards with pride, he didn't dare attempt to correct her. There had been many Demons here in these tunnels – dozens of them – and it'd taken him a long while to get rid of them. They either died, and he dragged their disgusting bodies out to be washed to sea, he ate them, or they fled to save themselves.

Still, the comment on his strength had his pulse spiking.

I am strong. Physically, emotionally, mentally. Even though he knew his mind to be a little broken, his will was strong from holding back the fragments.

He knew his capabilities, his weaknesses.

He was a formidable Mavka, and she'd chosen a good protector so long as he didn't lose his lucidity and turn on her. Nathair was surprised he hadn't already.

Her scent seemed to be soothing the worst of it, as did her voice. Her face may be beautiful, but it did little to keep his horrid human memories at bay, other than shadowing them when he incidentally became lost in his slips of lucidity.

Now that she felt at ease again, she inspected the size of the room while remaining near his light.

The orange glow that matched his orbs gleamed against her skin. Seeing her washed in it, something that was solely his, had a dark emotion twisting around his heart. Somehow, she looked even more alluring in it. It brightened all her features and highlighted her high cheekbones and soft angles.

If he wasn't careful, he was aware pretty creatures like her could become the light in the darkness for a Mavka like himself — just as his glow chased away the shadows for her in this otherwise dreary alcove.

Wanting to escape such thoughts, he gently slipped his wrist against her hand. Despite her hitch of breath, she didn't recoil. She seemed to sense he wanted to move them on.

Many other areas matched the alcove he'd just shown her. He'd already rifled through the items belonging to the Demons he'd evicted, taking anything that sparkled or gleamed for himself.

Many ceramic pots lay broken or on their sides from disuse. There were a few human items they'd taken, like fishing rods, swords, and rusted plates. There was even a carriage wheel that was mostly rotten due to the constant moisture in the air.

Linh occasionally shivered under the weight of her cream-coloured hide jacket, but she never complained about the cold. He did notice she came closer to him when wind rushed up the tunnel, but he doubted his low body temperature aided her in any way.

She was the warmer one of the two of them.

She pressed her freezing fingers against his forearm when she grabbed it with both hands, and it felt like shards of ice against his scales. He didn't complain, instead soaking in the fact that she sought to be closer to him.

"Is that light up ahead?" she asked, her eyes squinting as if that would help her see.

She didn't look at him for an answer, so he didn't give one.

The answer was revealed as they came upon brightness. He could have led them further into his cave system and into darkness, but her expression stated she wanted to explore *why* there was light.

Nathair ducked into an opening and lowered his arm, since she no longer needed him. Except he had to quickly shove his hands out to catch her when she tripped the moment he moved his arm away.

Her gasp cut short when he propped her back on her feet, and her cheeks darkened at almost falling face first. That would have resulted in her going off the ledge and into the water below them.

"Thanks," she grumbled, her cheeks puffing as her lips pursed into a cute pout.

He snorted out a huff to let her know he heard her and didn't mind catching her. Once she was settled, she stepped closer to the high ledge with her lips parting.

A sharp wind gusted into the wide, open alcove and ruffled her clothes and hair. A large and somewhat deep puddle of water remained unmoving in a recess of rock and sand. A beach spanned between them and the ocean shore hundreds of metres away, where waves crashed and frothed.

The air was heavy with the scent of brine, and salt particles clung to his scales.

Nathair followed her gaze as she took in the massive area they were in. Rock had been smoothed over time by waves, sand, and salt, leaving a giant hole in the side of the mountain cliff.

Within the water below them, parts of a small ship lay

wasted and eroded after hundreds of years of lying there. There wasn't much to it since most of it was under sand, and the mast had long broken in half. At night, during high tide, water nearly came to the ledge they stood upon.

He guessed that the ship had sunk not long after the Demons' arrival on Earth, and it had been used in a futile escape attempt. There was an abandoned and dilapidated port only a few kilometres south of here.

"I didn't know we were so close to the ocean," Linh stated at his side, her voice raspy with awe.

The pond in which he'd met her may be close, but Nathair was lightning fast beneath the water, and no creature was speedier while submerged. The tunnel they'd swam through just to get to his own nest had required her to take a breath halfway through when she'd started kicking at him. That had been after minutes.

Adding to that, they'd been walking on a slight decline at a rather brisk pace for a little over an hour. They didn't linger long anywhere.

The cliff here dips in more than anywhere else along the shore. It was as if the ocean wished to shape this part of the land.

"Can we go down?" she asked, peeking over the ledge to look at the water. "I want to check out that broken ship."

Nathair inspected the water from a distance. He didn't trust it.

He held his hand up for her to wait as he climbed his way down. He entered the shallow pool without sparing her a glance. A small rock landed on his head from her trying to peek, but he ignored it as he lowered himself.

The moment his torso was beneath the surface, and he lay down, he opened his mouth and let water rush into his lungs. His gills flared, and the change of breathing technique made the iciness of the liquid suddenly bearable.

All seemed silent. Everything seemed empty. All he saw was muddy sand and rock, and the underside of the overturned ship beneath the water.

He waited, closing his sight to concentrate.

Then the surface stopped rippling from him disturbing it.

Subtle, minute thumping eventually vibrated in the water, and Nathair opened his sight. The moment he launched himself in that direction, with his long back fins flaring from underneath their hidden flaps, a bubbling shrill sounded.

A Demon leapt from the sand to swim away, but Nathair's unmatched speed had him grabbing it by its back flippers. When he lifted it from the water, it hissed and squealed with a seal-like face. It even gave a deep bawk as it tried to swipe at him, its red eyes dazed and confused.

Considering its lack of human features, he knew it'd rarely, if ever, eaten a human.

While it wiggled, he merely tossed the small and mostly defenceless Demon into the sun just before the cave opening. It rolled against the sand and immediately began to scream.

The Demon writhed, its void-like, skinless flesh immediately melting. Sulphur wafted from it as its purple insides were exposed before they, too, began to bubble. It writhed to bury itself beneath the sand as it flung it around in waves.

It didn't matter. It couldn't get itself underneath quick enough and disintegrated halfway buried. The rest bubbled and stained the yellowy grains in a melted blob of dark purple.

Rather pleased with himself that he'd been wise enough to double-check no Demon had come to seek shelter in his territory, he lifted his skull to Linh on the ledge with bright-yellow orbs. The colour instantly snuffed out to white, since she'd fallen back on her arse and looked utterly horrified. He tilted his head towards the now deceased Demon.

I did not consider how gruesome that may be. He thought she'd be relieved that she now knew for certain the water was safe.

He climbed back on the rock next to the pool and then cautiously slithered up to her. The scent of fear coming from her was light, but enough that he halted his breathing the moment he emptied his lungs.

Dark orange lifted into his orbs when he took in how frazzled her expression was as he drew closer. Her eyebrows were scrunched in obvious distress, and her lips were parted as though she'd silently screamed. She stared at the obvious puddle in the sand that had once been a Demon.

The moment his head height came to hers, where she sat on her rump, she gasped and recoiled to the side. Only to settle immediately upon looking at his skull.

"Holy shit! You were so fast!" She brushed her hand over the top of her hair as she averted her gaze. "It was like you knew where it was. You just leapt towards the sand and suddenly a Demon sprung from it. A-a fin even came from your back!"

Her little heart was racing, her breaths shallow and short.

Without being able to speak with her to soothe her, Nathair just rolled his skull in annoyance. He folded his arms and let out a guttural groan from his throat.

"You're right," she grunted out with forced nonchalance, throwing her hands up. "Sorry, didn't mean to freak out."

His head reared back at her sudden change of tone. *She got over that remarkably easily.* And her response had a quiet snicker rasping from him.

As she was standing, she shouted, "Did you just laugh at me?!" She placed her hands on her hips and narrowed her brown eyes into a tight glare. "That's not fair. Demons are freaky, okay? And I was about to go walking right to one."

Nathair waved his hand down his body, gesturing at it. *I'm a Mavka, female. How am I any better?*

As if she understood what he was trying to say, she wrung her hands together as she averted her gaze once more. Her cheeks darkened.

"You're different." Nathair waved at his body again and even lifted his tail. Her eyes darted to him due to the movement before looking off to the side. "You aren't trying to eat me."

Don't be so sure of that. He may accidentally hurt her, and the scent of her blood or fear would send him into a frenzy.

Nathair finally risked taking in a breath, and the scent of her fear had practically disappeared.

"I don't know why, but I trust you, Nathair," she grumbled while wringing her hands, making him tilt his head in surprise. "I know you're a Duskwalker, but you haven't hurt me once in the many *days* I've been with you. I'm afraid of a lot of things, and I'm so terrified of being alone out in the forest, but I'm not scared of you. Even though you're bigger than any Demon I've ever heard of, and quicker and stronger than any creature I've read about, you've proven how... compassionate you can be. You have no reason to protect me, and yet you've done so multiple times."

I did not know she feels this way about me. Trust? He didn't think he could obtain such a strong emotion from her.

Her faith was ill-given.

She does not belong in your nest. But with each pretty word from her mouth, each smile, and each acceptance of touch, Nathair was feeling the burning desire to put her in it. If he did, he knew he'd fucking keep her there.

Nathair darted his head away to avoid looking upon her when that burn radiated behind his sternum. He had half a mind to pick her up, throw her over his shoulder, slither to his nest, and shove her round backside into it.

Suddenly the pale skin of a man dipping his hands into a small chest of battered coins slipped across his conscience. They were counted nightly, as he coveted each coin like they were a rare beauty. His bald head and clean-shaved face reflected in the window of a fancy room, highlighted by the flame of a candle that showed the twisted greed in his stare.

The era didn't feel like the same as this one, as if the man lived hundreds of years ago. When riches and fine things could easily be kept, hoarded, and stolen.

Fuck, Nathair flung out mentally, clutching at his skull.

The greed of the human fragment boiled with his own that

was beginning to fester. The human's possessiveness of coin mingled with his growing desire to keep this female. *Mine. All mine. It's all mine.* Dark green entered his orbs, and suddenly her sweet scent wrapped around his scales like a discarded fishing net.

A small rock clunked against the side of his head, thankfully jarring him from the memory. With a snarl, he turned to Linh in anger. *How dare she throw–*

"Don't you groan at me like my feelings are bothersome, you silly snake!" she snapped. The mingle of hurt was evident in the slight glassiness of her eyes. "I was trying to be nice to you."

This time, she removed a shoe and launched it at his chest. Her toss had been soft, and it didn't hurt at all.

Did I groan? He didn't mean to, especially not after what she'd said to him.

Swiping her shoe, Nathair climbed up the rocks until they were the same height. He gave it to her, and she lightly snatched it in irritation before stomping it on. Unsure of how to apologise to the little female, he patted her head.

Her glare deepened, and he halted when he realised he was making it worse. She probably felt it was condescending.

He did the only thing he could think of. Nathair leaned forward quicker than she could react and slipped his tongue across her cheek. She let out a tiny gasp and stepped back. His forked tongue darted forward at the tanginess of her scent upon it, tasting it with his special glands.

"Y-you licked me." She covered his saliva track with the back of her wrist, but he noted that she wasn't attempting to wipe it away.

It seemed she didn't mind *why* his saliva lingered on her skin this time, or the action that had caused it.

She trusts me enough, which was why she felt brave enough to toss things at me. She'd be an idiot, otherwise. And the fact he'd hurt her feelings by accident had a warm fuzziness tingling his chest. It meant her words had been genuine.

So, he leaned against the ledge she was on until their faces were inches apart. She didn't back away, didn't even look afraid despite the concerned crinkle that formed in her forehead.

He attempted his apology a second time, as well as his gratitude for her bringing him out of the fragment with something as simple as a rock toss. Placing his hand on the small of her back to stop her from escaping, he rubbed the hard skeletal bone of his cheek against her soft one.

Nathair offered a short and sincere nuzzle, hoping that would better suit her tastes and convey what he wished to more effectively.

Within seconds, her cheek felt warmer. Her hands trembled as she held them together, and yet she never backed away.

He didn't know what any of that meant, but her eyes flicking away, only to come back before leaving again, seemed bashful.

She purposefully pouted, her cheeks rounding out. "Fine. I forgive you."

Pride in her made his chest feel swollen. *She is intuitive, even with a Mavka who cannot show his emotions with flesh.* He could tell she was young – she said she was in her early twenties – but she was wise enough to deduce most of what she needed to.

She was willing to try, which he would be forever grateful for. It made his lack of speech not feel so oppressing for him.

He hoped his voice one day returned, if only ever to thank her, or say her name.

Backing away, Nathair gestured towards the lower level of the cave alcove and the sunken ship. She leapt into action, and whether that be from excitement or embarrassment, he didn't know.

Linh slipped on wetness and a loose rock, and flew into him. The shock of it had him recoiling backwards, which made his tail slip down a boulder, and he fell as well. Unable to get his tail under his own body to catch himself, he wrapped his arms around her so she didn't crash against the ground.

Her scream echoed while he just patiently waited for them to stop falling. He tucked his head forward to avoid bashing his skull or horns and grunted at the impact.

The moment they halted, he dropped his arms to the ground, and closed his eyes to concentrate on not bursting into a fit of chuckles. *This human is rather clumsy. If I or a Demon don't eat her, she'll fall to her death.* He'd seen her trip four times now since the first day he'd met her.

"Oh my god," she groaned, covering her face and burying it against his exposed ribs. "That was so embarrassing. I'm so sorry."

Nathair, finding this rather humorous and wanting to needle her, pushed his tongue forward and let it droop down the side of his open maw. Unmoving, his sight closed, and halting his breath, he waited with his arms splayed.

"Thank you for catching me." She finally lifted her head. When he didn't do anything, she asked, "Nathair?"

Five. Four. Three. Two—

"Oh my gosh! Nathair!" She leapt off his body with a gasp, just so she could begin shaking him. "Oh no, I killed him." Then, for some weird reason, she began kicking his torso with the underside of her foot – albeit softly. "Now who will protect me from Demons? Hmm? You just had to go and die on me, didn't you?"

With a growl, he opened his sight to his usual orange and lifted his head. He lifted an arm to ask what the hell she was doing.

"Most dead things don't stick their tongue out when they die." Her eyes glinted with humour as she leaned over him with her hands on her hips. "Next time, make it more believable."

Nathair let out a loud chuckle as he twisted to push off on straightened arms, getting his tail to support his weight by shifting it under his heavy torso. Then he pulled himself upright and folded his arms.

Linh merely lifted her chin and walked around the lower level they'd fallen to.

From his spot, he stayed where he was as he watched her with mirth. *She is rather funny.*

If anything, Nathair was two things: lazy and bored. He found entertainment when it came crawling to him, and he enjoyed collecting things that sparkled because he adored playing with their reflective lights. Things that entertained him within his own spaces were what he coveted, and it made him greedy to keep them.

Linh filled the silence and radiated a beauty he hadn't truly understood could dazzle him. She was warm, both physically and towards him already. And she was brave enough to not be afraid of him, and he found that commendable.

I liked her weight on top of me. Her heat had instantly bled into his torso, and he yearned to wrap himself around her. He'd like his own personal heat source, one which was soft, smelt sweet, and could glitter if he showered her in sparkly, pretty things.

A shudder rippled down his body at just the thought of how much he knew that would entertain his bored and listless mind.

"Oooh! There are chests here!" she exclaimed from the other side of the pond she'd walked around.

Nathair already knew this, as he'd been the one to dig them out of the ship and had ripped them open with his claws. None of it had gained his interest except for what he'd already taken – a few bits of silver plates and cutlery.

A chest had been so waterlogged that the clothes inside had deteriorated the moment he'd tried to take them from it to cushion his nest. Another had coins and jewellery in it that he'd managed to scrape the rust from until their centres gleamed again or gems were revealed.

"There's a lamp and candles. Oh! And even some torches."

I'd forgotten about those. They had been in one of the chests that had managed to remain dry until he broke them open.

"Nathair, can you help me?" Her face was bright with cheer, as if the discovery of these ugly trinkets was wondrous. "If we fill that chest, we can light your cave so I can see better. I can use the carry lantern for the tunnels too."

She wants to change my home? Well, not change it, but add to it? *Does that mean... she does not intend to leave it?*

A dark emotion rippled down the exposed vertebrae of his spine. That shudder only deepened when she shone a bright and cheerful smile in his direction, and the red rubies dangling from her ears caught the bright sunshine that reflected against the sand.

This female had been in his home for less than two days, had pestered him and lingered on his territory for far longer, and now she sought to change his personal areas for herself. To add to and evolve them, as if she wished to leave her mark upon them until she forever changed them.

The places she'd left her peach-and-vanilla scent suddenly scalded his cool scales, and his heart picked up.

NINE

With the Duskwalker looming at her back, Linh shoved everything that may be of use into one of the chests that wasn't completely broken.

Okay. So he's laughing with me and playing pranks, she thought, as she shoved in another candle. *That's good... right? If I keep on his good side, maybe he won't make me leave? Hopefully I can convince him to be my friend.*

Linh was trying her hardest to not upset him, even when she stupidly kicked him for joking with her. *My emotions are so all over the place, I don't know what the hell I'm doing anymore.* She liked him a lot, but he also freaked her out.

She internally grumbled, while shoving an oil container into the chest.

Most of the items didn't have much rust or water decay, so she figured that the contents of these chests had only been taken from the water recently. The outsides, however, were caked in sediment and barnacles, which likely protected the insides as well as locked them shut without brute strength.

She asked Nathair to help her break open a large ceramic jar that was nearly the size of her torso. She thought it may have been wine, due to its mauve colouring and smell. Unfortunately, she'd accidentally knocked it over immediately after he'd opened it, rendering it useless when it shattered.

Gosh. I am not having a good day.

She'd slipped twice, fell on Nathair, and now broke something delicious. Thankfully, there had been a few smaller jars, and she took two, so she had something to cook with. The calories would do her good, and it was better than eating food with no spices.

Wine stops fermenting. Considering it'd been so airtight that not even seawater had leaked inside, she considered it safe for consumption.

Once Linh's loot was safely packed, she turned to Nathair.

"Is there anything else inside the ship?" She spared it a glance, her gaze roaming over it where it lay decrepit on its side.

He shook his head and picked up the chest to take it to the upper level.

"Actually," she started, fidgeting with her hands. Nathair paused and tilted his head at her, and her shoulders lifted in uncertainty. "I was wondering... is the beach safe? I would really like to go into the sun, and I've never seen the ocean up close before."

She tried not to be horrified by the creepy way his head turned a near one hundred and eighty degrees as he looked over his shoulder. Seeming to think on it, or maybe he was doing his weird senses scan or something, he eventually nodded. He placed the chest down at the bottom of the incline.

He seemed extra cautious about her and her ability to misstep even on a flat surface as they climbed down from the rocks. Linh removed her shoes to leave them behind and toed the sand.

It's warm. She hadn't expected the sand to heat, especially not in the first week of spring. A smile curled her lips.

For the first time, she heard Nathair slither as the tiny grains shifted and even squeaked under his tail. He appeared to put more strength into his slide.

I guess it's too loose for him to cross the sand properly.

"I've always wanted to go to the beach," Linh stated quietly as she walked, feeling the ground, the sun on her back, and the way the salty wind caressed her. "If you go to the highest point of my village, you can just see over the cliff. I've always wondered what a beach looks like, as I was only able to see peeks of cream along the shore."

Linh halted and turned to look at the gigantic cliff wall that had to be a kilometre high. Then she closed her eyes and lifted her face to the sun. She took in its warmth, and the way the light filtered past her eyelids. It felt like heaven against the chilly wind.

"It's so peaceful," she muttered, letting the song of the ocean cascade behind her.

She heard the froth of water, the crashing of waves, the whistle of the wind slicing over it, and even the occasional gurgle.

Her cheeks twitched when a strong hand wrapped beneath her jaw. She didn't flinch, nor recoil, even when she opened her eyes to Nathair. He hadn't steered her, but he didn't need to.

Towering over her with his daunting height, he peered down at her with bright-yellow orbs. He swiped her cheek with a clawed thumb, yet was careful with its glossy black point.

She didn't tear her eyes away from his snake skull and the golden hairline cracks that glittered brightly in the sunlight. Even one of his dark horns had a ring of gold just halfway.

The sight was quite mesmerising.

It looks like his entire face was broken. Most of the fractures appeared just behind his eyeholes, and the right side of his split jawbone had a gold line in the middle, as if it'd been snapped in half. *Whatever shattered his skull sure did a good job.*

Her heart both swelled in pity for the pain he must have been in, but in relief that he was alive and well.

This is the first time I've truly seen him in the light. At least, not while she was fretting.

His scales gleamed with oil-slick rainbows more than ever, each one reflecting the sun differently. He was a mass of darkness, nearly black from neck to tail tip, but the white of his rib bones, backs of his hands, the inner parts of his hip bones, and vertebrae were bright in contrast.

Light and shadows danced across his muscles, making them more noticeable than usual. His stomach was defined and tight, as if he had little fat but plenty of strength. His pectoral muscles were defined, and they moulded between each of his ribs and around his exposed sternum that looked to be sinking.

The light-grey fish fins appeared like frills down his sides. They were more rigid down his forearms, as if they had spines, and were currently slicked back.

His belly was a lighter colour than the rest of him, highlighting his navel, and was the same colour as his nipples. His gills were similar, as if the skin there was thinner.

Sharpness ran over the tip of her ear, and her earring clinked against the smooth edge of his claw. The sound startled her when she realised she'd been admiring Nathair, despite him being so different and utterly a monster.

With her cheeks heating, and noticing her nipples had weirdly hardened in response to him, she stepped back to put space between them. Then she turned and tapped her cheeks as if to smack sense into herself.

I totally wasn't ogling a Duskwalker... again. Her entire head grew hot when she couldn't even convince herself of that lie. *He's a monster, Linh. And not just any monster, but one other monsters are frightened of.*

The Demon from earlier had *fled* the moment Nathair dived for it. It hadn't dared risking an attack and was overcome within a split second.

It was his tail, she knew that. He was just so fucking big with it, so long, and his body was rippling with muscle.

And she'd been coiled *inside* it protectively while he soaked in her warmth. Unable to escape, trapped until he was finished with her. Had he desired it at the time, he could have done whatever he wanted to her, and Linh absolutely wouldn't have had a say in the matter.

He could stop her screams with nothing but a big hand. He could hold her legs and arms down by wrapping himself around her from neck to feet, rendering her completely incapable of kicking, punching, or doing anything to defend herself.

Linh was then, and still now, utterly at his mercy.

What had he done with all that power? Fed her, made her warm with the fire, kept her safe, and even... made her laugh.

He has all this power to be cruel, and he's shown me nothing but kindness. Every minute she spent in his quiet and calm presence, her trust for him was growing.

If he was human... She shook her head. She didn't trust that her thoughts wouldn't turn dark and complicated.

Her relationship with men was mixed between what she'd been through with Bragg, and the many friendships she'd had in her village. She didn't even know men could be cruel until the bandits had come to this part of the world.

Maybe dad hid any crimes. She also just... wanted to believe that the people of their village would never have done something so horrific to women.

She was scared of being ignorant and naïve. She was scared that she'd been too sheltered by her loving parents. *I don't want to think of the world as cruel.*

Linh faced the Duskwalker again. Seeing him in all his monstrous magnificence, she chose to believe that if Nathair could be good, then humankind could be as benevolent as she'd once thought.

I don't care what he is. Nathair could have two heads, wings, or six arms. He may be a monster on the outside, but his heart didn't seem to be.

Not like the villains who had recently dug their nails into her skin.

Nathair tilted his head, always silently conveying something. She figured he was wondering what her expression meant, and why she'd been solemnly staring out at the ocean.

She didn't know how to answer that, or if she even wanted

to.

Instead, she walked a little closer to the water. Just when she was about to reach where the waves lapped at the moist sand, he grabbed her arm and yanked her back.

He held up a single finger and wagged it at her.

"It's not safe?" she asked, her heart sinking.

He shook his head and lifted two hands. He put his palms together and open and closed them like a set of large, jagged fangs.

"Demons?" she asked, letting out a sigh. She should have figured as much. "But I wanted to feel the waves."

She gave a little pout, but otherwise stepped away so that she wasn't as close. Nathair cupped the underside of his chin as his skull scanned the damp shoreline.

He put his finger up again and then slithered into the water. Like before, he ducked beneath the waves, but this time moved and scouted back and forth. The large and frightful fins from before lifted from his back and pressed their tips together, making it look like a singular sail fin. Nothing leapt away, even when he seemed to purposefully disturb the sand.

Eventually, he stuck his torso out of the water and waved for her to come closer.

Linh released a quiet squeal of joy. Rather than just getting her feet wet, she retied the bottoms of her pants above her knees and ran into the waves.

"Eek! It's so cold," she shouted with a laugh.

Linh pushed up her sleeves until they were bundled around her elbows, and scooped up a handful of water. She watched as it drained through the gaps in her cupped hands. She sniffed it, taking in its oddly refreshing smell.

As much as she wanted to, she didn't dare run up and down the shore like her heart told her to. She remained where Nathair had already scouted, never going past his depth and the wide curl of his tail.

Waves broke around him as if he was stone, whereas their shoves tried to push her to her arse. He dipped under occasionally, likely to double-check that nothing came to disturb her moment of joy. She got to watch the way his tail pushed up and down, rather than side to side. It occasionally breached the surface in loops, and he truly did look like a giant sea snake as he swam.

He really is magnificent.

A deadly predator. A lethal killer both on land and in water. A creature of nightmares.

She was rather giddy that he was her protector.

I'd like to see anyone take me now, she thought with a laugh.

Linh was aware she was growing rather dependent on that idea. It might be why she'd had little anxiety about being recaptured, or what had happened to her.

Ever since he'd saved her, he'd been frightening enough to chase away those fears.

She needed that so fucking much.

There had been nothing worse than suffering nightmares while currently experiencing one. The relief from it was such a balm to her soul that she wanted to weep.

Before her thoughts could trail back any further, Nathair popped out of the water.

Although she'd been enjoying herself, her feet were frozen.

"I'm going to get out now, okay? It's too cold."

Nathair tilted his head, then straightened it. He patted his stomach.

"Am I hungry?" He nodded, and she shrugged. "Not right now, but I will be when it's time for dinner."

He waved her back, telling her to leave. When she did as she was told, he pointed towards the cave, and she figured he wanted her away from the water completely.

She wasn't going to argue with a Duskwalker.

"Oh, a shell?!" She crouched down to pick up the small clam shell. She ran her fingers over its coarse texture, brushing sand from between its pale-pink ridges.

She found another and picked it up as well. *These are so*

cool. I didn't know they'd wash up on shore. Oh! That one is even bigger. She ran over to a big white one that looked like some kind of critter could have lived inside it. Spikey and twisted, it reminded her of a snail's shell, but with a point.

She didn't know what animal it was from, but took it anyway.

I would love to take this home and show my mum.

Her parents would be so relieved to see her return, and she would like to give them something to show that not all of her days apart from them had been horrid.

A pang radiated around her heart and twisted her stomach into knots. *I hope they're okay.* She'd thought that many times, and hated that she knew the answer.

They wouldn't be okay.

Clenching her eyes and biting back the sudden strike of her thoughts, she turned once she was close enough to the cave entrance. The sun continued to shine on her, and with her out in the open, no Demon could attack her.

For a long while, all she saw were waves rolling before they crashed. She thumbed the large shell in her hands, gripping onto it for dear life. She'd obtained a new item for herself.

Other than the clothes she wore and the spare set she had in her bag, she had nothing else. Nothing that belonged to *her.* At least, not anymore.

Her bedroom was filled with everything a young woman could want, but it'd been so long since she'd seen it. She felt so separated from it and from who she'd been since she last slept in her bedroom.

Her reflection would feel wrong if she saw it again.

Linh groaned and palmed her face. *I wish these thoughts would stop.* She was trying so, so hard to push positivity to the forefront of her mind, but she couldn't seem to stop from spiralling.

Just smile, Linh. Just grin and bear it.

Thankfully, Nathair popped out of the water with his skull already facing her. A fish wiggled in his grasp, and he pointed at it with his chest puffed, obviously prideful that he'd caught it.

She threw her arm into the air with a thumbs up, trying to give him the best version of a celebration despite the distance. *Whatever keeps him happy.* A happy Duskwalker was surely a good thing.

Nathair slithered out of the water, and droplets sparkled as they dripped off his entire body. He crossed the sand, sluggish as if his weight on land made him slow.

Linh just waited.

A frown marred her features when he looked up at the sun as if to note its location, only to come to an utter standstill most of the way to her. Her brows drew together tighter when he just stared at the sky for quite a few minutes.

He'd frozen, as if he'd gone into some kind of trance.

His orbs turned white, and the fish fell from his grasp to land on the sand. Nathair opened his maw.

"The sun rises again..." he said, instantly making heat rush out of her veins and a crawl of dread trickle down her spine.

The voice was masculine, lacking any depth or bass she had expected from a creature such as him. It sounded *human.*

"A new day has come," the voice continued, just as Nathair's mouth parted further and his head tilted back more. *"The shadows fade, and God's protective light shines upon us again. Herald the light."*

"N-Nathair?" Linh stuttered, stepping forward hesitantly.

"He cleanses the world of human sin." He tipped his skull down slowly, and twisted his head to the side in an eerie fashion. *"He sends the Demons to cleanse us of evil. Forgive us, oh Lord, we see your deliverance."*

Her heart pounded against her ribs as she found what he was saying and his movements unsettling. Even more so when his head snapped into its normal positioning.

"You're scaring me," she admitted.

To make matters worse, it sounded as if he was speaking like a preacher of the past. Humanity had long felt like the old

God had turned his back on them. Over three hundred years of watching their kind dwindling into the mere thousands had that effect on people.

"Repent, my children."

Her stomach twisted, and her shaking hands cupped it in an attempt to settle it.

"Repent and stay in his light!"

A harrowing, bone-chilling roar vibrated her entire being, just as Nathair dived. Lying on the ground, he frantically bashed his head against the sand.

With a gasp, she watched in horror as he writhed and hissed. Sand flicked in harsh waves as he dug and clawed at it.

Then a language she'd never heard before came from his maw. The voice was feminine, leading her to believe it may be a woman. She shouted, her voice filled with anger rather than terror.

All the while, Nathair bashed his head against the sand. He twisted it, squirmed, as if trying to bury his skull. His tail swiped in every direction, wrapping around itself in loops and figure eights.

Oh my gosh! What do I do? Did she go over there, or was that stupid and dangerous?

Her eyes crinkled when she thought she could hear whimpers and whines beneath the many hisses he gave. A new man's voice trickled in, the language foreign but different from the first.

How many people has he eaten? And more importantly... *how* had he eaten people who didn't speak the language of the country they lived in?

I only know a few Vietnamese words. Much of that had been lost over the many generations of her family. But this? These were full sentences, *conversations* from what she gathered.

Nathair eventually stopped bashing his head the moment it was buried. The voices became muffled after he filled his entire mouth with sand.

He continued to writhe, but it was weakening, just as he

reached behind himself and clawed up his own back. He gouged deep, causing purple blood to well and instantly drip down his sides.

Unable to take the sight any longer, Linh ran towards him despite the obvious danger.

She lifted her arm to shield her eyes when sand flung on her and pressed forward. She fell to her knees and started pushing on his back, hoping to startle him back to normal.

"W-wake up!" she shouted, even though his orbs were white and not black like she'd only once seen them – the one time she'd ever heard him snore. "Wake up!"

His massive hand shot up and grabbed her forearm. She winced at the pressure, but he didn't squeeze any harder.

His squirming ceased. Instead, it was replaced by full-body shudders that caused his muscles to visibly leap all the way down his ridged back, then his tail, before making the tip vibrate. Muffled words continued to come from his buried mouth, as more shudders wracked his entire body like seizures.

Then he locked up.

Tears instantly welled in her eyes when she noticed that his whines and whimpers never stopped. *He sounds like he's in pain.*

Unable to leave due to his grip on her arm, Linh was forced to remain at his side. She didn't know how long she knelt there, if it were an hour or more, but Nathair didn't break from his whines, his tremors. He seemed to bury his skull further and further until all she saw was his hooked ram horns. Even the top of his chest was sinking.

Every time she patted his back comfortingly, his grip on her tightened until she cried out in pain. She stopped, unsure if it was even aiding him.

Sand bubbled up when his nose hole exhaled, clearing the grains away, only for them to slip back inside. Over time, water sloshed around his tail as high tide quickly crept towards them.

Then, finally, his hand lost tension and dropped to the

ground. She wished silence fell upon them when he shifted to the side just enough to unbury his head.

Instead, he hacked out sand, wheezing and whimpering, and he wildly huffed as if he'd been sprinting. Noticing grains in his gills, she wiped at them, sure they were uncomfortable.

He didn't react, but she couldn't stop herself from trying to dust him off further as tears fell. Shell-shocked and confused, she trembled as she tried to soothe him from whatever the fuck this just was.

Just a few hours ago, he'd seemed so formidable. Now, he lay there weakly.

He lifted his head just enough to show that he was looking at her. Then, within the blink of an eye, he recoiled from her, making her start and fall back. His orbs shifted to dark orange, and she was beginning to wonder what the colour signified.

Her eyelids flickered when he ducked forward and cupped both sides of her head. He brushed over the top of her head before grabbing her left arm to check it.

"I'm okay!" she shouted, shoving at him before he could continue. She slyly hid her right arm while rolling down her sleeve. "Are *you* okay? Your back is bleeding."

Nathair lifted his head to look at the sky, as if it hadn't just sent him into a weird trance! He darted his skull towards the cliff, the ground, and the water sloshing around his tail.

She realised then that since they were north facing, they were in the shade. The sun would go down soon.

Without warning, Nathair swiped up the fish and dived his claws into the sand around her body. He lifted her. Her legs and arms kicked in surprise before he secured her into a bridal cradle and bolted for the cave opening.

Along the way, he crouched down to grab the larger shell she'd dropped, like he'd seen it in her hand before he lost his ever-loving shit. He gave it to her, and her heart squeezed that he stopped to obtain it despite everything.

Still unrecovered from earlier, he let out deep huffs of exertion that echoed within the rocky alcove. He shifted her until she was seated with her legs wrapped around his side and his arm locking her in. He swiped up her shoes with his tail tip and shoved them at her.

He must be worried about the Demons. If his blood scent didn't bring them upon them, her human scent would.

"L-leave the chest," she offered when he reached for it, noticing how much he was shaking and how sluggish he was being.

She immediately clamped her lips shut when he bit out a menacing growl. He placed the fish inside it, scooped it up, and shoved it under his armpit. Then he slithered up the boulders carefully.

Did I make him feel weak? She hadn't meant to make him feel that way. She could just understand the need for urgency, and she hadn't wanted to burden him further with the chest.

With both of them coated in sand, he climbed the slight incline of the tunnels. Minutes ticked by, and she counted each one by his large heartbeat resonating from her ear pressed against his chest.

It was fast and pounded heavily.

"Nathair... what happened?" she asked, despite knowing she wouldn't get a response. She nibbled at her bottom lip with stress. "Does that happen often?"

He halted their climb and then sighed. When he knew she stared at his orange orbs, they bobbed up and down in the darkness.

"Is... it normal for Duskwalkers?"

They swiped side to side.

"It's not? So you're the only one who has to deal with... *that?*"

She felt his shoulder lift, as if he'd shrugged. Then, as if he thought better of it, his orbs bobbed again.

Unsure of what to ask, or how he would even be able to answer the many questions she had, she nodded to show she understood. He pressed on.

Does he normally... hurt himself? He had multiple gashes

down his back and shoulders. *Gosh. I feel so bad for him.* She couldn't imagine going through something so distressing.

When they entered the main area of his home, she noted the familiar trickle of water. The chest thunked and echoed when he placed it down before he slipped Linh to her feet.

Linh put her hands out, trying to orientate herself in the darkness.

Clunking and scraping of wood came from behind, followed by sharp clanks as sparks flickered. Nathair started her fire, providing her with light and the ability to orientate herself.

"Thank you," she stated, her stomach clenching as she fisted her shoes and the shell in her hand.

She appreciated his care, but she felt so awful that he needed to do it for her when he was in pain. The fact he'd had the foresight to aid her meant much.

Don't cry. Don't make it worse. He probably already feels bad enough. She held her tears back, but she was still so shocked and startled that she didn't know what to do other than awkwardly stand there like an idiot.

Her nerves were fried, and her brain was so mushy that she couldn't think of a single thing to say to make him feel better. Should she say sorry that he had to deal with his trances? She didn't want him to think she pitied him.

She didn't want to be pitied for her problems.

Even though flames began to flicker to life, Linh was too chilled by the events to feel warmed by them. Even the light seemed muted against the hard pounding in her veins, but she was relieved when it allowed her to see him by the flames glowing against his scales, his protruding bones, and the whiteness of his skull. His orbs dipped lower, just as clawed fingertips touched the inside of her wrist.

Nathair gingerly lifted her hand. He pushed her sleeve to her elbow, then his palm brushed over the flesh of her arm.

She wondered why he was inspecting her, only to rip away from him when she saw the palm-print bruise marring her.

Covering her forearm, she ignored the tiny, distressed wheeze that came from him. His orange orbs darkened in their hue, and it didn't take a genius to figure out the colour reflected his guilt.

"It's fine," she said honestly, hoping her trembling voice held the weight of her sincerity. "It was an accident."

Linh then lifted a reassuring smile to him before needing to avert her gaze as the glowing colour deepened further. She reached for him instead.

"L-let me take a look at your back. We should wash your wounds. There must be sand in them."

Nathair darted back, evading her touch before her palms could land on him. Once more, he gingerly reached for her arm. When she attempted to pull away, he let out a dark growl, causing her back to stiffen. She complied, offering it to him.

Orange light glowed and glittered around her arm when he laid his palm over the top of it. It looked the same as the light magic he placed, and she watched with rapt curiosity as coolness radiated beneath her skin.

When the magic dimmed and then faded, he pulled his touch from her. She let out a surprised gasp when she noticed the bruise was gone, as if he'd never hurt her to begin with.

"I didn't know you could heal," she stated with awe. "Thank you."

She offered him another reassuring smile, this one stronger than before.

Nathair reached out and cupped the side of her head, his thumb brushing over her skin. His palm and fingertips had been smooth and soft, like his flesh lacked any callouses or roughness. *Is he saying sorry for hurting me?*

Why did that twist her insides further?

"It's fine, Nathair." She had meant what she said: she trusted him. Her bruise was an accident, and she wouldn't judge him for it.

When she leaned into his palm, trying to show him it was okay and all was forgiven, a strangled whimper choked out of him. He twisted, walked on his hands as he headed for the freshwater lake, and dived. Liquid splashed in an arc as his tail flopped in, causing droplets to crash near her bare feet.

The surface rippled, seeming to vibrate, as bubbles popped. By the muted sound she could faintly hear, she thought he may have roared. Tiny waves formed near the middle.

She had assumed he intended to release whatever emotions had overcome him for a long while, but he flung out minutes later.

Orbs glowing with the depth of his guilt, Nathair flopped back out of the water. He didn't return to her, instead moving over to the entrance of the cave like the night before, as though he wanted to block it. He coiled himself up like a snake, as if hiding from her, the world, and how he felt.

By the lack of his glowing orbs, she knew he wasn't watching her. He must have completely hidden himself under the wraps of his tail.

He thought to grab the fish, the shell, the chest, even my shoes. He apologised, rather than shrugging and blaming something he couldn't control. He'd healed her and made amends by communicating the only way he could.

Nathair had proven just how much he didn't want to hurt her and cared for her wellbeing and feelings.

And that he was exceptionally tender-hearted.

TEN

With her spare clothing in one hand, and a lit flame lantern in the other, Linh wondered how she was supposed to get past Nathair.

Throughout the course of last night, the Duskwalker hadn't moved from his spot. It'd been difficult to see him in the dark, and her concern for him had grown when she heard small, distressing noises echoing off the stone walls.

Figuring he wanted to be alone, she'd distracted herself.

She investigated the iron lantern, then noted the candles were a little worse for wear. The ones at the bottom of the box were almost unusable, like the chest they'd been in slowly leaked once dragged from the ship.

The first candle she burned constantly sputtered, threatening to go out before it did finally die. She slowly heated the ones that were useable over the fire to try and remove any water or air pockets that had formed, hopefully preventing that from happening in the future.

Then she made sure she had all the supplies she'd need to get the torches going. The cloth in the chest was a little stained and crusty from sea salt but should still burn.

Whatever burning oil was used smelt pungent and gross, but two of the four containers had managed to not leak.

She put them to the side, wanting to utilise them at a better time.

Linh also washed the fish of sand, then prepped and cooked it. The wine was bitter, but gave enough flavour to make eating bearable. She wasn't used to consuming this much fish, so her dinner made her a little queasy.

Sleep had fallen over her with great difficulty, especially when her lazy eyes had kept drifting to where she knew Nathair to be. Only when the hour had to have been late, did she finally pass out.

Linh had woken to stray streaks of sunlight, which allowed her to see that Nathair had not moved from his spot. Eventually two desires had clutched at her: to remove the smell of fish from her clothes and skin, and to go to the bathroom.

Which is why she now stood next to this snake Duskwalker's huddle, assessing how to squeeze past without disturbing him. The sliver of a gap meant she had to press herself hard against the opening.

Once through, she turned to the left with her lantern barely lighting the way.

She removed her precious Ao Dai garment her grandmother – on her father's side – had made for her twenty-first birthday, and dropped it under the subtle waterfall to soak it. She also removed her pants, underwear, and the undershirt she wore as a bra.

She went to the toilet, hating how she had to do that over some strange hole. She tried not to think about it, or the weird paranoia that a Demon hand might shove its way through with swiping claws.

Linh sat down in the sprinkle of water to scrub at her clothing with soap before washing her skin. She also untwisted her braids so she could rinse them of grime, and used a bone comb she'd brought with her from when she'd originally been taken.

Once she was done, she placed her washed clothing over a jutting section of rock to dry. She donned a new undershirt and underwear, but paused at the knee-length dress in her hands.

I haven't worn this in months.

If she hadn't been naked, Bragg made her wear simple, plain dresses – for the cruellest of reasons. She'd then forced herself to wear his pants, wanting a barrier even if it was a pointless one.

But this dress... It had been her mother's. It'd been gifted to her, and she'd packed it because she just wanted to bring her family with her in the wake of her upcoming loss.

She'd refused to wear it. It was too pretty and delicate for the eyes and hands of dirty, sweat-covered bandits.

It'd also been too short for her own comfort, swaying just above the knees. Part of her had wanted to appear as unappetising as possible. She'd even smothered her face and body in mud – which had merely gained her a bucket of water tipped over her head many times.

It's only Nathair. He was a Duskwalker. Surely, he wouldn't look at her with a leering eye.

Yet, she thumbed the silky material while thinking, *I wonder if he'll find me pretty in this.* She blushed at herself, unsure of where that thought came from. *I'm starting to have weird thoughts about him.* Why did feeling safe make her like him more than she probably should?

She considered waiting for her pants to dry, but shook her head. She put on her mother's dress and patted down the pink silky skirt that had green leaves sewn into it. A green sash had been stitched to the centre and sat just below her breasts. Her cleavage would have threatened to spill out due to the wide vee down the middle, but her undershirt thankfully covered it. The garment bore no sleeves and was relatively simple in design.

She shivered at the coldness surrounding her bared skin. *I should have brought my jacket.*

Wanting to head back swiftly, she picked up her lantern and left.

Her lips pursed when she got to the main entrance to discover Nathair had shifted and completely blocked it. His black scales glistened with rainbows against the muted light of her lantern.

I don't think he's sleeping. His entire body rippled, constantly shifting. She hadn't been able to see it before, but he seemed to be twisting slowly, like he couldn't get comfortable.

"Nathair, I need you to move over," she requested with a quiet voice, not wanting to bother him. "I need to get past."

Her gaze flickered down the dark tunnel, and she swallowed thickly. She was a sitting duck right now; a Demon could come frothing up the incline at any point.

Nathair didn't respond, not in sound or movement, as if she'd been unheard.

She gingerly brought her fingers to him and pressed in and out, trying to stir him. Nothing. Her heart clenched when the candle sputtered, making the swallowing darkness flicker. She shook him.

Realising she hadn't fixed the candle like she thought she did, she leapt into action before it could go out. She climbed over him, figuring he was in another trance and couldn't be disturbed. He felt like climbing soft boulders, and she kicked and kneed him before crawling on the outer ring of his wrappings.

A small scream tore out of her when his coils suddenly opened and she fell. The lantern was lost, *thunking* against the ground after she accidentally tossed it to catch herself.

Linh was rendered quiet when Nathair surrounded her from all sides, blocking her escape from the centre point of his serpent coil. She refused to feel fear, but did squirm until a set of white orbs lingered barely a few inches from her nose.

They are colourless, like before. So, she'd been right – he was in a trance then?

Her skin prickled when claws tickled up the bare flesh of her thighs, his hands dipping up under her dress before they slid up her sides. Anxiety instantly clutched her throat, choking her at the intimate touch beneath her clothing. Her stomach bubbled with repulsion, which made her skin crawl.

She clenched her eyes shut, only to peek them open moments later when his arms crossed behind her back and locked her in. He'd laid down and seemed to be twisting tighter and tighter around her.

He did nothing.

He didn't try to touch her further, didn't squeeze her until she couldn't breathe. After a few panicked breaths, she realised his... shudders were beginning to settle, and became non-existent when he buried his snout against the crook of her neck and shoulder.

He's just... hugging me. And she understood, for whatever reason, it was soothing him.

Perhaps it was her warmth, or maybe even her scent, since he'd buried his nose against her. Whatever it was, the innocence of it allowed her to settle. She relaxed into it, and her loss of tension made him soften as well.

For a long while, they just laid there, unmoving in the silence. It grew warmer the longer she was there, as if her heat bled into him and filled the rest of his body.

This is actually remarkably comforting.

She never thought she'd like being restricted like this, but it felt different to being pinned down. It was like being cuddled in utter protection, shielding out all the light and cold, so the only thing that existed was them.

Her heart and breaths lost their rapid speed. She didn't realise her pulse had been racing every second of every minute since the day she'd been taken, and had never truly managed to return to a normal state, until now.

A scent slowly trickled into her senses. *He smells like... waterlilies, and moonflowers.* She'd never been able to smell them behind the heavy aroma of brine and salt. She liked that he didn't have an overly masculine scent, and instead found the femininity of it pleasant against the balm of her damaged spirit.

Despite her alertness, her eyes drooped in contentment, and she rubbed the tip of her nose against him.

A strong pulse resonated from all around her, as if she was nestled within his very heart. She could feel it everywhere, softly pulsating against every bit of skin: her hands, chest, calves, and even from the part of his tail that had nestled itself between her thighs.

It should have been alarming that something was pressing against her underwear, breasts, and arse, but her contentment never waned and only deepened. Even the bumpy texture of his decently sized scales was lovely.

She didn't know if it was minutes that ticked past, hours, or even days. Linh just soaked it all in as her mind went hazy in a stupor.

It'd been forever since she'd felt peace, and now she floated in it, basked in it, revelled in it. She was currently being snuggled by the most dangerous creature in existence, but not one part of her being, not a fibre or cell, was scared.

She even deepened it when she was able to wiggle an arm around his torso. Linh regretted it when she felt an open gash and he tensed. Everything got tight and the overall softness cushioning her hardened like stone.

"Don't," she whispered before he could react. She didn't really want him dumping her on the damn ground like last time. "It's fine. This feels nice."

Nathair's head pulled back, revealing orange orbs.

"Did you have a good sleep?" she whispered, her voice croaked and groggy.

Linh was choosing to ignore the uncertainty that he may not want to hold her like this. He'd started it, and the hold was innocent on both sides – she guessed.

Nathair never responded, and just continued to stare at her. The stiffness eventually dissipated, and a small smile curled her lips.

"If you're wondering how this happened, I swear it was an accident," she informed him with a subtle laugh mingled in. "You were in the way of me returning from my washing area, and you refused to move to let me back in. I climbed over you, and you opened up to make me come in here."

His head dipped as he pulled back a little, creating a pocket of room so he could look down at her body – and likely the way he'd coiled himself around her. His tongue flicked forward, much like how a snake would but with a thicker limb.

Her eyelids flickered rapidly when his orbs momentarily glowed bright purple. *I've never seen that colour before, but it was pretty.* Lilac purple happened to be her favourite colour, and a small amount of excitement at discovering what emotion it signified ran through her.

Too bad it faded, just as he began to pull away again.

"I like it," she quickly stated, before he could get the wrong idea. "I feel really safe. It's been a long time since I felt that way."

Nathair paused and tilted his head with his orbs flaring dark yellow. She was beginning to wonder if the darker hue conveyed curiosity or questions. Then he moved, making gestures, and she laughed.

"I can't see anything but your orbs, Nathair. It's too dark."

He let out a purposefully loud huff. She recoiled when he brushed over her breasts, but his intention glowed brightly seconds later as the light symbol shone on her dress.

Oh my gods. I didn't know he could make me glow! It was both cool and weird to see her chest alight.

Nathair patted his skull, ran his hand over a hooked horn, and tilted his head in question again.

"Are you trying to explain that you're a Duskwalker?" she asked, gaining herself a nod. A smile lifted into her features. "I know what you are, Nathair. Hard to miss that. But, like I said yesterday, I trust you. You haven't tried to hurt me and you haven't been... *weird.*"

Suddenly, the places he was touching, which almost happened to be everywhere but her chest, felt warm. He was against many delicate places, had her trapped, and she wasn't fretting to get away.

Quite the opposite, in fact.

Something about it, perhaps his waterlily-and-moonflower scent, or the feel of his smooth scales, or even his mild warmth, had her skin tingling. Now that they were talking, her drowsiness waned, and she became more alert to everything that was him.

With the increase of her strangely fluttering chest, places on her body began to throb. The inside of her wrist, her thighs cupping him, her clit pressed against him, and even her nipples as they hardened.

The arousal was subtle, and very much startling, but she didn't mind. He didn't know, and Linh absolutely didn't want more than this.

In some ways, she was relieved she felt desire, even if it was for this strange moment, for Nathair. A Duskwalker, a frightening monster, who would make any other human scream in terror being held like this. It meant she wasn't broken, and that side of herself wasn't as... *lost* as she feared it to be.

What a relief.

I don't understand this human, Nathair thought, as he drifted his sight up her body splayed on him. *She does not have sense.* That, or a complete disregard for her own safety. Who approached a crazed creature?

She does not mind being held like this? By me? What was that supposed to mean? After the previous day, when he'd wounded her, he expected her to no longer trust his presence.

She also didn't know of the twisted, dark thoughts that were beginning to stir.

Nathair currently had a very soft female within his trappings. Her dark, straight lashes frequently caught his attention, and he often wondered what they felt like fluttering against his scales. Her flesh was smooth and giving against the hardness of his own, and she moulded into the space he'd provided.

Her scent was sweet, and he flicked his tongue forward to taste the aroma of it completely filling up the gap of their bodies. Her heart was tiny – a cute little flutter he'd like to clasp onto permanently.

Nathair currently had a lax female on top of him, and the voices in his mind pushed back at his musings on how he could make her even more docile.

He choked back his groan when a tangy and body-tingling scent lifted into the air. He panted, his tongue flicking forward again, as his sight shifted to purple and held it. Although he'd never smelt a female's arousal before, the fact his groin jerked hard gave him the impression he'd just discovered it.

And what a remarkably tantalising scent it was.

It didn't matter that it was light, and barely a drop. His throat instantly dried, like he may be experiencing human thirst.

Although many of his fragments were rather unpleasant, fornication was not unknown to him. He'd experienced it, as both the male and the female in those fragments, and already knew it could feel amazing. The experiences were often muted, but he knew the sounds, the touches, what it felt like to bury and to be buried within.

His sight slipped to her generous chest, wondering if her breasts were perky or droopy. If her nipples were brown or pink, and if that colour would match the slit between her thighs.

This wasn't his first time having perverse thoughts of the little female he had in his keeping, but it was the strongest. He'd ignored them before, often shoving these fantasies away with the impression she would not want them. She'd never indicated otherwise – not with words, touches, gazes, or even scent.

But now? A small ripple danced down his spine all the way to his tail tip.

She also had his magic marking her, and that satisfied a rather possessive part of him. *She would look pretty in my nest.* She would fit there, among his other pretty treasures.

He started to reach out, and the glow of his magic upon her clothing glinted against his claw. It looked sharp, deadly, and the exposed part of her chest looked remarkably soft. His protruding knuckle bones looked... *wrong,* and not like the many human hands he'd worn in his fragments.

He took in the gleam of his black scales beneath her, and how she appeared delicate and pure – and that she didn't belong against them. Against *him.*

Her arousal is not for me. It couldn't be.

She thinks of me as safe, not as a mate. Parents, friends, and even pets could make humans feel this way. *She is likely thinking of a male of her own kind.* One with flesh upon his face, and who had two legs and not a lengthy body. Someone who did not have claws, scales, or who could accidentally envenom her.

Realising he was about to do something idiotic, Nathair gently spread his coils apart. She slowly slipped to the ground, and he released her for his own sanity.

I am not fully lucid. He couldn't be to have such fantastical, groin-pulsing thoughts of this little female. *I have not rested fully.* If only he could sleep peacefully.

His life was sleepless, and he was growing tired of existing in it already. This female was not helping. He didn't feel like himself, especially when the yearning to lick every part of his own body where she'd left her scent on him itched at his tongue.

He'd also never felt so hot before, and the air felt chillier than usual at the loss of her heat. He could see himself growing addicted to her, which would only hurt him when she inevitably chose to leave.

Which she would. Nathair was just waiting for the request.

He was entertaining her here because he liked her. Her personality was docile, but she was also willing to be playful.

She gave him smiles that mostly appeared sincere, complimented him on the smallest of things, and was compassionate enough to talk to him even though they could not properly communicate.

I long to speak with her. To ask her questions, and figure out who she really was, where she'd come from, and why she'd latched on to him so readily.

As he backed away from her, his gaze drifted to his nest hidden away on the other side of the crescent floor. He missed resting in it. The way its tall walls surrounded him made him feel secure, but he'd been blocking this entrance for her sake: to prevent Demons entering even if he was in a trance, and to minimise her human scent from flittering down the tunnels.

Linh stood, and she tilted her head down at her chest. She brushed her fingertips over his magic symbol.

"This is really cool. I don't need a lantern if I have this."

He wouldn't do it often. Magic came with costs.

Healing her meant he'd taken on her bruise on his arm. The light required a drop of his blood. Both dimmed his mind, stealing more of his limited strength.

She likely thought him strong, but Nathair was constantly at the edge of collapsing.

He watched her walk around, seeming to inspect everything properly now that she had the light. *My scent is all over her.* She was on him, he on her, and the mingle of it was rather gentle and pleasant. Once more, the purple of deep desire flickered in his sight as his groin clenched and spasmed.

"I didn't realise how deep the lake was." She pointed to it while shining a cheerful smile at him, and he gave her a lusty purr for it.

Folding his arms, he covered his face with a palm and shook his head. *Think of other things.* Like the risks involved in her simply being here. *She will likely be hungry soon.* He didn't want to go far, nor did he wish to leave her alone.

She seemed to like the beach. Perhaps he could offer she join him each day, rather than slithering off while she was asleep like he'd originally intended. *I worry if I leave her here by herself, and my fragments render me useless for a time, she will be unprotected.*

Demons often pulled him out of them, as their smells were putrid and instantly had him shoved into aggressive alertness. She would be safer with him, unless he went into a rage from fighting.

She padded around the area barefoot and appeared to be checking every nook and cranny, while Nathair was having a life crisis about what to do.

He wanted her, but doubted she'd want him in return. He wanted to protect her, but he'd likely be her demise. He wanted her to stay, but...

"Holy *shit*," she rasped from the other side of the cave.

Wait. He lowered his hand and looked up, and his chest tightened when he saw her next to his nest.

Dark green flickered in his sight, and he was unsure if it was because *she* was so close to it, or from the greed of her possibly touching his treasures. She bent over the tall edge.

Stay away from it! He let out a menacing growl.

As if she didn't hear his warning, she said, "Where the hell did this all come from?!"

Nathair darted towards her with his growl deepening. The clinks and clatters of coins, gems, jewellery, and polished cutlery burst in his ears.

Linh tipped forward, hand outstretched, then she squealed, her legs kicking at the air as she fell inside the deep recess. Nathair received a flash of creamy thighs, of pale-green underwear, and a round backside before she disappeared... into his *bed.*

Like a whiplash of fire slicing across his entire torso, Nathair halted when possessive rage bashed his being. Tension shot into his hands, prepping his claws, while his flesh seemed to tighten over his bulging, blood-filling muscles.

Her head popped up, as did her hands cupping two necklaces: one pearly, and the other silver with little white gems and a large sapphire in the middle.

She is in my nest... A shaken pant fell from him, his tentacles swirling behind his seam. *Admiring its contents...* He crept closer to observe her, trying not to startle the little prey sitting in his predatory den.

He bet the contents were cool against her skin, and that she'd warm it all for him. That she'd replace the many metallic smells with her peach-and-vanilla one. It'd all glitter around her with his light brightening her.

His tongue flicked forward as he licked at his maw in interest. Desirous venom flooded his veins at just the mere *thought,* just the imagery that plagued within his mind.

The moment his hand rested on the edge, and he leaned over to look at her, purple blasted in his sight.

He was right: the hundreds of coins, gems, and even chalices sparkled from her radiating light. A bracelet had hooked around her foot, while an unmatched set of earrings had tangled into her long, single braid.

One word echoed as a growl within his darkening thoughts: *mine.* Metal shifted under his weight as he entered it with her.

Unaware that the Mavka approaching her was filled with an inferno of untapped and unbridled lust, Linh stared at the necklaces in her hand with awe. Dizziness swam in his senses, like the dark desires of his kind were suffocating for something such as a Mavka.

They were insatiable, and always hungry for *something.*

"This is amazing. I've never seen these many riches in one place." She tipped her glorious, smiling face at him, and her brown eyes shone. "Do you know what this could do for my village?"

She gasped when he shoved his hands against the wall of cloth and hide just behind her, trapping her in. She dropped the pieces of jewellery and rolled back until she was almost lying down. Shock marred her features, but she didn't smell afraid.

She climbed inside my nest, my bed.

She put herself there.

This pretty little fucking human, and she looked wonderful in it. Smelled wonderful in it. Like she belonged there, the treasure adding to the beauty she already beheld.

She made herself *his.*

His growl turned into a thunderous purr.

Did she know what she'd just done? He wanted to think she'd done it willingly, knowingly. To have wordlessly made that statement to him. His hazing thoughts believed so.

His mind felt clouded, like his lucidity was about to slip. Nathair didn't even know if it was his fragments clouding him, despite their mildness currently.

Smells nice, he thought, as he leaned down and drew his tongue against the side of her jaw. He groaned, just as the pressure behind his seam pounded. His tentacles swirled tighter, holding back his girth and stopping him from extruding.

He laid down on top of her. He pinned her with nothing but weight, and her thighs were forced to spread around his narrow hips.

"N-Nathair?" she asked, trying to wriggle her arms between them.

Her voice is so nice. He never thought just his damn name being spoken to him could make his entire body tingle. *I want her to call it.* Over and over again, as if to make up for all the times he'd never been able to say it.

Coins clinked around them as he wound his arm underneath her back and lifted her so her stomach pressed against his. The pumping pressure behind his seam became unbearable at her warmth pressing against it, and he thoughtlessly thrust his hips against her once – just once. It was enough to lance him with profound pleasure, and he extruded forward with a quick dart.

"What was that?" she whispered shakily when the protective shielding of his tentacles brushed against the crook of her thigh and pelvis. "Please, Nathair. I-I don't like being pinned down."

He cocked his head at that, his murky thoughts puzzled.

Considering he'd been pinning her from all sides not even a few minutes ago, he didn't see how that could be true.

"Oh-oh my gods." Her eyes widened when she looked down. "You're hard."

Unbearably so. What other Mavka wouldn't be after a female just crawled into their *bed*?

He'd been hoping to experience the return of that arousal scent from earlier. She'd gifted him with it and then crawled into his nest. A sense of hope had washed over him that maybe this female did desire him in return.

That bubble of optimism popped the moment he heard a quiet sob. Then it felt as though he was punched in the side of the skull by a brutal wave of fear. His orbs flared red, and he almost launched his maw at her head to swallow her whole in an instant.

Nathair cut off his breath and froze as his claws dug into the wall. Branches, sticks, and ship planks creaked and cracked while he quaked above her.

Want to eat her. Rage tickled at the back of his skull. *Her fear smelt delicious. Just another taste.*

His lungs tightened with the greedy desire to huff in that tangy perfume of delicious terror. ***Hungry.*** His stomach clenched in emptiness, before twisting in agonising starvation. His torso hollowed.

"Please," she cried, her voice broken, cracked, and pleading. Linh trembled as salty tears fell from her clenched eyes. "Please, don't." Just as a set of invisible hands squeezed his brain and he truly did turn on her, the rage receded when she whimpered, "I'm scared."

He knew she was scared. He could feel it, had smelt it, and could hear it in her voice.

But that wasn't why it knocked him back to temporary sanity. It was because she'd said she was scared... of *him.*

And he could see she was utterly terrified, even when he rose to put space between them. *No? She does not want me?* She did not want to be a permanent piece in his precious nest?

The moment she was free enough, she curled into a ball on her side. She wept and covered her chest and stomach, as if she was trying to protect her body from him.

I was mistaken. He did not mean to frighten her, and should not have let his Mavka instincts make him act foolishly, or so aggressively.

He went to cup the side of her face in apology. She recoiled from the touch – one she had accepted the night before and had even leaned into. She let out a screaming cry, as if the mere brush had burned her, and tried to make herself smaller.

The scent of her utter terror was so strong, it flittered into his closed maw to touch his tongue.

Nathair darted to the side to escape and give her space. He slipped into his cold lake with a splash, shifting into a more aquatic and monstrous state as he did, wondering what he'd done so wrong to make the little female weep that intensely.

He did not realise his desire could be rejected so strongly.

I should not keep her here any longer. He covered his face as lucidity broke into the dizziness of his haze, and his orbs shifted to dark orange. *Why did I do that?* It was like something had come over him...

Now that he understood the depth of his own desire, he wanted this female more than he realised. To not only keep her, but to make her his.

Where his magic light had radiated from her chest, her soul simmered just beneath her flesh. He wanted to take it, to consume it, and bond it to him.

I cannot. She does not wish for the same. I will only vomit it out.

If she stays... He would want it more and more.

He whimpered into the water. *Fuck... what if I took away her consent in a trance?* He could reach out and just take her soul for himself, and may be too insane to realise what he was doing.

Would him eating it and then spitting it out kill her?

I don't want to hurt her.

Now that he was growing attached to her, the fear of doing so had his hungry gut gurgling with a familiar nausea.

ELEVEN

With water trickling over her head, Linh covered her tear-swollen face with both hands. She put one foot on top of the other and squeezed her knees to her chest in an attempt to make herself smaller.

To hide – from Nathair, and how she felt. The shame of how quickly she'd broken under the weight of her fear. The way guilt twisted in her chest at knowing he did nothing wrong.

I said I trusted him and then immediately broke into tears when I felt his dick.

And she felt so awful that the only reason she was even bathing was because something slimy had rubbed off it onto her thigh and hip. Even when it'd dried, it itched, irritating her skin and making her cry harder.

She wanted to remove it, and the subtle warmth that it'd left behind. She'd needed to douse and shock herself back to normality, and yet she hadn't stopped crying since.

I just locked up. They'd been having such a good morning. *I went from trying to keep him cuddling with me to screaming. He must be so confused.*

Why did I do that? She knew why, and the horrible memories only made her overwrought.

She hadn't been scared until she felt his dick. She'd known he must have had one hidden away, but she hadn't been anxious about it before. The moment it touched her, she remembered being pinned down, choked to quieten her screams and cries, and she'd been terrified of it happening again.

No. It was worse.

Although Bragg had been undoubtfully cruel to her as her 'husband,' she'd never trusted him. She'd never cared for him. The moment he'd beaten her father, she'd hated him.

If Nathair had continued, Linh knew she would have felt unequivocally... betrayed.

I care about him. He makes me feel safe. She'd even felt desire towards him, and all his inhuman qualities. *Oh gods. Do I like him because he's a Duskwalker?* Nothing about him felt human.

Not the softness of his large hands, his scaly skin, the coolness of his body temperature. *Even his dick felt weird.* Like a gigantic, spirally flower bud she knew would tear her in half.

The size hadn't frightened her, just *it* – what it was, what it could do. How it could make her feel, not physically, but mentally and emotionally. What it could take away.

I didn't want to be broken, she mentally lamented as she cried. *I didn't want my first time to be filled with tears.*

She'd always thought she'd fall in love first.

"No," she whispered, pushing her hands up to fist her hair. "Don't think about it. It didn't happen," she insisted to the air around her. She covered her mouth when her trembling lips irritated her, yet her shaking hands only seemed to make it worse.

She didn't mind that Nathair desired her. She was actually a little giddy about it, despite her current panicked state. Linh was a woman, and he was a man of sorts – she wasn't overly surprised he'd developed those kinds of feelings. He was probably lonely, and they did seem to get along well.

She knew her trust in him was utterly warped by her trauma. She didn't *want* him to be human. She would have been constantly watching her back had he been one, worried he was only being kind to her so she'd let her guard down.

I was never that way before. She was once carefree and *happy.* A silly girl who thought the world was filled with butterflies, rainbows, and fairies. Who, while knowing Demons existed, had loved her life.

In her village, she'd been quiet because she *had* to be. She'd wanted people to respect her, and her father, but simmering beneath the surface had been an immature brat grinning ear-to-ear with mischief. Behind closed doors, she'd pranked her mother, her father, and even her grandmother before she passed away.

Now all she knew was that pain had nestled into her heart, and she was so scared of being touched intimately that it physically made her want to hurl.

The fact that she'd felt desire towards Nathair, only to lock up when receiving it back, hurt so deeply. She probably looked so pitiful curled up into a ball on her side.

Would the old Linh have teased him and tried to rile him up in hopes she could make him crazed? She wanted that to be the old her, and she wanted to take back the possibility of that side of herself. To be the kind of woman who was confident enough to open her thighs and crook her finger while coyly singing, 'Come here, big boy.'

Linh palmed her nose as she tried to settle her tears. She sniffled, but her nostrils were so blocked she couldn't take a breath through them.

She wanted to calm down and apologise. Her bottom lip trembled when she felt so bad for thinking: *At least he can't ask me about it.*

Honestly, Linh just hoped he pretended nothing had happened. It'd make her feel better; a lie surrounding the resolution of how she'd acted.

She didn't know what to do about his desire. If she hadn't felt her own during the cuddle, she would have detested the idea, but she couldn't ignore it.

I liked it when he held me like that. And, right now, she kind of wanted him to squeeze her tightly with his entire serpent body. To wring out the sickness and trauma trapped beneath her skin until she shed it.

His claws had felt nice dancing across her skin, and his smell had been mind-lulling.

He's so nice. He took care of her needs to the best of his capabilities inside a cave. He made sure everywhere she went was safe, and even allowed her a moment to splash in the ocean while making sure no Demons would eat her. *And he's funny.*

Who the hell plays dead when someone falls on them?

She brought her hand up and closed it until it looked like a snake. She flapped it open and shut, mimicking the way he moved his mouth.

I didn't think I'd be able to smile or laugh again after everything. If someone had cracked a joke, Linh had a feeling she would have just stared at the person blankly. She'd needed the humour to be ridiculous. For her saviour to be out of the norm.

For life to be completely and utterly skewed in reality.

For it to feel so wrong that it felt right.

The cave, his home – she shouldn't be here. She adored it for that reason.

She was living in the dark, and she found that far less scary than being in the sunlight in a bandit camp.

Once more, Linh sniffled but otherwise was finished with weeping. She felt worse from crying. It hadn't been therapeutic. It hadn't felt good to shed her tears, simply because the reason behind them was so horrible. No human, regardless of their gender, should be forced to cry for such a reason. No one deserved to feel so raw inside that their mind was littered with scars no one could see.

Utterly thankful for the glowing magic circle on her chest lighting the way, she crawled towards her clothing. She donned her lavender dress and grey pants, even though they were still damp from washing them.

They felt safer. If his dick decided to pop out and say hello again, she wouldn't feel it against her skin. She wouldn't feel so exposed.

She hated that's why she was putting them on.

It wasn't that she didn't trust him. Nathair literally showed her he had no intention of violating her without her consent. He'd given her more respect than she'd received in the past two months.

She didn't trust herself. *M-maybe if I wear pants, I won't get scared again.*

She'd like to experiment on how she felt regarding his desire, and the possibility of her own, without instantly locking up and panicking.

She blushed at her thoughts, her mind feeling scattered. Her heart was all over the place, confused and wary.

Picking up her pink-and-green dress with leaf patterns, she cringed. *Gosh. I feel so pathetic that I can't even wear this right now.* It was a dress, and suddenly she was petrified of it. A piece of clothing.

Fisting it in her hand, she stormed her way back to the main area. Nathair wasn't there.

The dust particles glittering in the streaks of sunlight made the dim cave bright. Now that she knew what the lump on the other side of the crescent-shaped cave floor was, her cheeks heated as she glanced at it.

Embarrassment combined with shame and giddy nervousness had her casting her gaze away like it was a spooky shadow.

Linh started the fire again, fumbling with the flint and steel due to shivering from her damp clothes. Then, with her back against the wall and her arms around her bent knees, she sat by it for what seemed like hours, waiting to dry, and for Nathair's return.

She never doubted for a second that he wouldn't.

She would have cracked a joke about how he couldn't

escape her because it was his home, but she didn't particularly find any of this funny.

Since she was staring at the inky water, she saw the moment the top half of his white snake skull breached the surface.

Her brows drew together when she took in his blue orbs, never having seen them turn that colour before. He didn't lift higher for a long while – just his head visible – and they stared at each other.

"Hey," she eventually croaked out to break the tension. She even offered him a cringing smile. "I-I'm really sorry about before."

His orbs darkened in their blue hue, and he swam towards the ledge. His movements were slow, calculated, and careful as he used his arms to drag himself out. Nathair looked tense, as if he worried any sudden movements might have her bursting into tears again.

He's probably upset with me. Sh-should I just explain a little bit about it? At least enough to ensure he knew it wasn't his fault, and that her rejection hadn't come from a place of disgust at him.

She knew her answer immediately: she had to be fair to him, even if it hurt her chest.

"About before..." she started, eyeing him warily as he came closer. She frowned when he picked up her special shell from the beach. "A-about before, it's not your fault..."

Her frown deepened when he picked up her shoes, then her water sack, before grabbing her bag. He placed them inside it. Then he gave Linh the satchel, and she took it while rather confused.

"Are we going somewhere?" she asked when he offered out his hand.

Wanting to show him she did, in fact, trust him, she put her hand in his big palm. She immediately noted how soft it was, even compared to her own, and how it swallowed her up. He gingerly lifted her to her feet, only to put his arms behind her so he could lift her into a safe cradle.

"Nathair?" she asked, eyeing the ground.

He started slithering towards the lake, and not the cave opening. She knew where it led: his pond. With every millisecond that passed, her heart doubled its speed. Realisation dawned, and her entire being went cold.

"No!" she screamed, shoving at his chest, his face, anywhere she could to separate them. He gave her the tiniest growl, and renewed tears instantly welled as she kicked and punched at him. "No! I don't want to."

Ignoring her, he began to drop into the water.

Frantic, desperate to stay on the land, she grabbed a jutting rock. She kicked him in the head before he could submerge her, and it forced him to let her go. A guttural noise tore from the Duskwalker, but she refused to listen as she scrambled to get away from him.

Linh, with tears freely falling, clawed at the rock with all her might.

Betrayal stung her chest so intensely she thought her squeezing, fright-filled heart would give out.

With a snarl, angry at himself and not at her, Nathair leapt forward and grabbed her ankle. She screamed when he dragged her across the ground and back towards the water.

It'd taken him hours. Long, agonising, conflicting hours to make this decision.

As much as he wanted to keep this little female, this cute creature that desired his protection, she couldn't stay. No matter what he felt towards her – affection, fondness, desire, friendship – she wasn't safe.

He was bound to hurt her; he'd already done so.

He was too unstable, too large, too *different.*

Nathair had tried to convince himself otherwise; maybe they could resolve his fractured mind and he could speak to her. He wanted to believe he could win her heart, obtain her soul, and make this alluring creature his bride.

The moment she sat in his nest, the nagging, deep-seated yearning clung to his scales like water. Linh as his female. For him to treasure, cherish, and covet. To protect, touch, and marvel at like a gem sparkling in the sunlight.

But she didn't want that, and he was too much of a monster to know that would not bode well.

Nathair was a Mavka.

They were stupid. Emotional. They thought with instincts rather than with sense.

He had just enough lucidity and humanity to know that if she smelt of arousal again, if she climbed into his nest again, he was doomed. She was doomed.

It was better they parted ways now, before she could envenom his heart even more with her wiles, her smile, and her lovely voice and scent.

"Please!" she squealed, sobbing. "Please don't make me leave!"

Linh kicked, threatening to strike him in the skull again, and his sight shifted to dark orange. *Why does she have to fight?* She didn't truly want to be here, not if she knew what he wanted. *Why does she fight?* She should be fucking running away from him!

She should *want* to be freed.

She was the most confusing captive. It was like she'd lured herself here. And her squirming was not *aiding* her. It only made his sight threaten to shift to red in hunger.

He let her go when it was too much. When the grip of invisible hands wrung at his brain to try to enrage him. Clutching the side of his skull, he shuddered at the vile thoughts of tearing her limb from limb.

"I'm sorry!" she yelled, backing away from him once more. He slipped beneath the water until his gills were covered to escape the dizzying scent of her fear. "I didn't mean to cry. I didn't mean to get scared."

With a groan, he darted his fuzzy sight to her.

Fuck, she looked horrible. Her face was so pink and swollen from tears, and the rest of her filled with fright.

"I promise I won't cry anymore," she stated, while crying.

Her heart was beating so fast it throbbed in the back of his throat and assaulted his ear holes.

Dozens of faces flittered into his mind, all of them tear-filled and crying. Strangers, friends, and even family members of the fragments. He choked on each one, and yet the silhouette of her face played behind them. Their sobs mixed in with hers.

Strangled by the onslaught, bubbles pushed out of his gills and he clutched at his throat. The urge to bash his head against something in a pointless attempt to stop them nagged at him. Fragments clutched at him, moments from disorientating him and stealing his lucidity.

"It wasn't your fault. I wasn't scared of *you.*"

That had to be a lie. He'd scented her fear. She'd recoiled from his apologetic touch. She'd curled up into a fucking ball like he was a villain, and he hadn't liked the way *guilt* weighed in his gut.

The first instance of him letting the human side of him slip, his Mavka instincts taking hold, and this female had turned from him.

He wanted to believe her.

He didn't, so he clawed back onto the land when the worst of the fragments stopped hounding him. She scuttled back, and only just missed the fire.

"Someone hurt me," she tried to explain, her entire body shaking. Droplets of water splattered against the ground, and he trailed a path of them to her. She cowered, shrinking against the ground and rocky wall. "I w-want to stay here with you!"

I don't understand. She was confusing him.

Nathair paused and just let out a fucking whine. *Why the fuck are you doing this to me?!*

"I know what you are. I know you're a Duskwalker. I know that every moment I'm here, you may eat me, and I don't care.

I don't care if you hurt me accidentally. I know I'm intruding on your home, but I just feel so safe with you. I know that doesn't make any sense."

When he didn't do anything but tower over her, his hands opening and closing with mixed emotions, she braved peeking up over her forearms.

"At first I wanted to stay here in hopes you would help my people, b-but it's okay if you don't. Just... please don't make me face the Demons by myself, d-don't let me be taken by the bandits again. P-please don't hurt me in the way they did."

His head reared back. *The way... they did?* Realisation began to trickle into his mind, and he turned his gaze towards his nest. *She did not mind being held, or when I cupped her face, or even when I carried her.*

There were two fragments that Nathair despised, and he tended to act rather violently when suffering through them. Two different memories, belonging to two different humans who had never met: one in which he was a victim... and one where he was the perpetrator. He hated the latter, hated he was forced to suffer through something he'd never done, would never do.

Neither were pleasant, and he often felt rather sickly afterwards. He'd long to shed his scales after both, and had even once done so on his left arm when desperate.

He brought his gaze back to her and tilted his head. *It's true she was never afraid of me until...*

The bitter snarl that burst from him was dark. Nathair darted his hands forward. He pushed her arms to the side before he shoved into her chest.

The little female gasped, her back arching, while her body wavered around his embedded fist. Blistering heat surrounded his hand as he carefully grasped what felt like a flame.

Nathair pulled her soul from her.

The moment he opened his hand, her soul sprung to life. It retreated to his fingers, pressing against them like skittish, cornered prey against a wall. It looked up at him in utter terror.

Markings on a soul could vary, and he'd seen countless different kinds in Tenebris. The darkness of depression, the whiteness of physical scars, the cracks and craters of sickness.

But this? Tiny red handprints left their markings on her soul, and were the evidence that someone else fucked with it while its owner lived. Actions so utterly cruel and unforgivable to the point they left burns on their victim's soul like a physical taint. There were only two kinds of violence that could cause them.

Weldir told him they could be healed, but while they lingered, they were like parasites. They messed with the human bearing them, making them act out of character – often with fear and sadness.

Without nurturing, the soul could be permanently marred.

And this poor female's soul had four burns from what he could see: on the left side of its face, its left inner thigh, its right breast and shoulder, and one that spanned over both wrists. There could be more on its back, but he couldn't tell.

He didn't know if all four were from physical violence, or sexual, nor did it inform him if it were multiple people or just one vile cretin. It didn't matter. Linh was tiny, petite, and *defenceless*. No one deserved these parasitic markings, especially not this alluring creature.

But, due to her earlier reaction, he knew.

Nathair knew why she did not mind his hold, but the feel of his arousal had given her such a concerning reaction.

She was right. It was not his fault, nor was it hers.

While he held it, Nathair admired her beautiful soul. It looked just like her, from her generous breasts, round backside, her narrow waist, the gentle shape of her face, to even her long, straight hair. He lifted his palm and nuzzled it with the back of his index finger.

It didn't particularly like that – her infected soul was likely untrusting of anything – but that was fine. He'd like to teach it that not everyone, or every*thing*, would cause it harm.

He lowered it to take in Linh's frozen gawk. Her eyes were

riveted to it, and she watched as he tipped his hand down and let her soul find its way back to its owner.

"What the *fuck* did you just take from me?" she asked, surprising him due to her swearing. He couldn't remember her doing so before.

I did not take it. I borrowed it – momentarily. I did return it. He thought all this to justify what he'd done.

Especially since... if he had ripped it, the little female before him would have died instantly. A soul was an exact replica of the current living body. Had he destroyed it, she and it would disappear forever – no human could survive being in two pieces.

It was why they could not be shared between Mavka; not that his possessive kind could handle sharing anything on such a deep and territorial level anyway. Weldir had been able to warn him of this, as well as many other things.

An eaten soul pieced back together within Mavka and Demon stomachs, and turned white to signify its death. However, to eat a soul while its wielder still lived... a Mavka's body bonded to it protectively.

They were delicate things.

Linh cast her gawk up at him, and he greeted it with understanding.

This tiny creature longed to be protected because the world had been undeniably cruel. She'd turned to him for it, latching onto a monster that could, literally, fight all her Demons – including the ugly ones clinging to her soul, should she allow it.

He'd scented her arousal before, so not all hope was lost.

The fact she'd felt it at all, and for him no less, meant much and made pride swell behind his sternum. She trusted him more than humans; she could see he wanted to be a benevolent spirit upon the world.

He did not wish to be violent, nor was this why he was created.

The need to remove her from his home for her own safety

waned. Instead, his heart ached to shield her from the world even more than he did before. To not only protect her from others, but from the parasitic wounds on herself.

He could not fight them for her; they were not his battle to face. However, he could be her armour, her sword, and her steed, fighting alongside her until she claimed victory.

Maybe she could save him in return somehow.

She makes the fragments easier to handle. His attention was often so focused on her that they grew quieter. Her face sometimes shone brighter than the fragments, her scent stronger than the ones in his mind, her touch grounding him in the present.

She was witty enough to understand him in the silence. Tender enough to try to listen to him when he'd never spoken a word. Her touch was benign, rather than handling him like the massive monster he was.

He hadn't wanted her to leave for these reasons. He'd never truly wanted to let her go, but he'd been worried she wouldn't trust him anymore now that he'd revealed his growing longing. He hadn't even realised how deeply he desired a bride until she came and refused to leave.

Nathair lowered himself and gingerly scooped her up. She recoiled, and her brows swiftly knotted in distress.

The moment she opened her mouth, likely to plead, beg, and cry, Nathair darted his skull forward. He licked her cheek, showing her she didn't need to worry, as he lifted her.

He slithered towards his nest.

"W-wait," she rasped when he placed her inside it.

Then, in case she now associated it with his desires, he curled himself around the outside of its walls. He didn't join her, didn't overwhelm her with his presence, and she watched as he settled down at a distance. Nathair folded his arms on top of the nest's thick ledge and placed his jaw on the x of his forearms.

She may be in danger from him. He may accidentally hurt her with his claws. He may even accidentally steal her soul in a trance.

What he did know was that he would not take this female unwillingly.

He would also try his hardest not to eat her, so that one day he could eat her soul when she was ready to give it to him.

Nathair had decided she was now *his,* and just hoped she longed to stay so. His home would be a cage for her, one in which he'd leave the door open.

She would need to make the choice, and he would try everything in his might to make her choose him.

With her face stained with tears, swollen and kind of dishevelled from crying, he watched her. She looked tiny in his nest, which was so large he had plenty of room to laze around in it. She sat on top of his bed of treasures, and he knew she was the most precious piece.

She looks like a baby bird. Startled, unsure of the world, and not ready to fly.

His heart radiated with pity and sadness for her, and her puzzled expression only deepened it.

She eyed him skittishly. "Y-you're not getting in?"

He shook his head.

He expected her to look relieved. Instead, once more, her eyes bubbled with liquid.

"You figured it out." As soon as he nodded, she threw her face into her hands and sobbed. "I was hoping you wouldn't! It's not fair."

Nathair hesitated before just reaching out to cup under her chin. She gasped, tried to tear away from him, and he refused to let her.

He made her watch as he opened and closed his maw, then let her chin go to point at her.

"You want me to talk about it?"

He nodded, and she shook her head.

"I don't want to," she whispered, hugging her midsection. "I'm scared that if I talk about it, it makes what happened more real, and I don't want it to be. I don't want to hear myself say it. I want to pretend it didn't happen."

Then we will pretend it did not happen.

If she wanted to speak of it, he would listen. If she never wanted to, then he wouldn't push her. Her path to healing was her own – he would just be conscious of it.

Her crying quickly settled, and he hoped it was because she was at ease in his bed, in his presence. That what he was doing, and trying to say without words, held meaning.

"Nathair," she started, before lowering her gaze.

Yes, little female? He tilted his head to convey his question.

"C-could you hold me like before?" She swiped the heel of her palm over her cheek to get rid of the liquid on it. "It was really comforting."

Permission to enter his own nest was all he needed, and he was rather gleeful she'd given it so swiftly. He pulled himself up and then dropped himself in slowly, so as to not startle her.

"But please don't get offended if I get scared. I don't feel like myself, and sometimes my stomach hurts."

He didn't need her to say this. The moment she was uncomfortable, he would release her. He would like to hold her as well, and had wanted to from the moment he understood what she'd been through.

He thought it was rather brave when she crawled towards him to quicken the pace. She even entered his arms as he started wrapping his lengthy and girthy tail around them both until she was utterly trapped. Until she was completely hidden and shielded from the world.

Linh never grew afraid, and Nathair didn't release her until she desired it.

You are safe in my arms, little female.

TWELVE

Linh scouted the beach in search of more seashells, wanting to add them to the collection she started over the last four days. When she picked up a new one, she placed it in Nathair's cupped palms.

The sun was bright, the wind light but growing warmer with each day. The sand was coarse against her bare feet, but she adored the way it felt between her toes. It abraded her, and she wished it would score her mind and heart so she could feel better.

Ever since Nathair had figured out why Linh had reacted so strongly and then placed her in his nest, they'd not spoken about it again. If he truly wanted to, he could have pestered her about it, but never did.

A nauseating, dark part of her had worried he wouldn't want to be near her anymore. That once he discovered what had happened, he'd no longer want to be her friend, or even... want something more.

She knew what happened wasn't her fault, but that didn't stop *other* people from being fucking stupid.

She'd worried Nathair would change.

And he did.

Her smile grew when he used his nose hole to huff away sand that clung to the shells in his palms. He meticulously cleaned each one for her, brushing them off and showing he cared about the task she'd taken on.

In the four days since she'd asked him to hold her after crying her heart out, Nathair had been even more attentive.

Not once did he try to touch her intimately, but he often caressed her cheek with the back of his fingers. The few times she waited for her hair to dry so she could restyle it, he'd sit her on a coil of his tail and comb his claws through the strands until it was untangled and glossy. He even just simply held her hand... and his thick thumb brushing over the back of her daintier one made her heart weep from its gentleness.

He'd carefully yanked his nest to a spot of the cave where a streak of sunlight hit the middle, allowing her to have brightness. He'd also managed to find more cloth from somewhere else within his tunnel system so he could cushion it better for her.

Each day, they came to the beach to collect shells. Or she would create sandcastles or dig a hole – only for him to help until it became a massive crater in the sand. *I kind of like that we're leaving our mark in the world.* Maybe they could dig all the way through the earth and find themselves on a different land.

Her mind directed back to the day before.

After they'd dug, a part of the hole's wall had collapsed and half buried Nathair. So, Linh had pushed more and more onto him until all that remained was his head.

"Now you know how I feel every night," she'd said, until she kicked sand on his face – knowing it wouldn't bother him due to the fact he didn't have eyes like a human.

His roar had been playful and instantly had Linh squealing as she ran.

He didn't grab at her, he never did, but he shot forward to block her path. Before she knew it, she'd been circled, and she'd burst into a fit of giggles.

I really like the beach.

It was separated from her old life. Nothing here could remind her of home, of what happened, and it allowed her to remain in the present.

Like most days, Nathair would hunt for all manner of sea creatures for her to eat. Oysters, prawns, and he'd even once tried to gift her a small shark – she told him to put it back since it was too big. She only knew what they were due to old books detailing animals that had been seen before the Demons arrived.

At some point, she planned to ask him to take her to his pond so she could forage. She'd been putting it off, worried he'd abandon her there.

I'll have to get over that at some point. She'd been struggling to forgive him for trying to get rid of her.

They also had not spoken of his desire, or her own, which was growing. In some ways, despite all its unpleasantness, she was thankful the other day had transpired. Knowing she wasn't the only one growing attached, and beginning to long for more, was reassuring.

She wanted more, wanted to touch him, to do more than just hold his hand, or cuddle in the security that was *all* of him.

Linh knew she'd first clung to Nathair for all the wrong reasons. But the longer they spent together, and the more she got to know him, the deeper her feelings evolved. *I like him.*

She liked his waterlily-and-moonflower scent. It was so gentle and refreshing, and often made her mind hum in its pleasantness.

She liked his scales and the way they felt inside her palms, against the tops of her feet, and against her face. She was beginning to want her pants or sleeves to ride up so she could feel them against her calves and forearms. She thought they would feel nice against her thighs, sides, and stomach – but she wasn't brave enough to do anything about that, even if it was just for an innocent caress.

I like his skull a lot. She'd never been particularly frightened of it, nor had she ever been disgusted by it.

Her mother was her mentor when it came to work, and they'd both often held skeletons out of fascination.

Understanding the biology of creatures, humans included, often aided their capabilities with their medicine.

The longer she gazed at his ethereal face, the more she wanted to cuddle his skull in her arms. It was Nathair's face. It was who he was, and that's what made it beautiful. Everything about him was magnificent, especially the mesmerising way his black scales gleamed with rainbows.

She had a funny feeling that he'd added her to his riches, but he didn't seem to realise he was the most breathtaking thing in his home. He took up the entire cavern with just his mere presence.

How can someone who's never spoken a word have such a loud personality?

Just as Nathair picked her up to climb the boulders of the cave alcove where the sunken ship was, she thought, *his body is also really handsome.*

She flushed at her thoughts, but only due to the way her heart shyly fluttered in response. His shoulders were broad, his chest firm, his biceps and stomach muscles pronounced. He was a very big boy, with a massive hand that spanned her entire waist as he carted her to the top ledge so she didn't trip again.

I like the way his hands feel touching me. Of course, that was only over her clothing, but their strength and size was impossible to mistake, even with a barrier between their flesh. How would that feel touching more delicate places on her body? Would his gentleness give way to needy roughness?

He placed her on her feet, and they made their way up the tunnel in the dark.

Every day, her trust in him grew, as did her fondness for him. It also brought on doubt.

Paranoid thoughts nagged at the back of her mind.

He'd shown he wanted her, but she feared all this extra kindness was just an act. He was being patient currently. What if he grew tired of waiting for Linh to figure out what she wanted, and then, more importantly, if she would act on it?

What would he do when his patience ran out? Take away

her choice, or give up and cast her away like he'd tried to before?

She had no idea what she was doing.

A human and a Duskwalker living together under some strange truce was *odd*. But... love? Lust? Some kind of relationship or bond? Was that too farfetched?

Was it... too wrong, even in the skewed reality she was choosing to live in?

And yet, all these pangs kept clenching around her heart whenever he did something nice for her. Each platonic touch to her hair, or even the nape of her neck, had her shivering for more. His claws tickling any part of her felt dangerous, but she associated that danger with Nathair, which meant safe, exotic, and heart-stuttering.

I'm scared of touching him, she thought, her stomach knotting. She bit her bottom lip and shoved her crossed arms – hands still clutching the seashells – against her abdomen when it twisted.

If she let a moment of heat take over, she was scared something would remind her of the horrible past. She didn't want to lock up in the moment, causing Nathair to think it was his fault and she was rejecting him, when she was the one who had instigated it. She also didn't want him to be so deep in his own desire that he didn't realise she'd lost her voice, her ability to speak out, and unwittingly betrayed her by not stopping.

She wanted to try.

However, the moment she felt her nipples bud or her pussy grow slick because he was coiled around her and his tail felt nice between her thighs, her damn throat squeezed. Her hands would shake, and she'd need him to release her before she hyperventilated.

I'm scared of my own desire. Because of what it meant, what it could lead to, and how much something going wrong could damage how she felt towards him.

The fantasy of touching him buzzed in her mind, and the idea of him brushing his hand over her naked body had her wanting to combust with need. Making it real, where she couldn't control what happened, made the unknown and unpredictable frightful.

She wanted control.

As much as she wanted to trust him fully, he was still... a male. He had his own needs, his own wants. Humans could be rather selfish, so how would a Duskwalker, who appeared more creature than person, be able to restrain himself?

It was selfish to only consider her desires, but if she didn't think of him as safe, then Linh was... fucked. If he became a source of pain and betrayal, then her only option was to leave and face the Demons.

She'd be dead within a week – she knew it.

She couldn't go back to her village without help.

What if travellers find me? What if they ended up being just as vile as the bandits?

Linh was willingly trapped here and was putting all her faith in another being.

She felt pitiful, weak, and vulnerable.

In the darkness of the tunnel, a strong limb coiled around her and lifted her into the air. Before she knew it, she was placed into one of Nathair's arms, and he carted her up the mild incline.

Did he realise I was feeling anxious? He'd brought her closer, as if he'd been able to see it in her face, her body language. Maybe she'd even smelt lightly of fear.

She pressed her face against his exposed ribcage for comfort, thankful he'd reached out. *It's okay. He won't hurt me. A-and if he wanted me gone, he would have done it by now.* She felt he was trying to convey that with just a simple action.

She adored him for it.

When they reached the main cave, Nathair put her down to get the fire restarted. Linh headed over to his nest when he dived into the freshwater lake to rinse himself of the ocean.

She placed the smaller shells next to it, rearranging them so they went from smallest to largest. She took the one really big shell she'd found and placed it next to the two others she'd put on the wide rim of his nest.

Since it was only the middle of the day, streaks of light brightened his home. The one hitting the centre of his nest made all his riches sparkle, and they reflected rainbows against the rocky ceiling above.

Linh was under the impression that Nathair hadn't thought to move his nest here before, nor did he know the shiny objects would reflect the light in the way they did. She could tell he was very excited by this discovery after moving it, as he often looked up at the ceiling or stared at his treasures as if enthralled by their glitter.

He kind of reminds me of fable tales of dragons. She laughed a little. *I wish he breathed fire.*

She gasped when a large set of hands spanned around her waist. He turned her, and made her sit on the edge of the circular wall of his nest. She didn't miss how he tried to slip between her knees.

Dripping wet, he pointed to the lake. Then, with his hands flat and downward facing, he placed one on top of the other and wiggled them up and down towards her.

Linh purposefully pouted her lips and drew her gaze to the side.

"I don't want to," she grumbled.

Nathair gingerly cupped her jaw and brought her eyes back to his skull. He nodded and then put his hands together to wave them up and down.

"It's cold."

He answered her with a growl and pointed at the lake again – only to clutch his throat and make gurgling sounds before pointing at her.

Nathair was being rather pushy about teaching her how to swim. Considering he was an aquatic creature, and he'd already had to save her from... drowning. *It's not like I tried to go swimming on purpose.*

Humans rarely lived near any body of water. Learning how

to swim was a rarity, and generally not necessary. However, Linh now lived in a home that was seventy-five percent water, and it was startlingly deep.

"I know I almost drowned, but the water is cold," she grumbled, arguing with him. "I also don't have anything else to wear."

With a huff, he turned from her, slithered over to her bag, and pulled out her pink dress. He waved it at her, likely calling her a liar in his head.

Shame prickled the back of her neck as she looked down to fidget with the seam of her lavender garment. "I-I don't want to wear it."

His orbs shifted to a darker shade of orange, and she'd already figured out what this meant: guilt. She felt awful that he felt bad, considering it was obvious she didn't want to wear it because of what happened between them.

It wasn't him, but her need to not feel so exposed.

He directed his skull away and brushed one of his hands over the top of it. Linh bit her lips and considered apologising and explaining her reasons. Before she could, he let out a sigh, nodded, and placed it back into her bag.

"Fine," he gestured with his hand.

Linh was beginning to understand his hand signing. He had his own language, one she wasn't familiar with. When she'd offered to teach him Austrális signing, he'd gotten annoyed with her. He'd eventually written against a rock: *Learn mine. Nathair speak.*

So, that was what she'd been trying to do, and what took up a fair amount of their time in the last four days. They'd also been bonding over it, especially as she was taking her lessons very seriously... while seated on the very *lap* of his lengthy tail. Of course, she found that distracting for the most titillating reasons.

Nathair came closer and picked her up before she could register it.

"Don't you dare!" she screamed as he carted her towards

the lake.

He tossed her, and her scream was swallowed up by water. Linh kicked, her legs going outwards as she clawed to get to the surface. She heard the crash of Nathair's body joining her before ripples swayed her to the side and pushed her further under.

Hands grabbed her hips and yanked her to the surface. Linh sputtered icy water when she sucked in a breath, goosebumps prickling across her flesh and tightening her scalp.

Since he was right in front of her, she bashed on his shoulders.

"How dare you! I said no!"

Ignoring her, Nathair pushed her away and released her, and Linh instantly began to sink. Her legs kicked outwards while her arms flailed, and her panicked breaths didn't help when she let them out under the water.

Within seconds, his hands were on her hips. This time, she didn't fight him. She clung onto his shoulders for dear life while shivering.

Opening her clenched eyes, her gaze landed on Nathair's skull. He tapped against the side of his empty eye holes. "See?"

"O-okay, I get it. I can't swim," she answered, her teeth chattering as she spoke. "B-but it's really cold."

He pointed at her, then put his hand straight up and made it fall backwards. He cupped his throat and gurgled.

"I w-won't fall in again, I promise."

He rolled his head.

They both knew that wasn't true. Linh had clumsy feet. She'd tripped, fallen, and stumbled multiple times.

Nathair pointed to himself. He put his hand up next to his skull with his fingers hooked and splayed, made his orbs white, then turned his hand back and forth with his claws pointing towards his temple. *He's saying if he goes into a trance...* He pointed to her, cupped his throat, and then made his head fall to the side with his tongue out. *I'll drown and die.*

He slipped in and out of trances at random, and Linh was always incapable of drawing him out of them. He never hurt her, although often brought her inside his wrappings like he wanted to hug her like a teddy bear.

A chattering sigh fell out of her.

"Okay. I get it, you're right." Annoyingly, she'd suffer the cold if it would put him at ease.

He pushed her back. Despite how much she clung onto him, he eventually ducked beneath the water. As soon as she was no longer supported, she tried to stay afloat.

She gasped when his hands shoved her legs together, but thankfully he pushed her up so her head stayed above the water. He let go, and she uselessly kicked like before. He shoved her thighs together.

Keep my legs together? She did that, and he released her.

She immediately found it easier to keep her head above the surface. He put her hands together near her chest, and then forced them outward underneath the surface. She tried to mimic him, although her mind told her that in order to breathe, she needed to claw at the surface of the water, rather than have her arms submerged.

Every time she kicked like a frog, he shoved her thighs together.

He's been under there for ages. If he'd been human, or didn't have gills, he would have drowned by now.

The moment she started to get the hang of it, she realised the chill of the water had started to fade. Her movements were warming her, and she wasn't shivering so hard. It also stopped her from fretting.

I'm doing it! Thank goodness. Hopefully he'd let her get out now.

When she attempted to swim towards the shore, she put everything out of whack. She realised she'd only learned how to stay afloat, but not how to move. Even now, she was growing tired. If he went into a trance for hours, she'd give up and sink.

"Eeek," she rasped when his hand pressed against her stomach.

Nathair finally breached the surface with his skull and forced her to lie on her stomach. When she just lay there, breathing, he tapped at the water. "Swim."

She let out a false cry and kicked her stupid legs. He supported her abdomen with one hand and grabbed one of her wrists with the other. He made her do that arm swiping thing, but against the surface.

I hate you so much right now, you overgrown water snake.

THIRTEEN

Every time Linh made headway towards the land's edge, the Duskwalker drifted her away from it against her will.

After what felt like an eternity, Linh considered just letting herself drown. She stopped moving – her arms and legs hanging while he held her up – and submerged her face. *Put me out of my misery.* She blew bubbles.

A chuckle sounded, and she lifted her head to glare at him.

"Don't laugh at me. I'm tired and cold. I'm probably going to get sick after this." She rudely pointed at his face. "If I do, your healing magic better fix me, or you'll regret it."

Nathair rolled his head, but did bring her to his body to hold her. He swam towards the rocky bank and placed her on it.

"Land!" she exclaimed.

She bolted straight for the fire, threw wood on it, and put her frozen fingers out to the subtle heat. She shivered, her teeth chattering when the cold air wrapped around her wet form. When Nathair approached, she threw her head to the side.

"I'm not talking to you until my clothes dry."

He snickered. Snickered!

Nathair lowered himself, curled around her back, and brushed his hand over the top of her head. He did it repeatedly, as if trying to soothe her.

She hated how nice it felt, and slapped his hand away with both her own. When she lowered them back to the fire, huddling for its warmth, he gently patted her again.

"I told you, I'm not talking to you until my clothes dry. Go away."

He opened and closed his maw mockingly, shaking his head around. She reciprocated by poking her tongue out at him. Like the bully he was, he retaliated, pretending to poke the tip of her nose with a claw. Except he retracted it, then bopped her with the end of his forefinger instead.

Linh gasped and grabbed his hand. Only the one finger was clawless, and she inspected it with wide eyes. "You can sheath your claws? I didn't know that."

As if to demonstrate, the rest of his claws pulled back, showing he had complete control of them.

"Why didn't you show me before?" she asked, turning her gaze up to him. Nathair lifted his shoulders in a shrug.

She guessed he'd never needed to reveal this ability until now.

Then she remembered something and shoved his hand away. *I forgot I'm not speaking to him.* Her gaze drifted to the lake. *I guess it is a little relieving that I could probably save myself now.* A small smile tried to creep onto her features, but she refused to give Nathair the satisfaction of her relief.

Her attention grew focused on the way he'd returned to patting her head. She noticed the distinct difference of how it felt now that his claws were sheathed.

She nipped at her bottom lip. *I didn't know he could do that.* Honestly, part of her worries of him touching her anywhere *delicate* was if he tried to shove a claw inside her. No woman wanted their insides sliced.

His fingers are so thick. They appeared nimble, the grey tips darker. She thought just one might be very filling if he were to sink it inside her pussy.

Shaking her head, she cleared her mind of any more potentially perverse thoughts. Her stomach grumbled, as if swimming had worn her out.

"If you want to make it up to me for throwing me into cold

water," she started, lifting her chin with a forced pout, "then you can prepare my dinner for me. I'm really hungry now."

Nathair did just that. He descaled the fish, gutted it, and then staked it over the fire. She was almost dry by the time it was ready. Nathair placed it on a silver plate – he'd been giving her all sorts of utensils from his special hoard – and she turned her back to the flames as she ate to remove the last of the dampness from her clothing.

He'd given her a metal cup a few days ago, and she sipped the wine to wash down the taste.

When she was halfway through the fish, she placed it down on the plate. He lifted it back into her hands and she turned a glare up at him; she was tired of having this argument with him.

She kept asking him to catch smaller, more manageable meals, and instead they got bigger each time. He probably thought she was thin, but she was a perfectly acceptable weight. Thin, but soft enough to give her generous womanly curves. He probably didn't realise he was just so big that *everything* was tiny compared to him.

Still, for his benefit only, and because he was more stubborn than a mule, she attempted to eat a little more.

As she did, she darted her gaze to him often. Now that she was warm again, she felt more inclined to be nicer.

"Thank you, by the way," she muttered. "For teaching me how to swim, and just... for everything."

His orbs shifted to bright yellow, and Linh fidgeted. Her cheeks heated, suddenly self-conscious. She placed the plate down and ventured over to the water to wash her hands – thankfully without falling in like she did two nights ago.

Like then, the area was dark. Dusk was likely falling on the world, and she couldn't wait until the longer, summery days arrived.

She turned to find Nathair preparing one of the torches for her. She would have been nervous about what that meant if she hadn't grown accustomed to it over the past few days. It probably meant something significant to him that they spent most evenings in his nest.

The proximity always brought on a wave of bashful stomach flips.

Linh had tried to sleep near the fire the night he'd tried to take her from his home, but he'd refused. No matter how many times she attempted to crawl out of it, he kept placing her in the middle of the large recess until she caved.

The first night, she slept inside it alone, as if he understood she was unnerved about being in a vulnerable state after what happened. The second night, he placed only his tail in. The third, he made her sit in it with him long before it was time to sleep, and started to teach her Nathair speak.

It appeared he wanted to spend the evening in it again.

I've kind of noticed that he seems rather content to do... nothing. Other than taking her to the beach, he didn't move around much. He often just sat there watching her.

He's laid-back and aloof. It's like nothing bothers him. Although she knew that wasn't true. *I kind of find his ability to do that really cool.* She wished she could be like that; her ability to fake it wasn't very good.

Linh approached when he shoved the bottom of the torch into the wall so it would stick out and give her light. Like she knew he would, he carefully lifted her into the nest before slipping inside it himself.

Seated upright with his back against the wall, he rested his arms inside. His tail was bundled to the left, as if he wanted to give her as much room as possible while forcing her to sit on a loop of it. She thought from where a human would have had knees, he was free and straight all the way up to his head.

He continued her lessons on Nathair speak, and she tried to remember each sign he taught her to the best of her ability. It would take time. To learn a whole new language in a short span was impossible. She hoped he understood that if she made mistakes in the future, it wasn't done out of disinterest.

They were not at the point in which they could have

complex conversations.

"It feels weird having to learn how to sign all over again when I already know how," Linh said with a small smile, repeating his version of day and night. "I never considered people from different places or cultures would have different ways of doing it. Some of them seem to be universal, so I may be able to remember them better."

Nathair paused to listen. He always listened, so Linh continued speaking, wanting some rest from her full day of *learning.*

She leaned her back against his waist and crossed her legs to make herself comfortable. "My dad is the mayor of my village. My mum works as a herbologist, apothecary, and doctor for our village. They are a perfect team; both want to support our people in different ways that matter."

A small smile lifted into her features as she thought of them, all the while trying to ignore the cold ache that swirled around her heart.

"My dad made me learn from a young age. He said it was important that I be able to communicate with everyone freely. As his daughter, I had to be respectful towards everyone." She paused, and with a low voice, added, "I ended up having to sign for him after the leader of the bandits came and broke both his hands for trying to fight back. He couldn't move his fingers for weeks."

She glanced at Nathair from the corner of her eye and lowered her head when she took in the blue of his orbs. Was it pity they conveyed? Sadness for her? Who knew, but looking upon them only twisted her heart.

She didn't want to talk about it anymore.

"I miss my parents a lot," she admitted, looking up at the torch so she could stare at its flames. "Sorry. I didn't mean to make the conversation sad."

The growl that thundered from him immediately had the tiny hairs all over her body standing on end. Goosebumps prickled over her flesh for the most titillating reason, and she clenched her thighs together.

Linh turned and folded her arms on his flat torso. To distract him, she poked next to his navel.

"You have a belly button. Does that mean you were born?" she asked to distract him and, more importantly, herself.

He made a fist and dipped it forward and back like one would nod, stating yes.

"So you have parents. Are they nice?" She gave him a smile, only for it to die when he shrugged. "How long ago were you born?"

He touched his elbow with two fingers and then made them leap to his wrist. She winced, since he hadn't taught her this yet. He did it again, and again, meaning he wanted her to figure it out.

"Jump?"

He shook his fist side to side to state no.

"Is it close to that?"

He nodded his fist, and she watched him do it again.

"Over?"

He nodded his fist, then put up three fingers and made two zeroes.

She slapped his stomach when she pushed up on straightened arms. "Are you saying you're over three hundred years old?"

He chuckled as he nodded his head this time.

"Oh my gosh. You're ancient!"

That gives a whole new meaning to the term cradle snatcher, she thought, rubbing her hand over the top of her head in disbelief.

"Have... have you been alone this entire time?" she asked, her voice breaking an octave. Just the idea of Nathair being all by himself for so long was deeply saddening.

He sighed and plonked his head back, tilting his skull to the ceiling. He wouldn't answer – or couldn't.

At least he didn't say yes. She held onto that.

She ran her fingertips over her lips in thought. *If not no, then...*

"Does that mean you kept other captive women here?" she teased. She wiggled her eyebrows up and down, while being completely uncertain of what answer would actually please her.

Once more, he let out a delicious growl – one that was utterly meaningless as her protector. She gave him a coy grin when he faced her and shook his head. Then, as if he was upset she'd insinuated otherwise, he curled his arm around her midsection and yanked her until she was seated on his pelvis.

She had a funny feeling that if she tried to get off him, he'd get annoyed. She assessed whether she was uncomfortable or not, especially since it probably meant something to him. Since his penis was hidden away, and the area was flat, she found she didn't mind. They'd already rested together, and had hugged far closer than this.

Okay. No other women... So that means I'm the first? She wanted to be giddy over that, but it just brought on more questions.

Does that mean he's never been... touched before? Or did he have his own kind to mess with? *He figured out what happened to me. He seems to be very knowledgeable about the world.*

Linh knew under all that silence he was a very intelligent person. He had to be. He reacted with calculated thought. He was hesitant when he needed to be, forceful when required, and had already shown he knew two languages – English to understand her, and sign language to speak. He could count, write, could hunt, prepare food, and already knew when to give her privacy and space.

Sure, there were times he acted a little more... animalistic, but she figured that was because he was a Duskwalker.

Maybe it's from all the human memories he has? The voices of different people were a dead giveaway.

Linh was smart, or at least tried to be. She didn't have many survival skills, but she had a keen eye and usually thought logically when she wasn't too busy screaming.

She had observed the dangerous being before her with an analytical eye because learning about him made her safer. She just... chose to disregard the constant danger she was in; she'd discovered there were worse things than *dying*.

Before she could open her mouth to ask another question, she paused when she noticed his orbs were white. Her companion had turned to stone, as if all his muscles had locked up.

He'd slipped into a trance.

"Ugh, *rude*," she playfully blurted out. "We were talking."

She knew it wasn't his fault and didn't blame him for spacing out. She also doubted he heard her or would remember it – she hoped.

She considered sliding off now, but decided against it. She was comfortable, and she didn't think he'd mind, considering he put her here in the first place.

I feel so bad for him, she thought, turning so her left leg was bent on top of him. She stared at the Duskwalker before her. *I can tell he hates this.*

Sometimes he reacted to the trances. He'd whimper or violently twitch. He hadn't reacted so violently again after the day on the beach where he'd lost his ever-loving shit, but he sometimes scratched at himself. Most of the time, though, he just froze up.

Sometimes he'd be out of it for a few minutes, other times for hours. It was always random, and she didn't know if anything in particular set him off. There were even times she'd seen his orbs be white, but he acted like normal except for breathing heavily – like he was still aware while the memories bothered him.

I wish I could help.

She drew her gaze away from his white skull until it landed on his gills. She wanted to touch them and find out if they were as soft as they appeared, or if his chest muscles were as firm as they looked. When they cuddled, she occasionally felt the dense plane of his stomach, and the way his tail muscles clenched in waves to help him move around.

His black scales looked like segments of glossy ink in muted light, dancing across his chest, his arms, and almost every inch of his body except around his navel. The scales around it were smaller, and more like a dark grey. That same grey matched the underside of his soft but thick hands, and his gills.

The white of his ribs was pronounced, and they looked unusually clean. They weren't entirely porous, like real bone, which made them only appear stronger and unbreakable. She eyed the light-grey fin frills going down his sides. Linh knew the location of his pelvis due to the half-sunken hip bones protruding out of his flesh.

She nibbled her lip, since she was sitting between both of them.

He really is spectacular. Hard and soft all over. Each scale was smooth on its own, the quantity of them making him bumpy, but he was rough due to his external bones. A mixture of different black, grey, and white tones, only to sometimes be dazzlingly splashed with rainbows.

She bit the inside of her cheek. *I really want to touch him.*

Linh placed her hands against his muscled abdomen to gauge their size difference. Even though his waist was narrow, her pinkies didn't even reach the sides of him.

Her touch was innocent, but the urge to make it less so tingled her fingertips. *Just a little bit?* In ways she didn't think she'd mind if he touched her?

Convincing herself, the pads of her fingers dug into hard muscles, just as her thumbs brushed up the sides of his navel. With how dense his abdomen muscles were, she didn't think they would *squish* as much as they did. She thumbed the dipping line in the centre of his abdomen, while her eyes drifted over the deep vee lines of his groin, admiring the way he was formed.

Bragg was strong. He was a big man with lots of muscles.

She thought she'd hate that quality in men after him. Whenever she imagined her future partner, it'd always been someone... small. Someone thin, who looked more like a bookkeeper, and maybe the same height as her, so he didn't feel imposing?

Nathair was the utter opposite of both those things.

He was muscled, he was gigantic, and she really, *really* wanted to knead his big chest.

She didn't, though, because she would be absolutely horrified if he did that to her while she was unaware. Or even aware.

However, she did caress the bottom rib protruding from his flesh, only to lift her hand up to lightly brush her fingers down the gills going down the right side of his neck. She didn't play with them, as she didn't know if it would feel bad – like someone tickling her lungs. She cupped down the length of his jaw, wanting to lean closer and give it a soft kiss.

Scooting herself up his torso more, she ran her hand over his round shoulder joint before going down his arm. A grin spread across her lips, flashing her teeth, as she squeezed his biceps. Then she found a strange, raised line, and petted it until she realised it was a thick vein.

She moved down his arm and grabbed his big hand so she could lift it to his stomach. Inspecting the fish fins that lay flat against his forearm, she pulled on the spike near his elbow until she flared his fin open.

Oh wow. I didn't know these were so big. The fin splayed in the middle to almost a foot!

She noted the black segments of cartilage, and how the light-grey flesh wasn't as see-through. His fingers twitched when she played with the fin, so she left it be and it snapped closed.

With both hands, she lifted his until it was near her face. She tapped the end of a black, glossy claw. *How do these sheath?* She pushed on it, and nothing happened. *His fingers are so thick and long.*

Her pussy clenched at what one would feel like inside her, and how it would feel if two stretched her. Slickness pooled at her entrance, as she thought about wanting to find out.

She pressed the pads of her thumbs against his fingertips, just so she could take in how soft they were. *He's aquatic, so I guess I shouldn't be surprised he doesn't have callouses.* She kind of liked that, as she didn't want to be abraded or for his touch to feel rough and sandpapery.

Her skin was soft – the evidence of a life that had been easy.

Linh curled his hand forward to look at his protruding knuckle bones. Only to turn it on its side moments later.

She placed his big, soft, and lukewarm palm against the side of her face and leaned into it.

I don't know what you want from me, but I know you desire me. And by the subtle warmed pulsing she felt in the core of her pussy, she desired him too.

She didn't know why. Was it because she adored how safe he made her feel? Not just from the outside world, but here, in this space, where they were alone but she didn't have to fear his presence. She didn't want her desire to be born from a place of desperation to ease her trauma, or a way to heal from it, but because he was so generous, altruistic, and sympathetic.

Because he was handsome, in all his weird, monstrous glory.

"I really want you to touch me, Nathair," she whispered quietly, unsure if it was so he couldn't hear, or in hopes that he might so he could take control for her.

I want him to erase what happened, so the only hands I remember are his, and the only skin I feel the lingering of is his scales. She wanted his feminine scent to flood her mind, and his growls to replace the disgusting sounds that echoed in her ears.

For a long while, Linh just sat there holding his palm across the entirety of her face. She brushed her skin back and forth against him, remembering the many times he'd caressed her cheek, her jaw, or just held it silently. She clung to him, to those memories, and feeling him doing it now made her so content she panted. She rubbed her lips against his palm, not kissing him, but caressing him with them.

Even his claws – his inhuman, semi-sharp claws – tickling over her skin had her stomach fluttering. The longer they innocently stayed there, the more her nipples hardened against her undershirt. Her pulse sped up in desire, but also pounded deeply with adoration.

She eventually let him go so she could lay her head against his chest. Her eyes closed when she heard his strong heartbeat.

It was fast, almost like it was semi-panicked.

She took comfort in it. *It sounds so nice.* The heart of a Duskwalker was surprisingly sincere.

Linh would like to scoop it from his chest and curl her body around it protectively. She'd like to shield it from the memories that bothered him, and the anxiety that currently had it sprinting. To keep it safe and nurture it in the exact same way Nathair did to her within the wraps of his lengthy serpent tail.

I've only been with you for a week, and I already care about you so deeply.

FOURTEEN

Nathair groaned and flicked his forked tongue forward at the sweet aroma in the air.

He'd grown accustomed to the little female in his keeping releasing subtle wafts of arousal, but it usually wasn't as strong as it currently was. Venom dripped in his mouth due to the way the scent relaxed every fibre of him, and he swallowed to rid himself of its lingering taste.

She is lying on me, he thought, since the light pressure of her waved up and down from his breaths.

He was lying flat and spread out to the point most of his tail had slipped from the nest. It wasn't uncomfortable, since his entire body could twist.

He went to lift his head to look down at her, and grunted when he couldn't move it. *My horns are caught.* He patted a hooked horn to feel how it'd slipped between tree branches and figured out the motion to unlatch himself.

Once freed, he tilted his snout downwards to take in the pretty female sprawled upon his torso.

He chuckled. *Fuck, that's cute.*

The side of her face was squished against the hard plane of his abdomen with an arm resting above her head, while the other hand dangled down the side of him. One foot rested on top of his tail, as the other tried to dig its way underneath him.

Trying not to jostle her awake, Nathair reached his arms

back so he could pull himself up and be seated. She slipped down a little, but otherwise remained how she was positioned.

Her hips dipped towards him, before she hummed out a pant.

What are you dreaming about to smell this sweet? Nathair thought, as he cupped the base of her skull.

He leaned his own to the side when he thought he felt wetness, and another chuckle threatened to fall from him. *She is drooling.*

When his claws slipped up the side of her kinked neck, she stretched it in welcome. Her hips dipped again, like she was wiggling to get closer.

Nathair flicked his tongue forward just to take in the taste of her arousal, allowing himself a tiny reward for his endless patience.

He had a pretty human on him, peacefully asleep, and filled with desire. A Mavka such as him couldn't have asked for a sweeter return to lucidity than this.

He would let her have her dreams. They were all hers; Nathair did not have to be part of them.

Brushing her long braid to the side, he pushed some escaped strands behind her ear so he could see better. He stroked the rounded top with his fingertip, and she let out a little rasp. Just as he was about to pat her hair down, she dipped her hips again, and her features tightened as her parted lips cracked out a moan.

Nathair froze and drifted his sight down to her rounded backside. Or, rather, the way her thighs were spread around his tail just below his groin. Her entire body was warm against him, but he realised then that he could feel a spot of muted *heat.*

He covered the end of his snout, closed his sight in distress, and let out a tiny whimper.

Her hips weren't *dipping,* she was *grinding* her clit against him.

Just to make sure he wasn't mistaken, he waved his tail to

do it back, and she squeaked out a moan and pressed against him harder.

All the softness of his return to lucidity evolved into hardness. He'd been able to handle her sleepy arousal, but the idea of her using his body as a masturbating pad to achieve completion was too much. He shuddered and clenched his seam when the hardness behind it truly began to swell. She was lying directly upon it, and he didn't wish for her to wake up mortified and then to scream, cry, or panic.

She was lying on him trustingly, and he would like for her to do so again in the future.

Opening his sight to find the edges of it glowing bright purple, he patted the top of her head. *Wake up, Linh.*

Her features screwed up in irritation, her lips cringing. She ground against him again before turning her head the other way.

"Five more minutes," she pleaded.

Now that she was half-awake, her movements *worsened.* She became more audible as little pants and quiet moans slipped from her parted lips. She even bit down on the bottom one.

Shit. Stop.

He palmed the top of her head until he made it roll back. Her eyes fluttered open when he directed her face to his, her gaze lazy and glistening with desirous heat.

Female... you are making it very difficult to be good.

Nathair was not infallible.

If she twisted him up enough with her sounds, scent, and movements, he may make a mistake. He didn't think any male, who had a vast amount of pent-up need, could last under such onslaught.

He could push her off, but he didn't wish for her to think he was *unwelcoming* of this. He'd rather she just didn't think he took advantage of her by allowing it. He didn't wish for her to regret it later.

Trying to make her understand, he produced a loud

whimper. It was a real one, as having her grind her needy clit against him when she was *looking* at him had him near shuddering in delight.

Her lost gaze narrowed as her lips shut.

Then her brown eyes flung open. A gasp tore out of her as she shoved herself up until she was straddling him, and the muted heat became stronger when her entire slit pressed against him.

"Oh my gods. I'm so sorry," she exclaimed, cupping her hands to her chest.

Her face grew so red he thought she'd pass out from all the blood rushing away from her racing heart.

She went to hop off him, but Nathair threw his arm out to stop her. He didn't touch her, and she immediately drew away from it to be seated upright on him.

You have the wrong idea, female. I don't want you to leave, nor to stop. He just wanted her awake.

She cast him a wary glance from the corner of her eye as she slowly brought her face towards him.

No fear entered her scent. With his maw slightly parted, the little sparks of her arousal continued to burst against his tongue. When she didn't try to escape again, remaining just to stare at him, Nathair waved his body so his tail would grind against her pussy.

Her thighs stiffened around him, a pant fell from her, and she pressed her hands against his stomach for support.

She didn't run; he chose to believe she didn't want to.

He slipped his tongue forward and licked across the seam of his maw to show his interest. He also waved his body again. *You smell like you are dripping, Linh. Like you are needy and achy.*

Like she desired just as deeply as he did and had been holding back for days.

Her lips parted in shock. "You want me to grind on you?" she choked out, and he nodded. "N-no. I don't..." She didn't finish, like the words caught in her throat.

Fuck. I want to see you come. He didn't care how. If he received his own pleasure in return or not.

Something, anything, to progress with her. He could wait, he could be patient. He didn't care if it took days or bloody *years*. Just something to show that he was desired, even if he could not touch.

He lifted his palms up, showing them to her, and placed them on the edges of his nest. When she didn't say or do anything, he patted the ledge where they rested.

"Are you saying you w-won't touch?"

He patted again.

"You'll k-keep them there?" Her brows waved in confused distress, yet the scent of her never dulled. Actually, he thought he felt the heat between her thighs *twitch* against his very sensitive scales. "A-are you sure?"

Her hesitancy waned as she repeatedly darted her gaze between his left hand and his skull. He nodded and patted one last time.

She smelt so damn good, her peach-and-vanilla scent hot and dripping in the back of his throat and nose hole. Her little sounds earlier had been cute, but he wanted her to claw at him with her cries.

The fact she wasn't immediately rejecting the idea had hope blooming in his gut. He could see she wanted to, but was struggling to convince herself.

"I don't know. I think it might be embarrassing to..." She bit her lip as her eyes crinkled and her shoulders lifted self-consciously.

Fucking grind on me! He waved his tail harder, trying to stir her into using his body. She'd been happily doing it in her sleep, and he wanted more. *Please.*

Just the idea had more hardness swelling behind his seam. He slipped his tail back inside his nest, just so he could wrap the end of it over his groin. He laid it there for now, but if he grew any more swollen, he'd use it to keep himself from extruding.

Nathair held back his desperate growl, and his pathetic want to whine at her to give *them* this. She was needy, and her desire had never been this strong before.

He wanted her to feel pleasure, even if he couldn't directly give it to her.

Silence, much of it forced and restrained on his part, echoed between them. He waited on her to make her decision. He would be disappointed if she chose to run away, but he wouldn't blame her for it. He just hoped she... didn't.

Use me, little human. Erase the ache you gave yourself.

She bit her lip hard, her head lowering, and his sight flashed with blue. It sharpened back into purple when her hips waved forward, and his muscles lost their tension. She peeked up at him, only for her frantic heart to stutter, and she shyly brought her gaze back down.

Her back-and-forth movements were tentative at first. Short, unsure, and slow. They grew more confident with each attempt until she placed her hands back against his abdomen and leaned forward. She hooked her feet on his tail behind her backside, and gave a hard grind, causing a soft moan to flutter out of her.

Nathair panted in delight and kept his seam shut by squeezing the tip of his tail against it. Pressure and thumping radiated behind it, but he'd grit his fangs through the pain to experience this.

Nathair flicked his tongue forward constantly and watched as Linh started to move in earnest.

Good girl. Grind your needy clit against me.

He'd kill to see her do this naked and feel the bundle of nerves moving against him. For her slick cunt to wet his scales and mark them in her pleasure.

As much as he wanted to move with her, Nathair remained still. He didn't want her snapping out of her lusty need in worry, and he figured she would know how to get herself there faster than him.

Her nipples are hard. He could see them poking against her purple dress, and he wished he could reach out and touch one. He'd never held her generous breasts, but he'd felt them moulding against him countless times. They were soft, as was all of her.

Her head snapped back, causing her chin to jut as she released small cries. Eyes clenched, her face stiffened as sweat began to dot her brow.

The desire to move, to lunge at her so he could grind against her, share in this with her with his own release in mind, gripped at him. To tear her clothing off, part her thighs, and shove himself inside her to rut them both into bliss. To see what she looked like, tasted like, felt like as her wet cunt swallowed him whole. To have her beautiful face screaming in the agony of release for him. To experience *sex* beyond his fragments.

Instead, he fisted the hide-covered branches harder until he heard them creaking under the stress.

Then she fucking *paused,* stopped, her hips ceasing, and he almost roared in anger. He managed to stay quiet, but his chest twisted. Her eyes opened.

Quaking, fighting his own need, he lifted a hand to ask, "What?"

Why the hell was she stopping?

"I-I don't think I'm going to come," she admitted, averting her gaze to the side. "Y-you, uh, you feel really nice, but your tail isn't hard enough."

He dipped his sight down. *If she removes her pants, she could mould against me.* They were restricting her, he guessed. He just really liked the idea of her reaching completion against his scales and hoped that dream might come true in the future.

Nathair unlatched his hands and inched them towards her.

Linh let out a whimper, just as her shoulders turned inwards to duck away from his claws coming towards her from both sides. As much as he didn't want to distress her, he couldn't speak.

At least he absolutely knew he could not touch her intimately.

He grabbed her forearms near her elbows, and directed her hands to where he wanted them. One against her breast, the other on the crook of her thigh. Then he retreated to place his hands back where they belonged on the ledge.

He waited for her to soak in what he'd done, and she looked down at her hands.

Play with yourself. Use your own hands then.

Granted, that wasn't the same as her using his body, but it sure as hell would *excite* him all the same. Perhaps even more so.

Linh squeezed her breast, and the triumph he felt had him purring. He did it louder when she cupped between her thighs and pressed against her clit.

Nathair bundled his tail behind her when it looked as though she wanted to lean on something, and she pressed her back against his coils over time.

As she fondled her breast, he could tell each squeeze became harder. Her moans were soft at first as she moved her fingers back and forth over her clit. Like before, she took time to relax into it, and much of that was gaining the confidence that he wouldn't disturb her.

Peeking at him while she licked at her lips, her hand lowered from her breast. Since the one on her pussy didn't cease, he knew it wasn't to take it away. It drifted to the side vee of her dress, and his heart quickened when he thought she might...

She pushed underneath it and touched her breast directly. Even though he couldn't see anything but the impression of her fingers, he could tell she plucked and played with her nipple now. She pinched it, then grasped the soft mound.

Her moans grew louder, her scent thickened in the air, and Nathair once more fisted the walls of his nest. He winced at the unbearable pressure behind his seam. He was fully engorged, and his tentacles had already wrapped around the girth of him protectively. They were long, reaching the entire length of his hardness, but they strained under the torture of this.

He swelled every time she let out a sharper cry than normal.

When he knew her hazy gaze was rapt on his face, a soft growl tore from him. He gestured his snout down. He did it multiple times, trying to get her attention, for her to do what he wanted.

Her eyelids flickered in recognition.

The hand between her thighs inched up, and up, and up, until she undid the ties on her pants. She hesitated, just enough to show she was wary, but eventually dipped inside to touch her pussy directly.

Feel how wet you are, he thought with a pant. She had to be drenched with how strong the aroma of her arousal was. So much so his next tongue flicker had it coated in sparks that sent him drooling.

You must be so hot there. He'd kill just to feel her heat.

Now that her hands were underneath her clothing, she squirmed and rested completely on his bundled tail. Her feet came forward, and her bent knees parted and closed as she ground the lengths of her fingers against her pussy.

Her cries were high-pitched, her moans airy and dripping with need.

"Oh gods. Nathair, I think I'm about to..."

My name, he thought with a pitiful groan, his hips darting upwards so he could grind himself inside his seam. *She moaned my fucking name...*

He whined when his insides clenched, shuddered, and convulsed in rapture. What would it sound like when the only word she could get out was his name as he pumped into her? Nathair crushed the edge of his nest until it cracked and splintered under his strength.

The hand between her thighs sped up, and her little legs kicked and squirmed. Her head fell back as her eyes rolled, and her back arched as she sped towards her climax.

"I'm going to... I'm..."

Come for me, little human. Let me taste it in the air, let me see it.

His tail waved downwards when his spine tingled just where the base of his humanoid torso met the rest of him. He didn't mean to move, but she didn't seem to mind as he ground his seam against his constrictive tail holding him at bay to ease the pressure. He was so damn hard, his entire body pulsed with need.

He'd never seen anything more *arousing* than Linh touching herself... for *him.*

His forked tongue shot forward non-stop, wanting to taste the moment she released. His seed sacs tingled and clenched hard. Her thighs spread, her feet arched as her toes clenched. A hot wave of her arousal smacked him in the face just as she released a loud, echoing scream.

The tingle in his back bolted through his entire groin.

Darkness slashed into his sight, robbing him of his view of this female coming, as liquid began to burst behind his seam. *Oh gods. Oh fuck.* His entire body rippled, causing his tail to subtly writhe behind her as he released inside himself.

His whimper strangled in his chest, like it wanted to squeeze his heart until it burst in two.

The entire time, Linh let out cries, drawing out her own orgasm rather than ceasing once it started.

Nathair collapsed against the inner wall of his nest long before she collapsed against his bundled tail. He opened his sight to find her wildly panting, with her thighs spread, her hand still in her pants, and her head turned to the side.

Dazed and limp, he'd never seen her look so utterly content.

The corners of her lips twitched, and she drew her gaze towards him. "I've never orgasmed like that before. It felt amazing."

As much as he wanted that to excite him, the meaning of it shadowed her admission with despair.

It was soon forgotten as tingles ran down his three limbs. Even his fingertips pulsed.

"Thank you," she whispered, giving him a sated smile. "Do you need me to leave so you can..." Her gaze darted to his covered groin, and her words faltered.

In his thrusting movements, his tail had slipped up. It was still covering him, but he could feel the bottom half of his seam had parted slightly by the air against the back of his tentacles.

Her eyes snapped open wide, but she didn't tear her gaze away.

"Did... did you *come*?"

Nathair winced at that. He'd been hoping she wouldn't notice the heavy stream of pearly seed leaking from his seam. Her eyes followed it running down the side of his pelvis, and he knew a decently sized puddle of it was forming beneath him.

His orbs shifted to reddish pink in embarrassment, and he covered his skull. *I came just from watching her.* Was that the equivalent to a human male coming in his pants, like in his fragments? He'd never felt such shame.

"It's okay. It kind of feels nice knowing that me doing that made you feel good."

Nathair groaned behind his hand, wishing she hadn't said anything. He could still feel it trickling from him, and every time he softened a little, it gave room for more to spill.

She giggled at him. Giggled!

Nathair shot forward with a growl bursting from him, startling the shit out of her. She recoiled beneath him when he slammed his hands against the opposite wall of his nest.

You are lucky your giggles are rare.

He didn't mind being teased for it because it meant she accepted his desire. She hadn't run away now that she'd come. She didn't flee to go cry in regret.

She'd been *giggling*, her cheeks still warmed from her sated desire, and that was better than any other alternative.

But Nathair had been good. He had been patient. He had not touched like he promised, even when he desperately wanted to. He may be understanding, but he wasn't a *saint*;

rather, the furthest thing from it.

He wanted a fucking reward.

She warily turned to him after a few seconds of him not doing anything. A small amount of fear had entered her scent, but he chose to ignore it for once.

What do I want as a reward?

His sight landed on her wet fingers, and the urge to lick them was strong. He wanted her taste directly on his tongue.

That was too much — for her, who may not take it well, and for him, who may instantly harden again.

Nathair slowly lowered himself. Keeping the pressure of his body away by supporting his weight on his straightened arms, his back muscles clenched as they squished together. The closer he came, the more she shrunk away, and she shut her eyes in uncertainty.

Nathair took his reward.

He brought the seam of his maw closer, right where the lower segments of his jaw could split apart, and pressed the hard bone against her soft, full lips.

Her pretty eyes flung open. He stayed pressed against her lips, stealing a long-awaited kiss from her, until she softened in acceptance. Then, and *only* then, did he pull back.

A kiss. He tasted her lips.

Linh launched forward and wrapped her arms around his neck to stop him from escaping. She pressed her lips against his maw herself. She clutched a horn, holding onto him, and he melted when she began lathering kisses all over him. She pecked at his skull with abandon, moving it around like she wanted to press her soft lips everywhere.

Yes. His heart raced as giddy tenderness chased it. *More kisses.* His chest rumbled instantly with a purr, and it grew louder with each soft, warm, and lovely pet of her lips. His cheek, his brow, nowhere was left untouched.

He'd just wanted one, but was utterly thrilled to have dozens, hundreds, *thousands* should she be so willing.

He pushed an arm around her back to draw her closer, and

her feet slipped against him. Linh froze and then cringed inwards. Just when he thought he'd gone too far by trying to hug her, her features twisted.

"Oh gods. There's cum on my foot."

That is the problem? Nathair burst into chuckles. He hadn't realised she'd accidentally swiped her foot through the track of his seed.

"Don't laugh!" She shoved at him, and he gave her space so she could climb off him and out of his nest. "There's so much. I need to wash it!"

He'd be offended that she didn't want to be marked in it, but he just found the situation too funny to feel anything negative.

She bolted for the lake, hopping as she did. The moment she stepped her cum-covered foot down, it came out from under her. Nathair utilised all his strength to leap forward and cushion her head before it hit the ground.

"Whyyyy?" she cried falsely. "I slipped on cum! Why does weird shit always happen to me?"

Fucking hell. That's really funny, Nathair thought as he snickered.

He couldn't remember if he'd ever laughed like this, or even felt the lightness in his chest before. Nor did he think his lucidity had ever been this strong, the voices that constantly battered the back of his mind softer than ever. He thrummed in the afterglow of Linh somehow bringing them *both* to completion this day.

Setting her down next to the lake, he waited for her to roll up her pant leg so he could help clean her.

Okay, little human. Wash your foot, and then we will find you more shells.

He hated them. They were not to his taste, as they were ugly things that didn't shine like his gems, but he would never tell her that. His contentment at watching her *add* to his precious home outweighed their ugliness.

She was making his home *hers*.

FIFTEEN

He seems... different, Linh thought, as Nathair poked another flower stem into her hair.

She regretted not braiding it completely, since she only did the top half while leaving the bottom half free. It was wet from their swim through his lake and up to his pond. Everything she wore was drenched, but at least the warm spring sun was drying her.

She fingered the fourth weed flower he'd put into her long hair, while staring up at his snake skull glittering in the light.

He seems more at ease ever since the first time I touched myself in front of him.

Her cheeks instantly warmed in memory, and she spun to hide her embarrassment from him. Her heart fluttered bashfully as her stomach flipped for the same reason.

She pressed on, searching for more herbs and any edible berries or nuts in the sparsely shaded forest.

An internal groan had her wanting to cover her face. *He made me do it yesterday too.* 'Made her' was a bit of an overstatement, considering she quickly gave in when he requested it. *I wish I'd known sooner he's always been able to smell when I'm aroused.*

It was pretty damn obvious now since his orbs would shift to bright purple, and he never once hid it over the past three days. It was like he *wanted* her to see it, to make it known that he could smell it, and he wiggled his long, forked tongue in her direction every time.

Which, being caught out, only made her scent deepen. He seemed so cocky about it, too, the jerk.

When a shrub caught her eye, Linh crouched down to inspect the blackberries on it. Firstly, to check to make sure they weren't poisonous, and secondly, to hide her blush from her next thoughts.

I can't believe I've been doing it for him. As promised, he never reached out to her. His poor nest had multiple dents in it now from where he'd crushed it with his mighty hands.

He didn't come with her the second time, but she had a funny feeling that when she went to her bathing area to semi-panic, he'd eased himself. That, or he was so good at holding back his own need that he could make himself soften at will.

If so, he was incredibly forgiving.

Wouldn't most men lose their marbles if they had a woman masturbating on top of them? And not just once, but twice?

It didn't help that just the brush of his tail against her body had her remembering how she'd ground on it. *I did that. I ground on a Duskwalker's tail.* She'd just been so groggy with sleep and turned-on at the time that it sounded like the grandest idea possible. Each reminder had her clit throbbing for her to do it again.

She wanted to be mortified by what she did, how she kept responding to the memory, but Nathair coming just from watching made her feel like the most sensual, alluring woman in the world. Even when he scented her desire, *teasing* her for it, her body would thrum.

Oh gods. What am I doing with a Duskwalker? It felt so perverted to have one watch her as she touched herself intimately, which made it all the *naughtier. Have I gone insane? Is that why I like it so much?*

Although she'd acted awkward afterwards, unsure of how to react to him or what she'd just done, she found she didn't... regret it. It didn't make sickness cling to her heart or make her feel ugly on an emotional level.

Instead, she'd grow bashful, her head hot with a blush that wouldn't settle for hours. She'd find herself eyeing him, wanting more, wanting to touch *him* instead, but then her hands would start shaking.

For three days, Linh had been trying to push herself. To shed her fears like a snake moulting its skin. To get herself to a point where she could finally let go and ease him like he was allowing her to ease herself. Gosh, she wanted his hands on her so badly she almost caved and asked for it today when he wouldn't stop purring.

I feel like a frigid teenager. Like a trembling virgin about to lose her chastity.

She was none of those things.

Once she determined the blackberries were, in fact, safe to be eaten, she picked the bush clean. She slipped them into her bag that already had some mint in it.

Due to the stream nearby, the area surrounding the entrance to his home was moist. Everything was green, flourishing, and ripening, even though it was only the start of spring. Despite them being in the north, the mountains on either side of this valley protected it from harsh winds, making it warmer.

It meant Linh had a garden to play with, so long as she was willing to walk and find it all.

When she stood, Nathair placed his hand on the top of her head. He wanted her attention, and she gave it to him. He pointed to his chest, swiped two fingers in front of his nose hole, touched his elbow and leapt to his wrist, before pointing away. "I smell something over there."

Like with most sign language, Nathair's gestures weren't technically grammatically correct due to the shortening of sentences for the ease of conversations, and some of the actions could mean multiple words at once. But Linh was interpreting them into fully formed sentences, since that was what was generally insinuated.

She knew what he meant, and the fact she was getting good

enough to understand Nathair meant every new word made her feel closer to him.

"Lead the way then," she said with a smile, thankful it was something other than *fish*.

That's what she thought, but as she came upon the orange fruits that had a sweet scent to them, she grimaced.

"That's a strychnos tree. The fruit smells sweet because it's decaying, and the nuts are highly poisonous," she explained.

His head reared back, just as his orbs turned a reddish pink. He circled his hand over his chest, which was very similar to how her people signed *please*, but she knew he meant "Sorry."

"It's fine," she said sincerely. "Not everyone knows plants as well as I do, and since you don't eat them, it's understandable that you wouldn't know. You're just lucky I know not to eat them."

Then, as if he wanted to make it up to her, he took her to a different plant.

"Can you eat this?" he signed.

"Can you lift me so I can check?" she asked, staring up at the dark-purple fruit protruding from the tree's tall trunk.

With a nod, he grabbed her hips from behind and lifted her to his shoulder. Her heart immediately picked up when he placed his palm over her inner thigh to keep her steady. She picked a bulbous fruit and opened it with her long thumb nails to get to its bright-red meat. Her mouth instantly watered at the sweet, juicy smell, but she checked its consistency.

"You're lucky!" she exclaimed, turning a grin down to his skull. "These fruit in summer in the south, but they ripen at the end of winter here."

He put her down when she began to pick them, just so he could do it instead.

"I could have done it," she stated with a forced pout, wishing to nettle him.

Nathair opened and closed his mouth mockingly, just like she knew he would. He lifted higher on the base of his tail, reaching heights no human could as he offered her fistfuls of plums. He turned to a second tree, as there were three huddled here, and gave her his back.

His muscles rippled around his exposed spine, and she could just make out the flaps next to the row of vertebrae, hiding away his massive back fins. Linh folded her arms to lean against the tree next to her, admiring each leap and clench of muscle. Dappled sunlight splashed across his body, making him shine with rainbows while the rest of him appeared a glossy black with grey accents.

He really is handsome.

She wanted to dance her palms over his scale-covered back muscles and see if they would respond to her touch. *Duskwalkers shouldn't have a nice body like that. It's not fair.* It made it harder for her to resist him.

Something in her periphery grabbed her attention, and she turned her lazy gaze to the side. She met eight eyes set in a small fuzzy cream-coloured face.

"Eeek!" she screamed, leaping away from the huntsman spider, which had been so close that if it had lifted a furry paw, it would have touched her chin.

Nathair spun while dropping plums to the ground, ready to defend her with a bone-chilling hiss. She tripped over his tail and landed on her arse with an oomph. He halted when he found her on the forest floor, rubbing at her arms like thousands of tiny spiders were crawling over her.

He looked around, searching for the danger, then threw his arms to the side. "What?"

Linh pointed at the spider that was the size of *his* palm.

Slithering over to it, Nathair cupped his thin jaw as he lowered to inspect it. He turned his head to her and tilted it questioningly.

"Sorry, but bugs kind of give me the heebie-jeebies." If he had been any kind of bug Duskwalker, she would have run for the hills, uncaring if a Demon got her. To her horror, he reached the claws of both hands out to it. "No! Don't touch it!"

Ignoring her, Nathair gently brushed the spider into his

palm, and it walked on willingly.

"Nathair," she whined, cringing through another shudder. "Put it back."

She didn't want him to kill it, even if it made her skin crawl. It deserved to live, but just... not anywhere near her.

To her disgust, he slithered over to show her it, as if telling her not to be afraid. Linh squealed. She shot to her feet and backed up, throwing her hands up to ward him and *it* away.

From what she could tell, Nathair held his breath, since his chest was unmoving. She bet she smelt of mild fear.

He came forward again, so she backed up a little more.

"I really don't like bugs." Even if he'd been holding a butterfly, she would have wanted to hurl.

Nathair let out a dark, morbid, and *evil* little chuckle. Her face drained of heat at what that could possibly mean. He wiggled the hand holding the spider at her, as he came ever closer and looked as though he was about to put it in her hair.

Linh, realising what he was up to, nearly burst into tears when she ran. He fucking chased her with it! Considering he was usually lightning fast and didn't catch up to her right away, he was letting her be a few feet in front of him, but still...

His chuckle was cruel, the game mean.

That was until he wrapped his arm around her midsection. She kicked and bashed at his forearm, even when she watched him free the poor spider by letting it crawl onto a random tree trunk. Then he turned her to him.

"You're a jerk," she bit out when she finally calmed – since fighting him was pointless. She folded her arms and threw her head away.

He forcibly turned her face back to his, and his bright-yellow orbs glowed with joy. He let out a snicker.

"It's not funny. I'm really angry with you."

He circled his hand over the left side of his chest.

"You're not sorry. Don't lie."

His snicker deepened!

When she refused to soften her glare, he shot forward. A

wet, forked limb swiped across her neck, just below her jaw, and her skin instantly prickled. She gasped and cupped her neck, her pulse fluttering faster under her palm.

He licked me.

Nathair then held the side of her face, staring down at her, and his yellow orbs seemed to say a thousand silent words. His chuckles morphed into a purr. She realised he was holding her, hugging her so they were torso to torso, and that she'd instinctually wrapped her legs around his waist.

He slowly leaned forward to lick her again, but down her cheek. The swipe ended at the corner of her lips, and the fork of his tongue ensured it was wide. His maw lingered near her mouth, and she dabbed her tongue at the seam of her lips, unsure if she wanted him to lick across them or not.

She was mad at him, and she knew the 'kiss' would be unfamiliar. She was also kind of... curious.

Deciding the betrayal of him chasing her with a spider wasn't as terrible as what he *could* have done with it, Linh nodded, hoping his lack of movement was a question. She wanted a proper kiss, and not just her giving him a bunch of them against his skull like that one morning.

When he slipped his tongue across her lips, Linh knew she'd made the right decision. She instantly melted for it. *It's so firm.*

In case he only intended to give her one, she panted as she whispered, "Again?"

Nathair groaned and held her tighter as he did it a second time. She opened for him so he could dip it into the crevice of her mouth. Her stomach instantly tightened and clenched as her pussy quivered in delight at the strangeness that greeted her. His tongue split over the top of hers, and its roughness felt weird – which meant it was *perfect.*

Thrumming with arousal, she wound her arms around his neck and drew him closer with her ankles. The rumble in his chest vibrated against her breasts, making her nipples harden further. His hands spanned over her side and the back of her opposing shoulder as he pressed her tightly against him.

Linh fought his tongue to dance around each fork. It was messy and uncontrolled, but tingled her lips with each back-and-forth stroke. *More,* she thought with a moan, her pussy spasming in welcome of the foreign sensation.

He pulled away too soon, leaving her panting and buzzing with want. His tongue flickered into the air, tasting her as his purr deepened. With orbs purple, he set her down. Yet, her stomach flipped to sucker punch her heart when he cupped the side of her face and caressed her cheek with a clawed thumb.

Linh knew he was pushing her boundaries on purpose. He was being patient, but he wasn't willing to wait for her to take each step on her own – especially as she'd shown she found it difficult to take those leaps.

It was all happening too soon, too quickly.

Two weeks ago, she'd been in the clutches of a vile monster parading around with a human face. The fact she even allowed Nathair to delve his tongue within her mouth wasn't something she had been able to foresee herself doing so soon.

The pains and aches constantly lingered, and she often shrank at the thought of being intimate. Yet, her utter faith in him only made her dizzy in this moment. She was nervous, but for the right reasons.

His tongue hadn't been hot like hers, but it had been long, dexterous, and wonderfully textured. It wasn't even overly wet, like it was drier than a human's.

Why did he stop? Was it too much for him to hold back? She hated that she couldn't gauge what he was feeling because of his skull, and that his purr could be hidden by his racing heart. The idea that Nathair might be spiralling, his desire twisting to a dangerous degree, sent a thrill straight to her stomach.

She shouldn't be teasing this beast, but she couldn't seem to stop herself – not when he kept instigating it.

As he turned, heading back towards the wild plum tree to obtain her more fruit, Linh followed him in a daze. Her appreciative gaze was more delirious as she took in the play of his back muscles, wishing she'd thought to dig her fingertips into them.

She eyed his bony maw and licked her lips at the memory of that strange kiss. *I really want to do that again.*

She completely forgot about the huntsman incident.

SIXTEEN

Nathair snorted a contented huff through his nose hole while his snout poked through a fold of his coiled tail. His neck was twisted in a way that would have put a strain on most creatures, but it felt utterly natural for him.

With his skull lying flat and facing upwards, while his body was twisting on its side, he tightened his arms around the little human in his clutches. Her face was buried against his chest, and her once-cold fingers were warmed in their cupped position against his abdomen.

The length of him wrapped around her in different ways, trapping her. Not much of an imprisonment when she willingly crawled into his space each night.

Although Nathair wasn't particularly warm, he was a shield from the cool air. Linh heated them both, and his mind grew dozy on the sensation of it sinking beneath his scales.

Why has my lucidity not slipped yet? The voices, ever persistent, still chattered in his mind. After a long while of being motionless, one would usually shove its way to the forefront and yank him semi-unconscious.

It was how it'd always been, and it was his way of sleeping.

He could completely fall asleep, but that never boded well. It was like the complete emptiness of his senses made his gruelling, ruminative fragments more realistic, more comprehensible.

More frightening.

He couldn't truly hear the outside world, couldn't smell it, nor could he see it. He'd even been partially eaten by Demons and never registered it other than the pain – which his fragments had utilised for their own gain to disorientate him.

Dreams and senses would swirl and bind, stopping him from separating life from human memories.

So, he rested but didn't sleep, and the result was the further twisting of his sanity. Coming back to Earth had worsened his mental state, and it had been unbearable for the longest time.

Until the pretty female in his arms rudely kicked her way into his life.

Nathair hummed in contentment as he squeezed her with all of his being, knowing she enjoyed the constriction.

She didn't like being pinned down or lying back with Nathair towering over her. Yet, being closed in on all sides had become some kind of stress relief.

He twitched when delicate fingers caressed over the scales of his sternum. He hadn't expected her to be awake still.

As much as he would have liked to bring his head into the folds of his body to check on her, he didn't. Or, rather, *couldn't*.

He snorted another huff, taking in the clean, cool air – which wasn't clogging him like her constant arousal scent. It'd sparked in his wrappings, and he hadn't been able to handle the way it fizzled in his lungs.

His sight shifted to bright yellow in both joy and humour. *She liked my kiss.* She'd been gifting him the salacious aroma on and off all day ever since.

At the time, he'd just wanted to figure out a way to get her to forgive him after scaring her with the spider. He really hadn't thought she'd be so upset, but he'd found it just too funny not to chase her with it when she squealed and ran away from him.

However, the moment he swept his tongue against her skin, the longing to taste her had overcome him.

She opened her mouth for me. She'd let him delve, and even slipped her tongue against his own in welcome.

He was still rather thrilled about that. He thought she may be put off by his forked tongue, or the fact he didn't have lips to kiss with. He also had fangs and venom, which he knew she'd seen him use.

Since then, the sweet, tangy smell of her arousal had clouded around her all day, thickening and softening. Her gaze also appeared shier, and he found her staring at his skull before quickly looking away with pinkness lifting into her cheeks.

Which he thought was rather weird.

He'd seen this female touch herself and come, so he never expected something as mild as a Mavka's kiss to make her act so fidgety.

His intentions over the last few days were to have her grow comfortable with her desire around him. To touch herself, and learn that he had the restraint to not take more than just the view and her smells.

The only reason he hadn't acted on her current state of need was simple. Nathair did not wish for this female to think he only wanted her desire and would steal any opportunity to make the situation sexual. He didn't wish for her to associate his precious nest with intimacy, and it was imperative she know he didn't expect anything in it.

He wanted to prove that she could be in any state, and he wouldn't *need* anything from her. No matter how strong it was, or how much he desperately wanted his own release and to touch this infuriatingly alluring creature, he would be good.

I don't want to be good. If she knew the dark, perverse thoughts that constantly bounced around within his skull, she'd be clawing to leave his home.

Nathair wanted to cherish Linh. His heart very much swelled for her, but he was a male, and one that did not know pleasure from another. But he'd seen it, he'd experienced it in his fragments, and he knew there were *so many* ways he could tease and play.

He was oozing with untapped and pent-up lust; it had been

rolling around inside him like a thunderstorm for *hundreds* of years.

Even if he was happy to be patient, he was still a Mavka. He was a species of monster that hated feeling starved, and they were insatiable. His stomach gurgled in emptiness, yet his seed sacs throbbed in fullness.

The only way to sate both was to consume her soul, then spread her thighs around his hips and rut her until he filled her up with every drop of seed he had.

She would need to be ready for that.

Their first time would require a lot of restraint on his part, as he doubted he'd be able to unleash all of himself upon her. *But the idea of connecting with her makes me feel good.* It would mean she asked him to be inside her, and not only trusted him with her delicate body, but her wounded heart and infected soul.

He would be gentle with her and teach her body pleasure. He wanted to show her that sex could be passionate, and he would adore it if she could allow him to discover that with her as well. She was the first female he had in his keeping. He'd never touched nor been touched, but he'd been both the female and the male in the many sex fragments he had.

Nathair would like to learn what it felt like to have a soft hand on his scales, rather than human flesh that did not belong to him. What it felt like to move intimately with his tail, rather than two spindly legs. He'd like to know what it was like when *he*, a Mavka, lost control in the throes.

He'd like to be himself and discover what it felt like to have a female coming around *him,* for him, while looking at him, touching him, tasting him. That all the things making him a Mavka were wanted, desired, and perversely *yearned* for. That everything about him which was monstrous and *wrong* to her kind only made it feel like he was some kind of sinful, evil devil-god about to broker a bargain by offering the touch of his inhuman flesh and depraved pleasure.

He wanted to be craved in the unholiest of ways, and

worshipped along the way.

He'd like it to be this female that taught him. Someone who smelt of peaches and vanilla, and had such a kind and feminine voice it tingled his mind. Who giggled and smiled, despite all the internal pain he knew she must be in. A female who was willing to see him as what he wanted to be: someone strong and protective.

Someone willing to listen to him in his silence.

A human whose personality and heart seemed so benign, he wanted to corrupt it just for his greedy self until she'd turned into an aching creature that clawed for more.

Linh, who was internally wounded in the ways he hungered, had drunk from the wrong pond.

A Mavka can hope, he thought with a joyous hum.

"Nathair?" she croaked, digging her thumbnail around the edge of one of his chest scales. "Are you still awake?"

I am always awake. He knew she meant if he was conscious and not in a trance.

He opened a pocket big enough that he could cup the back of her head and patted her silky hair. He combed through the loose half, purposefully tickling her neck. He liked the way she styled it today, and that she often changed it.

"I'll take that as a yes." Her legs shifted through his coils, and her hands fidgeted against his torso. "I was wondering..."

She paused, and Nathair let out an annoyed sigh. *Spit it out, Linh.* It likely was a question he couldn't answer, as her lessons on Nathair speak were slow going. She liked to ask complex questions that required explanation, which he couldn't do just yet. She'd gotten the hang of his alphabet, so he was able to finger spell many words, but it was too arduous to have a lengthy conversation that way.

However, she was willing to learn, and that was all that mattered.

"Could... we kiss again, like in the forest?" she whispered, and he instantly stiffened around her.

She wants to kiss again. He almost groaned.

They'd only kissed twice: her kisses as she pressed her lips all over his skull the first time he'd watched her touch herself, and today... *his* kiss, which had been messy and confusing even to him.

His chest swelled that she'd asked for another. That she'd asked for anything at all. Linh was, understandably, hesitant.

The temptation was too hard to resist, and he slipped his head into the centre of his wrapped self.

Nathair instantly choked on the thick, clogging aroma of her arousal. It was so heavy that the air itself felt charged and hot. His skin tightened around his muscles and bones as he held back his full-body shudder.

She had, apparently, been thinking about kissing him for a while. Had he known that something so simple and innocent from his side could instil such a strong reaction, he may have done it sooner.

With his orbs threatening to shift to purple, he utilised every bit of willpower to keep them their usual orange hue so as to not startle her. He cupped the side of her head and directed her face towards his bony one. She tilted back to make it easier, as he pressed the seam of his maw against her soft and plump lips.

Linh immediately pressed against his mouth harder, and brushed her lips in waves, seeming unbothered that he didn't have his own to mesh against. Nathair wanted to try something new, and he attempted to utilise his partible lower jaw segments to mimic the movement of her lips. Surprisingly it worked, and he was pleased he could almost kiss like a human.

But I want the taste of her. He snuck his chance when her lips parted again, and he swiped across them with his forked tongue. She opened them more for him.

A groan caught in his throat, and he shoved his tongue as deep as he could. Their tongues clashed and were messy due to the fork he had in his own. Despite being split like a serpent's, his was flatter and wider, and she slipped hers between the two halves.

All the while, her lips pressed against his closed maw. Nathair had only separated the segments of his jaw, as opening his mouth could make his fangs dip and his venom leak. He had to be careful, as he didn't know what would happen if she were to ever ingest it.

Of her own accord, she ended it by shutting her lips and pulling back. She panted, her breaths sweet and filled with her scent, and the taste of it lingered within his maw.

"Can I touch you?" she whispered breathlessly, as her gaze moved back and forth between his orbs.

He clasped one of her forearms to push her hand against him, then covered it to show she could do whatever she pleased. He wanted her hands upon him, and had been waiting for her to grow the courage to do so.

Linh leaned forward again, pressing her lips against his skull, and he was slightly taken aback that she wanted more. He gave her his tongue again, and she greedily accepted it. Both her palms lay flat against his abdomen, and she swiped them to the sides, feeling his body and the muscles that leapt under her caress.

Her hands are so soft against me. He hummed in contentment, as his wobbling sight finally defeated him and shifted to bright purple. He clenched his seam to make sure he didn't begin to extrude, and kept his hands where she'd find them safe: her back.

He would not ruin this for his own selfish longing.

Her hands glided upwards. He almost chuckled when she gripped both his pectoral muscles and kneaded them. Although firm, they squished against her fingers. The longer she did it, the more her thighs squeezed around his tail.

Her breasts pressed against his abdomen, and her hard nipples scraped him through her purple garment.

The arm she lay upon remained to fondle his chest in obvious appreciation, which made his body puff with pride and tenderness. The other palm began to caress him everywhere as their tongues danced: his biceps, his forearm, before darting to his back to touch his exposed rib bones. She explored everything that was different to her, including the flexible fins going down his sides.

With each foray, lightness pushed into his skull. Her scent choked him, while the fascinating nuances of her body – the way she released soft 'mmm' sounds around his tongue, and how her pretty face became docile and relaxed – all had the voices softening. They remained, ever present, but the ease of pressure had Nathair turning into a puddle.

Her hand descended the front of his body, and she tickled the muscled ridge between his seam and hip bone. He let out a quiet, shaken whine when he had to clench his seam so hard it pinched all the way across his pelvis.

Seemingly unaware of the danger she almost put herself in, how his tentacles almost lost their battle at keeping him at bay, she brought her hand up. Then she took it away, twisted it, and he felt the backs of her knuckles against his abdomen instead.

Her hand descended once more, but into the confines of her pants. Her movements were slow, and her lazy gaze bore into his orbs as she slowed their kiss.

"Is this okay?" she whispered against his maw.

He could feel where she was going, what she intended. Nathair tightened his arms around her and leaned forward to lick her lips with a nod, hoping to continue their leisurely kiss.

He knew the moment she grazed her clit because she released a raspy moan around his tongue. Her mouth became unresponsive as she began to play with the bundle of nerves, going in circles before moving side to side.

Nathair pulled back to watch her features twitch with pleasure, overjoyed that he could hold her while she did this.

It wouldn't last much longer, as he could only hold back his tentacles for so long. He'd like for her to come in his arms, so he could feel the way she tensed up, and experience her release on a much deeper level.

Don't extrude. Don't ruin this, Nathair pleaded to himself when her hand worked faster.

Her little cries were like mild waves rolling over him, and he took in their decadence with strain.

She leaned forward to press her face against his collar bone.

"You smell so nice," she whispered around hitches of breath.

She kissed at his scales, and he swore her little tongue darted out to taste him. Then she went higher. She licked across the side of his neck, his fucking *gills*, before giving them a messy, lewd kiss too.

A choked groan burst from him. Nathair shot his hand down to physically stop his deep, throbbing arousal from shooting forward. He doubted his tentacles would have been able to keep ahold of him if he didn't.

She stopped, likely due to the back of his hand now being nestled against her thighs, and very close to her pussy.

Linh, he whimpered, panting against her.

He wanted to release the pressure throbbing within; it would be more bearable than keeping it hidden. He longed to replace her hand with his own and bring her to release.

"Did I hurt you?" she asked, the desirous heat in her gaze softening as she frowned. "I-I didn't know if your gills were sensitive or not."

That was why she stopped?

He was so damn thankful that it wasn't in reaction to his hand placement, and he cupped the back of her neck with the other and pressed her face against them.

Nathair was torturing himself. He didn't know how he had the willpower for such agony, but he was so content in his suffering that he didn't care. Not when she kissed his gills again and her hand started back up between her thighs.

He was swallowing up her moans as they vibrated against the thick flaps of skin, and each moan tingled the bottom of his lungs. It was like she was caressing him all the way to his sternum, and it felt so damn good his maw parted to drip venom.

And yet, the closer she seemed to get, the harder it became

to stay *sane.*

His muscles swelled with restraint against the nagging desire to strike at her with his hands, his tongue, his damn cock. He needed release. Fucking *ached* for it.

He yearned for her.

I can't! Nathair's mind bellowed as he flung his wrappings open.

Linh gasped at his jarring movements as he writhed and slithered to separate them before he did something he would regret.

Fresh air greeted his senses, giving him back just a semblance of control. He shifted until he was able to reluctantly wrap the end of his tail over his seam to hold himself at bay as he positioned her behind it. He seated her against a wall of his limb and sat back as he wildly huffed.

"Nathair?" she asked, her voice higher pitched and shaky, mingled with arousal and obvious uncertainty.

His orbs flashed a reddish pink in shame and embarrassment, and he released a curt whine in answer. He shuddered, utterly thankful for the separation, as it allowed his mind to sharpen – even if that meant the voices chattering grew louder.

The lit torch gave low light, the oil mostly burned off, but he thought it would be enough for her to see him. Still, just in case, he pricked his palm and touched the side of his nest to give her his light symbol.

"T-too much?" She gave him an unsure smile, her face cringed into an expression of what he thought may be hope.

He nodded, showing her his quaking hands, and they trembled as he placed them on the ledge of his nest like usual. A safe placement, one where he could let out his strength and need by partially destroying his nest.

Her eyes softened. "Do you want me to stop?"

The growl that came from him was unhinged, beastly, and *dangerous.*

I will not be tortured just for neither of us to achieve

release. Harder than normal, Nathair rolled his tail between her thighs to get her to play.

He just needed space to ensure her safety from *him.*

Hesitant, she began to touch herself like before, and he purposefully let out a purr to show he was pleased.

She bit her bottom lip hard, and her gaze turned meek. Her movements slowed before pausing as she eyed him almost cautiously. She removed her hand, grabbed the bottom of her purple dress, and lifted it off her body.

The pressure behind his seam throbbed in delight. *She removed it on her own.* He thought it'd be forever before he'd be allowed to soak in the skin of her navel, to just *see* the tight curves of her narrow waist, her wide hips. She even pushed up her undershirt as well and exposed her round breasts for him while still keeping it on.

All his aggression and irritation from earlier bled out of him at seeing them, and Nathair gave her another encouraging purr.

Pretty, he thought with a deep huff, licking across his snout to show his interest. *Kisses and I get to see her breasts?* He was getting all kinds of gifts today.

They looked soft, like one would pool in the very centre of his palm should he touch it. Her fawny-brown skin was lighter on her breasts and stomach, while the top half of her chest, her arms, and even face were darker. Her nipples were a pinkish-brown, and he watched as she pinched one.

Her other hand went back to play with her clit, and her eyes never left his skull.

She trusts me. Knows I won't touch. And he was rewarded with a tantalising view. *I wish for her to lower her pants as well.* He'd like to see her fingers teasing her little clit and pussy, rather than just the imprint of her knuckles through her grey pants.

Once more, she bit at her plump bottom lip.

He was beginning to read this as the first step into her leaping forward. Her gaze always turned shy and uncertain, but he'd already observed she was strong, as she often caved to her own wants.

"You can..." She averted her gaze momentarily, and her heart rate spiked in a way that had him tilting his head in curiosity and *worry*. She peeked at him, her cheeks reddening. "You can move your tail."

He rolled it in a wave between her thighs, but she shook her head. Her right foot lowered, and she gently pushed against the tip of it where it was keeping his seam closed.

"It's-it's okay. I've already seen it."

His skull tilted as he looked down. *She wants me to extrude?* He hadn't thought she'd be comfortable with this, considering how intensely she reacted last time.

When he didn't, the trickle of hesitancy strong around his heart, she pushed her toes against it again.

"Please? I want to see it."

Tenderness swelled in his gut, and his pulse quickened. *She wants to see me...*

He'd like for her to see how much he wanted her, to see what had been buried within him for days while she flittered around him. Nathair wanted to reveal just how *much* he was holding back, so she would be at ease in his presence, no matter the state of her body.

Lifting the end of his tail, he forced himself to slowly extrude, while also keeping it hidden from view. The relief at releasing the throbbing pressure had his clamped muscles softening. He let out a contented pant at the freedom.

When the tips of his tentacles shielding him were visible to her, he waited to see how she would react. Whether it be encouragement for herself, or for him, she kneaded her breast and played between her thighs.

He let his tail slip to the side and fall off his pelvis to fully reveal his purple tentacles and the way they wrapped around his full girth. *Should I open my tentacles?* They were long, able to encompass him fully.

"You are really big," she rasped, her voice shaky and quiet, before nibbling at her lips. "I-I don't think any human would be able to take you."

He looked down at it. *No, not like this.* Not that anyone was supposed to fuck him while his tentacles encompassed him. But he knew beneath them would be more manageable.

He jerked each time she made a little noise of pleasure, and her eyelids flickered in recognition as if she noted it. Her need didn't seem to be waning, but rather... *deepening.*

Her arm dipped further inside her pants, as if she was reaching lower. His sensitive ears picked up the minute squelch, but he didn't know what that meant – only that her toes curled in reaction as she let out a higher-pitched cry than normal. Nathair just panted at her, desperate to do something but unable to.

She stared at him with a hooded gaze. It sharpened, then she glanced away, only to look upon his arousal sticking upright in excitement.

It didn't seem she knew where she wanted to focus her gaze, and he had a feeling that was due to his own locked on her. He was observing her in what he knew most humans considered an intimate and private moment, which was even more nerve-wracking for someone as wounded as her.

"Do you want to stroke it?" she asked, before her knees turned inwards.

Yes. Absolutely, he wanted to stroke himself.

Still, he pointed to his chest, made a stroking motion in the air, waved at his groin, while tilting his head to convey his question. He wanted to make sure she really wanted this.

She nodded.

This will not go well.

Nathair would usually find it rather humorous when it came to knowing something the other person didn't, and they were about to get a rude awakening.

He didn't find this funny.

He knew how this little female was about to react, and he prepared himself for it – and that he likely wouldn't be stroking himself in her presence this night.

He released his tentacles. They swirled backwards, wiggling in their freedom as he completely and utterly revealed himself to her.

Her gasp was so loud that if it hadn't been sucked inwards, it would have come out as a scream. Her hands ceased, her back grew rigid, and her eyes widened.

"That wasn't your dick?!" she squealed, her eyes riveted to the writhing purple limbs, and more importantly, what they surrounded. "You have *two?!*"

Yes, little female. I have two cocks.

None of his human fragments had more than one, nor were they purple like he was. Each of his cocks was slightly tapered, and both were puffed in the middle to keep their tips apart as they sat side by side. However, they did mesh together to create one large shaft he could pet if he held the bases in one fist.

Both were long and lacked foreskin like in humans. Instead, his dripping lubricant protected the hard, jutting muscles that were sensitive all over. He thought a human may be able to take one with little resistance, as they were thick but manageable, but two meshed together would require patience.

Each cock had two rows of small nodules, while the tops had a singular line each, as if they'd perfectly split in the middle. A large seed sac was embedded into the very base of each one.

As much as he didn't want to frighten her, Nathair considered it wise to let her know about this difference between him and other males. *She gave me permission,* he thought, using that to alleviate his guilt. He hoped the earlier she learned of it, the sooner she would accept them.

Despite the current twitchy hardness at having her gaze upon his two cocks, his pulse began to slow. Her shock was enough to soothe his desire into a more manageable state, and he waited for the inevitable.

She will run.

She would seek to go to the one space in his home he

wouldn't enter: her bathing room.

Her tiny heart fluttered wildly as she gawked for longer than anyone could say was comfortable.

Air began to cling to them as his excessive lubricant started to dry. He let out a quiet, non-aggressive hiss, and made his tentacles swirl to protect him from the sting.

"Wait!" she cried, reaching her hand out before second-guessing the action. "Wait. I-I'm sorry. I didn't mean to stare."

Dark yellow infiltrated his sight as confusion settled in. He still closed his tentacles to save himself from the sting, and was thankful they reached all the way to both tips. *She does not want me to put them away or leave?*

"I just... I know you're mainly a serpent in nature, but I didn't think you'd actually have two penises like a snake." She lifted a hand and made two fingers open and shut. "Talk about double the trouble," she stated with a forced laugh.

"I don't understand," Nathair signed.

Her cheeks re-pinkened. "I don't want to stop. I was just surprised."

His cocks jerked, making a small amount of fresh lubricant seep to the surface.

"Un-unless you want to," she added, showing she didn't want to force anything from him.

He almost chuckled when fondness radiated behind his sternum, as well as relief that he'd been wrong. He'd much rather this turn of events, despite the awkwardness of it. Nathair enjoyed watching her, and was thrilled she'd taken so many steps herself this evening.

He waved his hand towards her while he nodded, then placed it back on the ledge of his nest. Her relieved smile and soft, appreciative eyes had his stomach clenching in want. *Pretty female.*

He waited for her to continue, and released a contented purr for her benefit when she did. Her scent still sparked with strong arousal even after he revealed himself, and he flicked his tongue forward to taste it in the air.

He'd never been this at ease while doing this with her before. She was touching herself for him, while he lacked the agonising pressure behind his seam. Her gaze landed on his tentacle-covered shafts that spanned up his muscled abdomen, and rarely left them except to look up at his skull. His desire was on show for her, accepted, and that was enough to resend his pulse into a deep pound of lust.

Her straight lashes tipped as she licked and nibbled at her lips, causing them to swell under her nervous teeth fidgets.

Only when her breaths turned laboured once more – soft and cute, with little pitches – did he raise his right arm. Lubricant had resoaked him, and he should be able to stand the air again.

He formed a ring with his fingers and then made a stroking motion in the air. Her toes curled, and she nodded. Nathair lowered his hand and allowed his tentacles to unlatch. They swirled back, and a small shudder rolled through him when he palmed the tops of his cocks before gripping them both at the base in a singular fistful.

Oh fuck, yes. Nathair groaned as he made his first stroke up and the ring of his fingers ran over the heads. The rims weren't pronounced, especially in the middle – like his cocks had once been singular and split apart – but they felt wonderful to stroke over.

Pleasure sparked throughout his groin and made his flesh ripple underneath and behind her. He sagged a little as he stroked himself, lubricant seeping over his fingers.

She squeezed her soft mounds in earnest, often curling her index finger around her nipple before flicking downwards over it. *I would like to put my tongue on her breasts.* He wondered how his forked tongue would work with her nipples, and if she'd like the way he could move it.

Her arm sunk deeper into her pants like before, and he wondered if that meant she'd sheathed her fingers inside herself. It was a new action. He hoped it was in want of what he was stroking, and Nathair quickened his pace as he rubbed up and down.

His black claws glinted in the light, and his dark-grey fingers were a stark contrast against the colour of his cocks. He observed her eyes dipping up and down with his movements. She seemed to like it when he slipped his index finger between them, splitting them momentarily, and he enjoyed the way it felt. Her lips often parted to moan or pant, but her teeth bit down on the bottom one when his abdomen and pectoral muscles bunched and leapt beneath his scales.

Each cute noise from her had his embedded seed sacs clenching until the bubble of precum overflowed to drip down the slightly tapered heads. He answered her with his own slow and airy groans.

Fuck this feels good. Being watched while he fucked his fist around his shafts, being *involved* in her pleasure, felt amazing.

"I really like the colour of you," she stated softly. "I like that your cocks are purple."

The purred groan that shuddered out of him had him quaking inwards like he was melting. *She likes them.* Fuck, she could *have* them. He wanted her to claim them. To touch them, taste them, mount one at a time, or both if she would allow it – he didn't care how.

He stroked his hand down to hold the bases so she could see how long his cocks were without his tentacles impeding her view. To see them for all their twitching glory, and how wet they were with his lubricant from how turned-on he was. He stroked the left one lightly before doing the same to the right, letting her see their sizes on their own, then gripped them both in his fist again.

Her cries became more consistent, her self-touches more erratic and hurried. Her hips waved, as if she wanted to grind on her fingers, just as her head tilted back.

That's it, Linh. Make yourself come.

Her eyes rolled, and her back arched, right as the heady scent of her arousal clasped at his throat. She let out a cry as her knees drew up to her chest and parted, and the hand between her thighs quickened.

She came, and Nathair worked his cocks harder, faster, gripping them with strength until they meshed tightly. His maw parted for ease of panting, and the venom on his stilled tongue was sweeter with the taste of her orgasm he'd stolen from the air.

Her sated look only lasted until she saw him still masturbating over what he'd just seen, heard, and smelt. Her limpness faded as her fingers upon or inside her pussy began to work again.

I am close, he thought with a groan.

And he was glad he wouldn't be releasing without the view of her.

In his lust-addled thoughts, it took him longer than it should have to realise something. Something that instantly had continuous bubbles of precum welling at the tips of his cocks.

Is she... He slowed his strokes to make sure, and threw his head back when a thrilled *whine* nearly felled him. *She is mimicking me!*

She was matching his speed, as if she was picturing them inside her, and Nathair's free hand clawed at the ledge of his nest. He played with her tempo himself, his strokes becoming rapid, only to slow. They were unpredictable, and she tried to match each one.

His tail uncoiled behind her when his embedded sacs clenched. He couldn't help it, not when a tingle raced outwards from his groin to shoot down the vertebrae of his long spine.

His groans evolved into constant quiet whines as his cocks swelled. Intense pleasure ran up them, and his hips jerked and twitched, right as he came simultaneously from both. Pearly white seed burst from him in thick and powerful ropes up his chest.

Nnhn, fuck. He couldn't hold back his hips from pumping any longer, fucking his fist as he worked through the rest of his orgasm. Then, as the release began to soften, a few voluminous drops dripped onto his shafts, tentacles, and fingers when it stopped violently shooting from him.

All the while, Linh didn't stop, her soft moans ensuring he'd come hard as bliss made him writhe behind her. Even when he stopped stroking, his breaths shallow, hard, and choked, she didn't cease.

After her first orgasm, he thought she'd lose her enthusiasm. She usually only came once, but she seemed to be in a worse state than before. Linh trembled from head to toe, her eyes glassy and wet, but there was no evidence of spilled tears. Her breaths were so high-pitched and strangled she sounded as though she was in pain.

Worry lanced his satisfied stupor when this little female sounded... *distressed.*

"N-Nathair," she called so sweetly, dripping with need, that it sounded like pure heaven. He was a monster, a Mavka, a corrupt and bloodthirsty creature; his name shouldn't be called so sensually and around sultry breaths.

The utter fucking delight of it slashing through him was wicked, and he was depraved enough to want more. It made him want to do obscene things to this tiny, vulnerable female.

Her hand drew back like she removed her fingers from her channel, and her voice was low as she said, "I-I really want you to touch me right now."

I can touch? he thought with a deep, rumbling groan.

Unsure if such a marking would make her uncomfortable, Nathair wiped his seed-covered hand clean on the furs of his nest wall. She was asking for his touch, and he didn't want her to retract her request before he got the chance.

He would take this leap with her. He'd come. He was feeling calmer and more in control, and would be able to focus solely on her needs rather than the ache of his own consuming him.

However, he knew she didn't like being towered over. Even though that would make it easier, he instead curled his semi-flexible torso so he could bring his head below her chin. He also ensured that not a single part of his torso, especially his cocks and tentacles, brushed against her.

She didn't stiffen, and worry never entered her heavy-lidded gaze, even when he placed his left hand down beside her to keep the weight of his torso up.

With the pocket of space separating them, Nathair tilted his skull as he drew his gaze all over her.

Her scent is so much better up close.

He noted the way her jugular fluttered fast at his proximity, and her heart stammered along with it in his ears. He took in the heat cascading off her skin, hotter than normal and warming him despite their separation. How her flat stomach grew concave on each quick and sharp breath as her generous breasts jiggled.

Nathair leaned forward and pressed the seam of his maw against her lovely lips, and placed his right palm on the side of her neck and jaw. He smeared remnants of his seed on her, but she didn't seem to notice. Her breaths came out shaken, as if with relief, and she cupped the corners of his jaw to hold him to her.

Brushing his thumb up and down the centre of her chin, he kept his touch light. She moulded kisses to him, completely unbothered that his mimicked lips were bony.

The tenderness he felt towards her only grew in that moment. She ignored the barrier of their differences because her heart was telling her to dole out affection, and it made him feel accepted.

Drifting his hand down the side of her neck, she shivered when his claws and fingertips brushed over her. *Her skin is so soft, so smooth.* It was hot to the touch for a low-temperature creature such as himself, and it felt divine.

He could have petted something as pure as her arm for hours and been enthralled with the task.

His hand slid to the side, letting her feel the span of his palm against her shoulder while he brushed his thumb over the ridge of her collarbone. He was fascinated by every part of her, and hoped she understood that by his light caress.

Nathair palmed down the flat portion of her chest and over her bundled-up undershirt. She arched into his touch, as if she wanted him to reach lower, faster. He brushed the outside of her breast before cupping it, and his purr of satisfaction tumbled in his chest. He clasped it softly, kneading it lightly, so he didn't hurt her with his strength. When he thumbed her nipple, she let out a little moan against his bony maw.

She pulled back just a little. "You're not going to kiss me like before?"

Nathair shook his head, despite the longing to. The dances of their tongues had caused her to be like this, and he wondered how doing so now would deepen her arousal.

The uncertain furrow of her brows softened. "Because of your venom?"

He liked that she asked this, rather than taking it as a rejection. It only proved she longed to see good in him.

He nodded. *I accidentally drained my venom sac when I came.* Not completely, but enough that he could taste the remnants upon his tongue.

Nathair did dip his head to the side so he could lash his tongue against the side of her neck. He could kiss elsewhere, if she liked, and he very much wanted to.

Her breath hitched, and she wrapped her arms around the back of his skull, grabbing each of his hooked, backwards-curling ram horns. The way she clung to him had a thrill racing down his spine.

He licked across her neck, jaw, and over her ear, giving back each of the many kisses she had just gifted him. The taste of her skin upon his sensitive tastebuds, the feel of her softness brushing against each one, left his mouth tingling. He also cupped the underside of her breast, weighing it in his large palm before drawing away.

As much as he wanted to linger here, there was somewhere that called him.

He drifted his hand down, and her stomach dipped under

his claws. He momentarily slipped back up to touch the curve of her waist, letting her know he appreciated there as well, before continuing his teasing path. Her sultry moan, like his descending touch sent sparks through her, was hauntingly beautiful. The moment he brushed down the side of her navel, she lifted her hips up towards him.

Then her heart stammered and her hand shot down to grab his fingers.

"W-wait. Can you use your other hand?" Her lustrous features twisted into a cringe. "You... you came all over this one. What if you get me pregnant?"

Her question elicited fiercely provocative thoughts. Ones that had cum seeping from the tips of his still-hardened cocks until they freely overspilled against the base of his tail.

This little female, so full and flooded with his seed that her stomach rounded with his youngling... A possessive dark green flickered in his sight, and he shuddered with deep want.

He shook his head as he dipped his fingertips into the waistline of her pants.

"No?" she asked, and he shook his head again. "You can't get me pregnant?"

Absolutely, I can, Nathair thought while shaking his head a final time to reassure her as he caressed the straight hair of her pubic mound. *However, I would need to consume your soul, and make you like me.*

Even though he'd hated it at the time, he was now rather thankful that Weldir had been a constant source of information about the living world. Nathair was aware of this possibility, since other Mavka had bred their own younglings. It was not something he thought he'd long for until he found this female he wanted to lay his claim on.

So, until she gave him her pretty soul, he could come inside her cunt until his heart's content, and there would be no reason for her to fear.

Now that the issue was settled, one that should benefit him in the future should she swallow his body within her core, he lowered his hand. He sheathed his claws at the last moment.

Mmm, so wet for me, he thought with a rumble, as he greeted the drenched slit of her pussy. She parted her thighs further in welcome, and her pussy lips spread, allowing him easier access to graze her clit. He resumed petting her with his tongue, while he gently nestled the bud between his thick fingers to touch it everywhere.

"Nathair," she breathlessly whispered, tilting her head back.

He took that as his opportunity to lower his head and lash one of her nipples with his tongue. He rubbed back and forth around her clit at the same time, and she melted for him.

She hugged his head and used it as an anchor to wave her hips back and forth.

He picked up the pace ever so slightly, while pushing the fork of his tongue directly over her nipple so it split around it, only to dip forward so he could nestle it between the junction. Then he pinched it.

His large hand felt unwieldy petting her clit. His fingers were too thick and long for such a delicate place, and he worried that her bucking hips meant he wasn't doing well on his own. This was his first time touching any female, and he wasn't sure if he was applying enough pressure or too much.

He pinched his fingers around it a little harder, and she choked out a breath and moved faster.

The flooded pool of her arousal beckoned him lower.

I want to touch inside. I want to know what she feels like. He yearned for her to swallow up any part of him within her.

He slipped down between the lips of her folds. The moment the leaking pool of her entrance dabbed against his finger pad, he pushed inside to the second knuckle. She tightened around him, rasping, "Wait," which was the only reason he paused.

Was that too fast? He may have let his curious excitement get the better of him.

Her features twisted up, and his lust-addled mind was a little lost as to why. *She was soft.* Despite the thickness of his finger, she'd easily swallowed it. Her deep arousal made it slippery, and she had stretched herself from playing earlier.

He pushed in slower, and she didn't soften. So, he wiggled his finger, doing that *digging* thing he remembered from his fragments.

"Ohhh!" she cried, her hot cunt quivering as it instantly let go.

Like this? He thought, pushing the pad of his finger harder against a textured spot inside her. Perhaps a little too hard for a human, as her back instantly arched, her hips lifted, and her eyes snapped open wide.

More wetness greeted him, and he realised he'd found the special, pleasurable spot for females.

Pride swelled in his chest, as did a rather dark and mischievous emotion. Now that she was soft, although very much snug, Nathair let the naughtier side of himself come to the front.

She had accepted him, seemed to be enjoying the way he was penetrating her, and now he wanted to see this female fucking lose it for him.

He shoved his finger in all the way, hooked it, and viciously attacked the same spot.

Her cry was unhidden, instantaneous, and exactly what he wanted. She didn't even have the strength to move her hips, yet she hugged his head even tighter until he couldn't lick her chest.

He happily nuzzled between both her breasts with his entire skull. *Mmm. Soft. I like being here.* They moulded around his hard head like two warm pillows of feminine curves.

"Oh gods. Oh *gods*," she moaned, her legs shaking and jerking as he wiggled his finger.

He'd never heard her moan so loudly before. Her legs had never kicked, nor had her body twisted and contorted. Liquid heat dripped from her pussy as it quivered, clenching and spasming like it wanted to crush his finger as she came. Nathair panted against the cuddle of her breasts, his cocks lewdly swelling repeatedly in blissful contentment.

Fuck me. She would feel amazing around my cocks. Hot, wet, snug, while her naughty scent messed with his senses.

He may not even need to thrust. He thought just the way she came would rip his own release from him.

When she eased, coming down from her blissful high, Nathair wanted her to do it again. Repeatedly. He wanted her to orgasm until she had given him every drop and could take no more.

He unhooked his finger, so it wasn't so intense, but kept the targeted pressure as he used it to give a tentative thrust. When she rewarded him with a lost moan, quiet and weak, he moved it in and out slowly.

Her head lolled to the side as she bounced with it. All that did was make her arch her back repeatedly, but he took it to mean that it felt wonderful for her. She was tangling her semi-loose hair, causing loops to form behind her head.

Parted lips spilled deliciously erotic cries as he brought her close to the cresting waves of her orgasm again. All the while, she hugged his head against her, refusing to let go, as if she needed it to stay centred.

I am sorry, little female, but I cannot take it.

Nathair was losing it. He couldn't take the onslaught of this as much as he'd believed he could.

Trying to balance his weight on nothing but his neck and the loop where his humanoid torso met his serpent limb, he lifted his left hand away from next to her. He darted it down to his cocks, wrestled them with his fingers to bring them both into his fist, and stroked them.

He didn't know what noise was coming from him. If it was a purr, a needy growl, or a desperate, quaking groan, but it bubbled in his chest.

Nathair masturbated to what he was doing to her, how she seemed to adore it, as he matched it to the tempo of his finger thrusting with her snug pussy.

Come again, Linh.

His cocks were jerking in such enthusiasm that he was moments from losing his seed. He'd like to do this with her.

He nuzzled her with the hard bone of his skull, twisting it side to side in hopes that would help her. He thrust faster, trying to be careful with her delicate body but demanding that she give him what they both wanted.

She let go of a horn to slap her hand against his shoulder, and dug her nails into his flesh. His muscles bounced and leapt under his self-stroking movements, and her pussy clenched around him.

"Oh gods. You're... you're..." she couldn't get it out, but he didn't need her to.

She knew what he was doing, and it only seemed to arouse her more.

Just before he thought he'd come alone, her body tensed as she let out a wild scream. When her cunt clutched his finger and flooded with liquid, Nathair ceased breathing as he released against his own tail and the base of his nest.

His sight blackened, and he swore life was expelling from him through his cocks, bleeding out of him as unfathomable pleasure jolted his entire body. His finger inside her slowed, and he had to stop his claw from unsheathing, as his control was almost lost in the wake of his muscles bunching into stone.

I want inside her. I want to feel her do this around me. He stroked himself faster, trying to drain his cocks, as rapture made him whine.

When they were both done, Nathair removed his hand from his cocks to hold himself up. He panted through his nose hole, his maw clamped shut by her weak hold and his refusal to pull away.

Limp against him, he allowed Linh's lovely face to enthral him. *That was very much worth every bit of suffering.*

He had not come since he released within his seam, as he didn't want to be found fucking his own fist. He could only imagine her horrified reaction; he doubted he would have been anything but rough with himself.

His reward was sweet. It was made even better by this cuddle that had this sated and well-pleasured female in it. He would have adored staying here, in her arms, as her drenched cunt fluttered around his finger.

That was until her face twitched and pulled back into a cringe, and her core delicately fluttering around his finger tightened. Her body locked up.

"C-could you remove your hand... please," she whispered, her voice croaked and cracked from crying out.

Nathair did as requested, slipping away from the depths of her pants. Her legs immediately snapped shut, and her knees turned to the side as she trembled. She didn't let go of his head, and the arm that had drifted away returned to squeeze it. Then her eyes clenched shut and her lips turned inwards as if with pain.

For a long while, she squeezed him as they both remained unmoving. When too long passed, Nathair's sight grew white with worry.

"S-sorry. My stomach hurts all of a sudden." Despite her cringe, she gave him a smile that looked horrible, as it was utterly false and only worn for his reassurance. "I really want to hold you, but you're covered in come."

I see. He'd be disappointed that she seemed to have an aversion to his seed marking her, but the rejection that stung was entirely unnecessary.

She did not understand Mavka, or his sudden and weird desire he had growing to smother her in it. To claim her body as his, and ward it from other males, especially those of his own kind – it didn't matter that they were in a cave where they absolutely wouldn't be disturbed.

She was a human; that was all he needed to remember.

Patting at the bottom of his nest, Nathair retrieved some cloth he'd obtained to soften the hardness of his treasures for her. He held it in his fist and nudged it against her arm until she peeked open her eyes to see it. Then he wiped down his body as best as he could, gauging where he felt wet, before tossing it.

Only then did he scoop his arms around her and lift her so she wouldn't brush against his softening cocks, both drained for the time being. His tentacles had already begun to swirl around them.

Nathair then fell back with her in his arms, one resting under her thighs to lock her legs to his abdomen, while the other curled around her back. She let him take her, and she eventually hugged his neck instead.

He didn't know how she went from being an achy, needy creature to one that felt unwell. He took it in stride when he realised that, even though it was likely due to the intensity of their intimacy, she had chosen to remain with him.

She felt unwell, but not unsafe in his presence. She had even reached for him, clung to him. She wanted his comfort.

At that realisation, his sight shifted to bright yellow in joy.

SEVENTEEN

Linh groaned when movement disturbed her sleep. With her hands cupped above her breasts, she curled into Nathair's chest more. Movement was often stiff when inside his coiled-up tail like this, which was why she liked it.

She was trapped, but it was so soothing. It was like she lay in the centre of a heart, as he pulsed all around her.

For two weeks, she'd been in his presence, and not once had he betrayed her. To feel so safe, with literal walls of muscle protecting her, allowed her to separate herself from life, the very world – where past, present, and future didn't matter. A few hours where *she* didn't matter.

Out of everything, the laughter that was caused by Nathair's gentle bullying, the moments where he was sweet as he combed her hair and it made her stomach flutter, the intimacy where she felt like she was taking back her body... none of it compared to this.

This intimate cuddle felt more healing than anything.

She hadn't forgotten what they'd done before she'd fallen asleep in his very arms.

Something about having someone else inside her, no matter that it was only a finger, had locked up her stomach. She also thought the intensity of her orgasm had twisted her gut; her heart had been beating too fast, her body frightfully weak afterwards.

Her chest had been exposed, as it still partially was – since she only wore her undershirt and pants. If she didn't trust him as much as she did, she would have been concerned about that.

Linh's brows twitched when movement slipped over the rigidness of her hipbones, as well as next to her navel. She opened her eyes to find darkness with the smallest hint of white light – Nathair's orbs.

Just seconds before, she'd been undeniably comfortable. However, dread prickled across her skin when she felt that rigid hardness slipping backwards.

His orbs are white. He was in a trance.

Wetness was pressed against her. It clung to her skin, making it crawl. She also realised limbs were clinging to her, and that the hardness pressed against her was split in *two.*

He's hard. He was thrusting against her.

Anxiety clutched at her throat as memories she didn't want to be associated with trickled into her mind. She pushed against Nathair's chest, trying to separate them to no avail. Instead, her squirming only made him thoughtlessly shove harder against her, like it excited him.

Oh god, I'm stuck! That was usually the point, but she'd never wanted to escape before.

Her heart began to sprint as tears bubbled in her eyes.

She knew it wasn't his fault. She doubted he even realised what he was doing, but she was partially bare, pinned, and she was *scared.*

Scared because he wasn't himself right then. He often moved when in a trance. Sometimes he'd move around his home or lift his arms like he was holding something that wasn't in his hands. He'd even reached out to her a few times, holding her arm like at the beach, or cupping her face.

What if he... What if he did something to her while like this?!

Unable to free herself, nor even move her arms to defend herself, Linh began to tremble. *Calm. Try to be calm.*

The thrusting stopped just as the smallest heart-bursting

growl rumbled. A choke was rent out of her when his large hand wrapped around her throat.

She should have kept her eyes on his hidden face, on the colour of his orbs reflecting against his scales. Instead, Linh darted her gaze up to find his skull now turned to her, red orbs ominously peering down.

Unable to get a hand up to claw at him squeezing around her neck, she clenched her eyes. *He's reacting to your fear. Stop.*

"Nathair," she whispered out, only to strangle when his grip tightened.

Her lungs suddenly felt too full as they attempted to depress on a trapped breath. *Don't be afraid. Control your fear.* That felt like an impossible endeavour when she couldn't even take a calming breath.

Instead, Linh focused on her heart.

Nathair slithered all around her, the walls surrounding her shifting and sliding. Although he freed her from his tail, he instead pinned her down by the throat, and she'd suffered that before at the hands of another.

So she reached down into the depths of her consciousness and escaped. With all her might, she pushed nothingness to the forefront of her thoughts, and forced numbness into her heart, her mind, her very veins. She utilised a tool that she despised because it was the complete opposite of who she was, but it had made the two months of hell sufferable.

Her eyes opened lazily as she disassociated from the present, and everything she saw was murky.

His skull was fuzzy, but she could just make out that he parted his maw wide. It came closer, and she didn't react when something lukewarm, wet, and hard slipped across her cheek and forehead. By the blackness that pushed into her gaze, she knew she was looking at the back of his throat, and that it was his fangs she felt.

His hand softened around her neck, and she managed to push out the tiniest breath so she could suck in fresh oxygen.

Linh didn't fight, she didn't even claw at his hand even though she was free.

Cold air swirled around them, washing away the thickness that had formed within their cuddle. *Wake up, Nathair.*

By the pain she felt in the front of her throat, she knew her windpipe and vocal cords were damaged. She wheezed.

Just as his fangs were about to finish their glide and would flick forward and likely stab into her, Nathair froze.

Linh was violently shoved to the side when the Duskwalker leapt back with a writhing tail. His bellowing roar blasted into her senses, as did the ability to breathe, and her body convulsed as she coughed. Forced back to the forefront, her numbness faded at the swift change of state, and she cupped her swelling neck.

The thwack of his body hitting the stone ground outside of his nest was loud, as was the constant flicking and smashing of his tail.

Renewed tears bubbled in her eyes as she rose to her knees, just as she saw purple cloth in the corner of her shaking vision. Linh grabbed her dress and drew it to her chest to partially cover herself before turning to Nathair when she heard him whimpering.

Dark-orange orbs crested over the edge of the nest. He was circling his hand over his heart repeatedly as he reached out to her from the outside of his nest.

Even though she knew he was saying sorry over and over again, was only trying to cup her face, she was so freaked out that her shoulders turned inwards to shrink away from him. She continued to cough, to wheeze, while trying to keep her tears at bay.

Usually he wouldn't touch her when she recoiled from him, but Nathair placed his palm on her shoulder. Orange magic glittered around her, and the swelling pain in her throat dissipated.

Eyes wide with panic, she attempted to cast him a thankful gaze. He was still signing sorry, his whimper not fading, and she took in how much his arm was quaking as he drew it back.

"It's okay, Nathair," she offered, trying to hold his gaze to show the sincerity of that. The whole event was a blur, and much of it was her fault. "It w-was an accident. I know you didn't mean to."

It was an accident, and yet she couldn't handle the way everything reminded her too much of her trauma. Her lips trembled as liquid fell from her eyes. She *had* to look away when her shock finally bled out to tell her just how fucking scared she'd been.

Had she almost been assaulted in a way she didn't think she could bear? She'd been strangled, and if she hadn't forced her numbness, she would have been fucking *eaten*. Or, at least, envenomed.

She'd known the likelihood of violence had always been possible, but she'd thought she would have been able to handle it. Yet even though he absolutely didn't mean to, she couldn't stop the way his betrayal made her want to be sick.

I-I care about him. I care if he hurts me and eats me now. For a long while, she'd considered him her friend, but she'd begun to see him as *more*.

"I'm sorry," she sobbed, before scrambling out of the nest.

She needed to be alone so she could collect her thoughts and settle her emotions. How she felt would fade: the feeling of betrayal would dissolve when her heart wasn't trying to come up her freshly squeezed throat.

Linh didn't even care that she shoved herself into darkness by going into the tunnel. Balancing and guiding herself up the wall, the way was paved by memory. When it opened up, trickling water sounded in her ears, and she moved over to it.

She sat next to it and let its cleansing rhythm play so it could give her something other than herself to focus on. She covered her face and shook her head in her hands as she placed one foot on top of the other to make herself smaller.

H-have we been touching too much? Well, had she been touching herself while he watched too much? *Or was last night just too much?*

I feel like I'm becoming addicted to pleasure. The lack of it had been horrible. Not because she was greedy, but because she'd been taught only pain, uncomfortableness, and sickness revolving around her own body. She'd been trying to erase it, and trying in the most fucked-up way possible to share it with someone she *wanted* to touch. But she couldn't because she felt so damn broken that reaching out to him felt like she could plummet.

I can't believe I asked him to touch me.

She'd been so desperate in the moment that her aching pussy had been purring for Nathair's touch. And it'd purred so damn loud that it'd snuffed out her trepidation and let her leap too fast.

She'd enjoyed it. It'd felt nice to have someone's gentle and kind hands on her. They had been slow, unhurried, and seemed to read what she needed. Even his strange tongue had felt good because it was uniquely his.

Why did he have to be hard? And, since he'd been in a trance, she doubted his erection had been for or about her. *Was it from all the touching and the scents?* Maybe they had made him fall into some kind of perverted human memory.

She dug her fingers into her forehead so hard her nails threatened to cut her flesh. *Why did I have to get scared?*

He probably wouldn't have hurt her; that's what she wanted to believe. Maybe if she'd just stayed still, he may have simply rubbed against her until he either came or woke up.

She... didn't think she would have minded that, but her thoughts had just instantly twisted.

I feel so awful. He was probably so confused, and likely blaming himself. *I feel like such a bad person.*

She felt selfish because her response to everything was unusually severe. Then she'd spend hours feeling so regretful and guilty for her behaviour.

He's so kind and patient. How could I suddenly just lose faith in him like that?

She sobbed into her hands. *What's wrong with me?*

Nathair sat on the high ledge that overlooked the sunken small ship. He did so with his arms folded and a sickness in his chest.

Two Demons cowered from him in the shade, shaking and trembling with his watchful skull directed upon them. They avoided the sunlight by just a sliver, but he refused to allow them to seek refuge within his tunnels – which is where he'd found them.

Rather than going left to travel up what he considered the main path, they'd gone southwest and deeper within the cliff.

He had not taken Linh that way yet, although he'd like to at some point. There was a specific chamber he thought she'd adore, and would likely share a beguiling, awed expression. He would like to see it shine from her and knew it would be pure and sweet.

He didn't know why he was putting off showing her, but he thought it was because he wanted it to be... special.

The path also needed to be safe, and he couldn't guarantee that. These vermin hiding away were evidence of that.

But Nathair was already feeling rather guilty today, and these Demons hadn't done anything wrong to him. Sure, they were in his territory knowingly, considering they hadn't come sniffing after the human he had in his keeping. He'd let them be free by half-heartedly chasing them.

They look like forest Demons. They must have gotten trapped throughout the night by exploring the wide arc of beach and cliff wall.

He couldn't use his voice to make them leave, but he knew his watchful gaze was telling.

His arms tightened across his chest when dark orange flared in his sight before the reddish pink of shame flickered.

I cannot believe I attacked her.

This day was always likely to come, but he hadn't thought his fucking cock would be jutting from him at the same time. He remembered what fragments had caused it. He could only imagine what he'd been doing to make her smash him from his trance, something he couldn't even do, by hurling him into a bloodthirsty rage.

The embarrassment he felt for not having control of his own body. The shame that it'd happened. The guilt that he'd squeezed her throat so hard it looked red and *dented*. The anger at himself that he'd been a split second from envenoming her so she wouldn't squirm while he ate her.

It all weighed on him.

The scent of her fear hadn't been strong enough to make him act in swift aggression, but rather trickled through his already weakened mental state to make him move sluggishly. His prey had already been caught, and his starved gut had wanted to *savour* her.

None of it was his fault, nor was it hers; they'd both reacted on instinct. It didn't stop him from feeling like shit regardless.

She knows I am sorry. He didn't doubt that. Like the day on the beach where he'd hurt her arm, she understood he couldn't help it and would likely forgive him. She'd seen him fade into his trances multiple times.

Despite this, he was finding it difficult to face her.

A maelstrom of thunderous and aching emotions tumbled inside him. He needed space as much as she did.

He'd hurt someone he didn't wish to harm, and he feared, truly feared, what would have happened if he hadn't managed to snap out of it. *How did I snap out of it?* She couldn't just erase her own fear... could she?

Fuck. I don't know. He enjoyed holding this female while she slept like a cute little bunny on his chest. He didn't wish for that to end simply because of this, but wouldn't that be wiser? If they went back to before, where she slept wherever she wanted and he blocked the entry to his cave, he thought he'd find that hollowing.

He liked her warmth; it came with her pretty scent. She was so damn soft it was like she was made of dough, and he fit perfectly around her. Her breaths were calming, her heart lulling, and her voice decadent.

Nathair let out a sigh and dipped his head to the side.

I wish I could ask Weldir for advice. His father had been with his mother for over three hundred and forty years, if not more.

Their relationship was a mystery to Nathair, as Weldir scarcely spoke of it. He had a feeling things hadn't been well for a long time, but Nathair was aware of Weldir's longing to keep his intangible hands on her.

It must be hard to be made of cloud and mist when you have a female you crave.

Therefore, Weldir could have bestowed upon him advice.

All he needed to do was call for him – shout his name, *speak* it. *Then again, I would need to be near his mist for that.*

No. Nathair was on his damn own, and he was making a mess of it.

When shade finally entered his home and the Demons could run along the path of the cliff wall, he released a growl. They immediately bolted with shrill cries, taking his mercy when he was offering it.

Annoyed that the shade finally came, he backed up and turned to go up the tunnel. *I have no other excuse to stay away.* Time to go face the human.

His tunnel felt arduous and longer than normal.

When he was halfway up it, he winced. *Should I have obtained something as a gift? Is that not what humans do when they seek forgiveness?* He couldn't remember what they gave, only that it had to be a physical representation of their remorse.

A fish? No. She'd asked to go 'foraging' because she wanted a break from eating sea creatures. *Then what else could I give her? A fucking rock?*

The closer he climbed, the more he heard... something. It

was soft at first as it echoed down the tunnel. *Is she... singing?* It sounded like a sorrowful song, her voice quiet and yet transfixing.

He ducked into the main area. Seated on her backside with her feet flat, Linh had her arms wrapped around her legs to hug them as she stared at the lake.

Does she think I went into the water? He'd considered it, but he wouldn't have been able to sense her properly, and if she had been in danger, he may not have saved her in time. At least going down his tunnels meant nothing could come up them to harm her.

With the way she was positioned, he tilted his head in surprise. *Has she been waiting for me to return?*

Not because she was hungry, or bored, but because she *wanted* him to return, *missed* him?

He longed for that to be the reason.

Nathair approached her, and his silent form meant he didn't disturb her. The voice grew louder, as did her scent, and both tangled and spiralled together in his senses. *Her singing voice is beautiful.*

Something about it had his sight wavering. His movements grew sluggish – even his heart slowed – and he thought his breaths would taper off and cease.

Time seemed to pause except for her song.

The chatter in the back of his head, the constant source of his suffering that had been going on for *centuries,* quietened. Then, suddenly, the voices dissolved altogether.

Silence greeted him. Blissful, long-awaited *silence.*

Nathair shuddered when lightness radiated within his skull. Lightness that was so breathtaking and heavy, his entire body lost every ounce of its strength. Sight going dark, his humanoid torso fell forward, and he didn't have the will to catch himself with his arms.

His body hit the ground with a thud, and his skull smacking it thundered in the cavern.

Linh released a sharp gasp.

Nathair clutched at his skull as his body shuddered, twitched, and writhed. The voices were gone, and he opened his sight to see orange floating droplets. He'd seen his own tears before, how they hovered and sparkled around his eye sockets, but he'd never previously shed them in relief.

He crawled to her since she'd stopped singing, following her beautiful scent like he was a leashed being returning to its master.

Don't stop, he *pleaded.*

"Nathair?" she asked, lifting her arms when he came upon her.

He weakly curled around her with what little strength he could muster. He couldn't wrap her up as normal – it required energy he didn't have.

Please, he begged, wishing she could hear him, could hear how desperate he was. *Please don't stop singing.*

Lethargy settled into every part of his being, his very essence. He knew he'd buried his skull against her outer thigh, while his arms curled around her, so she couldn't escape and might give him what he wanted.

Contentment made him whimper when she started her song once more. Her scent was so close now, her voice next to his sensitive ear, and she was so warm that it melted him. All three of these began to pull him under.

His broken orbs leaking ethereal tears blackened again, and he huddled around his salvation.

A snorted huff came out muffled from how his nose hole was pressed against this heavenly being. Finally, after years, he truly and deeply fell asleep.

Quiet, blissful *sleep.*

EIGHTEEN

Eyelids fluttering in surprise, Linh stared down at the Duskwalker who snored *loudly*.

Each one was muffled, and long. The kind of snores that were evident the person was exhausted and so deep in sleep, it'd be near impossible to wake them.

She didn't even try.

His orbs are black. I've only seen them remain like that once. On the first night he'd brought her into his home, and it'd been for less than fifteen minutes, if that.

Has he really been awake *this whole time?*

Pity filled her. Linh continued to sing, and petted his bony forehead softly as she did.

He... spoke. She'd heard him *ask* her to keep singing.

It hadn't sounded like a human's voice. His mouth had also been closed, when usually he opened it to 'speak' from the memories he stole, like they came from his gut. It was creepy and made her skin crawl in dread.

This had been nice. His voice was deep, and kind of growly. Since he was a monster, she'd expected more bass in his tone, but it was smooth.

When minutes, maybe even an hour, passed, Linh finally stopped. *Is this all you needed? For someone to sing you a lullaby?* A small, but saddened smile curled her lips. *I'll sing you one every night if you need it.*

Her eyes drifted to what she could see of his body. His torso was pressing against her back, while his hips had partially curled around the opposing leg his skull pressed against. The length of his tail pushed around her feet, but then swayed back and became a wiggly line leading from the cave entrance.

In some ways, it almost looked like he was in the foetal position, the first bend of his tail like a set of knees.

He appeared remarkably innocent in that moment.

As silence dragged on for a long while, Nathair eventually stiffened. He pulled in tighter, just as white flickered in his orbs like the beginning of a trance. *Are the memories returning?* Linh quickly sung, and he instantly softened. His snores resumed.

I guess singing a lullaby isn't enough. Her brows drew together.

When she stopped again, she had about thirty minutes to rest before his orbs flickered white. She started back up, realising she needed to keep going to keep his trances at bay.

My throat is starting to hurt. She hummed instead, wondering if that would be enough. He remained asleep, and she took that as a win.

As boring as it was, Linh pushed herself to stay awake, even when the hours dragged by. She did accidentally nap, but upon waking, she instantly started to hum to keep him resting peacefully. She also got up to go to the bathroom, eat, and drink some water, but she always returned for his sake.

Nathair had barely moved an inch, and she always came back to be seated where he originally held her.

He's done so much for me. This is the least I can do.

Only when he stirred of his own volition did she stop.

Lifting onto a singular arm while clutching at his forehead, Nathair groaned. Linh twisted to greet him.

"Good morning, sleepyhead. Well, afternoon really." He'd been out for what could only be a day. She patted herself on the back for making it that long with little sleep, and she bet she looked frazzled and tired.

"It's been so long since I slept like that," he stated, his voice rich and soothing like before. *"Fuck. It's been forever."*

Oh, he swore, Linh thought, her cheeks heating a little. She didn't think a Duskwalker would swear, since it was a rather human thing to do. *He's also still talking.*

He shook his head, as if trying to shake it of sleep. He'd never really shook it so hard or fast before, so when she heard the quietest rattle of bones, it took her aback.

"How long have I been out?" he asked, removing his hand so he could stare down at his palm and claws. *"I cannot believe her voice and scent made me fall asleep. Why? I know she doesn't have any magic."*

"You've been asleep for about a day," she answered, as a mischievous grin formed.

"A fucking day? That's it? No wonder I'm still so tired." He snorted out an annoyed huff as he pushed himself higher and shuffled his tail underneath himself to support his torso. *"I thought when I finally slept, I'd pass out for years. All I get is a day? At least the fragments are gone."*

A sort of giddiness fluttered in her belly. *Did my singing heal him of his trances?*

"The memories aren't returning?"

Nathair looked up before tilting his head up at the ceiling. *"I... don't think so."*

"I'm glad I could be of help then," she answered. She kind of liked that she had this magical power – although she didn't really think magic had anything to do with it. *Unless...*

"Little female, you have no idea." She heard the sincerity of that, but also how his voice had been slightly louder than before. It quietened once more as he said, *"I'm tempted to start calling her a siren."*

"I think a siren is a bit much," she stated with a laugh.

He chuckled along with her until it abruptly cut short.

His head darted down and then twisted so hard it almost went upside down. His orbs morphed to dark yellow. *"Wait... did she just respond to me?"*

"I did." Her brows drew together as she tilted her own head. "Did you not know you were talking?"

"What?" He leapt back from her before halting. He cupped the end of his snout. "I'm talking? *Am I really?"* Once more, Linh noted that his voice changed. It didn't change in tone or bass, but was either softer or louder. He lowered his hands. "Can... you really hear me?"

"Yes," she giggled.

He cupped his snout in a thoughtful gesture. *"Why now, though? Is it because the voices are gone?"*

She raised a brow since she'd been expecting him to be overjoyed. "I don't know, but isn't it a good thing they're gone?"

"Well, yes, but–" His head reared back, as if with surprise. "Wait, did you hear my question?"

"Well, yeah. Did you not mean to ask me?" *He's being really weird.* "I didn't expect you to be this chatty," she said with an awkward laugh.

White flickered in his orbs. *"Can you hear this?"*

"Yes?"

She didn't expect him to suck in a loud gasp, or for him to suddenly cup both sides of his head like the world was ending. His muscles bunched, as if with tension, while a curt whine escaped him.

"Fuck! She can hear my damn thoughts!"

Linh, surprised by the horrified tone, fell back from kneeling to land on her backside. "I can?"

"No!" Nathair clawed down his skull, seeming to fret under the power of this realisation. *"I don't want her to hear my damn thoughts. She probably heard that, and that. Shit. Shut up. Shut up!"*

"I-it's okay, Nathair," Linh reassured, reaching out to comfortingly palm his biceps.

He darted away from her. "No, it's not. You have no idea the kind of thoughts I have."

"It'll be fine," she offered, her brows furrowing. "Now that

I know you're not meaning to say them, I'll try not to take them seriously."

With a soft growl, Nathair ducked closer until the tip of his snout was less than an inch from her nose. "You do not *want* to know the kind of thoughts I have, little female. I am a Mavka, and we are not pure creatures. *And my thoughts about you are wildly perverse and impure. You would not be able to handle knowing what I really want to do to...*" His orbs flashed a reddish pink. *"Shit."*

"At least it makes you honest?" she attempted to joke, while trying to not let what he said, or rather *thought,* make her eyes widen.

He was so irritated, his growl had a sharpness to it that almost gave it a hiss-like quality.

"I cannot stay here," he stated, turning towards the lake.

"No!" Linh shouted, lunging forward to grab his wrist. "Wait! Please don't go."

"Linh," he warned, likely only halting so he didn't drag her across the ground.

"We've never been able to talk freely like this before, and I have so many questions. Please? I promise not to get upset if your thoughts slip something out. I can ignore them."

"You say that–"

Her cheeks warmed, and she clenched her eyes shut in courage as she shouted, "I know you want to touch me! I know you probably want more than that. I'm not an idiot. But I-I don't think I'll mind hearing things like that, even if they are... more bloodthirsty. They are just words, and I know you aren't going to purposefully hurt me, nor are you saying them to make me uncomfortable or get a rise out of me. I'll trust what you do, not what you say, e-even if it makes me uncomfortable."

Gosh, she was rambling, but she really did want him to stay.

What if this is only temporary? If she missed her chance to get answers, she'd be really upset.

Yes, she was learning what he'd called 'Nathair speak,' but

it was taking time. She'd only been learning for a week, and it was all new to her. It'd take forever to understand a whole new language.

Nathair turned to her slightly, seeming to assess her and weigh his options.

"Please? I want to know why you are suffering from human memories when you told me it isn't normal for other Duskwalkers. I want to know where you came from, how you came to be, why you're choosing to... *protect* me."

The wrist she was clinging to for dear life pushed through her hands towards her. He gently cupped the side of her face, and she let out her held breath as her eyes flickered open.

"I am protecting you because you deserve to be shielded." He fully turned towards her and retracted his hand to fold his arms across his chest. "Fine. I will stay unless something rather difficult to bear slips out. I will try to remain thoughtless. *She has aided me, so the least I can do is answer her questions.*"

The smile she gave was fully of relief. "M-my questions, then?"

He grunted in answer at first, his arms tightening, before he loosened them in defeat. "You asked about my fragments and why it is not normal. The reason is because I ate souls in the afterworld when I should not have."

Her brows drew together, her lips puckering in uncertainty along with them. "Afterworld?"

"The afterlife is what your kind call it." When her lips parted in understanding, he tipped his head to the side like he often did when annoyed. "Yes, little female. I died."

"B-but you're alive!" she exclaimed, her eyes roaming over his very alive body.

"I was brought back to life by my father, who is also the demi-god of that world. He is a soul eater, and he collects all the human souls that have been eaten by Mavka and Demons and gives them a place to rest, while also taking their life force for power."

She covered her mouth, unsure if it was in shock or rapt curiosity. She wouldn't dare argue with him in disbelief. "How long ago, and for how long were you dead?"

"I was brought back around three months ago... For how long I was dead, roughly two hundred and eighty years."

Heat drained from her face, and she gawked at him. "You were dead for that long?!"

Linh was trying her hardest to not freak out, but he couldn't suddenly throw insane information like this at her without letting her react to it. He hadn't even done it softly! Instead, he'd sucker punched her with it.

Nathair sighed. *"She's a human. Humans cannot comprehend Mavka."* At the slip of his thoughts, he stiffened. "Sorry."

"All good." Her apologetic smile was forced, and likely came across as a grimace. "Your memories are because you ate souls in this afterlife? Why would you eat them then?"

"I did not know. I was rather underdeveloped when I arrived. And, before you ask, it means my humanity was low, and my body gaunt and thin. Mavka gain physical strength by eating any creature, but intelligence by consuming humans. What we first eat before our horns form will dictate our characteristics. Obviously, I first ate some kind of serpent."

Linh was rendered utterly silent from the sudden bout of information he dumped on her. *Is Mavka what they call themselves?*

"What this meant is I was too stupid to realise that while my father was asleep, consuming so many souls was damaging for me. I also harmed him in the process and almost forced him into an endless sleep. I was confused about my new life, and despite no longer feeling hunger, I was still affected by my rages because Mavka like to chase their *prey.* When Weldir, my creator, woke up and realised what I'd done, it was too late to save me despite his efforts. I'd consumed too many souls, had been harbouring them for too long, and parts of them had burrowed so deep into my own soul that he wasn't able to completely remove them. I infected myself, and what remained are the fragments of dozens of human memories that constantly speak. I cannot sleep, as my trances are far worse when I do, so I rest by letting them play. However, I am tired, I am weakened, and sometimes a voice will shout louder than the others. When that happens, a fragment will take hold, and then it becomes a barrage of them."

Her lips pursed in thought. "Does this mean that, technically, you haven't actually eaten that many humans?"

"I am surprised she is not running away in fear after learning all this." He tilted his head at her, and his folded arms lost some of their tension. "Well, yes, technically you are correct. Most of my mass and intelligence comes from already deceased humans. *I shouldn't tell her they all screamed, regardless.*" His orbs flashed a reddish pink in embarrassment. *"Fuck."*

Her eyelids fluttered in trepidation, unsure if she should answer his thoughts. She decided not to.

"Do you..." Linh licked her lips nervously. "Do you regret harming humans? With how kind you are to me..."

"Why ask me such a question that will only make her harbour resentment?" Nathair covered his face and sighed behind his palm. "Yes, and no? I do not regret developing, and my past is lined with bloodshed in order to do so. But, yes, I regret hurting people, especially as this is not my task."

"Task?"

"I am a soul harvester for Weldir. I am supposed to eat Demons and cleanse the souls they incidentally carry and then ferry them to my father. This is why all Mavka were born. It is why we *exist*. However, we have an insatiable hunger he did not foresee, and the only way to remove it is to... *No. I should not tell her that we seek a—"* He stiffened and let out a vicious snarl that overshadowed and hid his thoughts from her.

Even his orbs flared bright red behind his hands, as if he was growing angered by his thoughts slipping from him.

Linh chose to ignore it, and instead lifted her hands. Then

she started counting with her fingers all she'd learned. "Okay, one, Duskwalkers call themselves Mavka. Two, they are soul harvesters for a demi-god, who is also their dad. Three, they gain weight from eating things, but humanity from people. Four, you are unwell, and my singing managed to aid you. Five, your memories are actually fragments, and I'm guessing that makes you more aware than others of your kind, and you can understand humans better. Is that right?"

As she spoke, Nathair lowered his hand. His orbs flared bright yellow. *"I knew she was smart, despite her clumsiness. Her face is not the only thing that is pretty."*

He called me pretty and smart. Linh's ears flared with heat at that, and he mimicked it with a reddish-pink glow. He grunted, like one might clear their throat.

"Yes, that is correct. However, there is much about humans I don't know, as the fragments are only pieces of their memories, and always their death. Some are unpleasant, and others are *very* pleasant."

Oh god, he probably means memories like sex.

As if to answer her thoughts, his thoughts slipped out. *"I have experienced humans fucking in so many different ways that I could show her..."* He growled again and clutched the sides of his head. *"Stop. Don't think about touching her. Don't think about spreading her thighs apart and..."*

Linh gasped when Nathair lowered his arms so he could rake his claws down his forearm until purple blood welled and gushed down the sides of it.

"Hey!" Linh cried, rising to her knees to reach out to him. "Stop. It's fine."

The Duskwalker parted his maw to hiss violently at her, warding her back and rendering her silent. "My thoughts are mine! It is unpleasant to spill them. When I decide to tell you what I want to do to your supple body, I will do so when *I* am ready." Then he darted forward so their faces were barely an inch apart. "And when I know you will *moan* like I have petted you with them."

Linh didn't back away from the menacing way he towered over her. Her heart fluttered, and she was unsure if it was in titillation or wariness.

"Okay," she conceded, then let an appreciative smile fill her features. "Thank you for talking to me, despite how uncomfortable it's making you. I also wanted to apologise for earlier, and how I–"

Her words were cut short when he placed his unbloodied hand over her mouth.

"Is this really what you wish to speak of now?" he asked, tilting his head. "I can... *feel* the voices returning."

He pulled back just enough that he gave her some space. "They are?"

Nathair nodded. "Yes. There is a familiar heaviness returning. Once they begin chatting, I am unsure if my ability to speak will remain. *I do not wish for us to waste what valuable time we have on pointless apologies. Both of us are sorry.*" Then Nathair turned his head to the side to look away from her. His voice sounded quieter than before. "I am... thankful to you. As much as I care about speaking with you, being able to sleep even for only a little... it means more to me than you can ever understand."

"I can sing for you every night if you like," she offered. She'd like to help him, especially when he did so much for her all the time.

His orbs faded to blue. "No. I do not think that is wise. If you were to fall asleep with me, and I slipped into a trance, I may harm you. Like I said, they are worse when I am asleep." He turned his saddened glow to her. *"I would rather not sleep than hurt her."*

Her heart squeezed in tenderness with how sweet she found his words, even if they were hollowing. "I can always do it in the morning, so I'm fully rested. That way, I'll have the energy to stay awake."

"Would that not... *bore* you?" he asked, his voice even quieter than before. *"To even offer this on my behalf..."*

"No," she answered warmly. "I'll just pet your skull like I did before. I really don't mind."

He cupped the side of his head. *"She petted me?"* She barely heard what he said, but the joyful awe in his tone was evident, especially when his orbs flickered a bright yellow. "Really? You would do this?"

She nodded, and he leaned down once more, this time holding his torso up with one arm. He reached forward with his free hand.

"Will you sing for me then, my little nightingale?" Nathair rumbled with a purr, raking his claws from her collar bones and up her throat.

Linh shivered in delight as goosebumps prickled all over her, and she let out a raspy breath. *"Yes."*

Nathair grunted as white flickered in his orbs, fighting with his usual orange. He flinched as he pulled back and covered his empty eye holes and bony forehead, then shuddered deeply before letting his arms fall.

He stared at her for longer than was comfortable.

After a small length of silence, Nathair signed, "Did you hear?"

Her lips tightened in sorrow, already missing his charming voice. "No."

She never expected him to chuckle. Even when he hissed out a breath of pain and dug his fingers into the crown of his skull, the sounds of his amusement continued.

Her eyes widened in disbelief. "You said something important to me, didn't you? Something that would have been okay if I heard it!"

A loud burst of laughter exploded from him as he nodded.

"That's *mean,* Nathair!" She stood and placed her hands on her hips, wishing she could tower over him. "Tell me!"

He shook his head to deny her.

"Come on!" she shouted while stamping her foot. "You can't leave me hanging like that. If you don't tell me, I-I'll... tackle you and beat you."

"I would like to see you t-r-y." He finger-spelled the last word, as he either didn't have a sign for it, or hadn't taught her yet.

With a childish pout, her cheeks ballooning in annoyance, Linh pounced. She shoved at his chest, and he fell to his side – she had a feeling he let her push him over. Then she lightly beat on his chest.

She giggled when he wrapped his arms around her midsection and squeezed tightly while licking at her cheek.

"You're such a bully," she exclaimed, her tone dulling in annoyance at his kiss.

He chuckled in return, his orbs flaring bright yellow.

He signed, "I know."

NINETEEN

Tenderness radiated from Nathair's chest as he caressed the curve of his claw down behind her ear. His fingers poked through black, straight hair as he tangled himself in its lusciousness.

Her hair was tied into two high pigtails that rested on the top of her head, with two additional braids swirling around the tied bases like buns. Every new hair style brought him joy, each one just as lovely as the last.

Linh's near-black, straight lashes tipped back, and her eyes greeted his orange orbs. The basking sun made the brown of her irises glow amber, and he found them just as mesmerising as the sable of them in the shade.

The round tip of her nose was cute, as were her expressive curved brows. Her rounded, soft cheekbones almost disappeared in the light, but cast in shadows, her jaw sharpened, making its usual gentleness strengthen. Her full pale-pink lips tightened as she looked up at him, but she didn't ask why he was caressing her thusly, nor did she stop him.

Considering she was seated on the folds of his tail, using him as some sort of beach lounge, he thought he should be allowed just a meagre touch. He kept the sand from dirtying her, and would stop the water from touching her once it finally reached them. Which should be quite some time, as they had not been here long.

A singular small shell rested on her lap, and she fingered it as she looked down at it.

This was all she apparently wanted to do today: just sit in the sun.

She probably feels unnerved constantly being in the darkness of my home. Linh asked to be taken to the beach every day since she'd learned of it, and it had become a pattern of theirs.

She would wake long after dawn, they would come here, and then he would find her more food – whether that be him hunting in the water or helping her forage in the forest surrounding his pond. If there was a spare chance, he would teach her Nathair speak; otherwise, that was a nightly lesson.

He'd only forced her to swim one more time to make sure she truly wouldn't drown and absorbed learning it. However, she'd grown unwell, as if the cold and damp of his home finally sunk into her bones.

Nathair learned the hard way that taking a 'cold' from her rendered him useless. He'd grown so weak he didn't have a single ounce of mental fortitude to keep his fragments at bay.

She sang for me while I was unwell. She had sung twice for him in the few days since they'd discovered she could vanquish the wretched human memories. *I still don't feel rested.*

A few hours of sleep likely wouldn't soothe the hundreds of years he'd only caught minutes of sleep. It'd take time before he was truly rested, but he did feel... stronger.

We have not been able to speak voice to voice again since that day. Nathair had been hoping they could conversate in this way, but the lapse of will due to the ease of his mind meant he'd instantly been swarmed by trances upon his waking.

It was like they were punishing him for trying to flee from their cruelty.

It mattered little. Although he wanted to use his voice to speak with her, she was learning his hand signs little by little. One day, they would be able to talk freely, and Nathair didn't care *how* they did so, only that they could.

She has expanded my vocabulary. There were signs he didn't have for certain words or short sentences. Linh would teach him her people's way of saying them and, although that made him grumble, he accepted them. He wouldn't be petty and make his own on the spot like he and Weldir had.

Being brought to real life came with new things to speak of, new things to learn, and this female was on that journey of expansion with him. It, in its own way, made adopting them into his signs special for him. It was becoming Nathair-Linh speak.

Linhair speak, he thought with humour.

He'd never needed the word beach before, or sand, or even rain. He and Weldir had not spoken of these things in Tenebris, nor had he seen any of them. Even if the opportunity may have come about to learn many other signs, Nathair had... turned inward. After so many years within the afterworld, he'd eventually given up speaking with Weldir.

Not because there was no point, but because there was little he could add. Weldir would sit with him, make sure he was lucid, and then explain all that had happened in the world – without him. He was updated, but only asked questions if he wanted something to be expanded on.

Other than that, Weldir knew everything about Nathair. Why have the same conversations repeatedly? It was the definition of insanity, in Nathair's opinion, and he was already half crazed.

But here, with this female, he yearned to know all about her. He wished to tell her about himself, about what he could remember before he died, and the afterworld he'd lingered in. He wanted to tell her of how he picked on his sibling, Aleron, and the male he'd chosen as his bride and was brought back to life with.

He wanted to speak with her about Merikh and the unresolved feelings they both likely had, and would never be able to fix. How Merikh had travelled to another – Elven –

world, and left this one behind. How that fucking pissed him off because he'd like to take that bull-headed Mavka by his horns and squeeze the undeserved hate out of him with his tail.

Nathair wanted her to be a place he could lay those things on, as he thought she would welcome them with resilience. She may offer an outside opinion that could help him shed his feelings of regret, guilt, and melancholy relating to them.

Especially when she lifted a warm expression to the sun with her eyes closed, and therefore, his very face as well.

He flicked her earlobe, making the red gem dangling from it clink, and she opened her eyes once more.

"How do you smile so freely?" he asked her, only removing his hands from her neck long enough to speak.

A glint of trepidation twitched her features. "What do you mean?"

An annoyed sigh blew from his nose hole. "Don't be c-o-y. Don't make me r-e-p-e-a-t myself."

Her gaze flicked away at that, her lips pouting. Then she drew her knees up so she could plonk an elbow on one, and placed her cheek on her fist.

"If you're asking how I can still be happy despite everything... I don't know." The usual softness in her eyes hardened and then darkened as she stared off at the rolling waves crashing before them. "If anyone else had asked me that, I'd probably lie, but I don't want to with you."

"Then don't?" he signed, tilting his head. When she wouldn't answer, he gently placed his fingers around her pointed chin to tilt her face to him properly. "You don't speak."

"I talk all the time!" she exclaimed, rolling her eyes.

Nathair released a small warning growl. Any other human would have stiffened their back or grown wary. Linh just half-heartedly poked her tongue out at him with the bridge of her nose wrinkling.

"T-o-w-n? Past? Memories?" Nathair wanted to know more about this female.

She had withdrawn from him in the past few days, while

still being kind enough to sing for him. The little female no longer wanted to be intimate, and was making him worry that she hadn't truly forgiven him for how he hurt her... and *frightened* her. Yet, she still desired his squeezing hold nightly, like nothing was the matter.

When she looked away again, this time with her lips tightening with a pensive expression, his sight shifted to blue.

I give up, then. Not on her, just on this subject. He vowed he would not push her to speak of things she did not wish to, and just hoped she would one day do so.

They would remain in their silence, then.

I tire of silence. Beyond his ears was too quiet, while the chattering in his mind seemed to grow louder because of it. He longed for her to fill it with her melodious voice, as it eased that chattering. To soften the voices himself, he often focused on her lovely features, the lulling rhythm of her heart and breaths, her pretty scent.

He caressed the side of her neck again, showing he was exiting the conversation as he looked up.

The blue sky was bright, the sun warmer with each day. Yet, a chilly wind came from the south as storm clouds inched their way closer with every minute. *Would she like to sit in the rain?*

Nathair loved the rain, even when the drops were icy. The sprinkle of it was nice upon his gills, and it felt like it was cleansing his body, mind, and soul. They were only less than three weeks into spring, from what he gathered, so the rain should be somewhat warm.

"If I smile, no one knows what I'm thinking," Linh eventually admitted softly. "I am at peace here with you, Nathair. My smiles are not false, so please don't think they are, but hidden beneath them... my heart does hurt."

Nathair brought his skull down to face her and observed the pain in her gaze. There were no tears, but her lips were curled downwards, and her chin did wobble slightly. The only parts of her that trembled were her hands as she picked at her nail beds and the sides of her fingers.

"I smile because I was forced to, or I'd be... *hit*. I wasn't allowed to cry, or scream, or show just how miserable I was. I wasn't allowed to grin, as it came across as snide or spite-filled, so I learned to just... smile. That way, no one knows how much hate I hold, how much I'm hurting, and what I'm planning to do next." She tipped her face up to him. "I don't feel like I have to do that with you. I've cried in front of you, shown anger, and even... *kicked* you for fun. I smile for *me* because it's meaning was stolen. I share them with you because you deserve them, because you make me want to, and they feel so good when they touch my heart."

Nathair parted his maw slightly and then spread his lower jaw bones like he was trying to emulate a grin. Her brows drew together, obviously puzzled, only for her to cover her mouth. A giggle sounded behind it.

"If that's a smile, I have to tell you it's creepy," she stated with renewed mirth in her eyes.

Nathair chuckled in return and snapped his maw shut. He'd wanted to ease the hardness in her features.

Wanting her to know that he'd listened intently, he brushed the back of his claw over the corner of her lips, admiring this simple part of her. He felt when it curled, and her expression grew tender.

It dimmed as she lowered her gaze and fiddled with her fingers again.

"And... I have told you something about myself. I told you my mum was an apothecary, herbologist, and doctor, and that my father was the mayor of our village. I come from Springrock Mountain. I think that's west of your pond, since I have no idea where we are right now."

"Your father is a..." He'd never needed to say this word before.

"Leader?" she asked, pressing the tips of two fingers together before pulling away as if she was lining the edges of a triangle.

"Yes, leader," he signed, mimicking the movement. He was

thankful she simplified it by giving him a less specific name for those who led humans.

He did it again to make sure he absorbed the new word, then tilted his head at her. He nodded, hoping she'd continue.

"He wasn't voted in. My grandmother on my mum's side was our mayor before this, and when he married my mum, he was taken under her wing. Everyone loves him, so he was forced into the role when my grandmother grew ill. My mum didn't care to lead, but she helped our people in her own way by taking care of the sick." She gave a small laugh. "Half the time, everyone talks to her rather than my dad. You'd be surprised how much patients speak to their doctor about their problems. She was already giving them medicine, so why not?"

The more Linh spoke, the more his sight shifted to yellow and grew in brightness. He was learning new things about her, and he'd been waiting forever to hear this.

When she didn't say anything for a while, he signed, "More?"

She laughed, but in the way that felt like she was calling him greedy. Nathair's insatiable need to learn rumbled within him, and he'd take every bite he could.

"Fine. I'll tell you more, only because you deserve it."

Nathair snickered. *I deserve more than that, and we both know it.*

"I'll be honest with you, I had it really easy growing up, despite all the Demon attacks," she stated, waving her arms into a small shrug. "Because of the positions my parents had, I was watched, and kind of... it feels weird saying this, but... adored? I did what was expected of me. I made sure I exceeded at my tutoring. I learned how to cook so I could help feed everyone, and went with my mother into the forest to pick herbs since I wanted to follow in her footsteps. She's one of the few doctors in our village. I was kind to everyone and learned to sign because my father told me I needed to be able to communicate with anyone and everyone."

Nathair tilted his head when her warm expression crept away, and darkness entered it instead.

"It was lucky I did. I ended up having to translate for those in my village who are unable to speak, when both my father's hands were injured due to..." Her features pinched and her face grew ashen as she darted her gaze to the side nervously. "He disobeyed the bandits, and they... they *bashed* them as a way to punish him."

Liquid bubbled in her eyes, but she quickly blinked it away. A blush rose on her cheeks as she peeked at him from the corner of her lids, her lips tightening. Seconds later, she gave him a forced smile.

"I'm the only one my age in the whole village," she said, drawing away from the painful conversation. "Everyone is either years older than me, or at least three years younger. It sucked being the only person who was twenty-one, and I only turned that a few months ago. Instead of getting to play, I just studied hard because there was nothing else to do. I followed mum to work or played by myself."

"Were you l-o-n-e-l-y?" Nathair signed, since he'd asked this of Weldir quite a few times. His father never answered directly.

"Hmm. Not really." Linh shrugged her lean shoulders. "Sometimes the other villagers would sit with me, and I managed to know everyone well, even though there's a few thousand of us. I know everyone's name, who their families are, and where they live. I made friends with everyone, no matter if they were old or just a baby. Everyone in the village was my friend, but the Jolston kids were the ones who followed me everywhere I went."

Nathair purposefully darkened his orbs to ask why.

Then again, she is like a pretty gem. From what she'd said about her past, he imagined she'd always been radiant. If what she was like with him was only a fraction of the loveliness she'd been before, then even Nathair thought he may have been hopeless to chase after her light.

"They are the closest to me in age, both sisters, and they both have hearing loss. So does their father. Not everyone knows how to speak Austlan, so they liked having someone they could speak freely with who wasn't an annoying adult or someone younger. We think the loss of hearing is hereditary. My dad made sure I learned because they grew up next door to him. They had a lot of boy troubles and wanted advice, not that I could give it!"

Her face brightens as she speaks about her family and people. It was obvious she cared about them very much and had deep bonds with them all.

She is so lovely. Her face had gentled, yet the corners of her lids were crinkled with effervescent fondness. It made his chest swell with gooey warmth, and he almost leaned down so he could taste the emotion curling her lips.

Nathair refused to steal this moment with a drive to kiss her. Linh was finally sharing. Every word was important, and each new thing he learned of her and her people was locked away in his mind to be kept forever. The melody of her voice would sing in his memories, as would his nightingale's song.

"Why could you not help?" Nathair signed, since she seemed to be rather witty. He imagined she'd have information to share with other females.

Other males would have tried to catch her.

Too bad for them – Nathair currently had his claws in this female, and he was reluctant to let her go.

Even if she asked to leave, he... may not let her. Just the thought had the heaviness of greed and possessiveness clamouring around in his veins. He'd rather bleed them empty than remove the way her essence clung to each drop. To each scale. Nathair would need to rip himself apart and scrub his entire being to cleanse how she'd burrowed beneath his flesh.

Just as his orbs were about to flicker a dark green, Linh snorted a laugh. "Well... like I said, I didn't really have anyone my age. I'd never dated anyone. My parents were planning to take me to Fayrest Town after my twenty-first birthday to see if I wanted to" – she jerked in his arm, her cheeks turning pink – "*date* anyone. There are more people my age there."

She turned away from him and scratched at the back of her neck, as if awkward about telling him this. Nathair couldn't care less about who she dated or what she'd done before he met her. He hadn't even been *alive* for any of it.

He had not existed in the same plane as her.

He could growl, huff, and fold his arms, but what would it change? Nothing. So, he'd rather just discover more about this female, while she was so willing to share.

Nathair placed his foreknuckle under her chin and lifted her face to him, then pulled his hands away so he could sign, "Did you find anyone?"

He'd like to know if he needed to constrict away the lingering of someone in her mind. This was all that mattered: that her heart was empty so he could swim his way inside it.

"No." Once more, her features fell. No, they didn't just fall – her entire body seemed to slump. Her heart sped up, while her lungs quickened in what would only be anxiety. "The bandits came before then, and they didn't allow us to travel between towns freely. None of us were allowed to leave in case we figured out a way to relay hidden messages. We became trapped inside our village walls, and then I was..."

"Taken," Nathair finished for her.

Her eyes lifted away, only to land on the storm clouds above them. "Yeah, I was taken."

Seeing this was likely the end of this conversation, since her eyes had reddened and turned glassy, Nathair lifted his sight to the sky as well. Then he tapped her shoulder to get her attention. "Do you want to sit in the rain?"

She sniffled quietly. "Isn't that dangerous, though?"

Head rearing back, and with jarring and annoyed movements, Nathair waved his hand up and down his body.

She gave a deadened laugh.

"True. You'll just keep them all back, won't you?" Her voice was utterly shaken and weak as she spoke. "Biggest and scariest thing around."

Absolutely, Nathair thought with a sharp nod.

Perhaps other Mavka would be wary, but he was larger, faster, and he had a wall of tail. No harm would come to this female, no matter how many Demons came. He would also take her into the cave and become a wall of aggressive wrath should they try to enter it.

"Y-you really are that strong, aren't you, Nathair?" she asked, her voice wavering even more. "Enough to keep *Demons* away in the rain, in the night. At... all times. Land or water, it doesn't matter to you, does it?"

Any pride or cheer he'd held was instantly strangled at her tone, the way her bottom lip trembled. The brimming of tears became heavier. *Perhaps we talked too much for her.*

He didn't know how the conversation of Demons and his ability to thwart them became distressing for her, but he rubbed her back in a comforting gesture. He even massaged his fingers into her shoulders and the back of her neck, trying to remove the tension that had stiffened her.

That only seemed to worsen her state, and she threw her face into her hands as a sob broke.

Since she'd covered her eyes, he prodded his foreknuckle against her cheek to get her attention. He wanted to ask her what was wrong.

She only shook her head, purposefully ignoring him. Except he didn't need to ask, not when the truth spilled from her lips.

"Where were you when I needed you?" Linh cried into her palms. "Where were you when my *people* needed you? I needed protecting from bad people, and then I needed *saving,* and no one came! No one came to save me, no matter how I waited every day. Every minute I prayed for someone to help me, but I knew... I knew no one would come. I knew everyone was as trapped as I was."

Linh lowered her arms so she could hug her midsection. Cheeks and nose swollen from tears, her wet lips quivered. Her small shoulders shook violently from unhidden sobs as she keeled forward, her long ponytails slipping over her shoulders to hang in front of her chest.

Despite his heart twisting in pity for her, Nathair did nothing. He didn't touch her, didn't try to comfort her, nor did he try to speak.

None of these things would aid her current state.

"I love my parents so much, but I hate them... I hate them for being who they are, for being so important. I hate that the reason I was taken was to control them, and therefore the entire village. And I *hate* myself... I hate myself for wishing I wasn't their daughter because it meant I wouldn't have needed saving. That it wasn't *me* who needed to suffer. He told me I was lucky I was beautiful because it meant I would be treated special. But... but that meant..."

Linh shook her head and buried her forehead against her knees.

"I can't. I can't say it," she cried, as a sharp gust of wind brushed around them. As if weak, or subconsciously using it as an excuse, she fell to the side until her body lay against his chest. "I-I'm sorry. I just... thank you so much for caring a-about me. I don't mean to blame you for something that isn't your fault, but I just wish, with all my heart, that I had met you sooner."

Nathair wrapped his arms around her and used a hand to lift her face to his. He nudged the end of his snout against her tear-stained cheek, giving her the affection she obviously sought, and to let her know it was okay.

He, too, wished he could go back in time and prevent the parasites from harming her soul, her heart. To be her shield. But Nathair could not do this – his magic was limited to the constraints of reality. He could bend his own Mavka essence, but there was little more he could do, and everything came with a sacrifice.

He pulled back so she could see him sign. "I am here now." Her brows waved in distress, as if that wasn't enough to stop her pain. "I am sorry for you, but I can only protect now."

"I know," she cried, shaking her head. "I don't mean to sound selfish. I know I probably sound–"

Nathair squished her cheeks to quieten her before letting go to talk with both hands. "Stop. I don't need your sorry." She gave him a hiccup, but he was thankful her tears seemed to be ebbing. "I cannot protect you from the past, but I can help you."

"Help how?" Her brows drew together as more liquid brimmed in her eyes. "You can't erase the past, what's happened to me."

"Heal your mind and heart," he signed.

I cannot change what has happened, but maybe I can help her forget. And, when she remembers, she focuses on me like how I focus on her to keep the fragments at bay. Both their minds were unwell, both difficult battles to face.

Both unlikely to ever be permanently fixed.

But if they could be a support to lean on for each other when their minds rotted in decay, wouldn't that be... comforting? They may end up hurting each other, but so long as they remembered it came from a place of confusion, disorientation, and pain, and forgave it, then their bond would be strong. They'd need affection and reassurance constantly to battle the darkness they both harboured within, so that any toxicity they brought forth was healed within the warmth of tenderness.

She may be volatile with her emotions, but it would never compare to the life-ending violence he could wield within a second. If she was willing to forgive the craze of his fragments, there would be very little she could do to hurt him, unless she wanted him to destroy every male within a kilometre radius of her.

He didn't think she'd do that, though. Hurt him with other males, or even females.

"It's not that easy, Nathair," Linh argued as she pushed off him to sit up. "You can't just snap your fingers and make me feel better."

She folded her legs under her backside and placed her face into her hands again. Seeing her distressed burned a cold hole in his chest. He prodded her on the shoulder again to inform her he wished to speak. She peeked at him over her fingertips.

"I know it will not be e-a-s-y," he signed, as his sight deepened in its blue hue. "But isn't it better than thinking you are a-l-o-n-e?"

Linh crawled off him with agitated movements, just as the clouds finally shaded the sunlight. Soon, Demons would come to inspect them, and he'd been hoping to ward them off with her upon his coils.

"What do you even want with me?" Linh half-cried, half-yelled at him. Nathair reared his head back, unsure of what he'd done to deserve being shouted at. "Why are you here, protecting me, caring for me? You make me do all those... *things* with you."

His sight flared red in anger at what she was insinuating. "I don't make you do a-n-y-t-h-i-n-g you don't want to."

"I don't know if you're planning to just eat me when you're ready or if you're just pretending to be nice to get me to have sex with you! There's literally no other reason for anything you do."

Unable to contain the flare of rage that crushed around his heart, he darted his hand forward. He gripped her cheeks and brought her closer until the rounded end of his snout brushed her nose. He didn't squeeze her, but his hold was meant to be possessive, demanding, and showing he was no longer *pleased.*

Her eyes widened as a quiet, waving hiss climbed up the back of his throat. His fangs dropped to rest against his forked tongue, and venom dripped from them slowly.

He shocked her enough into shutting up, her lips snapping closed, but she didn't smell of fear. *Good.* He would have been upset if she'd shown that she couldn't trust him after stating something so callous.

Twisting his head, getting his point across that he wouldn't tolerate her saying he was so unfeeling, or disgusting, he let her go. He pulled back, his shoulders rolling superiorly, and his reddened glow remaining.

"I can ask you the same." His fingers were more pointed in his gestures, his movements sharper and harder to show his anger. "Why do you c-r-a-w-l into my arms every night? Why do you desire me? I am Mavka, and you're a human."

Her features grew ashen, and she attempted to look away. Nathair threw his arm into her view, showing her he wanted answers to his questions.

"I don't know," she mumbled, as shame seem to fall over her features.

"You asked me to touch you." A small growl escaped him. "I did not ask for that. You did."

Linh folded her arms across her torso and rubbed her biceps as if hugging herself. "I know. I'm sorry."

"You are using me to take back your body because I am not a human m-a-l-e," Nathair signed, daring her to say otherwise.

"No. That's not–" She bit her lips, unable to finish the denial. Tears bubbled in her eyes as she began to tremble like a wave of sadness washed over her. Her arms lowered, and she clutched her stomach with sickness. "I promise I care about you. I do."

"I care about you, too," he answered, tipping his head.

She shook her own and gave in to her wobbling legs to kneel before him. "I swear I don't desire you for such a selfish reason."

Nathair sighed, wondering if she truly believed that or not. Of course she desired him. He didn't think her arousal was solely for her own self-pleasure, not with the way she'd bitten her lips in want at his cocks while he stroked them.

He was not normal to her, and that was likely why she considered him safe. He had two cocks, double the trouble as she'd said, and he had more strength than multiple humans combined. If Nathair wanted to, he did not need permission, and there was little this female could do to stop him.

He could take, and take, and not care for her feelings or the state of her body, mind, and heart afterwards. But he cared how she felt about him, what she wanted from him, and what she thought of him.

Nathair would only use his power to protect and adore her.

I only realised what I was beginning to feel recently. It would be unfair of him to pry into her heart when his own was just as confused.

Yes, he desired to protect his little nightingale; he'd wanted this from the beginning. To add her to his treasures, and guard her as he would them. To stare at her like a greedy creature, snickering as he placed her in different lights until she gleamed the way he wanted her to.

Her scent had been pleasing, and instantly wrapped around his mind like a silky cloth. She stole his focus and had lowered the burden of his fragments. Not enough for him to notice the true impact, but enough that it meant he wasn't... insanely lost to them all the time.

Before her, his lethargy had been worse. The headaches, the clogging of his lungs, the sickly twists of his gut – Linh was a balm to them.

But something had shifted in his mind and heart for this delicate female when he figured out what had happened to her. This insatiable need to shield her with his entire body had come upon him violently and with unbreakable force.

He wanted to hunt down those who hurt her and snuff them out – all the way down to their putrid souls.

However, he would have to leave her here. She wouldn't be safe. The moment his presence was gone from his home, Demons would chase down her scent and eat her within a night. She had nowhere to run in the main area of his cave, and everywhere else was filled with darkness.

Nathair could not take her with him. He may turn on her, should he succumb to a rage. He also didn't want her to face her attackers. She wished to forget them, so dragging her back for his own selfish need for retribution was... *cruel*. Nathair may be selfish enough to hunger for her body, but he would not hurt her heart in this way.

It was too fragile.

Nathair desired her. Part of him longed to have such a beautiful, trusting creature belong to him from the first night he saved her. He'd ignored it, as the potential of a bride was a poor decision on his part.

Yet he wanted her soul to protect. He wanted to be the one to help heal it, and teach it that his touches were different from the selfishness of others. He wanted to be able to hold it in his palm, and not have it skittish or backing away from his skull as if it feared he'd consume it without permission.

The only way to obtain this was to capture her heart.

Her heart is locked from me, he thought, as he gazed at her breaking apart before him. *It is hidden away from all.*

This female may care for him, but everything about her was too guarded. He hoped it didn't matter that he bore a skull, and that he could win her regardless, but he knew what he was for her.

A tool. One which he was dubious enough to wield until he'd picked the lock around her heart's cage and was able to reach into her centre.

If she wanted to learn how to touch and be touched with faith, then she could stroke his scales until she was content. If she wished to learn what it was like to share heat with passion, rather than sweat in fear, he'd scald her with kisses, heavy breaths, and intertwining groans. If she wanted to be intimate in order to take back her body and heal from this, then Nathair would find a way to fuck his way into her heart.

I am... in love with her. At least, he thought he might be, since he'd felt the fragments react intensely in this way. He'd realised just how deeply he was falling for this female when she became his songbird. His nightingale. His damn salvation. A dark obsession.

With one song that gave him the peace he'd sought for

centuries, she'd become the most important creature in existence.

Nathair was aware he could discard her at any point and find a different human to become his song. It did not *need* to be Linh. It did not need to be a human who came with battles just as deep as his own.

Their issues were so vastly different, and yet she constantly *tried.* For him, for herself. She was strong, passionate, and stubborn, and so innocently sweet he wanted to corrupt her in ways she obviously desperately needed.

Nathair leaned forward and cupped under her chin to lift her sobbing face to him. She did so willingly, even as she continued hugging herself in a position that made her small.

"Use me," he signed before giving her space.

"P-pardon?" she asked, her voice cracking an octave.

"Use me," he repeated. "I am yours to take in any way you want. Use me to take back your body, to heal, to finally feel p-l-e-a-s-u-r-e – pleasure." He repeated the last word to show her the sign for it.

"But why?" she whined. "Is sex really all you want?"

Nathair let out a small rumbling growl at that. "No. I want more."

When she shook her head like she didn't understand, Nathair wanted to roar his words. *I have never wanted my voice more than now.*

His movements hastened, became more jarring. "I want to f-u-c-k you until all your body knows is the feel of me taking it. Until it only knows the t-a-s-t-e of me within it, and only remembers me. I want to c-l-a-i-m your body like this because you will not give me your heart first."

Her eyes grew wide as her lips parted in disbelief.

"You will be mine."

Her shock gave way to a glare. "I don't *belong* to anyone. No one owns me."

Her feistiness had his back muscles leaping with a shiver, his orbs daring to flicker to purple. Nathair chuckled.

"For now." Then, within the blink of an eye, Nathair darted around her until she lay on the sand with him creating a circular wall of scaled muscle. He positioned his torso upright in front of her, with less than two feet separating them. She was trapped, caged, and imprisoned. "I am yours, Linh."

He hoped she knew the sincerity of that, even if he didn't think she was ready to hear the depth of it.

"When you are ready, c-l-a-i-m – claim – me and yourself. Then, when I claim you, I will be yours to do what you will. I will follow you anywhere."

"R-really? Anywhere?" she asked, her tone cracked and raspy. The light from the greying clouds reflected in her rich brown eyes. "Will you help my people?"

He should have expected that question.

"Do not do this for such a s-e-l-f-l-e-s-s reason." His heart hurt a little at the idea that she might. "If you do, I will r-e-s-e-n-t you."

"You'll resent me?" She signed it back to him, filling in the word he did not have a gesture for.

He purposefully slowed his gestures, wanting to convey the depth of his next words. "I want more than your body, Linh."

"What do you want?" she asked, sitting back in her kneeling posture. Thankfully, her crying had eased. "You still haven't told me."

Linh flinched when he reached his arm out. He sighed at her reaction, but used his magic to dip his claw tips into the rippling well of her chest. They both watched her soul emerge, floating just behind his fingers.

Since he didn't touch it, her soul didn't awaken from its slumber. It hugged its midsection, digging its nails into its back. A back he had not seen before that was blackened like coal with the evidence of mental decay. Her little soul was in a worse state than he'd realised.

Still beautiful, just like her.

He signed the word soul with his right hand – his fingertips together before he drew his thumb down his palm with his fingers flicking forward flat and together – and gestured at it so she understood the new word he was teaching her. The most important word to him. Linh stared at it floating between them, before darting her horrified gaze between it and his skull repeatedly.

"You want my soul?!" Grasping it with both hands, she retreated until her back met the wall of his tail. She held it tight, and he winced when he feared she'd crush it.

He just hoped she couldn't destroy it, since she was human. It didn't even seem to notice her, as it never woke.

Her features fell when realisation dawned. "You said you were a soul eater! I knew you were trying to eat me," she said, but she didn't sound very convincing, as if she didn't truly believe what utter crap she'd just spilled.

With the way she was cowering, despite not even having a single drop of fear tangling in her sweet peach-and-vanilla scent, he knew she wasn't ready. She didn't know what she wanted, what she was doing – she just wanted to feel safe while she nurtured herself through her trauma.

Nathair sighed and dipped his head to the side until his skull rested on his shoulder. "I want you to give it to me w-i-l-l-i-n-g-l-y."

"Why willingly?" She looked down at her slumbering flame. "Is it like the devil of old? You must bargain for it?"

The snicker that escaped him was an accident. It immediately made her back stiffen.

"It will make you my b-r-i-d-e – bride. We will be b-o-n-d-e-d – bonded – forever. Where you go, I go. Where I go, you will go. I will protect you with all my might. We will be... one."

"What...?" She bit her lip and lowered her gaze as she looked off to the side. "I just fled from one person, but what you're saying sounds permanent. I-I, Nathair... I don't know if I'm in the right place to make such a large commitment. I feel like I barely know you, or myself anymore."

Nathair slipped into her view. "I will wait."

"What if I never want that?" She shrunk under his gaze with

her knees to her chest, clutching her soul tight like her life depended on it. "That sounds too important, too heavy. What if I'm the wrong person for you? There are other people... those who aren't... broken."

"You are not broken, Linh," Nathair signed, tilting his head. "Just hurt."

She pressed her lips together tightly. "You didn't answer me."

"I will do whatever you want, and h-o-p-e it is enough. You do not have to give me your soul. I am not expecting it in e-x-c-h-a-n-g-e for anything. I will not try to c-o-n-v-i-n-c-e you, or take it by force."

Her brows drew together in deep puzzlement. "You won't convince me?"

"You now know what I want. My goal is you. If all you will allow is a t-a-s-t-e – taste – then so be it." Despite what Nathair said, he still let out a chuckle. "But I will not play fair if you claim me, Linh."

Her cheeks heated, and she shrunk under his gaze for a different reason. Her eyes darted everywhere, as if looking for an escape, before relaxing. "B-but I have a choice?"

His heart swelled, and he nodded. "Always."

When she loosened her hold on her delicate, wounded soul, Nathair pushed at her hands until she was forced to let it go. He squished it back inside her chest, where it currently belonged, but he vowed he would win this female. He would feel her flame tied to his horns one day, no matter how long that took.

That, or he would pine for her for an eternity, and wait for someone else willing to sing for him instead. They would have to be special to erode the way her essence clung to his own. *I doubt anyone would be able to compare.*

Droplets splattered against his scales, the yellow sand, and her hair. Linh appeared a little lost as she stared at the sand, as if she was struggling to absorb all this.

When he spoke again, she gave him her attention so she

could see. "Inside, or play in the rain?"

She lifted her face to the dark sky and flinched when a raindrop splattered on her cheek. Then she closed her eyes and let more land on her face, and the swollen redness in her cheeks and nose appeared to cool.

Nathair enclosed them with his tail, while digging it underneath Linh until she was seated upon him once more. She didn't try to flee, nor did she react as she kept her face pointed upwards.

The rain it is.

TWENTY

Tucking away handfuls of lemon ironbark into her bag, Linh continued to search the forest. It wasn't particularly edible, but she thought she may be able to stew it long enough to make a dull tea with the water mint she'd found a week ago.

Placing her hand to her brow, she noted the sun's afternoon location. *We've travelled far from his pond today.* They'd been foraging for hours.

Nathair slithered off to the side, and she followed. He only left her if he wanted her to check a new scent, something they hadn't encountered yet.

He brought her to some flowers, and she knelt so she could check them properly. They smelt sweet, almost like vanilla, and she gingerly pulled one of them from the ground by grasping its base. She assessed its tubers, brushing them of dirt, to check their colouring.

These are pale vanilla lilies. She tucked them into her bag and then hunted for more in the area. They wouldn't provide much sustenance, but it was better than only eating plums and fish.

Once she picked all the lilies she could, wanting to use both the tubers and edible flowers, Linh moved them on.

She followed the stream that took them further north towards the cliff edge. *There are probably better plants south.* She shuddered at the thought of heading in the direction of

Bragg's bandit camp.

Still, she stayed near the stream and waited for Nathair to point out a new smell for her.

In some ways, she tried to ignore the hulking Duskwalker.

They'd barely spoken since the day they sat in the rain together. Linh had been introspective in their shared silence. *My heart still hurts.* Her ponderous mind wasn't faring any better, whirling wildly until she gave herself a headache.

Gosh, she felt so damn *petty*. She also felt insanely pathetic, weak, and... selfish. *Use him? How the hell am I meant to do that when I now know what he wants?* Her soul? She didn't want to sell her soul to any devil, no matter how much his scales felt sublime rubbing against her.

And yet... she wanted to crawl on top of him so badly, her pussy literally dripped at the thought.

I know I don't just desire him for the reasons he said. She hated that he thought so low of her.

There was something about his skull she found attractive, and she longed to lather it in kisses again in hopes he'd purr sweetly for her. She wanted to grab his horns, stroke them, see if he could feel through them since his skull was sensitive.

His humanoid torso... well, what female *wouldn't* be attracted to that? It was muscled, hunky, and covered in pretty black scales that gleamed with rainbows in the light. Even his dark-grey nipples often grabbed her attention, and she wished she had a shirt she could throw at him. Not to mention a skirt to hide his seam because she was beginning to want to pet it longingly so she could make his dual cocks spring from it.

They're purple, she thought, kicking a rock. *Why do they have to be my favourite colour?*

His tentacles were strange, but she wanted to explore them and know if they were firm or squishy, if they felt good to be touched or were just an external tool for something.

Then there was his waterlily-and-moonflower scent, both which could be found in her village. *I think... he'd like my village.* They had springs all around it and flowing through the mountain side. A waterfall literally flowed out to the beach a few kilometres away.

I like the way he looks. A lot. Enough to disregard *what* he was. He was a monster, something freaky – and sometimes freaky was too much of a hurdle to get over.

But Nathair was magnificent in all his Duskwalker glory.

He was a serpent in nature in so many ways. Even his mannerisms felt snake-like: lazy, territorial, calm until not, and always watchful.

His fins and gills just added to his beauty, and she'd learned the ones going down his sides really were soft. With a velvety texture, she thought they might feel nice rubbing against the softer parts of her, like her inner thighs. She liked that his entire tail would shiver all the way to his tip if she caressed them; the intense reaction stimulated her with tingles.

None of this was enough for Linh.

It was his patience, and his... mind. His deeply disturbed mind, constantly making him feel relatable. He was as messed up as she was, yet his problems were more physical than her own, more pressing and harder to break. To heal him of his voices? It felt impossible. All she could do was sing for him, and she did every day just to avoid *talking* to him.

Even when he didn't slip into a trance straight away, I didn't have a single thing to say. She'd had the chance to hear his deep, mesmerising, cocky voice again, and she'd missed it. All because she suddenly felt really nervous and unsure around him.

I wish he didn't tell me. She'd rather not have known the depth of his desires, that apparently weren't so two-dimensional like hers.

Nathair slithered off.

He brought her to a flowering shrub of melastoma affine – better known as blue tongue plant – and she lowered to inspect the ripeness of its berries. *The soil must be loamy for these to grow so big here.* Considering how little clay appeared to be in the moist, fluffy dirt, she wasn't surprised. The northern cliffs were plenty fertile for these.

Her vision blurred as her painful thoughts rambled.

Although it'd only been two days since the rain, Linh hadn't touched herself in front of him for days prior to that. She'd been so worried that all the intimacy was the reason he'd had an erotic trance, and had just been trying to gain the will to be okay with it if it happened again.

Waking up with a set of cocks pumping against her had set her back. She'd relapsed on her healing, and she wished it had a definitive end – that she could note down the time when she would be *free* from her inner turmoil. She'd been hoping to try again that night after the beach, but her stomach had been so sickly since then that she couldn't.

It would be unfair of me to lead him on when I don't know what I want. When a stick cracked under his tail, likely from him coming to see why she wasn't checking the bush for berries properly, she hastily jumped to do so. His shadow blocked out the little sun shining through the forest canopy.

Her lips tightened as her sinuses grew tingly. She quickly blinked to disperse any possible tears.

I hate that I think he's right. I like him because he's not human, because he doesn't feel human. It's wrong of me, isn't it? To be intimate with him to get over what happened to me?

But what had happened to her... what Bragg had done... how was she supposed to get over something like that?

Part of her wanted to tell Nathair. She wanted to let him know that what he sought from her was probably a losing battle. That Nathair wasn't the problem, and she was; she thought she was... *ruined.* Not physically, but within the recesses of her mind and heart, where she didn't know if she could be with anyone without constantly feeling afraid. Where doing anything intimate came with a stomach ache that was physical, despite her not eating anything unpleasant.

The only unpleasant thing she'd eaten were her own unspoken words that she swallowed as emotional lumps.

He said I was lucky I was pretty. Her 'marriage' to Bragg

was entirely political, and was a way to force her father into being compliant. If her father didn't do as he was told, the threat of her life constantly loomed over his head. She was a bargaining chip.

Of course, her father refused – which resulted in the intense spectacle of everyone watching each of his hands being clubbed. Even then, he'd still said no, as did her mother, as did everyone in the village.

As did Linh.

She never got that choice in the end. He'd ended up just taking her despite everyone's outrage, forcing her to pack at knife point, and then told her father to be thankful marriage was his choice.

He didn't love her, but he'd always given her a disgusting appreciative eye. He gave the same one to many women in the village. But his need for control was why it was *her* he'd taken.

Bragg couldn't destroy their homes, or they'd revolt. The promise they'd protect them from Demons, which they did, was the only reason they were even tolerated to begin with. The reason they didn't have soldiers was because they stopped them from reaching out to the south for aid.

But when Bragg asked for more – more crops, more clothing, more medicine – choking them of the supplies they needed to survive, the angrier everyone became.

And the more he set his sights on Linh, the more worried they all became. He kept hovering around her, kept finding a reason to be in her vicinity. A random scrape she needed to tend to, a concoction to help one of his men with a stomach bug, anything he could think of.

He'd even offered to take her and her mother personally out into the forest to find herbs they couldn't safely get on their own. He'd been rather forceful with his ugly attempts to woo her, but her mother's proximity had kept him at bay.

His patience had run out, even more when her father bartered too hard to protect their village. When her father had... tried to send a message to the south for aid against the bandits, and had gotten caught.

Bragg had grown enraged. He'd finally had enough of her father. He'd turned to Linh as his option for control, but she knew it was more than that by his continuous creepy stalking.

Death or pain did not frighten her father; he'd already proven that by his injured hands. It also hadn't frightened the men who fought back. They'd all constantly argued with Bragg's men and forced them back, tried to stop them from... *taking* her.

The moment her throat was in his rough palm, her potential death frightened everyone.

The last hug she'd gotten from her mother had them both shaking and in tears. Her mother had promised they'd find a way to save her, and all she had to do was live. Survive. To just get through each day and know they were trying every resource to bring her home.

But every painstaking day felt like eternity, and Linh had feared she couldn't survive the next as she promised to. That she couldn't bear it if her hellish life continued the way it did.

She knew no one was going to be able to save her. They hadn't managed to stop her from being taken in the first damn place. What chance did they have running into the belly of the beast – Bragg's camp – where there were more men, more weapons, and the potential for more Demons to sniff out the bloodshed?

Linh thought she could bear to share all this with Nathair, but doing so was really fucking hard. It felt easier to just stay quiet, and hope everything slipped from her memories permanently.

The rest? She didn't think she'd ever be able to explain the way Bragg didn't want to mark her face and body, but it didn't mean he hadn't been unkind. He'd just found many other ways to be horrible. Violent in ways that didn't leave marks, and he was emotionally abusive until her spirit was crushed.

I was so scared I'd never want to be intimate with anyone ever again. She took in the towering, oppressive shadow of

Nathair, and only felt calmness in his foreboding shade. The fact she'd found someone already who was constricting those anxieties away was a miracle. *If he'd been a man...* Linh would have never let him within ten feet of her.

Yet, with Nathair, part of her desire was intrigue. He was so different that it put her at ease. It made it less daunting and became erotic instead. Like her own virile, sinful god coming to shine his dark light on her.

Checking to make sure the melastoma affine berries had all broken from their pods, she tucked them away. She nibbled on a few, hoping to ease her queasy gut.

But he offered it, and I really do want to touch him. She wanted to see what it was like when Nathair let his unbending control slip under her power, rather than Linh be a shaking, needy mess.

Her inner walls gave a tentative pulse at remembering his big finger inside her. She'd been so soft around it. She didn't think she'd ever come through penetration before, and if she had, she'd completely locked those memories in a *'do not fucking open this'* hellish box because she knew she wouldn't be able to handle it. She'd dissociated herself from those scenarios to escape, and that came with memory slips.

She'd rather keep it that way.

Honestly, those two months had been a nightmarish blur, and she absolutely did not want to wade through any of her recollections for clarity. *I wish he had the power to make me forget.*

Linh had asked him if it was possible, and he said no. She knew he wasn't lying.

Once she was done eating until she was full, she turned to the Duskwalker, who had been staring at her back with his arms folded.

She tucked a few strands behind her ear, since her hair was a single braid swinging down the side of her neck.

I adore how sweet he is. In everything he did for her, he showed utter care and consideration. He appeared to be completely devoted to her needs, her comfort, while disregarding his own – often making her wish she could take the leap and meet him halfway. *But he's also... funny.*

Nathair was charming, but a little creepy at times with the way he stared at her, not to mention his intense mannerisms whenever she sat in his nest by herself. He'd stopped entering it when she'd tried to get out of it the first night they'd gone to sleep after the rain.

She'd wanted to sleep alone and put space between them, but he'd been very, *very* displeased by this. He'd literally carted her to his nest and then coiled around the outside of it like an additional wall.

She'd woken both mornings with his head plonked on the ledge, watching her like a weirdo. A pretty weirdo, with mesmerising orange orbs that seemed to want to inhale her into their fiery vortexes.

"I think I'm done for the day," she stated quietly, somewhat evading his orange orbs.

Now that she was done foraging, he snorted a deep huff and turned to lead the way back to his pond. Linh followed a step behind, and watched as his tail created a massive, continuous wave for metres. He'd folded his arms and lifted a hand to his cheek as if he was ponderous.

It made him come across as more daunting and grumpier.

I don't think he's grumpy, though. Brash, absolutely. Nathair lacked a filter for his movements, and sometimes she thought she could read his mind with them alone. He also didn't seem to be hiding his orb changes, even the purple of his arousal, and offered them freely.

She liked that he was kind of rough. His movements could be sly and smooth, and she thought that may be his serpent nature, but the Duskwalker in him was harsh, brutish, and jarring. He was also very direct when he signed, getting to the point despite possibly being insensitive.

I like that about him. He comes across as honest.

Linh eyed how he ducked underneath branches she

wouldn't even be able to jump to graze with her fingertips. She even tried and almost stumbled when she landed on a damn stick.

Quickly righting her footing, she flushed. *Of all the spots I could have landed, it had to be on a stick?!* Come on, the universe was just fucking with her at this point.

A grunt caught her attention, and she looked up.

His dark horns and the back of his skull glittered gold in the dappled light before he turned it to the side to look at her over his shoulder. Orbs yellow, he signed, "I saw that."

Her cheeks flared with such a heat that even her ears went hot. "How could you see that?" she yelled, waving her arms up in disbelief. "Your face was turned forward."

"I see everything."

Embarrassed, she sneered before sticking her tongue out. She barely had time to gasp before he suddenly spun to her and grabbed the end of it. She froze with her tongue caught between his big fingers.

"It's..." He purposefully changed his orbs to blue and pointed to one. "Blue."

Crossing her eyes, she looked past the tip of her nose to her blue-black stained tastebuds. He let it go so she could talk.

"Well, yeah. The berries I was eating stain your tongue."

Seemingly curious about this, he dug into her bag and stole a few. He sat back on the base of his tail and pried a berry apart with his thumb claws. Then, to her surprise, he threw the rest into his mouth.

He instantly shuddered inwardly. All the way to the tip of his tail, his entire body convulsed in what she figured was disgust. He squished them, his jaw segments moving and parting, while his orbs flickered with black.

She giggled behind her fist when she figured this was a Duskwalker's way of cringing like a human might when eating something sour.

When he was done, he scraped his tongue clean, rather than swallowing, and poked it forward. His orbs didn't move, but she knew he was inspecting the way his purple forked tongue had turned blue-black.

He turned from her to lead the way once more, but he never drew his tongue back in. He even grabbed the forks and pulled them apart. Linh ran up beside him to watch intently, and something became apparent.

He's more curious than I thought. Because he could speak so well, spell, and just in general seemed to be knowledgeable, she often forgot he was a monster. *He hasn't been alive for long – as he'd been dead for most of it – and I'm guessing there's not actually a lot he's seen and done.*

And this monster apparently wanted to be very curious with her. *He always leads so well that I forget that I'm the first... woman he's ever kept.* Linh was his first.

She could be his first for many things, if she chose it. *I want him.* But becoming his bride... did that mean he wanted her to be his *last* as well?

How many souls can he bond with? Because, if Linh was being truthful, she'd rather not be one of many he kept. *But with two cocks, he wouldn't have an issue pleasuring more than one person at a time.* Was that why he had two? And did that mean all Duskwalkers did or just him?

She covered her mouth, suddenly feeling nauseous. She didn't want to give herself to him to have to deal with that kind of emotional anguish.

Rather than sitting in her sickly thoughts, she just asked the question. "You said your father can eat many souls. How many people can you bond with?"

As if he didn't care for the conversation over his stained tongue, he lifted a singular finger in her direction without turning his skull to her.

Okay. So just one. That did make her feel a little better. *More for me, then?* Her back stiffened at her thoughts. *I-if I decide to, that is.* She palmed her face. *Oh, who am I kidding? Resisting his charm and barring touching just isn't going to happen.*

It'd already been five days, and she was ready to squirm. She wanted pleasure, and he'd already shown her she could take it by her own hand, or around one of his fingers. And she really did want to erase all touch until she could only remember Nathair's.

His palms were so soft they were silkier than her own. They felt so nice caressing just her cheek, her neck, and from what she could remember, her breast.

I want to learn him, and see what happens when he learns me. The first woman he's ever touched. *That* should be scary, being with someone so inexperienced while she had trauma, but the idea turned her on so much it had to be a sin. To take his firsts with everything, like they were her own, but wanted, pleasured, revered.

He'd be her first Duskwalker, or the first male that had two cocks, scales, a forked tongue, claws, and no legs but a tail. So many firsts to have with him, when she'd thought she'd been all out of those.

She wanted his sexy, smooth scales caressing every inch of her body to the point her nipples hardened with hope that he'd scrape them too. She wanted him everywhere, all at once, and he was so damn big and long that he might be the only creature in existence that *could* do that.

Linh wasn't sure about sex, but why hold back when they both wanted to get closer, and could in other ways? *I know that if I was to reach out right now...* He'd cave within an instant and give her whatever she hungered for.

Because he hungered for it too.

So she did. In the most innocent of senses, Linh tentatively reached out to him and placed her palm on his humanoid waist.

Her heart nearly wept when he grabbed it, and just held her small, nimble hand in his overbearingly large one. His claws stabbed into her delicate wrists, but they didn't hurt. All her loneliness and self-loathing... all the unbearable, gut-twisting sick that had been haunting her for days, unravelled itself in his soft palm.

Nathair didn't do more than that. He didn't turn to her now that she'd given him an opening, didn't try to cart her into his arms. He didn't try to shove his tongue into her mouth or expect anything from her.

He just held her hand in a simple gesture, and her being radiated in tenderness.

It only made her want him more.

TWENTY-ONE

Linh had this big scheming plan for when they got back to Nathair's cave.

Bathe so she felt clean, dry up with the fire, eat some of the fruit, and then ask Nathair if they could cuddle again. It'd been days since she'd been coiled up in his tail, and she'd missed it – her sleeps had been restless.

She'd had no intention of getting rest straight away.

Linh pouted as she blinked within the darkness, her head pressed between his pectoral muscles, and her arms squished between them. *Dammit. I fell asleep as soon as he held me. Gone – unconscious within seconds.*

She'd just been so comfortable, the familiarity and closeness of the hold whisking her under.

I wanted to try touching him. He obviously wanted it, and she was tired of letting her mind hold her back from taking that leap. For once, she wanted to let her heart take the lead – or pussy, rather. *But now he's in one of his trances.*

Twitching, he was tense around her. His claws dug through her dress as he clutched at her back.

Tilting her head to follow the white light of his glow, she nibbled her bottom lip in thought. *I wonder if I can...* She began to hum, worried if she snapped him out of his trance too fast, it could mean trouble.

He didn't soften, so she incrementally increased the

volume. When his rippling clenches eased, she smiled. A small, short whine broke from him, and he brought her closer. Linh gasped when he squished her face against him, incidentally rendering her quiet as her hums were muffled against his pectoral muscle.

Lying on their sides, Nathair panted around her. Then he patted the back of her head before drawing the tips of his claws up and down the side of her throat.

She pulled her face free.

"Did that help?" He tapped at the side of her neck before just tickling it again. Her eyes crinkled with humour. "I'll take that as a yes."

He snorted out a huff but didn't move an inch. He was usually a little lethargic after his mind was lost.

Linh took that as her opening. She pushed upwards now that he was awake so she could be higher, knowing he would move and wiggle to let her. He dipped his skull to her, halting her when she'd made it less than a foot.

Linh hesitantly chewed the inside of her bottom lip before sucking in a courageous breath.

"Can I touch you?" she whispered, placing her hands against his broad shoulders.

Nathair grabbed one of her hands and made it cup the back of his own. He chuckled as she felt him sign, "Always."

"You can't say always, Nathair," she stated with a weak laugh. "That would mean whenever–"

Before she could finish, the arm behind her darted up so he could cover her mouth from behind. In the dark, she once more felt him sign, "Always."

Her features softened at that, and she reached up to cup the corners of his jaw. She brought his head lower so she could press her lips against the smooth length of his jawbone.

"I want you to know that I don't desire you because you're not a human man, but because I find you... beautiful." She kissed where she thought the side of his nose hole was. "I like your skull, Nathair. I'm used to seeing bones in my line of work, and snakes often have deep symbolism that holds a lot of meaning."

Now that she'd uttered that, she realised that may be why she'd found him so comforting from the beginning. Serpents, in many lores, represented rebirth, transformation, immortality, and healing. They shed their skin, in the same way Linh wished she could shed the past and transform, bigger, better, and brighter than before.

Nathair nuzzled into her kisses as she softly lathered him in them.

She brushed her hands down the sides of his neck, her lips following on one side, until her fingertips grazed the hard pebbles of his flesh. His muscled chest dipped beneath the press of her finger pads, showing he was soft underneath despite how dense his skin was.

"I like your scales," she continued, whispering her lips over his throat. His entire body lightly writhed when she kissed his gills. "I like these. I like how sensitive they are."

He clutched the back of her head, and she was unsure if it was to press her harder or to draw her away. A high-pitched moan came from him when she licked across them, and Linh beamed.

She cupped both of his pectoral muscles, and her thumbs managed to flick across his small nipples at the same time.

"You feel so soft, and yet so strong. You feel masculine. I like watching your body flex, and when your scales reflect any light."

Linh wiggled herself lower so she could plant kisses on his chest, following a rib bone from the outside to the centre. She even licked up his half-sunken sternum.

His abdomen muscles twisted and contorted when she grazed her fingers lower before pushing the hand she wasn't lying on to the side.

"I even like your fins," she complimented, caressing the frill of them starting just above his hips. "They're soft and malleable. And I like the way you smell; it's so gentle."

Nathair's orbs had long ago turned purple, but they flickered with black when she began a path inward. Against her pelvis, she thought she could feel intense twitching from him. He quickly grabbed her hand and began to unfurl his tail. Tension clamped her muscles, and she gripped his sides.

"N-no. I don't want to change how we're lying," she whispered against his chest. "I want to stay like this."

A slip of light broke through a small gap between his tail coils, and it made the scales on his shoulder glitter. With her hands high on his abdomen, she kissed at his chest as she lowered her palms down his rippling muscles. She dipped one between her stomach and his torso, and Nathair clamped up.

His arms shot down, and she squeaked when he grabbed the bottoms of her arse cheeks to shove her hips against his own. The press was hard, and she knew exactly what he was doing with it. If he thought Linh was intending to touch herself, then he was wrong.

Linh unravelled that thought for him when her fingers grazed his seam. When she noticed he shot his skull down to her fully, she lifted her gaze to him. She caressed it repeatedly as she ducked her hips back, biting her lip at his purple orbs.

He grunted just as his cocks came forward, and by the spiral surrounding them, she knew they were encased by his tentacles.

"I like here too," she whispered, thankful she didn't feel any worry or aversion. "I like that you're purple, that you have two dicks, that you have these tentacles."

Nathair let out a growling purr, and it only deepened when those four limbs released so his cocks could extend to their full lengths. She petted the dual heads, but struggled to do so at the same time with the way their centres pushed them apart.

I want to feel him against me. She doubted her dress felt nice brushing over them.

She would have questioned why she was suddenly okay with all this, but Linh thought it might be because of what he told her. She'd been really lost before, wondering what he wanted with her, what his reasons for everything were. Now that she knew... yes, they were scary – the depth of what he wanted was too intense and more everlasting than she could wrap her head around.

But it revealed he wanted more.

That he didn't want to just use her because she was available and had just been playing the long game to get into her pants. She'd needed someone to not only desire her body, but *her*. There was more to Linh than her exterior, and she doubted he would make the decision to bond with someone solely based on whatever beauty he saw in them.

She didn't see Nathair being vain like that.

It meant he cared enough to not damage her heart. Could she give it to him? Linh wasn't sure. Her heart currently felt small and caged, and she didn't know how he was supposed to fit into her life.

She wanted to go back to her people. She wanted to be with them, live among them, and do the work she'd been training to do. How could Nathair fit into that when he was so different?

She didn't know if her parents would accept him, let alone the rest of the village.

But she'd lingered on these thoughts uselessly for days, and right now she just wanted to focus on him, on this. On how his cuddle always made her feel cherished, and finally be *brave*.

"Nathair," she whispered, petting down one cock as best as she could. He shivered for her. "Can you help me remove my dress?"

Within a heartbeat, he made an opening in his tail and fisted the garment to yank it over her head. He grabbed her shoulder and the hip she was lying on, and pressed her a little lower. Her undershirt rode up, exposing her breasts to his flesh.

It also gave her room to pet both his cocks with both hands, and she greeted the strange slime coating them willingly. His tentacles wriggled against her exposed belly, and they felt so odd and tickly that she arched into them for more. Since she was lying on one arm, it was hard to stroke both cocks properly, but she gripped the one to her right with enthusiasm.

She was thankful he wasn't questioning her and just letting her be in control.

"Does that feel okay?" she asked, tilting her head up at him.

He bucked hard into her hands. Then he cupped the back of her head and leaned down to swipe his tongue across her lips. She went to open them for him, but he quickly moved to the side of her neck.

A deep, unhidden groan purposefully rumbled right next to her ear in answer, and her pussy clenched in response to it.

Her nipples were hard, and she was finally feeling them scrape against his scales, his muscles, while savouring his mild warmth. His cocks felt so hard in her palms, their texture smooth and velvety but bumpy with their nodules, and her pussy pulsed for them. They were squishy until she gave even just a little pressure, then they felt as hard as steel.

Both were blunt in their tapered points, like they'd split in the middle as if they'd once been a singular dick. They felt like one large cock when she pushed them together. Each time she stroked him, gathering the lubricant making him slick, she could feel her pulse quickening. It was faster than his currently pounding below her lips.

His fingers dug into her before the hand on her hip lowered slightly. Those fingertips dipped into the back of her pants, but didn't go far.

Linh released a cock to loosen the tie of her pants before returning to it. "Touch, Nathair. It's fine."

Surprisingly, more than fine, actually.

As if permission was all he needed, Nathair's hands darted into action. The one gripping her shoulder pushed forward to grasp a breast with a tight knead, pinching her nipple in the process when the sensitive bud slipped between the lengths of his fingers. The other shot down into her loosened pants, and cupped between her parted thighs with ease, his arms longer than her own.

A soft moan caught in her throat at the sudden direct caresses, and it only grew louder when his fingers played. Suddenly her skin was ablaze, and the arousal heat simmering in her veins grew hotter. She panted and ground on his fingers when he moved them in circles against her aching clit.

She stroked him faster while kissing at his chest messily. Wetness squelched between her thighs as the pool at the entrance to her pussy overflowed, and it echoed the squelch radiating from her hands as she petted him.

Her eyes snapped open wide when he drew back a finger, sheathed his claw, and penetrated her deep. Her back arched as her core clamped around him in surprise and pleasure. Her moan was loud, and it continued when Nathair thrust it over and over, dipping in and out of the pool.

Her ears tingled when she thought she heard something, maybe a deep whisper, but she was too busy trying to stroke him while he pushed hard against her G-spot to hear properly. Her hands went lazy when she thought she was already close, and Nathair pumping into them only sent her further into a lather.

His cocks pushed against her abdomen, the tips splitting as they slipped back and forth.

Linh didn't mean to bite him when she clamped up, but her mouth latched onto his flesh when her inner walls clenched his big finger as she came, which only seemed to make it press into her harder. Her eyelids flickered, her breaths muffled against him. Her cry was constant.

"That's it, female," Nathair said softly, as if his voice was distant, whispered. *"Come for me."*

He spoke? she thought, trying to piece it together while she was squirming in bliss.

How? Why? She hadn't sung, so it didn't make sense. It was also so quiet she barely heard it over her own moans.

Just as she was settling, she unlatched her teeth so she could lift her face and tell him. Instead, she choked on a strangle when he rumbled, *"Let's see if your hungry, wet little cunt can take more."*

A second finger penetrated her. Linh scrambled to raise her hips away from the snug stretch, and her hands squeezed his cocks as nervous tightness clamped her muscles. Only for her to melt lewdly seconds later when he wiggled them against the swollen ridge inside her; the one that had her seeing white flashes in the darkness.

Her leg shifted to part her thighs more, and she wasn't sure if that was due to her own movements or because Nathair moved his tail to lift it. She straddled him and bucked against him as she moaned.

He only paused to pump his cocks into her loose hold. *"Fuck. Don't stop stroking me."*

Linh restrengthened her hold and moved her fists up and down. She gave up with her left, having to dig her nails into his stomach when he moved his fingers rapidly. She just kept stroking with her right arm, trying her hardest not to stop.

Taking gulps of his gentle, feminine scent, Linh squirmed against him as they worked in tandem together. Her eyes closed as she released cry after cry, but something became apparent. The louder she got, the louder *he* got, as if... her constant noises were acting like her singing.

His groans always overshadowed his words, but she caught his stray thoughts. The idea of telling him that she could hear fell away at how honest they were, how heated, and showed that despite his outward calm and control, Nathair was *excited*.

When he signed, he was direct, but he withheld his thoughts and wants – much like anyone. This? This gave Linh free rein to hear his deepest desires, and each husky word petted her mind.

"Fuck. She smells so damn good. I want the taste of her in my mouth. I wonder if she'll suck me with my tongue deep in her sweet cunt."

The perverted image of her lying on his stomach with her thighs around his serpent skull blasted in her mind. What would his forked tongue feel like against her clit? She clamped his fingers as a moan broke.

Nathair shuddered all around her and let out a deep pant. Although most of his focus was on thrusting his fingers, he squeezed her breast tighter.

"Look at how wet she is for me." He pulled his fingers out just to spread her entrance and rub against her clit, only to shove them knuckle deep again. *"I want to fuck her so bad. She'd be so fucking hot around my cocks, drenching them as she comes. I want to pump into her hard, until she's a senseless mess around me, singing her sweet cries until I make her scream my name."* He bucked into her hand and released a light growl before quietening. *"Shit. Why does she keep stopping?"*

Linh blushed at that and renewed her grip once more. She dipped lower, made her strokes longer in hopes of making him feel good. With her arm trapped beneath her, all she could do was palm the head of the cock lowest to the ground.

"Good girl," his mind said with a purr, slipping his tongue just below her ear. *"Do you like touching my dual cocks? Do they feel nice in your hands? You're making my lubricant seep everywhere. Are you getting a good feel of what I'll be pumping between your thighs?"*

Both his cocks grew warmer as they swelled in her palms. Sticky liquid clung to her abdomen. Nathair threw his head back as he huffed loudly, his chest rising and falling swifter than ever before. His fingers worked faster inside her, gouging against her most sensitive spot on each pump with surprising precision.

"I cannot wait until she's ready to have me inside her. I hope she clings to me, claws at me. She smells so good, sounds so good, and she's so fucking pretty she makes my damn chest hurt."

"Nathair," Linh moaned, as a shiver ripped down her spine. Her hands stroked harder, but that was more because she was using them as anchors to ride his fingers as she came. "Oh gods. Nathair, *please.*"

"That's right. Call my name. Soon enough, I'll have you fucking screaming it, Linh. All you have to do is sit this tight pussy around both my cocks, or one in your ass if we cannot get them to fit. Whatever has me deep inside you as I fill you with seed, covered and filled with my scent, my marking. I hope you spread your thighs in welcome for it."

Linh bit down on his chest as her orgasm continued on and on, her pussy wildly and violently spasming around his fingers with bliss. His unfiltered thoughts wouldn't shut up, wouldn't stop, and the fact his words felt like a naughty secret had her losing her senses.

His voice was so rich and unfamiliar, yet it had the tiniest growly tinge to it. What he said was too much, and yet it only made her want to claw at him for it.

She wanted everything he was saying. For him to shove his cocks inside and bounce her as he took her hard and fast with deep, longing passion. She could tell how desperate he was for it, how excited it made him, and it only made her wonder how the hell he could hold back.

His mind seemed to be more twisted up with need than hers, and yet he always showed unending patience and control.

"I'm going to come soon," he groaned, his hips shoving against her in jarring movements. *"How do I warn her? I don't want to take my fingers from her. I want to touch where I want to fill."*

Her dazed mind tingled in its lust-filled haze as she rubbed her face against him.

"Come for me, Nathair," she whispered softly, feeling her tremors easing.

"Shit. I'm sorry, Linh, but I cannot take it anymore. Your hands are too small and you're not holding them right." Holding her arse tight with his fingers buried, his other arm squeezing her to his chest, Nathair fucked his cocks against her hands and abdomen. *"Sorry,"* he repeated as he picked up speed, grinding against her harder. He shuddered violently against her. *"Fuck. Oh, fuuuck."*

A whimper broke from him as the cock in her fist swelled. Shudders wracked him before he let out a choke, just as liquid burst between the tight press of their bodies. He continued to pump against her. That was until he removed his fingers, and the slither of light allowed her to see him shove his hand covered in her slick into his mouth.

His second cock swelled. She realised both were now releasing by the opposing jerking and ropes of liquid. Within seconds, she was not only wet, but the front of her was drenched in copious amounts of Duskwalker seed.

Even her tits weren't spared, and they became slippery as they moved over his body.

When his groan quietened, he popped his hand from his mouth and just held her tightly. His heart was sprinting against her cheek as she frantically huffed against his chest. His pants were loud, unhidden, and cracked.

Linh just digested everything with her lids lowered in satisfaction, her body radiating bliss.

He... can come with just one dick at a time? She clenched her thighs together, and she felt how wet the lips of her pussy were. *Holy shit. He's a fucking pervert.* All the things he said! *Is* that *what he thinks every time we're intimate?*

Here Linh was, thinking he was just calm, collected, and always in control while she was letting herself be lost to bliss. She almost let out a laugh. *I didn't expect him to be so intense.*

She felt not an ounce of fear or worry.

If his mind could be so chaotic, and he still held back for her sake, then this naughty, sinful Duskwalker was a damn saint. He was a good guy, and she just wanted to lather him in affection for it.

Her stomach fluttered with butterflies, as her chest felt swollen with tenderness and trust. She waited for the nausea to come on, the gut-churning tension, like she should feel guilty for receiving pleasure, but none came.

Instead, she just basked in this afterglow with all of Nathair pressed against her chest, back, and arms. *I feel really at ease.*

However, a touch of guilt *did* trickle its way into her satisfied stupor, and she nibbled at her bottom lip. *Should I tell him I heard everything?*

Absolutely, but she had two reasons for this. First, because it was the right thing to do, and secondly, because she wanted to tease the bully.

"Nathair?" she cooed, lifting her head.

She squeaked when he suddenly unwrapped his tail, and she figured he'd mistaken her intention for calling out. He made her straddle his abdomen, hiding his cocks by placing her above them.

"Sorry," he both said *and* signed, making her wince. *"Was I too forceful at the end?"*

He calls that forceful? He humped her stomach. Considering that he'd said it was because she'd been doing it all wrong, she... didn't blame him.

She blushed in memory, as embarrassment singed at the nape of her neck.

"No, it's fine." She offered him a genuine smile and then placed her hands on his chest so she could lift up and slide forward. "That was fun."

Bright yellow overtook his purple orbs, and he tilted his head. "You are okay?" he said and signed. *"She's covered in my seed. I thought she'd want to wash straight away."*

The second half of that had only been his thoughts, which were barely a whisper now.

"No, I don't feel like washing just yet," she stated with a coy hum in her tone. She kicked her feet up behind her as she lay on him and pressed the pads of her fingers to her lips. "It kind of feels nice. You sure do like to apologise a lot as you're coming, though. You should work on that."

Nathair's skull reared back in what could only be utter confusion. Then he paused, as realisation settled in. He shot forward and cupped her chin with his fingers digging into her cheeks.

Silence greeted her, and she laughed.

"I think whatever makes you fall asleep while I sing has a similar impact when I'm moaning and you're touching me. I can't hear you anymore, though."

He let her go, although with a slight rough toss. "Why didn't you tell me?" he signed, his gestures jarring and very much angered.

Her cheeks, which had been cooling from their conversation, rewarmed. Her gaze flittered away. "I was too busy coming, and it was really turning me on. I'm sorry. I know I should have told you, but it was... *nice* to hear your unfiltered thoughts. It made me feel really good, especially since you kept complimenting me."

With an annoyed groan, Nathair fell back and covered his skull as a reddish-pink glow flickered behind his fingers. He slowly lowered them and peered at her from beyond his claws.

"It felt good?" he asked, and the colour of his embarrassed orbs deepened. When she nodded, they turned bright yellow. "I thought the voices were quieter."

"Quieter?" Her brows drew together. "They weren't gone?"

He shook his head. "No. But your voice, scents, and touch kept them back. Your singing is more p-o-w-e-r-f-u-l."

Maybe that's why his ability to speak out loud faded so quickly in comparison to usual? They would normally get about thirty minutes of voice-to-voice conversation before it faded.

"Well... after I quickly wash, since I do feel sticky, do you want me to sing for you so you can rest?" she offered.

"I would like that. Thank you." Then he cupped the back of her head to pull her forward and licked the underside of her jaw. He leaned back just to sign, "I hope your c-u-n-t – cunt – feels good."

Linh squeaked and pressed her thighs together. "You did not just say that! I didn't even think you had a gesture for that word!"

He let out a devious chuckle. "Of course I do. I'd be happy to teach you them all, so I can t-e-a-s-e – tease – you with them next time."

She opened her mouth to refute him, her head about to explode in bashfulness. In the moment was different! Yet, she did kind of want to know them. If he could only speak when she sang or moaned for a while, then she wanted him to have the ability to pet her with mental caresses *before* she was crying out with lust.

"Fine," she bit out in a low voice, waving her hands. "Show me now, before I change my mind."

"Good." Then he did a sign she'd never seen before. He pinched his fingers together. Then, in a fluid motion, he waved both his arms in front of his skull until his forearms met like he was signing the word 'night,' and brought his right hand next to his maw to pinch his index and middle fingers to his thumb repeatedly like a bird.

She mimicked it, and her lips pursed together when it didn't really look perverted. "What's this one?"

"Little n-i-g-h-t-i-n-g-a-l-e."

Her gaze softened at that, and somehow, her heart tried to flop out of her chest so he could gobble it up.

Did he make that one just for me? When would he have ever seen a nightingale? Perhaps in the human memories he has knocking around in that big skull of his? Not even Linh's people had a sign for it, as it wasn't a bird that was native to here – she figured it was some kind of songbird.

How could one person be such a deviant and so sweet at the same time?

Little nightingale. I like that he calls me that.

She'd be his songbird whenever he needed.

TWENTY-TWO

I keep having this dream, Nathair thought, as he struggled to open his sight.

"What kind of dream?" his little songbird asked, making him groan and curl his arms around her torso tighter. He nuzzled the underside of his short skull against her lap more.

Nathair thought back on it. Rather than words that came to him, that likely would have shared with her what he experienced, his other senses picked up on it.

They radiated in the blissful, although temporary, inner silence she gifted him.

The recesses of his mind were dark, like hollow night. Like the void of endless nothingness. Like the inside of Weldir's mind, where nothing lived, could live, and that utter blackness was *comforting.*

No light reflected, other than what shone from him... and *her.*

Two-inch-deep water surrounded him. It didn't have a colour, as it wasn't inky like one thought it might be.

His view was always from a third person perspective, as if he was a disembodied bystander. Yet, he could feel contented pleasure vibrating through his ethereal, orange, and intangible form. As if his emotions were heightened to the point they took on a physical spark in the air, his outer self experienced the laziness in him, the quiet relief, the tranquillity he'd never felt.

The voices were gone, giving him freedom to hold this female in his arms as she lay cradled on top of his tail folds. But, much like his spiritual self, she lacked a physical form. Instead, Nathair held her soul.

Not in the palm of his hand like a little bunny, but as if she was the same size as she was now.

And she was *warm*. She gave no breaths, and neither did he, but a pulsating came from within them. At first, his thumping had been fast, sprinting in the cold, lonely darkness by himself. But she always came. Her feet rippled the water she walked on top of, leaving behind little flames that sputtered out as she made her way over to lie with him.

She never spoke a word, never disturbed the silence he'd sought for so long, and just trusted that he wanted her there. She would hold one side of his skull in her lava palm, and tenderly blink up at him with glowing eyes that lacked any whites or pupils in them; they were just a solid brown, pretty glow.

The moment she was with him, his pulsing would slow, only to eventually match hers.

There was no evidence of her soul being tampered with, and he wondered if this embrace would be what it felt like when, or if, he one day consumed it. Would she touch him in such a deeply profound way, like a balm to his very essence? When she gave it to him, could he incidentally destroy what continued to linger and hurt her?

He'd like that to be so, and for her soul to one day feel as comfortable with him as the dream version did.

The only light in his vision came from them and the way they reflected in the colourless water around them. He felt peace, and could have lived there forever.

But, when she knew he was awakening, she would cease singing, cease humming, and the calm waters would begin to violently ripple. White shards would sprinkle in the blackened sky, like pieces of broken glass that gave the tiniest whispers of vibration.

Nathair always knew, before long, those shards would grow and lance the waters around him like falling rubble.

A warm hand stroked down his cool skull, and he finally opened his sight to look up at the female he lay his head upon. Her smile was small, but it twinkled in her expression as she gazed down at him.

Look at the way her eyes shine. Even her black eyelashes were long as they delicately framed them. He reached up to brush a claw beneath one of her molten brown eyes.

Her eyelids flickered, and her cheeks darkened in colour as if they filled with heat. He paused. *Shit. She probably heard that.*

The giggle that came out of her was sweet, and instantly had him sighing in annoyance. *This is the part I hate. I cannot stand that she hears my thoughts.*

Would anyone? *I'd rather remain voiceless.* It seemed like an unfair sacrifice for just a meagre amount of peace.

Now that she was growing more adept at his sign language, the use of his voice felt unnecessary. Before long, they would be able to have complex and deep conversations with little effort.

As he was rising so he could give her space, he noted the crinkle of hurt in her eyes. He sighed again.

"Sorry," he stated out loud, his voice remarkably groggy from sleep. "It is not that I don't wish to speak with you, but that I don't like my innermost thoughts spilling from me as if my mind is a sieve."

"I-I know," she offered, giving him a broken smile. "I wouldn't want my thoughts shared either, to be honest."

He nodded, thankful she understood, before looking up at the ceiling. The streaks of sunlight were dim, revealing the day was late but not yet over.

I'm not sleeping as long as I did the first time. He received only a few hours, like any normal Mavka. He sat back on his tail, and hollow feelings grew in his gut. *I cannot ask this of her for much longer.*

Her gaze darted away nervously, and he palmed his fucking face because she heard it. She was choosing not to comment on it for his sake, as if she didn't hear his thoughts, but he saw little point to it.

"Just ask," he stated with a grumble, licking at the inside of his maw in irritation.

Her features lifted to him with appreciation. "Why? I don't mind doing this for you."

"Because I cannot sleep the day away and keep you from doing the things you wish. There is little to do in my cave, and you miss the sun when you help me rest."

I do not want to keep her in the dark. Linh should glimmer in the light, and not be snuffed out within his cold, watery cave.

"Maybe I could do this in the afternoons instead, then?" she asked as she knelt. She fiddled with the sewn-on leaves of her pink dress.

I am surprised she chose to wear this today, after last time. Once more, he cringed, knowing she likely heard that. "It looks nice on you. I am glad to see you trust me while you're in it." Then, before she could speak on it, as he'd only commented on her choice of clothing to reassure her, he said, "The afternoons may be better. Once the sun goes down."

She nodded, but in general, just looked weirdly awkward seated before him. Her heart was even racing, as if a hummingbird had taken flight within it. *Is she uncomfortable with my voice?*

"No!" she exclaimed, shoving her hands up. "I'm just... I'm not used to it." She self-consciously tucked a few stray hairs behind her ear. "It's really nice. Husky and smooth. I expected it to be deeper, and kind of..."

"Monstrous?" he asked with a chuckle, and her shoulders turned inwards. "It was much different before I died. It was deeper, growlier, and even my mother struggled to decipher what I was trying to say."

Even Aleron's voice was scratchy when he spoke to me.

That bat-skulled Mavka had been very pushy to talk, without knowing it just hadn't been possible. He'd climbed all over Nathair before eventually giving up to just lie next to him with his feathered wing resting over Nathair's coiled-up form.

Aleron had been seeking comfort in his new life in Tenebris, and Nathair willingly allowed it – rather than rushing into the lake to be alone.

"It's nice," she complimented.

Says the female who puts me to sleep with a song. He grunted and scratched at the side of his neck in annoyance.

"Do..." he started, lowering his arm to wave at her with his claws facing upwards. "Do you always sing the same song?"

Whenever she started, a numbness rode within, and everything became inaudible. All he registered was her scent and the melodic cry of her voice changing in pitch. It always sounded beguiling, like she could tame even the wildest of animals with it.

"No. Sometimes it's different." She shrugged. "My parents used to sing to me when I was little, but they weren't really lullabies. I just sing whatever comes to me, and when I can't think of anything, I just make up my own song."

I see. No matter, they all had the same impact.

"I'll be honest," she mumbled, rubbing her arms as if a chill had crept over her. She looked away, avoiding meeting his gaze. "It makes me miss home whenever I sing to you."

He tilted his head at that. "It does?"

Nathair wished he'd known that sooner. He would have been less inclined to have her sing to him if it made it more difficult to gain her affections.

"I would have sung to you regardless," she stated, as if she'd picked up the stray thought. "It helps you, and... I want to give back for all you have done for me."

Nathair didn't know what to think, nor to say.

He had no soothing words, nothing that could make her feel better. He could offer her a condescending head pat, but that was beneath him. He didn't intend to do anything that could incidentally convince her to leave, but he also refused to pressure her to stay.

Their relationship was built on the foundation of nothingness, because there *had* to be nothingness from his side. No pressure, no devious plot – at least not yet. She needed to feel in control, without realising she had very little of it.

He didn't think this form of manipulation was evil, considering his intention behind it was pure-hearted. Or, rather, had become so.

I want her soul. And that wasn't a decision he'd made lightly. He wanted all the feelings that came with it, and all the affection he hoped to give, as well as receive.

Her gaze darted off, and he sighed once more at his wretched thoughts.

"I *do* want to ask something," she stated quietly, before chewing the inside of her cheek.

A tingle began to trickle in the back of his skull. *She better speak fast. The fragments are returning to pester me.*

"Can I ask... *why* you won't help my people?"

His orbs flared in their orange hue, highlighting a small amount of his guilt when she fluttered those pretty eyelashes at him.

Yet, his response was direct, harsh, and steadfast. Nathair folded his arms and tilted his head to the side, coldly stating, "Why should I?"

"Excuse me?" she squeaked, her voice turning higher pitched.

"Why should I help them? What reason do I have to do so?"

She gave him a cute pout. "Because I asked nicely?"

"You could ask me nicely to kill you too. Should I just adhere to every wish you may ask of me?"

Linh flinched at that and cupped her hands to her chest self-consciously. "Well, no. But... they're good people. They deserve to be helped. We all do in this valley. You're so strong that if you went between the mountain peaks south of here and destroyed the main bandit camp, you would save us all."

"I could do that. I very easily could rid you all of this problem," Nathair stated, tilting his head the other way. "But the question still remains. Why should I? Why should I help humans when, given the chance, they would turn on me simply because of what I am?"

"T-they wouldn't!" she yelled, throwing her hands up defensively. "I would tell them that you're there to help."

His laugh was dark and filled with malice. "Ah, so they would need *convincing* to spare me? Did you not just say they were 'nice,' Linh? If I were to crawl my way into your village, they would accept my help and, once I did, could turn around and attempt to capture me, stab me in the back."

She opened her mouth to refute him, and Nathair let out a sharp, maw-snapping snarl.

"Humans are unkind creatures, little female." He lifted his hands, his claws facing upwards, before he fisted them. "I have *seen* them be vile. They steal, they lie, they murder, they..."

He didn't dare utter his final word, and he made sure his mind didn't echo it. But she seemed to understand anyway, and her features drooped and grew ashen.

"They think of me as a monster, when their hearts drip with malicious selfishness. You want my help, but if I needed it, would they come to aid me?"

"I would be there to make sure they did," she argued. "I know my people. I even know the people in the eastern part of the mountain ranges. We're good people, Nathair."

"So are Demons," he bit out.

Her eyelids flickered in surprise as her jaw dropped. "Pardon?"

"Demons can be good as well. I've heard of it, not just here, but in another world. There is no difference between humans and Demons to me. Both are cruel, both can be good-natured. Should I side with the Demons just because they can be 'kind' and band with them to fight against humans, your species, instead?"

"I-I don't understand, Nathair. What are you saying?" Linh

shook her head, struggling to digest this new bout of information he was sharing.

But he knew it was true. Weldir had told him of everything that happened here, and the trickles of information his mother, the Witch Owl, had managed to gather on her own in Nyl'theria, the Elven realm. Nathair had been gifted so much knowledge of the outside worlds, and never thought he'd ever need it.

He'd been wrong, and now this female sat before him, asking him to be selfless.

"I am a monster, Linh." He placed his hand on top of her hair and tilted her head back. He cradled it in his claws, being gentle when he could crush her skull with little effort. "I am hated by everyone and everything. Just because you have decided to see me as your saviour, does not make me a holy being. I am violent, I am depraved, and I am *tired*. I have suffered enough, and the wars of humans are not mine to fight."

"Is there really nothing I can do to convince you?" she whispered from beneath his reaching hand.

He slipped it down the side of her face and brushed his thumb up and down her cheek. He took in the softness of her supple skin, how smooth it was, its gentle warmth. Then he admired the cute, rounded edge of her ear before touching the ruby gem dangling from her lobe.

"I am unstable, little nightingale. I would only do more harm than good." When she didn't respond, not even a twitch of a muscle or a softening gaze, he asked, "Did you hear that?"

He received no answer.

He huffed out a sigh and spoke with his hands. "My voice is gone, so I will say it again. I am u-n-s-t-a-b-l-e. I would only do more hurt than good." Then he added, "I am of no help to anyone. I may turn on you or your people should I try. I cannot even be with Mavka, Linh."

Her brows drew together to frown at his hands, before her eyes rose to his skull. "Your own kind?"

"I don't know why your presence eases me, but you have done so from the beginning," he admitted as his shoulders drooped. "Before I found you at my pond, I was much more violent. The day on the beach was a r-e-o-c-c-u-r-i-n-g issue that happened every day."

"I didn't know that." Her eyes bowed in sympathy for him, and he tried not to be annoyed at that. "I'm so sorry. I wish there was more I could do for you."

Why doesn't she see how much she has done for me already? These past few weeks had been like heaven to something with such a twisted mind as him. He'd been able to *sleep.* He'd also been able to avoid his fragments for the most part unless *she* slept. Only then would they usually pull him under, as if he needed her to flit and dance around in his senses to keep him steady and focused.

That relief... if he'd been a softer being, may have made him weep.

"As much as I wanted to meet my b-r-o-t-h-e-r-s – brothers – in my return to life, I worried for them and their brides. I do not wish to harm them, nor have them h-a-t-e me for things I cannot control. They would not forgive it if I accidentally hurt one of their brides or ate them in a rage. I am a big Mavka, I am strong, and I have much humanity. I am dangerous, and my tail means I can i-m-m-o-b-i-l-i-s-e and kill another of my kind with ease."

The only reason Merikh managed to win against me was because of his echidna spines. He was the one Mavka Nathair couldn't hold.

Much like Nathair, Merikh's outside was just as monstrous and dangerous. He was a ball of blades, something Nathair couldn't stand wrapping his body around.

As much as Nathair trusted Linh, he realised then that his trust only ran so deep. *I do not want to tell her how my kind... die, in case she leaves me.*

He would not be the reason one of his kind might materialise in Tenebris, the afterworld. His brothers were breeding, and Nathair didn't want to be the reason a young, mindless Mavka had their skull crushed. The idea left him feeling hollow.

He knew how it felt and wouldn't wish it upon any Mavka. His trust in humans was, justifiably, low.

"I came here for a r-e-a-s-o-n – reason," Nathair continued. "I came to this part of the world to be away from my kind, from humans, and to be near the beach. I..."

He paused when he realised his hands were beginning to shake. He was trembling because the future he'd decided for himself was unravelling due to this female before him. It was still a possibility, and it was a saddening one.

Sucking in a calming breath through his nose hole, he let it out with renewed strength.

"I had planned to see if I could fight the fragments on my own. I found my pond, and this cave, by accident, but I chose to remain for a reason."

He'd originally slipped inside the pond to escape his mother pointlessly mothering him like a weakened baby bird. She had been undoubtably kind since his return, and what did that do for her? *I attacked her multiple times.* All due to his fucking fragments.

And there was little Weldir could do. He'd merely saved his female by calling her back to his realm before Nathair could eat her, and likely his siblings she carried beneath her cloak.

He'd gotten a little better on his own. He controlled them better in the few months since he'd forced his family's departure. Eating a few humans seemed to have balanced him a little more. *It isn't enough.*

"Why did you choose it?" Linh asked when he didn't continue.

He hadn't realised he'd looked away and just placed his hand over his chest because it was hurting.

"To leave," he signed, bringing his sight back to her, and he hated the blue that swirled in it. "The world is v-a-s-t. I have eaten the souls of humans who come from other lands. I planned to leave if I could not fight this, and find a place to r-e-s-t-a-r-t. To swim in the ocean until I was l-o-s-t – lost, and let it be my life, find what treasures lay on the ocean floor. My only e-n-e-m-y would be the s-h-a-r-k-s and the Demons, and it meant I could not harm anyone that did not deserve it, humans i-n-c-l-u-d-e-d."

"Y-you were planning to leave?" she asked, her voice breaking an octave.

Nathair shook his head. "Nothing is set in rock."

Her dark brows furrowed. "What do you mean?"

His orbs deepened in their blue hue. "I cannot answer that without breaking my p-r-o-m-i-s-e – promise – to you."

Her brows furrowed again, and her soft lips pursed along with them. "Your promise?"

"My answer could be considered m-a-n-i-p-u-l-a-t-i-v-e," he signed.

"B-but it's not meant to be, right? I won't take it that way." She looked up at him expectantly. When he didn't answer, she hooked her pinkies together. "Promise."

He waited to see if there was truth in that, but what point was there in hiding the facts? It was how he felt, and likely what he would do.

"Will you stay here with me if I help your people?" When her lips parted, as if in surprise, he didn't like that her next words were likely to be a garbled mess of unsure. "T-r-u-t-h-f-u-l-l-y, what point would there be in your staying? You s-e-e-k to feel safe. If I destroy everything that makes you scared, you have no use for me. I will no longer matter."

"That's not true, Nathair," she stated, her eyes crinkling in sadness. "You're making it sound like I don't feel anything for you. I care deeply for you, and you mean more to me than you seem to even realise. My feelings for you are not hollow, Nathair, and I wish you wouldn't think that."

"But is it enough?" he asked, his usually steady fingers twitching in uncertainty. "My home is here, in this cave, where I cannot hurt anyone. You miss your people, your family, your home. Is what you feel for me more than your desire to return to those things?"

"That's not fair," she cried, licking at her lips.

He let out a soft growl, and his gestures became aggressive. "You promised!"

She flinched and then nodded. "I... I don't know. This feels like it's moving too fast, and I'm scared." Despite her bubbling tears, she did meet his gaze. "W-would you come to my home with me?"

The tension bunching his muscles eased a little. *She wants me to go with her?*

He'd already stated why he was afraid to be near his own kind, let alone humans who could smell of fear or blood – although that would be mostly nullified if she gifted him her soul and removed his hunger. But the fact she'd even *offered* it... proved he'd been wrong.

She does hold me in her heart.

Perhaps a small piece, but enough to ask him, a Mavka, a literal fucking monster, to greet her people by her side. Would she have done so proudly? Would she have held his hand and said he was her partner, or even a friend?

He wanted to. If that was the answer, then he wanted to go with her.

"I cannot. I will kill your people by accident," he signed. "If you do not remove my hunger, there will only be d-e-s-t-r-u-c-t-i-o-n where I go. Even if you do, I may harm you, or someone, due to my fragments."

"But if you clear out the mountain springs, we could stay there. It's currently filled with Demons, and no human dares go near them or into the cave systems, but it's right near my village."

Well, that sounded dangerous for her people. Demons inhabiting a place so close to their village only made him wonder how they'd all survived so long.

"What if I slip into a fragment while I am near your people?" He took in a long, calming breath once more, just to steady himself and stop his hands from shaking. "What if you change your mind, Linh? You may find another male, one that is pretty like you, and is kind to you. I am a Mavka. I have a skull–"

"I know what you are, Nathair!" she shouted, her eyes clenching shut and her fists bunching. "Why do you keep stating it like I care? I've already told you how I feel about your exterior. T-this morning, I even tried to worship it my own way, so please stop referring to yourself as what you are, like I need *reminding*. I can see you, have seen you, have even touched you, and have desired you since the beginning, even when you were a little scary."

His head reared back in surprise. With her little hands balled into fists and her eyes clenched shut, she'd roared her words. It only made him swallow the truth of them with a heavy lump of emotion.

But it wasn't enough.

I am not human. He couldn't escape this nagging worry that if he were to travel with her to her people, she'd realise just how much of a monster he was. Right now, he was comforting, he was safe.

When she felt that again, what use was he? There were other males, ones like her, ones that didn't have voices screaming at them from inside their heads. Ones who had soft flesh, and two legs. Who could give her the kisses she obviously sought whenever she lathered them over his skull.

As I said to her, I am not a holy being. And his orbs shifted to dark orange in crushing guilt when he realised just how much he selfishly wished to keep her. Enough to separate her from her people forever, enough to not give her the chance to realise how odd their pairing was.

This is doomed to fail.

He hated that. He hated that he could see how deeply she wanted to protect her people, and would likely resent him when he continued to deny this wish. He hated that no matter what he did, whether he helped them or not, she would eventually go back to humankind. Nathair doubted he, and what he could offer – this life – would be good enough for not just her, but *any* human.

Being with her own kind was not unjustified, but this relationship just wouldn't work otherwise.

He also hated that he... didn't care.

As he'd said to her, if he could not have her, he would like a taste of her. To be someone she remembered fondly in the future, as someone she had temporarily desired, and someone who may have helped... *heal* her. Someone he, in his own selfish way, hoped she regretted leaving behind.

I want her for as long as she wants me, and then more. His heart radiated with tender affection and a sickening cold pang.

"You promised that you would take my plans as what they are: truth. If you do not stay, I do not think I will be able to fight my fragments on my own. I worry about how much they will crush me in your absence."

He worried they would return tenfold and obliterate him from the inside out. They'd tortured him more violently than ever when he'd returned to life. He kept wondering if her being here meant he would need to restart.

Her lips trembled as she took in his words. Nathair revelled in the heartsick he could see in her expression because it was proof he *meant* something to her.

"It will not be long before I leave." If it wasn't for her, he would have been scouring the bottom of the ocean by now.

She opened her mouth to say something, only to shut it. Her sweet tears, all for his sake, doubled in their strength. "But what if I change my mind?"

His head tilted. "It will be too late."

He just hoped it wouldn't be. That, once again, he was wrong, and she came to love him so deeply that nothing else mattered.

"Let's not speak about this anymore," he signed, before leaning forward to cup both sides of her head.

He nuzzled one of her wet cheeks with the blunted tip of

his bony snout, then licked across it. Linh gripped his horns to anchor herself and bumped against him as if to return his affection.

"Thank you for answering my questions, even though it upset me," she whispered, burying her face against his skull. She wrapped her arms around his neck to hold him tightly, and he slipped his hands around her back to do the same. "In retaliation... here, have all my tears."

She rubbed her puffy and wet face all over his. Nathair chuckled, accepting each drop with fondness. He was just pleased she'd decided to be cute with him, rather than be a sulking mess on her own.

When they pulled back, she had the saddest smile curling her lips. He did want to make it up to her.

Perhaps I can take her to the forest again.

TWENTY-THREE

"I wish we could stay a little longer," Linh stated with a sigh, noting how the shade of the cliff side was about to touch the water.

Apparently sea Demons would shift beneath the sand of the beach, creeping ever closer for when they could emerge in the shade of the afternoon. As the tide rose, they chased the night along with it.

"I'd love to see dusk," she continued, picking up a shell to see if she wanted to add it to her ever-growing collection. "It's one of my favourite times of day."

She turned to Nathair to show him her new piece. He cupped underneath her hand to inspect it, pretending to care when she'd already figured out he didn't like her shells. This big Duskwalker was sweet enough to lie about it.

She pushed one of her loose pigtails over her shoulder — since she'd restyled her hair again this morning. She had a feeling Nathair liked seeing the change whenever she washed it.

"I am feeling well today," he signed, before looking back at the cave entrance some metres away. "Would you like to see what the night sky looks like over the sea? If I do slip into a fragment, you can just hum for me."

After testing it a few times, they had come to learn that if Linh hummed softly while Nathair was in a trance, she could ease him out of it. Singing, apparently, was too abrupt, and he'd slip back into the trance like the voices were angered she'd interfered. Humming brought him out gently, and only quietened them to a point to where he could push them back on his own.

They battled them together.

Her lips curled with fondness, and her eyes flicked side to side between his orange orbs. "I would say 'What about the Demons?' but I already know that answer."

Nathair chuckled, and with a satisfying purr that had her tingling, signed, "Good, little nightingale." Then he turned to head back to the cave entrance. "Dusk will not be here for quite some time. We can put your shells away and feed you before then, and return when it is closer."

She eyed the fish dangling from his tail tip. Now that she had some herbs, wine, and even ginger root, she thought she may enjoy the taste a little better.

The return to his main cave was uneventful, as it always was, but she'd begun to notice the distinct difference in the quiet darkness. Rather than Linh holding his wrist for guidance, Nathair would place his arm across her back and hold her shoulder.

She thought if he was able to sink lower on his tail without falling due to his heavy torso, he may have held her side. *I would have liked that.* But she didn't mind this.

It felt like he wanted to hold her intimately without having to cart her up the tunnel like a weak-hearted, frail maiden. She wasn't one, and she appreciated not being treated as thus.

She also took him preparing her food as a gesture to take care of her, rather than that she was incompetent. Nothing he did made her feel less, and sometimes she forgot that she was so much smaller than him. He treated her as his equal in heart and in mind.

Humour crinkled the corners of her eyes as she took in his serpent skull staring upon her while she ate. *I kind of enjoy how he treats me like a princess.*

He even had a crown in his nest of riches, which he liked to place on her head. *I should try to make him dance with me, like in those fairytales and history books.* The idea of dancing with Nathair, who bore a tail instead of legs, was rather humorous.

I bet he would try for me, anyway.

Finishing her food, Linh moved to clean up, the patter of her bare feet echoing against the stone. Nathair just tossed the bones in his lake, apparently not caring where they lay. She turned to him, brushing her pants and dress of any potential dirt and herbs, and gave him a smile.

"Alright. Is it time to go back now?" She couldn't contain her excitement.

"Sure," he signed with a nod. "But first, I would like to teach you some words in case we need them. You must also make me a promise."

"Oooh, a promise," she teased, making him huff.

"You must promise that no matter what happens, you will not be afraid."

Oh, that was a lot more serious than she was expecting. "Of course. I'll have you to protect me, so it'll be fine."

"Yes, but..." He paused, only to lift one of his hands and brush it over the top of his skull as he looked away momentarily. He brought it back down with a sigh. "If we are attacked, you must remain calm. I doubt your singing will pull me from a rage. I can battle Demons, but if your scent of fear is overwhelming, I will turn on you. Trust that you are safe with me, no matter how frightening it may be. No matter what I must do to keep you safe."

Linh reached forward and grabbed one of his hands to hold it in both her own. "Don't worry, Nathair. I'm a big girl."

He pulled his hand away to sign, "You must also not interfere. Do not try to help or get in the way. If I hurt you with a stray claw..."

Linh put her hand up, pressed all her fingers together against her thumb, and flapped it open and closed. "Blah, blah,

blah."

Nathair dived forward and scooped her into his arms before she could get a single step away to escape. He opened his maw to clomp it against her neck and nibbled while being careful of his sharp lower jaw fangs.

"Oh nooo! I'm being eaten. Whatever shall I do?" Linh placed her hand against one of her temples and went limp as if she'd fainted.

Then she let her tongue fall out. He chuckled deeply and pulled back to grab the tip of her tongue, giving it a light yank.

"See. I told you it's not believable when you stick your tongue out," she stated with a laugh.

Like he wished to punish her, he shoved her over his shoulder so she was forced to lie over it. He slithered over to her belongings, and her black slippers were waved in her face.

"I don't need them if you're just going to be a brute and carry me the whole way, like I'm a sack of potatoes."

She squealed when he accidentally tickled her foot as he was shoving her shoe onto it. Once they were both on, he bent forward to tuck her fire-starting kit into her lantern and picked it up.

"Why are you bringing that with us?"

He didn't answer her, just headed into the dark opening of his tunnel. She shrugged.

"I have a question for you," she started, digging an elbow into his shoulder so she could put her chin on top of her fist. "If you were to wear pants, would you just wear one leg and let the other flap about? That would look silly then, wouldn't it? What about a skirt? I think you'd look cute in a mini-skirt. Should we get one made for you? With ruffles like your fins?"

When he paused in their descent just to laugh, Linh giggled along with him.

Linh proceeded to have a one-sided conversation, all of which was designed to humour them both on their travels.

When they were closer to the exit, he slipped her forward so she could fall into a cradle. He didn't put her down as he ducked into the opening where the damaged ship lay. She looked out beyond the alcove.

"Oh wow. Look how close the water has gotten now."

Usually it was a rather large distance to walk to the shoreline, but it'd crept halfway up the sand. The sky was dim, and she could tell it wouldn't be long until dusk coloured its expanse. The shade of the cliff side reached way past where the shore would normally be.

As Nathair climbed down the rocky ledges, Linh remained unafraid. Even when he exited the alcove and she spotted a legless Demon flailing in the shallow waves, she wasn't scared. Nervous, sure. Her heart did pick up at seeing it, but she felt safe in his arms even when he took them further onto the sand.

The legless Demon looked like some kind of furry sea animal and completely lacked any humanoid qualities. Two large fangs shot down from its mouth, and it roared as it bounced towards them on its flabby gut. Its red eyes never left her face.

Surprisingly, Nathair placed her feet upon the sand.

Moving so fast she only saw him as a blur, he spiralled around her until she was protected on all sides with two rows deep of tail walls. Then he placed his clawed hands on the ledge of himself, bent towards the Demon, and let out a horrible, high-pitched *hiss* with his venomous fangs on full show.

The Demon cowered a little.

Nathair got in her line of sight, just to shield her from it, and let out a loud, beastly growl. The sound of it had the little hairs on her body sticking up as a titillating shiver rushed down her spine to sucker punch her in the pussy.

With her thumbs pressing into her cheeks and her fingers wiggling up near her ears, she leaned to the side and stuck her tongue out at its retreating form.

Honestly, the Demon had been so small she was bigger than it. No wonder it wisely chose to back off.

The walls collapsed, and he scooped Linh until she was seated on top of him. Nathair placed her back against his front, but in a way that was obvious he could quickly sink her into the middle and make her stand like before. His tail tip would usually find a way to curl around her ankle, but she noted a few feet of it were straight and outside of their cuddle.

Before long, the west began to turn purple. She couldn't see the sun, as this beach faced due north and the cliff walls blocked its descent from view.

Still, it was beautiful. She looked up and soaked in the white clouds beginning to turn purple and orange, as if fire had broken out in the sky. A few stars twinkled, and even the waxing moon already shone through the last of the day.

She stared up at the moon for longer than she should have. *It's almost been three weeks since I met him.* Had it only been that long?

It felt like forever since she'd met Nathair.

She lowered her gaze to his skull and took in the way thin gold cracks glittered in the muted light of the sunset. Even with his orbs red as his skull followed what she suspected to be another Demon, he looked magnificent. His black scales had taken on a more red-orange gleam in the dusking light, and she petted a few in appreciation.

His head darted to her, his orbs shifting to dark yellow before he looked down at her hand placement.

"Oops, sorry," she said, taking her hand away from the side of his pelvis where a human's thigh would have started. She hadn't meant to touch so precariously to his groin, and she flushed when his seam clenched before she looked away.

Nathair returned to warding off Demons with hisses and warning rumbles.

Linh ignored all the scuttling she heard, and the way sand shifted around them. She did flinch just as dusk was settling and the chill of night began to truly creep in.

A *euk* sounded to their left, followed by lots of flapping as sand shifted and sprayed. Linh braved looking over his tail to see the tip of it caught around a Demon's neck while the rest of it had coiled around its arms and legs to keep it from clawing him. It flailed but made no noises as he strangled it.

Blood sprayed from its mouth when Nathair tightened his tail and crushed its body. He tossed it towards the approaching sea, and water writhed and splashed as Demons fed upon it.

"I have an idea," Nathair signed in the bright light of the moon shining down upon them.

She trusted him when he placed her hands over her ears, then covered the backs of them within his palms as an additional sound shield. Nathair let out a roar, the majority of it muffled through their combined press over her ears. He did it towards the sky, as if he wanted the full use of his lungs and throat.

His entire body rippled, to the point his frills danced from the strength of it.

Even she could tell it was a frightening warning to all those within earshot. It was so loud it vibrated her, and her body instinctually curled in aversion to the monstrous way it tingled her. It also, somehow, had her pussy spasming along with it.

She had no reason to be afraid. Instead, she bit her bottom lip, wondering if he were to produce such a beastly roar while they were being intimate, if her inner walls would ripple again and it'd make her come.

When he pulled away, the area became quiet.

A Demon sat nearby, watching them as if waiting for Nathair to lower his defences or place her upon the ground. All the rest had fled, and even the water had gone still except for a small crashing or gurgling wave here and there.

Nathair cupped the side of her head and placed his snout against her neck. He took in a deep draw through his nose hole, obviously sniffing her, and let out a quiver.

"Did you like that?" he signed, a chuckle nearly over-shadowing the small purr he let out.

"Nope!" She squealed the lie while shoving her legs together.

"I smell your arousal, Linh." He tilted his snout down her body and flicked his forked tongue towards her pelvis – *tasting* it in the air. "L-i-a-r."

She squirmed and shoved his head upwards with her cheeks so hot she thought she'd melt. "Aren't you supposed to be watching out for Demons?"

"I can do it again for you." When his purr mixed in with his damn chuckles, it came across as devious. "It's loud, so you would still need to cover your ears, but I only covered them as well because I thought you would find it frightening. Had I known your pussy would–"

Linh grabbed his hands and gave him the foulest glare she could muster. "S-stop it."

She wanted to watch the sky with him, not be a fidgeting, horny mess. *I shouldn't have let him teach me all his sexual signs.* Now he was able to use them against her!

Nathair rolled his head and fell back against his tail as he slipped his humanoid torso down. With his arms over the ledge of a wall made up entirely of himself, he patted at his chest.

She considered denying him, but easily gave in. With her back nestled between his torso and left arm, she placed her head against his rounded shoulder joint and leaned into him.

Daring to look over her shoulder, she connected with red eyes gleaming in the moonlight. The Demon was fairly big, and seemed to be one of the rare few who could withstand the moonlight for long periods of time. It relaxed whenever a large cloud passed over it.

Humans knew the moon reflected sunlight, but it was muted enough that it didn't give them a sunburn, and apparently not strong enough to harm many Demons. She shuddered before turning back to Nathair.

"It's just sitting there... like a creep," she stated with a bleurgh.

"I watch you all the time," he argued, making her eyes roll.

"Yeah, but I like it when you do." She hiked her thumb at it. "You don't do it with red eyes and an ugly face."

Thankfully all the brine in the air stopped any unpleasant smells coming from it. The wind also came from every direction, seeming to disperse it further.

"I know you like it when I watch you," he signed slowly, purposefully, and in a way that made her stare at the points of his claws. He licked at his maw purposefully.

How have I never noticed how... nimble *his fingers are?* Although his hands were large, she'd never noticed how precise he was with his signing before. How he could make her focus on just the minutest things about his claws, how a finger twitched, how grey some of his pads were. She took in the plumpness of his palms, and the natural lines in them. Even his protruding hand knucklebones seemed more pronounced.

He signs delicately, but with strong and direct movements. They were always assured.

She never realised that they were almost a perfect reflection of who *he* was.

It took her a moment to understand what he was insinuating before her face heated until she felt faint and wanted to expire. *Oh god! He's talking about when I touch myself in front of him!* Her mouth opened and closed, as her body tensed in embarrassed outrage.

He chuckled and shuffled her close.

"You are safe. That is all that matters," he signed to distract her, then placed his hand underneath her thigh to lock her to him.

She grumbled, even as a small smile curled her lips. *That's true.*

She lifted her gaze to the sky and took in the stars as she attempted to calm her bashful heart rate. Galaxy dust sprinkled like a rip in the faraway horizon. Linh had seen it many times, like most humans, but somehow it looked even more mesmerising over the beach. The ocean reflected it, causing stars to glitter in the water like an endless, vast world had fallen upon it.

The waves occasionally crashing upon the shore played a

melody of water meeting earth, and it was lulling. It felt cleansing, like if she were to let them smash into her, they could score her clean against the gritty sand and wash away all her worries.

I'm so glad he offered to do this for me. No human would ever dream of sitting out in the open world at night like this. In the time they'd been here, three Demons had come sniffing for her.

Yet, here she remained, protected.

Like she couldn't stray away from looking upon Nathair, she turned a smile to him. Only for it to fall when all she saw was the dark underside of his jaw. With a worried gasp, she leaned up.

His head shot down to her, his orbs orange before he tilted it in question.

"Sorry, I thought you fell into a trance," she muttered.

Nathair patted the top of her head before dragging her back against his chest. Then he lifted his arms around her, and she was forced to translate his signs while seeing them from his perspective.

"Don't worry. Like I said, I feel well today."

She wondered why. *We haven't been intimate since yesterday.* She hoped it was because the sleep she'd been giving him aided the weight of his mind. *He hasn't even fallen into a deep trance like usual.*

She'd even woken up to Nathair already aware and ready to be a playful jerk. *He's a bully.* He took every chance he could to tease her.

The arm she was leaning on moved, and a soft hand came up to hold her nape. She used to hate such a possessive and controlling hold, but she only arched for Nathair when he tickled his claws up her jugular on the opposite side of where his palm lay. Had he brushed just his fingertips up the central column of her throat, she may have thought he wanted her to sing.

I want to tell him. On her mother's side, Linh's family *did* have a secret they weren't supposed to share. One they all had to vow not to speak to another person when they turned eighteen, and they'd done so in blood and in magic.

But the vow we spoke said human *being.* Their lips were locked, regardless, and any attempt to write it was broken and blurry.

She'd said it aloud while she was by herself and faced no issue. *Nathair is a Duskwalker, so maybe it'll be fine?*

He caressed her lips, since she'd been chewing at them in thought, and it caused her to lower her gaze from the stars to his serpent skull. His orbs flared dark yellow, his way of silently asking what was on her mind.

"I've been wanting to tell you something," she muttered, holding his stare. "I'm not supposed to tell anyone. I'm not sure why, but I think it may explain why my voice makes you sleep."

Nathair tilted his head, and the white light of the moon glistened off his dark horns.

"Do you know about the humans who can use magic? We call them Priests and Priestesses, since they don't share anything about their identities, not even their faces."

"Yes." His following dark chuckle said he found humour in this for some reason. Once more, he refused to take his arms from around her and forced her to read his signs backwards. "They are all over this world. Many of my fragments have seen them and their m-a-s-k-s – masks. Why?"

"Well," she grumbled, fidgeting by playing with the seam of her dress. *Come on, please be a loophole.* She clenched her eyes with hope, and stated, "We are descendants of them, on my mother's side."

Oh wow! That was so easy. She really thought her lips would lock and she'd appear like she was throwing a silent tantrum.

Realising how easy this was going to be, the words spilled from her lips with excited enthusiasm. "Apparently my great-grandmother used to be a mask-wearing Priestess because she could wield magic, but my grandmother didn't have any power, so she wasn't allowed to stay with them. My people made her their leader because we have an excellent relationship with the masked occult."

"Are you saying that you think you carry magic in your voice?" Nathair asked, his hands slow, and somehow they looked... weighted. They sagged after each word.

"Maybe? I do think my mother has magic, since she's able to tend to plants better than others. I think it's why she became a doctor and a herbologist to begin with," she stated, squinting one eye as she lifted an arm to shrug. "Maybe as descendants, we have powers that aren't strong and come out in subtle ways that are unnoticeable. I just... I don't think it makes sense any other way."

Her brows furrowed deeply when he seemed to wince. His orbs shifted to dark blue, and he turned his skull away. As he stared off to the side, there was a forlorn way his shoulders drooped, and his body tensed subtly around her.

Even his hand resting upon his tail wall fisted.

"Nathair... what's wrong?" She thought stating all this would be helpful, like giving him an answer he may have sought.

"Nothing," he signed without even looking at her.

Linh lifted up and cupped the sides of his skull. She turned his bony face to her, and she moved her palms to hold the undersides of his segmented jaw. "Please tell me?"

He stared for a long while, gauging her. He sighed, and the strength of it billowed stray hairs back towards her high pigtails and the thin set of braids she'd wrapped around their bases for extra design.

"Those people are not human. They are not even from this world. They are called..." He paused, his fingers twitching. It was the first time she'd truly observed them appearing unsure. "I don't know how to properly spell it, as it has a special symbol in it."

He twisted until he laid his stomach over the wall of his

tail. Then he wrote the word 'Anzúli' in the sand, with the pronunciation 'An-zoo-lee' along with it.

"Anzúli? If they're not human, then..." Her frown returned, deeper than ever. "Then who are they? *What* are they?"

He twisted back to her before snapping his head to the side with a hiss. Linh froze when she looked in the same direction to see the Demon had dared to come closer while he was distracted. It backed up and up until Nathair's following growl ceased. She noticed a few sets of eyes coming from the dragging waves in the water, and she gulped.

She gave him her attention so he could explain.

"They come from another realm." He pointed an index finger upwards on either side of his skull, showing her a new gesture. "E-l-v-e-s are the reason for Demons being here, and they acquired the help of Anzúli" – she guessed the sign via context – "to aid humans as a form of sorry. All their people wield magic, and by the souls I saw of them in Tenebris, they only look partially human. It's why they wear masks."

"So, they wear masks to hide their inhuman features?" she asked, gaining her a sharp nod. "What do they look like then?"

"They have glowing eyes, and a third one upon their forehead." He tapped a claw against his brow.

Her lips parted and then drew back into a cringe. She cupped her forehead with horror. "Are you telling me I could have been born with three eyes?"

"They are mating with humans to keep their numbers. Unless you were to breed with another of their kind, I doubt those features will return."

"Okay," she rasped with widened eyes, brushing her stray hairs back. "That's kind of freaky."

Linh eyed him cautiously and considered pointing a finger at his bony face and telling him to stop spinning wild stories to bully her. He liked to play pranks, so that wasn't out of character for him.

He isn't joking. What he said made sense, and now that she thought on it a little deeper, their secrecy became more telling.

They didn't share their names, their faces, nor allow anyone bar themselves into their small temple within her village.

But all this, none of it answered her original question, and she realised he'd only told her to... distract her.

"Why were you sad, Nathair?"

His rolling growl, curt and ending on a huff, gave away that he was annoyed he'd been caught. He snapped his skull away, only to lower it and direct it upon her again. Then he hooked his pinkies, but in the opposite way a person would fingerspell the letter 's'.

"Promise," she answered, knowing it meant he didn't want her thinking he was trying to manipulate her.

"If your singing puts me to sleep through magic, then..." He paused, his hands sagging, before his orbs flickered back to blue. "Then no other human will be able to help me, unless they have Anzúli blood."

Oh. If I left... then he couldn't just find someone else. He would have to wade through many other people to find someone rare like her and then hope they would want to be with him. *But... I want to be with him.*

She also wanted to go home.

Being his songbird for his sake wasn't enough to make her stay, but... Nathair himself? His kindness, the way he made her heart swell with tenderness at his desire to be affectionate and care for her, his humour... all these things constantly made her want to throw her old life away. He was naughty. She could tell he *adored* being intimate, and his thoughts slipping from him when he had clarity gave away he was rather perverse.

Then there was his exterior. His monstrous, lip-biting exterior that she just wanted to laze around on top of and touch like he was a sensual virility god. The idea of slipping and sliding over him like how he did around her very body often left her tingling with desire.

Linh nodded to make sure he knew she understood and curled back into him to show it was okay. He played with the long, loose strands of one pigtail, and Linh picked at one of his scales while making sure it didn't hurt him. He never seemed to mind that she did this.

Do I really have to choose between him and my home? Why couldn't she have both? Why couldn't he just come with her and meet her village to see that he was wrong?

I know they would accept him, just like I do.

Just like she wanted to.

Linh knew he *very* much wanted her to mount him. The more she saw his cocks, and even gained the courage to touch them, the deeper her desire to connect with him became. She wanted them closer until they meshed into one being and she forgot about everything: the past, the present, and their uncertain future. What was right and what was wrong.

But it was more than that... If she finally gave herself to him like that, and he didn't change, or only became sweeter, more charming, it'd be proof that Nathair wanted more than just her body.

Despite already knowing the truth, her paranoia refused to ebb. How was she supposed to know the true depth of why Duskwalkers wanted to consume a soul? She'd had someone lie to her to get their way before. Pretty words that meant nothing in comparison to their actions.

The last two times, I felt fine after being intimate with him. She didn't feel unwell, or like her heart was about to vomit out of her mouth in anxiety.

Instead, she kept wondering how she could make things work, hoping they could resolve the obvious problem between them: where they would live – which couldn't be here in this cave.

I want him. Not just his body, but *him.* More and more, she wanted to be with him. She wanted nothing else to matter, even if there were things and people she couldn't let go of.

Then Nathair did something that made her heart weep. He slipped his hand over her stomach, grasped one of her nervous, fidgeting hands, and held it. It was a silent gesture, telling her she wasn't alone, even if she never voiced her trepidation.

He listened to her silence, as much as she did to his.

She gazed up at the stars once more, feeling a lightness in her heart. *I think... I'm ready.*

TWENTY-FOUR

I'm glad she enjoyed seeing the stars over the water, Nathair mused, as he climbed onto the top ledge of the ship's alcove.

Now that it was safe to do so, he placed her feet on the ground and bent down to lean on his elbows. He sparked her stupid fire rocks together until the oil-soaked cloth caught flames and then proceeded to quickly light the candle with the use of his claws so he didn't get burned.

He gave it to her to hold, knowing he would need his arms free to speak soon, and led them towards the entry of his tunnel. However, instead of turning left to return to his nest area, he took her southwest.

"Where are we going?" she asked, just like he knew she would.

"There is somewhere I wish to show you," he explained, taking in the subtle way his claws clicked in the darkness as he signed. "I made sure there were no Demons earlier today while you were playing in the sun."

"Ohhh," she stated, lifting the lantern towards him. "So that's why you left me to defend myself alone." She chopped the air with the side of her hand. "Do you know how many Demons I had to fight while you were gone?"

He chuckled at that, soaking in her lies. "Must have been a formidable fight, then."

She lifted her free hand to shrug. "I won, of course, and

tossed their bodies into the ocean before you returned, which is why there weren't any left for you to see."

She's cute when she's playful like this. It was nice to see her being this way on her own, rather than Nathair instigating it.

Nathair's chuckle deepened as his orbs flared bright yellow.

The deeper they went through the declining tunnel, the warmer it seemed to grow. He would have preferred to make his home in the bowels of this cliffside due to the heat, but he didn't like being trapped and cornered. His underwater lake gave him an escape, whereas down here had no exit.

They passed a small alcove, in which her lantern light showed nothing but vacant nests. They journeyed on. A few times in their travels, he had to squish himself down shafts and have her carefully slide down to him. They went further down below sea level, sometimes moving through twisting, narrowing paths.

She occasionally mentioned her ears popping, when going deeper made them pressurise. He did not have the same issue.

A cavern opened up. There was nothing notable here, just different coloured rocks and sediment, but he did show her the area to appease her curiosity. Then Nathair lifted off his tail to place her in a dark hole in the ceiling. Seated near the ledge, she shuffled back to make room for him with the lantern shining right in his bony face.

"Holy shit, Nathair," she rasped as he pulled up the heavy weight of his torso while pushing off with what remained on the ground. "Just where the hell are you taking me?"

You'll see, little female.

He'd been wanting to bring her to a special cavern for days, but... he hadn't trusted his lucidity. If his consciousness slipped in here, she would be utterly trapped in the dark.

He did truly feel well today, the voices not as pressing as usual. It was temporary, he knew this, but he was pleased nonetheless. Between her quieter hums, the sleep she often gifted him, and just Linh feeding him joy, he had plenty of energy for once.

Energy he hadn't felt in centuries.

He cupped the underside of her chin affectionately, his orbs bright yellow in appreciation for all she'd done for him, then lowered his face to hers. He opened and closed his maw to mock her silly question, since he had no intention of ruining the surprise.

Her cute, full, and pouty lips quirked with humour. "Is this the part where you hand me a shovel and tell me to dig my own grave?"

Nathair licked across those pesky lips, letting a single fork of his tongue press between them. Her soft moan in return was the sweetest sound, revealing how at ease she was in the dark with him, how much she trusted him. He continued to lead, and she came up beside him since it was wide enough for her to do so.

The night was early, and she seemed invigorated by all the movement and the adventure. A smile shone constantly, as if the very emotion behind it thrummed steadily beneath the surface.

Regardless of what happened between them in the future, he just hoped she remembered the beauty he was about to share with her.

The area opened into a large cavern that looked fairly similar to his main cave. An underwater lake reflected the low light of her lantern, but the water was even more blue, clear, and clean than his.

He gingerly took the metal handle from her and placed it on the ground. The air was light, but there was enough of it coming from the way they'd ventured to give them both oxygen, as well as what already lingered here. It was too deep beneath the earth for anything to grow.

"I don't understand," she said, her cheer falling. "I-I don't mean to be rude, but isn't this like where your nest is?"

The humour in his chest was evil. His surprise wasn't ready, and it would require his intervention.

"We swim," he signed, before waving his hand towards the

water.

The bottom of the lake was pitch black, and he doubted she could see what glinted on the bottom of it with her measly human vision.

"Ugh, really?" She groaned, letting her head fall back. "Another swimming lesson?"

"You swim fine now," he responded, leaning down to pick up one of her feet to remove her shoe, before doing the other. He then pushed up her pants until they were bundled around her knees.

"I... don't want to get in the water and be cold," she admitted, hesitating when he slithered backwards while clutching one of her hands to bring her with him.

He placed his palm over his heart and brought it to the middle of his sternum. *Trust me.*

Nathair slipped into the fresh water, and bliss had his scales puffing along every inch of his body. It felt so good it rippled his muscles until even his seam clenched and his nipples hardened.

He didn't pull her in; he just waited for her with his tail swivelling to keep him afloat in the deep water.

"Fine. Let me see how cold it is before I stupidly follow your reptilian butt in," she whined, just as she went to dip a toe in.

She gasped, only to shove her foot in. He caught her when she almost fell, not wanting her to enter the water fretting. He wanted this whole experience to be enjoyable.

"It's warm," she stated with a smile, her face barely an inch from his own as he pushed her back onto the ledge. "Like... *really* warm."

Nathair knew there was a reason for it, although he hadn't worked out the why. He also didn't care. The water was warm, blissful even, and she had no idea just how close she was to her people's mountain. At least... he believed so from his mental orientation.

The entire time, he'd been taking them southwest. He

figured the lake next to his nest eventually drained into this one in an underground network of tiny tunnels he couldn't access.

She backed up when he thought she would have climbed in to be with him now that she knew the water was agreeable. He tilted his head and forced his orbs into a questioning glow. He reached his hand up, claws facing upward, and beckoned her closer.

She gripped the bottom of her dress garment with tight fists. "I-I don't want to get my clothes wet," she grumbled.

Disheartened, Nathair lowered his hand in disappointment. *But I cannot show her without going to the other side.* He didn't wish to force her, but if she didn't get in the water, all of this was pointless.

To his utter shock, she lifted her dress off her body. When she pressed the bundled material to her chest, her softened gaze was shier than normal. He noted that her knees had knocked inwards, yet she still dropped the garment to reveal the white cropped undershirt beneath it.

Warmth, hotter than the water surrounding him, swelled in his chest.

He didn't believe his sight when she then pulled at the ties of her grey pants, and suddenly his mouth went dry. Nathair had seen peeks of Linh's creamy thighs, but only when they flashed at him yesterday with her pink dress and the day she first fell in his nest.

Which was why, when she lowered the material and kicked it off from around her knees, he lowered himself to drown his immediate purr. Her underwear was a strip of pale-green cloth, with two ties resting over her curved hips, and she looked like fucking *heaven.*

With his gills submerged, he also stifled his groan when pressure surged behind his seam with a desirous throb.

She looked so awkward standing there, barely clothed for him. Her knees were still knocked, and her arms had crossed to hide the fullness of her generous, weighty breasts and her pubic mound. Her flush was so deep it blotched on her chest and biceps.

But she looked so damn cute, with her long pigtails and curved yet petite body, that he considered her divine. Her breasts propped up by her arm offered more cleavage, and they sat above a narrow waist, wide hips, and perfect-looking thighs.

There didn't seem to be a mark on her, and her fawny skin reflected the glow of the firelight like a hypnotic dance.

Had she stripped completely, he may have taken it as an invitation, and he would have forgotten why he brought her here in the first place.

So, instead of trying to see if he could rut her like he *desperately* wanted to, he reached his hand out once more. He didn't need to ask her to trust him; he knew she did by the fact she was scantily and teasingly dressed.

Bring that little arse here, female, he thought, waving his fingers at her.

Linh came closer. As soon as she was at the edge of the water, she removed her hand from her pubic mound and slipped her palm in his. Nathair helped her to sit on the ledge so she could glide into the water with ease.

He didn't let her go, even when he swiftly dragged her to the centre of the large lake. Her underwear clung to her plump, round arse cheeks, and all he wanted to do was grab them both with his hands. They looked soft, had felt soft in his palms the occasional times he'd kneaded them, and he wanted to play with their moulding forms.

Just as he halted them, and was about to sign something, he had to sink his gills beneath the water again to drown out his groan. *Fucking hell. She should have kept her damn dress on.*

Her white undershirt was apparently so thinly made... it'd turned completely see-through. How was he supposed to keep his hungry hands to himself when her perky breasts were showing? Even her pale-brown nipples didn't look a shade different from how he normally saw them.

The garment was pointless, and now his cocks were threatening to push through his seam. Given his aquatic nature, he *did* have extra feeling around his seam within the water to know when or if he was about to extrude, but it still softened the muscles. This could become awkward at any given time, but he just hoped he could contain his control on his dicks and not ruin this for her.

With strain, he signed, "I need you to hold your breath."

Her lips tightened, but she nodded obediently. She did as he asked when he wrapped his arms around her torso, making sure not to grab her anywhere she would be uncomfortable. Her body slipped against his, and he drowned any sound that could come from him in the euphoria of it.

Her soft, sinful thighs nestling around the scales of his sides and hips felt divine. Just her breasts and bare abdomen against his scaled torso clamoured at him to bring her closer. Even the weight of her arms around his shoulders felt wonderful.

Ignoring all this, Nathair stopped swivelling his tail and let himself sink. The moment they were a foot below the water, he arched backwards to tip them upside down. The long length of his tail crested the water in a loop before he flailed it to dive.

Nathair saw well in the dark, but even he had to partially navigate by the vibrations of the water speaking back to him as he moved through a narrow tunnel. He protected her head, just in case he didn't see something jagged, and swam as fast as he could.

Linh clung to him, but she didn't need to hold her breath for long. Within seconds of passing through the sharp and deadly spiking walls, Nathair swam towards the surface.

Darkness greeted them, and her breaths echoed in the large cave. He chuckled from the way his orange orbs glinted all around them, so he directed his skull in a way that would minimise it before she could notice. After sputtering for a moment, she lifted her face to his.

"Okay... so now what?"

Since she couldn't see, Nathair lifted one of her hands and

placed it over her eyes. When he pushed away from her, she flailed in the water. She wasn't confident with swimming, so he steadied her and made her cover her eyes again.

"I'll keep them closed," she argued, while lowering her hands so she could use them to keep herself afloat. Nathair answered with a soft growl. "I promise!"

Fine. You better keep them closed. With a snorted huff, Nathair sunk once more.

He made an incision in his palm. Pressing it against a large and smooth edge in the ground, he waited for his magic to come to life. The moment it did, he shot to the surface to make sure Linh had kept her promise.

His heart sped up in excitement, and he softly poked her cheek.

She opened her eyes, only for them to immediately widen as she took in all the white quartz crystals glowing around her. Her lips parted as she gasped, and she turned, seeing that every part of the wall, the ceiling, and even the floor had crystal jutting from everywhere.

She looked down to where it was brightest in the water. It also had an orange glow due to his magic circle having the strongest reflection in the quartz shards.

"Oh my god, Nathair," she muttered quietly, as she sightlessly reached for him while gawking at every surface. "This is breathtaking."

He didn't drown his purr this time. Instead, he took her forearm and pulled her towards him until she crashed against his torso. It vibrated into her very hands, her arms, and her chest, and he nuzzled the end of his snout against her neck.

Lying back, he propped her against his chest, and she subconsciously mounted his waist as she looked up at the ceiling. Flaring both his forearm fins, he stopped them from moving too far as he used his tail to keep them buoyant.

"I can't believe something like this exists," she continued, and her surprise evolved into pure adoration.

Nathair observed the glow mirrored in her pretty brown

eyes, and his chest swelled at the way they glittered.

The red jewels dangling from her lobes glinted, only adding to the treasure before him. Her pink lips were parted in awe as she relaxed with him in a magical place so deep beneath the ground. Her long hair seemed darker while wet, and clung to her chest on one side to curl against a breast and highlight its fullness. Her dark lashes sparkled from the water, and the many droplets covering her reflected the light, *his* light, as much as everything around them.

When he removed one arm from the water, they slowly spun in a circle, and that seemed to please her more. Cupping the side of her head, he brushed his thumb back and forth beneath one of her eyes to touch her captivating face, and she didn't even seem to notice. He liked that she didn't; it meant his touch felt so natural to her that it didn't steal her attention from the mesmerising beauty surrounding them.

This cave, this place... he'd lingered here for a long time when he first found it. There was evidence of his violence if she searched for it; places he'd broken as he tore at himself when the voices were loud and refused to leave him be. Times when he tried to sleep, only to wake up writhing and in pain.

Every time he'd slipped back into lucidity, he allowed this place to fill him with hope and enthral him into a peaceful stupor.

There was even a large and flat prism in which four of himself could curl up to rest upon right near the ledge. Water trickled throughout the cave, and all of it led to the lake they floated in. The sound was soothing for an aquatic being such as himself.

It was one of the few reasons he'd been hesitant about leaving this continent before he met her. He didn't know if he'd find a place – untouched and not ruined by Demons – like this again.

I'll always remember her face in this moment, he thought, as he continued to caress it. *How I was allowed to come back here, and finally appreciate it in the quiet she gifts me.*

Even just her echoing breaths seemed to lull him, and his orbs bled with bright pink for the first time as he gazed upon her against his chest.

Part of him wished his magic would reflect the colour of his emotions, so she could see it in everything around them. So she could see... the way he adored her, as if this very cave was the inside of his heart and they lay within it.

I want it to glow in her eyes, like she feels it with me.

She did eventually turn her smiling gaze to him, and the tiniest dots of his pink orbs merged in with the mess of lights in her brown eyes.

"Even the cracks in your skull glitter," she stated softly, cupping the sides of his head. "You look really beautiful right now, Nathair."

A tremor racked his spine, and they sunk a little as it disturbed his swim. To keep them afloat, he flailed his tail faster, and they shot through the water. She giggled, and the sound had him sinking his head beneath the surface to escape the way it ripped at his heart with elation.

Resurfacing until only the back of his skull and horns were submerged, he kept his humanoid torso flat and moved them through the water. He directed with his arm fins, while using them to keep his dense and heavy torso from sinking as she partially knelt upon him.

He moved close enough to a jutting quartz, and she did exactly what he thought she might. She touched it.

"It's warm." She smiled down at him. "Can we take some of it home?"

Home? Nathair slowed. *Did she just call my nest, my cave, home?*

His heart doubled in its pace, and he nodded.

She could take whatever she wanted. If need be, he'd fucking claw through the very earth to bring her the biggest damn shard so long as it kept her content. So long as it kept her with him.

Because, with every waking moment in her presence,

Nathair knew he was losing his will. If she kept stealing all the pieces of his battered heart, she'd find herself trapped in it like this cave – without his aid in escaping.

His cocks were already half swollen behind his seam. Everything she did, everything she said, every tiny breath, had them jerking.

Needing to separate them before he did something foolish, like attack her with his growing need and affection, he took them to where the ground was a horizontal flat shard of quartz. He found something to hook his tail around to keep them up so he could use his arms.

He let his body and the wall of crystal behind her keep her steady, while ensuring she had space so she didn't feel trapped.

"Do you want to explore deeper?" he asked, pointing to the back of the cave. "There are other c-r-y-s-t-a-l-s and o-r-e."

There was more to be seen, although he would need to carry her through all this so she didn't potentially cut the bottoms of her feet. *There are even opals in a deeper chamber.*

She wrapped her arms around his neck with her lids low, and whispered, "No."

Linh shot forward and pressed her soft lips at the very centre of his segmented jaw – right where his tongue could slip forward with ease.

Fuck! Nathair's arm darted out next to her head so he could let out the aggression that suddenly burst within his muscles. He bashed the crystal ledge. He clawed it as he dragged their bodies closer to the wall and cupped the side of her head to keep her to him while also protecting it.

More, his mind groaned. *Just a little more.*

His tongue flicked out so fast she didn't have a chance to stop it from penetrating past her lips, and he whimpered at the sweet taste of her. She moaned in answer and parted her lips, willingly allowing him deeper. Nathair took it and slid more of his forked tongue inside to forcefully brush it over the top of hers.

Claws gouged into the quartz as his pink sight deepened

into purple, and he huffed against her lips moving against the bone of his maw. Her legs wrapped around his waist as he squished her against the wall, her arms clinging to his neck and her breasts pressing against his scaled chest.

S-shit, he groaned, jerking in the water as he fought against the hold he had on his body. *Shit. If I don't stop, I'm going to extrude.*

Nathair pulled back with strangled chokes. They were nullified the moment she yanked him back into the kiss again.

Fuck, Linh. He quickly gave in as his seam parted and his cocks and tentacles came out in a mess; his profound lust and the heat of the water disorientated his insides. Nathair licked across her tongue as the pressure within released and he panted against her.

He gripped her thigh to shove her against his waist. When she didn't flinch or react, he grabbed her arse and squeezed. She *moaned,* and he knew he was irrevocably *fucked.*

She was half naked against him and kissing him. All he could think was: *I want to fuck her so hard I split her in two.* He wanted to shove into her sensual, feminine body until her mind broke and she did nothing but scream in relief.

With his claws latched onto the crystal and keeping them together, he released her head to sign, "Stop." Stop as he twirled the forked tips of his tongue around her flat, softer, singular one. Stop as she danced it with his, as her lips moulded and brushed the bone of his maw like he had lips to play with. Stop as every urge, every instinct, demanded he cut the crotch of her underwear, rise up, and slam one of his cocks inside her.

"Nathair," she moaned in an airy tone, giving him just a sliver of a chance to back his head away from her.

He obtained a second of relief before she lowered and dipped her head to lick across his gills.

Once more, Nathair signed, "Stop," but he realised her fucking eyes were closed.

His cocks swelled and released bubbles of precum when

she sucked and kissed the sides of his neck, over the flaps that tickled his lungs and around his heart.

With a curt whine bursting from him, he rose up while grabbing a fistful of both her hair tails and yanked her head back. Her eyes, half-lidded and almost delirious, peeked up at him.

Fucking stop! He signed both words, and her lips pouted into a devious curl. She was killing him with her wiles, and she didn't seem to realise how much a Mavka didn't like to be beaten.

A hand descended their bodies, and he instantly bucked into her soft, wet palm when she grabbed the head of a throbbing cock. *Oh fuck, so soft.*

"Inside me, Nathair," she rasped, before licking at the seam of her mouth. "I want you inside me, *please.*"

His entire body pulsed. With the last tether of control over whatever sanity he had left and his hand shaking, Nathair asked, "Are you sure?"

Shit, even his fingers were trembling.

She caressed her free palm down the side of his skull. "The fact you asked means I know I'm making the right decision."

Nathair released a growling purr as a heavy pant fell from his maw. He released her arse so he could pull on one tie of her underwear, then the other, and let it slip away to wherever he would find it later. His cocks thrummed in unbearable anticipation, as weeks of need made him feel like they'd turned as hard as the very quartz around them. They jerked so much, pressing apart and curving slightly from being this engorged, he felt the vibration of their movements against his scales and frills.

Sheathing the claws of his right hand, he grabbed her arse while dipping his fingers into the slickened slit of her pussy. Even in the water, she was so wet that her arousal clung to her.

He slipped his middle finger up until he petted her clit.

"You want me inside your pussy, Linh?" he signed with one hand, hoping she understood the half-gestures. His purr deepened when she bit her bottom lip and nodded, only to let out a shallow rasp as he penetrated her with his finger. "Fuck, you're so wet for me. If you wanted me this badly, you should have just mounted one of my cocks while I was swimming."

Nathair pumped before quickly adding a second finger to stretch her in preparation.

"Hurry," she pleaded, her long nails clinging to his shoulders.

"All you would have needed to do was place your cunt over my seam, and I would have emerged straight inside you."

"Oh gods. *Please!*" she cried, her pussy clamping around his fingers.

"Off," he signed, pulling at the bottom seam of her undershirt.

When she struggled to fight the clinging material, Nathair helped her and threw it into the water.

He removed his fingers, thinking two should be enough to prepare her so she didn't feel pain, but not enough to take away how he planned to stretch her tight little cunt. Because, as much as he would like to remove all possible aches, he *wanted* her to feel him spreading her.

Nathair lifted and held onto the ledge to prop himself up while keeping her neck-deep in the water. With her lathering kisses against his pectoral muscles, her hands against the sides of his back, and her arse in his palm, he lined up one of his purple cocks.

He nudged the hole of her pussy. Her slick was removed by his earlier prodding, but his cocks were covered in thick lubricant. She lifted her knees and spread them further by pressing her feet against his sides when he sunk the partially pointed tip inside.

Heat touched him, and his entire groin spasmed in pleasure just from the meagre contact.

He'd meant to enter her slowly; it's what he'd always planned. He'd intended to be gentle, and good, and not let his excitement get the best of him.

However, the moment his groin spasmed, his cock jerked and his hips along with it. She gasped as he mounted her halfway, fast and hard, and a curt whine burst out of him like a fucking scream. *Hot!*

His claws unsheathed and stabbed into her arse and the crystal behind her. *Fuck! Hot. She's so hot inside.* He tore at the quartz as he tried not to smash his way deeper inside her until that blissful heat swallowed every inch of his cock.

His body temperature was too low, and he needed her to cuddle him with hers while he lost his ever-loving mind.

She did tighten around him, but she was quick to soften despite the snug fit. Linh bucked against him, using her feet to draw him in, and Nathair's head tilted back. He slipped further in until he bottomed out inside her.

His mind dissolved into goo, just as his cock wanted to melt within the heat of her pussy. The other nestled right against her clit, and when he pulled back only to shove forward, he grazed it.

She moaned as she reached up to grab a horn, yanking his head down. This little female then proceeded to use his horn as an anchor to fuck herself with his cock like she desperately needed it.

Unable to deny her beckoning, Nathair began pumping inside her.

"Yes," she cried, lathering his collarbone in kisses. "Oh god, Nathair. I've wanted this for so long."

The groan that fell from him tasted of venom. With the way his fangs had extended down to press against his tongue, it flooded his mouth. He swallowed it as he buried the end of his snout against her hair and wildly huffed against it. He gave her measured thrusts, trying not to go too deep or too hard.

Her sweet pussy clung, rippling around him like his coils did to his prey. Each time her walls spasmed and clenched hard, his dark-purple sight flickered with black in bliss.

From his cock, tingles spread throughout his groin to clutch at his muscles surrounding it. Even his hip bones threatened to disintegrate in her warmth, only making him want to be more ruthless with her as it radiated to his spine. She was so snug, so soft and plump.

Fuck, she feels incredible inside.

Yet the way her body caressed his scales, her thighs brushing over them, had him aching for more. Her breasts slipped up and down his chest, and he could feel her hard nipples gliding over him. Her nails bit into his shoulder, threatening to pluck a few scales from him, and he wanted her to dig harder.

I want deeper. Already he could feel his fingertips buzzing with the desire to lance her abdomen so he could dig into her body until she mounted him to the base. So she could swallow both his cocks with a moan. So she could claim him fully, and give him free rein to fuck her like the rabid beast he wanted, *needed*, to be.

Nathair wanted to fuck like a Mavka, a monster, like the horny creature she'd twisted him into becoming. He'd panted after this female almost every second of every hour for weeks.

Her little cries made him want to pump into her faster until all she could do was scream and shatter the quartz around them. Yet the anchor for his tail was deep, everything else too small for him to latch onto properly. His frills did little around his hips, as they ended shortly above them. He could only pump slow, with Linh attempting to aid him as she moaned against his chest.

"Faster, Nathair," she pleaded hoarsely. "Please, I'm so close."

I cannot, he thought, yanking her arse down to meet his thrusts, only to realise that made him hit deeper, harder, despite aiding in speed. He immediately stopped when she cringed. She softened for him the moment he backed up.

His cock was too long for her. He tried tilting her hips and changed the angle of his thrusts to make it feel better for her. To hit the places she needed until she exploded for him. For his four tentacles to do more than brush against her inner thighs rather than clutch them together.

Then she did something that had his claws flicking crystal dust everywhere as he gouged into it with a horrible, bubbling snarl. His orbs flared bright red when she licked and sucked his gills at the same time. *Fuuuck!*

I cannot do this in the water. Not like this, not until she swallowed him whole – then it wouldn't matter how slowly he pumped when he could just take her hard.

With his snarl never ceasing, Nathair yanked his cock from her. She gasped, only to make a weird, strangled noise when he clasped her tightly and leapt out of the water by a violent flick of his tail.

Placing her against the flat quartz, Nathair slammed his hand down next to her head as he grabbed her thigh with the other. He gave himself the barest glimpse of her pretty, pink folds, her loosened entrance, before he dragged her across the ground while lifting her. Linh's back arched as he mounted her as deep as she could take him, and his groan was so profound it was palpable as it shuddered out of him.

He thrust fast, and his damn heart almost gave out in rapture. It deepened when she tightened, strangling his cock, just as the wicked scent of her arousal finally pervaded the air. It sparked on his tongue, in his nose hole, until it tickled his lungs.

Nathair thought she may be coming, but she gave no moan. His hips immediately stilled when the tang of fear mingled with her arousal.

Lowering his skull, he looked down at her beneath him. Her face was contorted, her eyes clenched up, with her hands balled-up above her breasts.

Fuck, his mind spat out. *Shit.* Fuck.

He'd scared her.

Dark orange morphed into his sight as he took in the way he was clutching her thigh and forcing her legs apart. How he towered over her much smaller form awkwardly bent to meet his higher thrusts. How the little female trembled in uncertainty beneath a monster, who had promised she could trust him.

A monster who had never done this before, despite the knowledge his fragments had shared. He'd been arrogant in thinking he was master of his control – even when he constantly lost the battle to an ill mind.

As he lowered her and let her thigh go, he tried to rein himself in with calming breaths through his bony nose hole.

Gentle, you idiot.

TWENTY-FIVE

Don't freak out. Don't freak out, Linh repeated like a mantra, while absolutely freaking out.

Even though the Duskwalker stopped, she couldn't bear to open her eyes to see the shadow of someone above her. When he released her thigh and let her arse touch the ground, she was still pinned on his cock, and it felt like her stomach had knotted around it.

A flinch ripped through her when he slipped his hands, claws sheathed, beneath her naked and exposed body. One cupped the back of her head and neck, cradling it gently, while the other clasped her hip as the arm supported her back. She felt the swirl of warm air as he rolled them until he was beneath her, and her heart lost some of its frightened speed.

The anxiety still lingered, and she didn't know how to unclench her muscles to continue. *I-I don't want to stop.* She wanted this, even if he'd suddenly become too aggressive, making her feel trapped and pinned beneath him.

She did kind of wish he'd removed his cock, and that she wasn't lying on top of the other.

I made it awkward, she thought, tears welling and squeezing through her clenched eyes.

A knuckle brushed her cheek, trying to convince her to open them.

"I-I'm—" Before she could finish, his hand pushed over her

mouth.

Her eyes flung open wide as her skin crawled from him doing so, only for the sensation to ease when he removed it. Her gaze connected with his orbs, just as he circled over his heart. *He's saying sorry instead.*

Yep, she made it awkward! *It's not his fault.*

Well, it kind of was his fault, but she couldn't blame him for getting excited. Hell, she'd been clawing at him like she was in heat, wanting him to go faster, harder, anything to get her to crash into a mind-boggling bliss. He'd given her both, but the position had just been too much.

The glow of all the quartz around them became too bright and seemed to burn against her exposed skin.

Linh went to sit up and remove his cock so she could feel more secure, but he held her hips down with one hand. He wagged his finger at her, and disbelief filled her. She expected betrayal to sway through her, but it never did.

"Who am I?" he signed, tilting his head.

"Nathair?" she responded quietly, her brows narrowing in uncertainty.

"What am I?"

Despite her growing confusion, her pussy clenched around him as she said, "A Duskwalker?"

"That's right. Keep your eyes on my skull. Whose cock do you have inside you?"

Her frown deepened. "Y-yours?"

"How many do I have?" To give her the answer, he wiggled his index and middle fingers at her with a devious, quiet chuckle.

Linh realised he was trying to ground her in the moment again. She softened around him, against him, as her stomach unknotted itself with every question. He would never know how much she needed him to do this, to laugh for her, and make her fears about ruining this fade.

Tears of relief bubbled as she stated with a fucked-up giggle, "Two."

"What colour are they?" He tapped a curved black claw against the bottom of his empty eye socket, pointing below his purple orbs.

"M-my favourite colour?" she tried to tease.

He released a small purr in appreciation, and the sound vibrated through her breasts squished against him. It tickled her nipples, making her want to scratch them against the scales of his pectoral muscles.

"Your pussy is very hot and soft inside," Nathair signed, giving her a desirous pant. "I feel like you're trying to melt me within you." Then he flicked his tongue forward. "You smell and taste nice too. I couldn't sense these in the water."

Linh nibbled her bottom lip, the compliments doing wonders. Her legs lost their tension, and they slipped down his sides when she parted them slowly.

"Sorry for frightening you." He cupped the side of her head briefly before drawing back to sign properly. "I am very horny, and you feel amazing. I want to fuck you hard, deep, and fast until all you can think about is the way I feel inside you."

A muffled moan clogged in her throat at the idea, and her pussy clamped in want around his cock. He answered her with a groan, incidentally slapping both her arse cheeks when his shaft swelled within her. Only then did she notice just how much he was quaking beneath her, and how his tail had coiled around itself until she thought it'd knot itself.

"Fuck, Linh," he signed after letting her arse go. "Your little cunt is so tight, and it feels amazing when you do that." Wetness returned swiftly, and Nathair's tongue flicked forward before it drooped between his parted jaw segments. "What's my name?"

"Nathair," she whispered, then let out a soft moan when he snapped his hips – drawing back, only to fill her to the brim swiftly.

"My name?"

"Nathair," she cried out when he thrust at the same time.

He groaned as he slowly began to pump up into her.

"Name?"

She stuttered it out as pleasure bounded its way into her being. The cock between them petted her clit with each movement, clamped between her pussy and the tentacle that managed to keep it in place. Linh began to release raspy moans as his cock hit deep, but not hard, and gouged against her G-spot with accuracy.

"Who is inside you?" Nathair signed shakily, his claws twitching, while his rich voice echoed at the same time like a quiet trickle.

"You are," she cried.

"That's fucking right I am," he quietly said out loud with a growl, and by the lack of hand gestures, she knew it was a thought.

Nathair grabbed her thighs with both his hands, keeping her hips locked in position for his increasing thrusts. Her breasts jiggled as they slipped against him, while her abdomen constantly brushed the scales of his.

Oh god, he's inside me. And she could feel the way his cock was formed. The tiny nodules bubbled on their way in and out, while the slightly tapered head pinpointed spots. It nestled inside her, and she hugged him to her as she absorbed it all.

She'd enjoyed the closeness of their bodies in the water. When he'd been above her, she'd hated the separation, but this? She rubbed her cheek against his chest, messily kissing it to show how much she adored him.

Within seconds, rekindling desire tipped over, and she let out a high-pitched cry. Her nails and fingertips dug into what she could reach of his back, her head snapping back. Her pussy milked his cock with hot squelches as she came.

Pupils dilating, the pretty glow of the quartz around her faded into a blur of light.

"Oh fuck," Nathair groaned beneath her, his head stretching back until the tapered ends of his horns came up the sides of his neck. *"So tight, so fucking wet. That's right, little female. Come over my cocks for me, let me feel it."*

Feels good. Feels so good, Linh's mind repeated when he began to wildly thrust. His second cock constantly grazed the lips of her folds, as well as her sensitive clit, and her body sparked.

She collapsed against him, her entire being spasming as her eyes lewdly fluttered.

"I'm so fucking hard." Nathair groaned as his cocks swelled inside and against her. She knew they were hard, their combined girth currently making her see stars. *"I want to come inside her so badly. Fill her with every drop of my seed. Should I ask? Shit. I don't want to stop to do that."*

Her inner walls clamped down on him, as if demanding that he stay. He couldn't get her pregnant, and the idea of that much liquid flooding her had her growing even wetter.

Nathair's thrusts quickened, and Linh spread her thighs in want, in need, as she tried to meet each one. She pushed up on straightened arms to help, and her feet almost slipped off him. She realised his tentacles had wrapped themselves around her calves when they halted her, and it gave her freedom to ride him despite the inhuman length of his cock.

She couldn't go upright, so she just bounced back and forth over him with her back arched.

"Her breasts are so pretty," he said, as she felt them slapping against her torso. *"She's riding me."* Nathair shuddered with a deep groan. *"I'm about to come."*

She didn't know what his plan was, whether he was about to pull out or not. But she knew what she wanted, and it was this Duskwalker's seed spreading deep.

"Inside," she stated around airy pants, her eyes closing. "Inside me, Nathair. Come inside me, I want to feel it."

Whatever thoughts burst from him were utterly drowned out when his back arched, his claws stabbed into her thighs, and he released a roar that caused goosebumps to prickle over her. His cock swelled repeatedly, thickening enough to make her gasp at the difference in pressure. Lukewarm liquid burst inside her fast, like it was racing to escape him.

His thrusts slowed, and he came in harder instead. But Linh was already losing herself, orgasming as she felt every spurt. He wasn't done when he yanked his cock from her pussy, ripping a distressed cry from her, as semen dripped onto his abdomen. He slammed her down on his second cock, and his hips were so rabid she jittered and bounced as he pounded into her.

Nathair wrapped his elongated arms around her. One hand kneaded one of her cheeks and thigh, while the other gripped the crook of her shoulder and neck. He squeezed her, constricting her against his torso, and it only made her more aware of how much he moved beneath her.

She felt every ripple of muscle, every dip in his stomach. His breaths were short and shallow, yet his big heart was beating wildly in her ear.

The hold felt passionate, despite the lustful nature of their long-denied intimacy.

A strange shiver tore up her spine when his milked cock slipped between the cleft of her ass. It was wet, almost slimy and over-lubricated with the mixture of their fluids, and warm from her snuggling it. At first, she ignored it, since it was semi-soft, but the longer Nathair pumped inside her, the harder it got.

A squeak sounded out of her when the tapered head lined up with the tight ring of her ass, and she tensed up. Pain assaulted her from the quick, sudden stretch, but he immediately stopped before he even got the rim of his cock head through.

"Tight!" he yelped beneath. All his muscles rippled, the ones between her knees, his pectorals. Even his tail as it flicked into her view, like he was letting it writhe to satisfy his need to move. *"I want to mount it."* He gripped one of her arse cheeks harder to pull it to the side. *"Have her swallow both my cocks."*

Yet, he circled around his heart to say sorry, while his mind thought out loud, *"Sorry. I didn't mean to do that."*

Her entire being radiated in adoration when he pulled away. He did what was right for her, not for him, and her heart flooded with tenderness.

He grabbed his left cock and pulled it forward so it rested against her clit like before. She didn't even get time to respond. Any words choked out when he started up again, and all Linh could do was take it until he was flooding her once more. It was swift, like it'd already been nearing release, and Nathair had ensured both his cocks had taken a turn pumping and filling her.

Seed gushed out of her this time, and her lips parted at the strange feeling. Her thighs twitched at the way it tickled up her clit and covered the second cock jerking in reaction without spilling. Her arms lost their strength, but she ground on him, hoping to be gifted every drop.

When he stopped moving, all Linh heard were his frantic huffs, his heart beating, and her own trying to match it. Her mind seemed to echo the erotic sounds that had just spilled from them in this quiet, yet mesmerising cave.

Nathair felt warmer than usual, like being inside her was heating him from the outside in.

Now that she was no longer moaning, he'd gone silent; the temporary lull of her voice was no longer in effect. But she thought she could have guessed what he was thinking when the shaft nestled against her clit, hard as ever, twitched.

Reaching up, she lazily petted down the side of his parted maw. "I don't want to stop."

This felt wonderful. Her mind and heart were light, and having him inside her felt perfect – it felt *right*.

He gave her a small, panted moan, as his orbs flickered with black and the softening within her pulsated and began to thicken again. Yet he pulled her up and off his cock.

Before she could voice her disagreement, the Duskwalker twisted his head and licked across one of her nipples. He clamped it with the centre of his segmented jaw to pinch it in place, only to soothe it with a lick seconds later. Then unlatched his mouth and he turned her until her back rested over his front.

Thighs parted, she arched her spine when two fingers shoved deep inside her. He wiggled his fingers and pulled to the side like he was trying to show her how much room there was now. *He stretched me*. Then he petted up her clit, smearing his seed all over it as he spread her lips apart.

The longer he touched, the more his recently drained cocks began to jut until they both bounced off each other sideways with each thrum of his pulse.

He glided her down his body until both tips of his throbbing cocks were nestled against her. Nathair fisted them, squeezing them together until they almost looked like one giant purple monster dick.

A growl rumbled against her shoulder blades as he nestled their combined tips against her entrance. Linh parted her thighs, trying to help their entry with heated pants. She wanted both – to have him completely fill her with his virility. His snarl got louder as he pushed his hips up and held her to him so she wouldn't slip away.

They twisted, one going down and the other going up, and that seemed to help. Her features twinged at the thickness as her pussy tried to give way, the stretch painful, and yet she bit her lip for more. Somehow the sting felt like a reward.

Nathair let his cocks go, giving up on the attempt, and one shot inside her. The other gouged against her clit so hard her toes clenched.

He then shifted his entire body until his tail circled around them and propped them up into a slightly seated position. The end slapped over her knees, pushed them together until her legs were straight, and twisted around her limbs so completely she couldn't even part her ankles.

With two clawed fingers, he pushed the cock nestled between her thighs until it forced her pussy lips to part and mould around it.

"Why didn't you put it inside me?" she asked, turning her

hazy gaze to his skull looking over her shoulder.

"Not ready," he signed, twisting his head and licking across her neck, making her stretch it to the side to give him more surface to play with. "Is this okay? I want us to watch."

Gosh, he *really* liked to watch her.

In answer, Linh lifted her hips as best as she could, only to wiggle her way back down. She hummed at the way he slipped inside her and against her clit. *I think I'm going to like this position a lot.*

When she did it again, Nathair ducked his hips down at the same time she went up. Then they met in the centre, and a moan broke when he dug harder against her G-spot. More noises only spilled from her when he took over, thrusting up into her.

His arm crossed her hips, while his other palm took a bouncing, jiggling breast in his large, dark-grey hand. Her body spasmed when she saw his tail all around them now, his scales reflecting the crystals and giving his entire body a glistening glow. She took in the contrast of how large and deadly he was in comparison to her.

She *watched* his second cock disappearing and reappearing between her soft thighs. His tentacles had wrapped behind the backs of them, and they did so snugly.

Linh reached back to grip the base of a horn, while her other hand gripped the backs of his protruding white knuckles as he cupped her breast.

"Do you like that, Linh?" his thoughts groaned next to her ear, making a strangled pant puff from her. *"Do you like seeing what's currently pumping inside your seed-drenched cunt by watching the other slipping between your thighs?"*

"Yes," she rasped, fighting her flickering eyelids to keep them open. "You feel so good there."

"She answered me?" A dark chuckle rumbled and his hips suddenly picked up speed, making her jaw drop. "I forgot you can hear my thoughts when I touch, scent, and hear your body intimately. Naughty little female. You should have told me."

"I'm sor–" A scream cut through when he pinched her nipple and thrust into her with strength.

Her knees knocked together, her body locking up at the pleasure that pounded into her. Linh yanked on his horn as she used it to anchor herself so she could bounce, could buck, but she could do little more than feel like trapped prey in a snake's coil.

"Sing for me, little nightingale," Nathair rasped against her ear. "Come hear all my thoughts of how much I've been wanting to fuck this cute body until I *ruin* it. Until I stretch you so open that I split you with both my cocks and have you come for me as I do." Then he groaned, his hips slowing as she felt them thickening momentarily. "Fuck, Linh. You don't know how hard it's been waiting for you to claim them for yourself. You've been driving me fucking *insane*."

He released her breast to palm down her stomach. Just when she thought he was about to fist the tip of his cock, he paused. He angled his thrusts slightly and her arse dipped. He pounded against a certain place in the front of her channel, the head of his cock hitting it repeatedly with hard shoves.

Grabbing her hand, he placed her palm where he'd been touching between her hips.

"You can feel me pumping inside you," he stated, and she felt the subtle movement beneath her sweat-soaked skin. "Here."

He covered her hand and made her push down hard.

Linh came within an instant as he shoved the swollen, hot, and sensitive ridge of her G-spot into his cock.

Linh nearly burst out of her skin to escape the intensity. Any hope she had of asking him to stop, to wait, to give her a moment, was suffocated in each of her strangled breaths. She couldn't even cry his name, her own, to any deity that may be watching her be railed by a Duskwalker – a legless, skull-headed monster.

All she could do was shake, tremble, and she gave up fighting as her head lolled. Her eyes closed as everything went dark, her vision too blurry and dazed to focus. A puddle of her own orgasm made his abdomen wetly slap against her arse cheeks. She'd never felt anything like it, but it was evidence that this was messy, and felt like utter bliss.

I love it. I love the way this feels. I've needed this for so long. To feel undoubtable, mind-bending, heart-stopping bliss.

"The way you come," Nathair rasped, just as his forked tongue licked down her jaw. "Your body is so needy for pleasure, little female. You slither and contort around me so easily, like you're hungrily sucking me within you for more. You get so tight, like you don't want to let go of me. You look absolutely beautiful breaking apart for me."

He removed his hand from on top of hers and cupped the side of her face. She didn't think to remove the pressure of her fingers, her mind too flooded with bewildered rapture that she'd gone immobile.

"Open your eyes, little nightingale," he coaxed, his words slow but his hips jerking with a sprint. A groan shuddered out of him as the constant tempo broke. "Watch me come."

Only because he slowed, grinding his way in and out as his cocks swelled, did she gain the strength to weakly peek her eyes open. His head fell back against the wall of tail supporting them, as rattling whines tickled her back. His claws suddenly lanced her, biting into her skin, as scales seemed to puff everywhere around her.

His abdomen dipped, his hips twisted to the side, taking her with him, before centring once more. The coil of his tail clamping her legs shut tightened and squeezed.

"Fuck, *yes,*" he growled with lusty excitement. Pearly white liquid shot hard and fast all the way to her throat in a heavy rope, just as a powerful spurt burst within her.

Both. He's coming from both!

She watched it drench her breasts, her sternum, her navel, as he pumped slow but hard, as he gave a long, *low* moan. His unhidden noise, the way his body squirmed, it all revealed just how euphoric it felt for him. His orgasm seemed to clutch at him deeply, like both cocks releasing at the same time ate away at his very being.

Duskwalker cum poured from her pussy onto him like a fountain, and even bubbled up like it climbed her clit.

She shook her head in disbelief at the perverted sight.

When he was done, they both fell back limply while panting. Even his tail loosened, and she thought he might melt with how soft he went around her, while his cocks continued to jerk with aftershocks and pulses.

Linh did nothing. She didn't move an inch. All she did was huff as her eyes strained to remain open in the sluggishness of satisfaction. Even when he dipped forward so she could see his arms, she didn't budge.

"Did I go okay for my first time?" Nathair signed, as a knowing chuckle vibrated from his throat.

Her cheeks couldn't get any hotter.

His first time, and he almost fucked her until her heart burst.

Her eyes crinkled as she produced a weak giggle. *I adored this*. He'd made her feel beautiful, wanted, and treated her like something to use while making her feel so respected and secure.

He'd completely cared about her pleasure and comfort.

"Don't stop," she croaked, her voice so hoarse and cracked from screaming. Linh twisted her upper body just enough to plant her face against his hard skull when she yanked him forward by a horn. "Just like this. I want more of you."

She wanted more of this. His intensity, his inhuman pleasure. She needed more of his waterlily-and-moonflower scent, his body, his big personality leaking through – unhidden and honest like she needed it to be.

He rumbled a purr against her. "Can I switch cocks?"

"Whatever you want," she offered, knowing those words held little value.

He would do whatever he wanted, so long as she wanted and enjoyed it.

TWENTY-SIX

Tired, physically worn out, and sluggish, Linh let out a tiny groan. She cupped low on her abdomen before she even peeked open her eyes from sleep.

A tender ache radiated deep within. Her pussy felt hot, swollen, while her clitoral folds were puffed from overstimulation. Her thighs felt overworked, while the rest of her legs ached from being squeezed straight for too long. Even her right breast, as if the Duskwalker mainly attacked just the one with his tongue and fingers, was warm.

Lying on her side with her back to his chest, she brought her knees up. She cringed at the smear of liquid she could feel in the creases of her body: between the crooks of her thighs, under and between her breasts, around her neck. Her body tightened as her gut twisted at the slimy way it felt, making seed drip from her core and highlighting how drenched the slit between her thighs still was.

The rest of her – areas that had dried – had been so saturated that trying to remove her palm from her navel had it sticking to it for far longer than comfortable.

My stomach hurts. The longer she woke to realise what state her body was in, how sore and well used it felt, the harder her gut knotted. A lead ball seemed to be growing within her.

Her throat clutched with anxiety, as memories that felt too similar, although not as intense, made her tear up. The lead ball moved, pushing underneath her stomach as she took in how wet and stained she was. Her skin felt unclean, wrong. It felt gross.

Lying here with Nathair felt wrong, and her flesh prickled with goosebumps as his chest moved from heavy breaths against her spine and sticky backside. Masculine breaths of a person who had been inside her, touched her everywhere, saw every inch of her body.

She wiggled away as her breaths turned sharp and shallow.

I don't feel good. She didn't know if the pain was real, or if her stomach was truly trying to turn itself inside out so she'd vomit, but saliva coated her mouth.

Trying to just accept her body, she curled into a tight ball with her arms across her stomach protectively. It only seemed to make it worse. She was naked, too exposed, and with her eyes closed, she felt weak and feeble.

Linh threw herself into a seated position, so her privates were protected from below as she huddled her legs. Both her fringe braids had unwound from the base of her pigtails during the night, and they swayed in front of her crinkled eyes. The rest of her hair clung to her skin.

Oh gods. It's in my hair. Seed was everywhere.

Memories she didn't want, things she hated, flashed behind her clenching eyes as she rocked. Disgusting sounds mixed in with the many from the wonderful night she just had, and scents and touches that once burned at her skin, did so again.

Her flesh itched, as if the liquid was trying to seep into her like needles.

Tears began to squeeze past her clenched eyelids, and they fell fast and with heavy drops. *Stop it. I enjoyed it. It's not the same. They aren't the same.* Yet, no matter how much she told herself the truth, she just felt sick. Everything felt wrong. In her heart, regret swelled, and her lips trembled.

Why?! She cried to herself, not understanding why she was having this reaction. *W-what's wrong with me? W-why can't I just be normal?! I don't want to feel like this – like my skin is crawling, like my own pussy feels wrong.* Even her breasts felt too heavy from being touched too much, highlighting that they *existed.*

Why am I broken? She thought she was ready!

She'd been able to touch Nathair's cocks without feeling like she wanted to expire or disappear afterwards. She hadn't been faced with sinking regret, fear, or anxiety.

So why now? Why after the amazing night they shared?

She lifted her head with stark eyes. *Where are my clothes?* She wanted to cover herself, so she felt safe again. They were the only barriers she had, the only things she could wear to protect herself, even if they could be torn away.

Even if it didn't truly matter.

She caught movement to her left and didn't even realise Nathair had awoken or wasn't in a trance until then. She'd thought he'd been out of it, giving her time to freak out alone. Knowing he was there, conscious, only made fear like she hadn't felt in weeks choke her.

When he came into view, she sobbed and flinched away from him as if she'd been struck. *Please don't hurt me. Don't pull my hair.* Her scalp tingled in preparation for a harsh yank in order to try and assert dominance over her tears, to try and get her to stop panicking – which only ever worsened her fretting.

"I-I-I'm sorry," she stuttered through hiccupping heaves. "I'll stop crying."

Refusing to unfurl herself, she let out a loud cry when he touched her. He scooped his arms around her body and lifted her off the ground.

Oh no. Where is he taking me? All she could do was tremble and let him do what he wanted.

Nathair lifted her above his head when he slithered into the water to stop her from going under. He settled her in the warm water gently to let it caress her skin, to let it *clean* her. It did nothing to loosen her fright-filled muscles.

She noticed he dipped down until all that remain above the

surface was his skull, and bubbles formed around his gills. *Is he hiding from my scent?*

Guilt only made her tears fall faster, and made her heave harder.

Nathair brought her to the ledge she'd kissed him, had reached for him, *begged* for him. Now she clung to the glowing crystals to get away, and was thankful when he let her go. She turned her head away as tears dripped on the ledge, and she brought her knees up when her belly just wouldn't stop quivering.

"I'm sorry," she sobbed around distressed hiccups. "I'm sorry."

She wished she had an answer for him, or that she could make herself feel better. That she could explain she didn't blame him, even if she couldn't stand the sight of him right then, even if his touch currently felt like it had set her skin on fire – and he'd touched her *everywhere.*

Just as she went to apologise again, he covered her mouth to stop her. Old habits burst into her, and she bit into his palm as hard as she could, only to flinch when she expected a reaction. She got one; he patted the top of her head in a single stroke.

She shuffled to get away from it, although thankful that was what she received.

For a long while, she clutched the ledge while trying to deal with her own body, her reaction. Being in his presence worsened it, but there was little they could do.

She doubted she'd be able to take a single breath and hold it to get to the other side of the underwater tunnel. She thought she may have preferred the darkness, rather than to be seen in the light like this.

Slowly her breaths calmed enough that she didn't feel like she was about to spit out her lungs. She refused to lower her bent legs, wanting to keep her feet shielding her privates, but her muscles did begin to unlock. She wished the knot in her stomach would unravel, but she couldn't do it with all the soreness she felt.

Looking for a way out, she finally braved talking to him.

"N-Nathair," she croaked with a sniffle.

He gave her a grunt in answer. God! He was probably watching her freak out. Was he pitying her? Judging her? Angry with her?

"C-can you heal me, *please*?" she asked, and immediately noted a blue flicker in her peripheral vision before it faded.

She wanted everything to go away. She wanted to feel normal again, like nothing happened so she could *breathe.*

Her neck arched when he ran the pads of his fingertips from her collarbones up her throat. She shook her head. He did it again with a loud huff.

"I-I don't want to sing."

He moved, and all her anxiety redoubled when he placed an arm on both sides of the ledge... with her between them. He trapped her, giving her no escape unless she was to dive. Then he traced her throat again with the smallest *growl.*

Linh, fighting through tears, hummed as loud as she could muster. It often cracked, and she struggled through her shudders.

"Can you hear me?" he asked, his voice so quiet it was almost a whisper. She nodded. "Good. Don't stop until I say so." He dipped his head over her shoulder just enough for her to feel the end of his snout against her cheek. "You want me to heal you?"

Linh nodded.

"No, " he said with a dark and unnerving undertone.

"Why?!" she yelled.

When he didn't answer, she hummed again.

"I am willing to remove my seed, but not the evidence of my touch," he answered with the tiniest *hint* of hostility in his tone. "You ask for too much."

Gosh, that made her feel so shitty. "I'm sor–"

Instead of covering her lips to stop her apology, he cupped the underside of her jaw and clamped it shut. It allowed her to hum still, but it jittered from her. She couldn't take this right now; it was too aggressive.

His voice was quieter, but no less powerful in its statement. He drew back a single arm and brought it underneath the water to glide his claws across her torso.

"This ache inside you is my ache. The pain you feel inside your pussy is one I gave you. The swollen thrum you feel is from you coming over, and over, and *over* again, as you pleaded for more of me."

Her inner walls clamped in memory, and she didn't know if that made her feel better or worse.

Why is he doing this? What happened to the Nathair that cared about how she always felt? The one who made her feel safe, secure, and comfortable in all scenarios? Now that they'd had sex, did he not... *care* anymore?

"My cocks burn from being buried inside you. My seed sacs throb from emptying myself repeatedly into you and on you. My groin aches, overused by giving you what *you* wanted. All. Night. *Long.*"

Linh's nails tried to dig into crystal to get away when he buried the end of his snout into the crook of her neck. He placed his arm back on the ledge until his clawed hands rested just beyond hers.

"I told you. I will not play fair if you claim me, Linh, and you claimed me until my cocks were raw," he rumbled with a warm pant wrapping around her skin. "So, when you are ready, little nightingale... come revel in the pain of our ravenous fucking *with* me."

He was telling her to wait it out, as if he knew how she felt would fade after time. Linh held onto that.

She didn't... *want* to regret it. She'd loved every second of it, had adored the way he moved within her, while he touched her all around. She'd liked the way his hard scales had glided over bare flesh for the first time, and the way he released pent-up and needy groans for her.

Even when she'd been passing out, she wanted more. Linh

hadn't wanted it to end – the pleasure, the feeling, all of it lasting forever so she could live in it until the world crumbled.

She thought she would have died happy if he'd fucked her last heartbeat out of her.

So, she battled herself while he secured her in place. She continued to cry, but she gritted her teeth to unravel the knotted lead ball within. It was so heavy that it felt like a ball and chain trying to drag her to the depths she floated in. She didn't know how long passed, if it was minutes or hours, but she weakly laid her cheek on the quartz ledge when she finally relaxed.

She sniffled and blinked lazily at the glowing world before her. It was still beautiful, even if she currently felt heartsick. Her gaze drifted to his hand, and she just stared at his glossy claws for what felt like forever.

Shudders fell past her lips as her tears continued to drip.

His hands are so big, she thought, her mind dozing.

She observed them until her right hand twitched closer to his. She hiccupped and sniffled, just as she brushed the tip of her index finger against the side of his thumb. He didn't move, even when she braved caressing the side of her finger over the white protruding knuckle bones and the smaller black scales.

Only when her ring and pinkie fingers brushed against his thumb did he finally turn it on its side. The last of her distressed sounds grew quieter as she tickled the inside of his soft palm. He cupped the back of her hand, so both their palms were facing her, and she took in the startling differences.

His hands were unnaturally big, even for his body, and she wondered if all Duskwalkers were like that. The tips of her fingers barely went past his second knuckle, and the heel of his cushioned around hers.

He bent his fingers until his claws lightly stabbed into her palm.

She reached for the other, and he gave it to her so he could hold both of hers in the lukewarmth of his.

When her heart finally calmed, and she felt normal again other than the throbbing in her pussy, she suddenly felt remarkably silly for crying. Which only made her want to start up again for an entirely different reason. Not in regret, but because of all the hurt she'd suffered to cause this.

How her emotional wounds had tried to ruin something so beautiful in their selfish cruelty.

Rather than apologising again, she whispered, "Thank you."

Nathair purred and nuzzled the end of his snout just behind her ear. He squeezed her hands, and finally brought himself closer until his chest pressed against her back. The vibration of his purr stopped her from tensing up, and she found the sound so utterly soothing in that moment.

Giving into the cuddle completely, she lowered her legs until her heels bumped against his tail.

"Can we stay here for a little while?" she asked, not wanting to change what they were doing until she truly felt better.

While holding her hand, he signed, "yes."

As he started licking the corded muscle of her neck, up her jugular, like he wanted to lavish affection on her, warmth radiated in her heart.

I really thought he'd be disappointed in me. Linh had just had a full-blown panic attack, all because she'd had sex with him. Part of her had feared how he would react.

Despite how much his denial of healing her had felt betraying at first, she was thankful for it now. Yes, her body thrummed in a way that was uncomfortable, but he was right. It felt good – an ache made from him, from their rigorous fornication of twisted need and surely many fond emotions as well.

When minutes ticked by in the complete silence, something crossed her mind. If he wanted her soul... did that mean what he really wanted was her *love*? Her heart did a little backflip at the thought.

"I-if I request something, will you promise to not take it as an offering?" she asked in a small voice.

"Of course," he answered, refusing to let go of both her hands, and she almost giggled at that.

"Can I..." She chewed at the inside corner of her lips. "Can I see my soul?"

He ceased moving. She wondered if asking had repercussions, or if he was pondering if there was a deeper meaning to her request.

Then he let go of her right hand and brought it closer to her chest. She looked down so she could watch him take her soul from her body. He tapped against her sternum, but nothing happened and that seemed to disappoint him. Her torso waved and rippled like water as he gently pressed the backs of his claws past her physical boundaries and reached deeper into the very abyss of her being.

Linh felt nothing, even when he had sunk base-knuckles deep. A bright red-orange light came from her as he pulled back, and behind his knuckles, floated her soul.

She hated that it was curled up in the exact position she'd been in right after she'd woken up.

Its feet were tucked protectively against the cleft of its backside, its knees against its chest. Its arms were crossed over its stomach, as if it, too, felt unwell. With its face buried against the nook of its knees, all she could think was... it looked uncomfortable.

It didn't appear to be resting peacefully.

Nathair pulled until it was hovering in the empty space between her outreached arms.

"Can I touch it?" she asked, her fingers itching to do so.

He tapped the back of her hand as he laid his right arm back to how it'd been before, yet he never let go of her left hand. Linh came closer to it until she could brush the back of her index finger against its side.

It dropped to the ground, and two brown eyes, with no pupils or whites in them, opened to look around. It darted its head one way and then the other before taking in her hand next to it. It crawled to it and tucked its back into her palm while appearing to cower, only to instantly calm.

It constantly covered its chest and pelvis, as if its nudity bothered it.

"Is this what I look like?" she asked with a cry, her eyes crinkling in distress. "A fucking shaking mess?"

"No," Nathair signed as he squeezed her left hand. He let it go, so he had freedom. "Your soul is your inner self. Your deepest feelings. It represents all parts of you, even those you may hate."

She didn't know if that made her feel better or worse.

She petted the side of her soul's stomach like she wanted to soothe it in the way she wished for when her anxiety got the best of her. Then as nonchalantly as she could, she asked, "Can I see yours?"

He gave a hum in thought. "I don't know how to do that. My soul does not sit inside my chest like yours. It is all of me."

All of him? Like the same size as he is now? Did that mean it filled every inch of his gigantic, monstrous body?

Linh chose to let it go.

Instead, she focused on her own and nudged it to stand. It was wary as it did, its face turning away from Nathair's skull with an awkward, inward shift of its shoulders. She made it spin so she could take it in fully, noticing that the dark, near-charcoal section she'd once seen on its back was much smaller than before.

She didn't ask what it meant, as she doubted she'd like the answer. She also didn't want to know what the palm print on its right inner thigh meant, nor the singular one that spanned across both wrists.

She did furrow her brows when she only counted two. *I thought there were more.* Then again, she'd only briefly glanced at it both times before she clutched it in worry he'd gobble it up.

The longer she gazed at it, the more a smile teased her lips. "That is nice."

The moment felt wildly intimate in the strangest but most

spiritual of ways. What other human could play with their literal fiery essence? The fact she was doing so, with a soul eater no less, showed the deep level of trust she had for the Duskwalker pressing against her back.

"Your soul is beautiful," he signed, before caressing the back of her free hand with the smooth, glossy curve of his claws. "Like you."

"Do you want to know what I think is funny?" With her small smile remaining, she placed her cheek against the quartz and tried to tickle the flaming version of herself. "My first name means spirit, and here I am playing with mine."

She managed to get it to come out of its shell a little with a soundless laugh. It crouched to hide from her torturous fingertip until it fell on its side. It kicked and slapped at her, trying to fight her off, which only made her laugh out loud.

Then it bit her, and she yelped when it hurt!

She hid her fingers from it, just as it cupped its own hand to its chest.

Did I... just hurt myself?

Which only made her wonder, "If I die, does that mean my soul dies?"

"Yes. It turns white."

She pursed her lips as she helped it back to its feet so it could hover properly. "Is it possible to harm a soul while the person it belongs to is alive?"

Nathair answered in the affirmative, and she just accepted it. She swiped it behind the knees so it could rest in her palm, like how the back of her left hand rested in his. Linh just held it, wishing she could feel its warmth or life other than pressure. It was light, like it weighed nothing, yet it was so unbelievably important.

I kind of want to give it to him, she thought, taking in Nathair's scaled arms, his light-grey fins, the way he was, but also wasn't, holding her.

But I want to go home. She wanted to see her family. She missed her parents, her younger sister, her friends. As much as she wanted to stay with Nathair in his cave, she had a life she wanted to return to.

A life she had been stolen from.

She didn't think she'd be complete again until she returned to it like she'd always intended. Like she'd promised the day she'd been forcibly taken from it. In the back of her mind, she kept thinking her journey of healing would finish there, like a circle of fate finally reaching its end.

It wasn't fair that she was being forced to choose.

Her village was so close, just a day's walk if she didn't stop to rest. Yet the person she *wanted* was here.

Why can't he just come with me? She didn't care what anyone thought.

Who cared if she was falling in love with a monster? His kindness and humour were not enough to fall for him, but his unflappable support towards someone who needed understanding was truly admirable. She knew she was broken, even if he stated otherwise.

She wanted to think of herself as broken, because it felt like he was picking up the shards of her mess and piecing them back together bit by bit. The glue he used was all the small things he did to make her feel safe when she thought she'd crumble. Then he held the shards in place as they dried, even when she kept wetting them with her tears.

He'd become her blanket of security from the very first moment she slept in his tail. He not only kept out the monsters lurking outside his shield, but also the memories in the boundaries of her mind. She rested, peaceful, in the middle of him.

No one else could do that for her.

No one else would look like him, feel like him, smell like him. His skull was bewitching, as were his hooked ram horns. His orbs glowed with fiery life, and they were so pretty no matter what colour they shone.

She giggled to herself as she thought, *No one else has two dicks like him, either.* A bit of a weird bonus, but one she was happy about. She'd been *very* happy about them last night.

An index claw tapped against the foggy quartz.

Nathair then bumped his skull against her cheek. "Can I touch it?"

I don't know why he's asking. He's touched it before... Her lips parted when she realised that the only time Nathair had ever actually touched her soul directly was the very first time he took it from her. *He's only ever beckoned it out of me.*

The day on the beach, and even now... both times her flaming self had floated *behind* his knuckles.

Oh, Nathair. Her heart stuttered at what she thought that may mean. *He doesn't like touching any part of me without consent.* Even this, and it only made her chest swell in tenderness for him to the point it panged and ached.

"Yes," she stated, her voice clogging with emotion. She trusted him not to take it while she was still so unsure.

She slid it off from where it sat on her palm, and she moved her arm back to give him room. Her smile brightened when he went to envelop it from the side, only for her expression to fall as her soul flinched and stumbled away.

Blue shifted into his orbs, and he backed off.

Linh, pissy with her literal self, pushed it towards his palm with the back of her fingers. He didn't move, as if not daring to, yet the moment its backside touched him, it clung to her fingers when she tried to slide away.

"Excuse me," she bit out, before she picked it up and placed it in the middle of his big palm.

It froze, then curled into the protective position it'd emerged from her in. *Stop being annoying,* she mentally willed at it. She poked it in the arm.

Nathair released her left hand so he could rub at its form, trying to coax it out gently rather than abrasively like she had. Folding her arms, Linh laid her chin on them so she could watch, and a knowing smile curled her lips.

He'll convince it. She trusted that, because he'd done the same thing with her.

He apparently had more patience. He also cared about what he was doing, made evident by the way he sheathed his claws like he didn't want to damage it.

My soul looks just as confused as me.

Even when he managed to get it to hold his thumb with its tiny arms in a loose embrace, Linh noted the way it inquisitively moved its face between hers and his skull. It sat there with its feet crossed, and she noticed how it slowly settled as he rubbed its torso. Nathair brought it closer as he pressed against Linh's back until her front was threatening to squish against the wall.

Looking over her shoulder, he inspected it more closely. Linh peeked from the corner of her eye to see his orbs had flared bright yellow in elation about being able to hold her fragile inner self.

Seeing him hold such a tiny but vital part of her felt so special. After last night, and then crying, Linh felt raw and emotional, and like her chest was on fire in the most tranquil of ways.

The water was just as soothing as having him at her back.

Her soul relaxed in his hold, allowing him to brush the back of his foreknuckle under its jaw, and Linh herself softened. She reached forward with her left hand so she could hold his wrist, wanting to touch him.

Maybe it was his strength pouring into her somehow, but she found her lips parting to speak... about things she didn't want to.

"My whole life, I've seen so many happy people. Even though the world is full of evil, it felt like our village was a barrier from what lurked outside," Linh started, while rubbing the pad of her thumb against the base of his pinkie, like he did to her soul's torso. "When I was taken... I thought maybe things would work out fine, and we would end up like my parents, even if I hated him at first."

She laid her chin on the quartz ground and then tilted her head so it partially lay on her outreaching arm.

"I wanted to believe that people weren't truly horrible. I chose to have hope and be ignorant, biased, and naïve. I was so scared... that I just told myself to try to be kind and accepting, as I had no other choice."

Her vision blurred as liquid welled, but her tears weren't followed with heaves or hiccups. They didn't feel like blood dripping and scratching at her eyes, but like the leak of her emotions she'd been bottling finally overspilling. They flowed but weren't important.

She wished she'd stop crying, and that she didn't feel like a mess all the time, but her heart and mind were so muddled she didn't know how to swallow her own reality. Her life was like a bone she couldn't gnaw through.

"I learned that first night that I was wrong. That people truly could have darkness inside them and could unleash it upon those undeserving. I was undeserving. I thought my kindness and acceptance of others with a warm heart would protect me from evil. I thought it would *save* me."

Linh touched the point of Nathair's claw. She stroked a part of him she knew to be dangerous and deadly. She petted a monster who could have been menacing and vile, and yet had been utterly wonderful to her.

"No part of me was safe. No matter what I said, did... no matter how I pleaded or cried, I only made things worse for myself. If I retaliated, I was met with harshness. I hate that I was forced to learn that if I didn't fight, I wouldn't feel pain, and yet that felt even... scarier." She brushed her fingertip against the cheek of her soul. "But inside, I was boiling. I wanted to fight, to run. Every second of every day for two months, I was looking for a way out that wasn't at the hands of death. When I first held a dagger, I considered killing to protect myself, but I thought if I did that, I'd lose myself. So much had been taken from me already, and I didn't want who I really was stolen by a single thrust of a knife, even if it was deserved. I was shackled, but I managed to slowly pry the bolt out over time. I ran away twice."

She lifted her eyes to Nathair, who had his serpent skull pointed at her soul, yet she could almost feel his gaze upon her. His orbs were bright crimson, but he didn't quake with the fury she thought may be simmering beneath the surface.

"The second time, I found myself at your pond. I was so tired from running all night and day, but I couldn't sleep in the darkness if I wanted to live." With her right hand, she lifted it to place her palm over his snout. "Thank you for saving me from the bandits that day."

Linh had no desire to elaborate on any details. She didn't want to describe the violence she'd been dealt, still wanting to tuck it all away so it could stay a horrible nightmare. This was as much as she was willing to face, or say out loud, and she realised then that she wouldn't speak any more about it, or again.

But she wanted to tell the one person she thought needed to hear this much. To explain her crying, not just today but in the past few weeks, so that he understood the depths of her pain he kept trying to shield her from.

No part of Linh had been safe, and as an apparent 'wife,' that meant doing her unwanted 'duty' every day for two months.

No person deserved that kind of hell.

She was no longer naïve, nor ignorant, but she wanted to pretend she was still innocent. With Nathair, she felt that way.

He was her first Duskwalker. The first person she'd touched with scales, claws, fangs, and even a long tail. He was the first person she'd started falling for, and she was starting to wish he'd be all her lasts too.

"Nathair," she uttered quietly, digging her fingers into the empty eye hole of his skull. "If I asked you to... would you kill for me?"

A growl, so soft and light, rumbled into her.

Cupping her entire neck with his free hand, Nathair licked along her jaw, the forks of his tongue always perfectly nestling the sharp edge of it. He pressed her soul back into her chest, so he could sign freely.

"Was already planning to."

TWENTY-SEVEN

After dipping beneath the surface to find her undergarments, Nathair took Linh back to the other side of the lake's narrow tunnel. The entrance to it glowed, showing the crystal reflected even when they entered darkness.

"Oh no," Linh stated as he helped her to the rocky ledge. "I forgot to blow the candle out before we left. I didn't think we'd be in there all night."

Neither had Nathair, but fucking hell was he *pleased.*

His whole being hadn't stopped thrumming in deep contentment. He hadn't lied to the little female when he said his cocks ached. The last time he'd come had been strenuous. It was like she didn't want him to stop, even when she grew so tired her eyes closed. The moment he stopped pumping into her, she'd whine at him to keep going with a groggy tone.

It was like she was trying to shove a lifetime of orgasms into a single night. Nathair had been absolutely delighted to find that Linh had an insatiable appetite for pleasure, to the point it almost combatted *his.*

Not even her tears after waking had managed to tamp down how he felt, although they had been concerning.

But, as Nathair kept reminding himself, it wasn't her fault, and wasn't his fault, nor should he wear a single ounce of blame for it. He also refused to. They would be intimate again – he'd make sure of it. He'd rut her until she finally woke up cuddling him.

Until then, he'd just be patient.

However, the part of her story she'd told him... his rage hadn't soothed since, and he felt it in each of his agitated and puffed scales.

I was already planning to find those who harmed her. He would have gifted her their heads as proof. *At least now I know it was only one.* Didn't make it any less enraging, though.

Does this mean I'll end up killing all the bandits anyway? Nathair shrugged. *I cannot do anything until she makes her decision.*

Whether she chose to stay or to leave, he could not leave her in his cave by herself. It'd take him a few hours to travel to the bandit camp. *If I fall into a trance while I'm gone, or if it takes me a long time to kill everyone, I could potentially leave her for days.*

All the Demons on the beach needed was a night without the strength of his scent, and they'd come for her.

He couldn't take her with him, as he'd likely kill her in the confusion of his bloodlust. Everything was foe, no matter who they were to him. His mother had faced that.

She must either give me her soul, so I can teach her to turn intangible, or... she must go back to her people without me. It was why he'd not already gone to destroy her attackers.

He did know one thing with absolute certainty: they would die, no matter if she chose to leave.

He'd like to destroy anything that could harm her, so he could feel as though he'd protected her from a distance. Then Nathair would leave this place, so he wouldn't be tempted to steal her from the very home she sought to remain in.

If she did not want him, then he wouldn't be like those who had kidnapped her.

I will be sad, though.

He could already foresee the pain that would linger in his heart. He'd live in these memories, and hoped they battled his fragments to be prevalent. He'd gnaw on them to pacify himself forever.

He'd cherish them.

Once Nathair helped Linh onto solid ground, he noted the way she covered her breasts and pubic mound. She'd been so annoyed with her soul for doing it and yet, here she was, doing the exact same thing.

"C-can I have my underwear now?" she asked, with her shoulders turned inwards.

Nathair looked down at her undergarments bundled in his fist. "No," he signed. "They are wet."

The way back would take time, and he didn't want her shivering from the cold.

Her brows drew inwards in concerned wiggles. "But I need them."

Rolling his head, he slithered to the side and picked up her dress and pants. He reached out to hand them to her. She silently obeyed, but he could tell the little human was cursing him out in her head as she donned them.

She was surprisingly spritely, even when he saw the tired wobble in her legs – a shakiness gifted to her by him. He wanted to *purr* at that. She even appeared to limp a little.

Nathair watched her breasts sway and bounce as she lifted her dress over her head, the sight enthralling. Even when one of her elbows got stuck and she fought the material, his feelings for her only grew rather than waned.

She cut him a cute glare when he laughed at her.

Little nightingale, you have no idea what you've just done.

He warned her that he'd no longer play fair if she mounted his cocks, and she'd done so *thoroughly.*

I'll be doing everything I can to keep you with me. As much as he thought he'd be able to let her go amicably, after last night, he realised he was irrevocably doomed. He'd adored every second of her. He'd gorged on the taste he'd had of her, and the insatiable side of him said it wasn't enough.

He was so utterly besotted with her – her wiles, her power over him, her cute face and sensual body, her giggles and tears... it was no wonder he dreamt of her.

Even his essence was begging to own her soul.

Nathair was attached. He was infatuated, and after the rather saddening conversation on the beach – where he learned she may have magic – he knew there was no one else for him. The chance of him finding another female who would not only sing for him, but also want to be with him, was so low he'd be better off asking a rock to do it.

I want to give her everything she seeks.

He wouldn't die for her; he'd spent enough time in the afterworld. But he would fight, he would live, and he would... love her with every one of his scales if she let him.

However... I cannot immerse myself in her people.

He doubted they'd accept him. He also didn't foresee them taking it well that he'd claimed one of their females. Would they attempt to diminish her affection by constantly whispering in her ear about the horribleness of him?

He thought he could bear that. He'd just convince her otherwise by doting every bit of his sensual attention on her.

He could take their snide remarks and sneers, their hate. So long as she caressed all that away and lathered him in kisses to soothe his bruised ego, Nathair could cope with hate.

But he had enough human voices in his mind. The idea of sitting in the middle of her village with his sensitive hearing, listening to thousands of voices chattering around in his ears... he didn't know if he could stay sane. Linh brought him out of trances. She steadied and focused him on the present, but a barrage of people speaking would only pull him under constantly.

It wasn't just because he was a selfish, greedy, and territorial Mavka. His mind was warped.

He could not live with humans, not when he already had dozens doing so in his skull. He'd go mad. He'd become violent. He'd harm, and he worried what would happen if she attempted to interfere.

How will she treat me if I accidentally kill her family? Her father was the leader, yes? That meant he would try to protect his people, and if Nathair lost it...

He shook his head. *No, I do not want to think of it.* He didn't want to imagine what would happen if this female's tender gaze towards him suddenly turned cold.

If he were to be the keeper of her soul, they'd be trapped with each other. He could not escape her, or she him, and their bond would fester and sicken.

She must choose him.

Not for her people, not to kill those who harmed her, but because she wanted to of her own volition. He refused to accept her soul as a bargain. The only cost for it would be her love; that's what he wanted in exchange for it.

I will try for her.

He wouldn't completely disregard taking her to her people, but he needed to know it wouldn't matter where he took her.

He wanted her to love him enough that she could forgive any transgression he might make because of his ill mind. Enough that she would be understanding if her people drove them away, and wouldn't resent him for it. Enough that it didn't matter where she was, only that she felt at home and at peace within the wrappings of his tail.

Only when Linh willingly chose him, and *only* him, would Nathair *try* to gift her all the things she wanted.

These were thoughts for when the day came that she chose. For now, he tucked her wet undergarments in her lantern for her to carry before diving back into the water to grab a gift for her.

By the time they were passing the exit to the beach, the day was late.

She appeared a little paler and drained than normal, but she was securely tucked into a bridal position within his arms. When he offered to take her into the early afternoon sun, she just shook her head, stating she was tired and hungry.

I really did not think she would offer her body to me while in the quartz cave. If he'd known, he may have brought food with them.

He'd just wanted to swim with her without her whining and shivering. Nathair was aquatic and preferred being *in* the water. It felt like a hug, no matter its temperature, once it filled his gills.

That cave, despite its beauty, had not been pleasant in the corner of his heart. Now it was, and if they went back there, he'd like to do it all again... but with food, so she didn't make them leave. *We can spend days there fucking, feeding her, and in between she can sleep upon my chest.*

The idea brought him immense joy.

He eyed the quartz prism she held in her delicate hand. He'd gone back to collect a thick shard so she could have a pillar of memory in the main cave. *I hope her face goes all cute every time she looks upon it.*

It sparkled, so he was rather content to add it to his treasures – unlike her ugly shells.

When they returned, she laid it on the ledge of his nest where a stream of sunlight would hit it. A ripple cascaded down his spine at her adding to his nest like this. He also liked that she'd been here so long her scent had greeted them upon entry.

My home smells like peaches, vanilla, and female.

Linh walked over to her bag, and Nathair came to crowd her as he often did. He observed her food resources were getting low.

Nathair dipped low to get into her peripheral. "You have eaten all your plums," he signed. "I am sure I can find the tree quickly on my own and return to you before dusk arrives."

Her lips lost some of their thoughtful pout.

If only I could find peaches.

"Can we look at the stars again tonight?" she asked, a small yet tired smile filling her features. "I don't feel like doing much else today."

If Nathair was honest, her face was all swollen. *She is an ugly crier.* Her eyes were the worst affected, as were her puffed lips, as if the salt of her tears had abraded them. He adored her even more for it, as it showed they were real, and that she trusted sharing her tears with him.

"We can do whatever you wish," he answered. "I will go hunt for you, so rest."

He'd rather hunt fish, but so be it.

The moment he entered the lake, it was like a coldness rushed over his very mind, as much as his scales. He shuddered when a voice screamed in the back of his mind, but he merely shook his skull to remove it before it could stick to his consciousness.

Yet, rather than leaving immediately, he leaned on the ledge of rock with straightened arms. Most of him remained submerged except for his torso. He waited for her to notice, as she'd been eating the weird berries that turned their tongues blue.

When she did, she came over to him.

"What's wrong?" she asked with a small furrow of her brows.

Since his arms weren't as long as most Mavka, as he didn't need them to walk in a four-legged position, he only came to her breast height. Nathair nudged his head up, bouncing it to obtain her attention. When she didn't understand, he came ever closer, waiting for her to figure it out.

The left side of her lips quirked, and she leaned down to give him what he wanted. She pressed those puffy, soft lips against the centre of his maw, and he swallowed thickly at the feel of their warmth moulding around his bone.

I like when she kisses me. It always made his heart flutter.

A purr immediately started up, only for it to drown when he slipped away into the water to leave.

TWENTY-EIGHT

With a drowned groan, Nathair weakly leapt out onto the lake's edge. He didn't make it far, only half his humanoid torso exiting the water. He clawed at the stone with one hand and an elbow to stop himself from slipping back in.

Unable to see Linh, Nathair heard her soft, steady breaths, as if she were asleep somewhere. His sight fell on the recess of his nest, hoping she'd crawled into it despite his absence.

It was her bed, as much as his own.

Dammit. I don't feel well, he thought, placing her bag of plums on the ledge.

He took a moment to breathe and settle the loud chatter of voices zipping past in his consciousness.

I don't understand. I was fine before I left her. He pondered as to why the fragments came in a rockslide. *Is it because I held them back for so long?*

It'd been over thirty-six hours since one had come to the forefront of his mind. He'd never had that happen before.

The day on the beach, their journey to the quartz crystals, their night of passion... It'd all drawn his focus to one big pinnacle point: her. It was always her. Somehow, she kept the agony at bay.

Then he'd parted from her.

With his hand reaching up to pick a plum in the daylight, he'd woken to it being... night.

Nathair had seen nothing, heard nothing, and scented nothing of the real world. A fragment had reached to take an orange from a tree, just as he did with a plum, and he'd slipped out of consciousness completely.

He didn't even think being attacked would have woken him.

Dark orange flared in his sight. *I left her for hours.* At least she was safe.

He'd been hoping she'd be awake to greet and soothe him.

Nathair crawled out of the water, having to bunch his tail underneath him to get leverage. Then he checked to truly take in how she'd chosen to sleep in his nest without his presence. His chest swelled before he choked at the fragment of a mother staring down at their child in a cot.

He shook his skull, then reached in to pull the cloth higher until it covered her exposed neck. *Her hair is loose.* Only when she planned to change styles did she briefly have it down.

After checking on her, Nathair went to the entrance of the tunnels to scent down them. He even flicked his tongue forward to fully sense whether a Demon was slowly infiltrating. Deciding it was fine, he came back to Linh.

I want to lie with her. His heart swelled to hold her.

He didn't. He didn't trust his current mental state, as it was weaker than usual. The voices were too loud, so he laid his torso over the ledge of his nest wall and gazed down at her.

Even though she was asleep, he craved her battling his fragments for him. His senses soaked her in.

His sight took in her beauty as she lay curled up on her side, with a folded bit of cloth under her head as a pillow. She looked uncomfortable, and he took solace in that; he was a better bed for her.

She smells so nice. The aroma of her peach-and-vanilla scent, and the utter sweetness of it, swirled in his nostrils until he let out a warmed pant. *She's so small and light.* His ears listened to her fragile heart, so tiny and delicate, and he let it lull him. He also noted how her even breaths were soft, perfectly rhythmic, and were at ease.

She really is a remarkable creature, he thought, reaching in to brush some of her black strands from her face. His claws were unsteady as he tucked them behind her ear, but he made sure to be gentle so he didn't scratch her.

Nathair allowed just a knuckle's worth of touch, and her heat shot up his hand like a spark. He caressed the curve of her ear, her lobe, until he trailed his thick finger down her jaw.

He didn't realise how fast and frantic his heart had been beating until Linh's unmoving presence calmed it. A sigh of relief flittered out of him, and he just let himself be lost in the female he had in his keeping. Back bent, the base of his tail straight before it looped to the left, he folded an arm on top of the nest's ledge.

I don't think she will mind that I am doing this. He was touching her face and neck while admiring her, but he had no ill intent with it. He didn't even care that she wasn't awake to realise he was being affectionate. The secret of it felt special.

Trying to keep all focus on her, he thought it would keep the fragments at bay. But he was tired – she had not managed to sing to him in days – and drained. By the time he realised what was happening, his muscles locked up and white bled into his sight.

It stole all of her from him. He experienced nothing but the many fragments that hammered for attention, as if angered he'd managed to shove them back for so long. His body went colder than normal, and he didn't even have the strength to shiver in repulsion.

How long he remained as unmoving as stone, he didn't know.

The tiniest hint of warmth bled into the bone of his skull, and Linh's face flickered into view in the background. Her head tilted as she cupped both sides of his jaw. In the back of his mind, he registered that hours must have passed, and she was now awake.

He even caught a glimpse of a sun streak hitting her cheek.

A tingle over his body informed him he'd slipped away with his arm in the nest, his head tilted on its side against his biceps, and his throat on top of his hand. His back was still bent, most of his body straight besides the last half of his lengthy tail. Thankfully he was bendy, otherwise the prolonged position would have ached him.

She spoke to him, her voice inaudible, only to get up and leave.

White took over his senses once more. Minutes, hours, days could have passed before he sensed her return.

Once more, she cupped under his jaw. This time, she attempted to lift his limp head until it was straight.

Her voice was so quiet and distant. "Are you going to wake up for me?"

Nathair wished he could, but he hadn't been this deeply impacted for weeks. He'd spent days trapped in fragments on Earth, and months in Tenebris when he'd first done this to himself. The heaviness in his body told him he likely wouldn't be coming out of this for a long while.

He'd always been worried of this happening, and how she may take it.

Then a radiant sensation prickled over his snout. It tingled up the bone of his face, his horns, and slowly made its way down his neck and back.

Linh *hummed,* and it brought her to the forefront of his mind, his sight, his sense of smell. Her touch blasted him, and Nathair choked as he was shoved back into consciousness.

Her face, appearing with a bright smile as he held up the weight of his skull, was the first thing he saw with clarity. He managed to catch that she'd changed from her usual purple garment into the thigh-high pink dress with the leaves sewn in. She smelt clean, as if she'd gone to wash, which is where she may have left to.

"There you are," she stated with a giggle.

The moment she stopped humming, he fucking slipped away again. His head thunked against his knuckles and tipped against his biceps once more. Nathair didn't even have the strength to *curse* in annoyance within his mind, but he felt the irritation in his chest.

Linh hummed again, only to give him a fleeting moment of control until she ceased.

Her voice echoed in the background. "I guess humming isn't going to cut it today."

She stroked up his snout and between his empty eye sockets. He wanted to lean into that gentle touch with his sight closed to savour it.

"I don't want to sing to you, though." Instead of lifting his head, she tilted her own until their gazes were centred – hers bright and aware, his dazed and unfocused. "I'm feeling much better, and I want you to give me attention. I don't want to put you to sleep."

Please, his mind whispered. Perhaps some rest would aid him.

Soft lips pressed against the centre of his maw. He managed to take in the impression of her pretty brown eyes staring into him from just beyond his snout. When that didn't work, she tried to coax him out with many more over the bone of his skull. He wanted to lean into each press of her lips and feel them totally, rather than the sensations of his fragments.

He felt his body limping as pain radiated up a *leg* he didn't have. A hand at his side kept him steady, while his arm was crossed over the shoulders of another. *"Who the hell twists their ankle going shopping, Sarah?"*

A sigh flittered over his skull.

"Fine. I'll just *play* around you, then," Linh grumbled, a pout obvious in her voice.

Fuck, he wanted to see her pout. She was cute when she did so, and it usually had a contented purr vibrating from him. She was such a soft creature against his overall hardness that he liked when her personality moulded against him like this.

"You did say I could touch you *always*." He noted the humour.

Something cold and hard thunked against the top of his skull between his horns. "There, now you're king of the nest," she stated, and he figured she'd put the only tiara he had on top of his head. It slipped right off and clinked against the coins around her knees. "Fine. I'll wear it."

The green gem caught a fraction of light before the silver ore reflected the pinstripe of sun. She placed something on his wrist, then a second, as her voice echoed, "You're so big I have to put necklaces around your arm since they won't fit around that thick neck of yours."

Nathair was thankful for that, as he didn't like anything hard against his gills. Even her flat teeth were too sharp.

Metal clanked and chimed in the background of his fragments as she placed more jewellery on him. A bracelet around his horn, a ring up to the first knuckle of his pinkie.

"I wonder if I can touch you out of a trance?" He figured she'd gotten bored when nothing seemed to disturb him from his 'trance.' "You won't mind, will you? Do absolutely nothing if you don't mind."

Her giggle was conniving.

She faded from view, only for weight to press upon his back. Circling her arms over his shoulders, she lay on him and spoke, yet little of it was registerable. He grunted when hands glided up his back, only to trace down the protruding bones of his spines. She straddled him and dug her fingers into the tense muscles of his back, as if she wanted to knead him of the strain clutching them.

A groan flittered in the back of his mind, her nimble fingers pressing in places that had his gut tightening.

Then she leaned forward as she did, and a growl burst within his conscience when she kissed at his gills from behind. His seam instantly clenched, his cocks jerking, only for a deep throb to thrum when she bit down on his puffed shoulder. She lathered kisses across his shoulders, her voice whispering something, before she licked at the other side of his neck.

Purple flickered in his sight when she sucked, only for it to immediately snuff out to white.

She straddled his waist, then slipped down, and down, until she'd brought herself below his hips. His body twitched when she gripped him just below his hips – where the base of his tail began. For a second, her voice became loud.

"I guess you do have a butt." She lightly spanked it! Her following giggle, as she did it multiple times, had his fingers twitching. "Ohhh, I bet I'd be in so much trouble right now. Too bad you can't do anything about it."

She wasn't gripping it, nor kneading it, but rather playing it like it was a drum. *How would she like it if I did that to her?* She was attempting to coax him out any way possible, and to his dismay, it wasn't working. She lightly spanked him a few more times.

But, as she lay down once more, and hugged his narrow humanoid waist rather than his chest, he flinched. She managed to glide her hands up his abdomen, and her tiny fingertips dipping into all the muscles made each one spasm. When she went too high up, he was too wide for her smaller frame, so she came back down.

His vision wavered and his cocks hardened the lower she went. If Linh didn't have any intention of playing *his* way, then he hoped she didn't caress his seam. She didn't, but she came dangerously close enough to tease him, tickle him, and make his groin tingle until he felt himself parting. *Fuck. Am I extruding?* Inside pressure was relieving, as central hard rods gave way.

Strength began returning, the voices quietening, but not enough to yank him free.

She came back around into the nest, and her features were clearer than before. He was able to take in the silver tiara on her head with a central green diamond-shaped gem. It flattened down her long, straight hair, and the lengths tickled into her cleavage. Her breasts looked softer in her pink dress than normal, as if she'd chosen not to wear her undershirt with it this time.

Oh fuck. Nathair groaned when, now that she was in front of him and his nose hole, he took in her scent.

The little female was aroused, and saliva instantly flooded his maw. Unable to muster the strength to swallow, it seeped from his downward-pointing mouth. His tentacle-shielded cocks fully extruded, throbbing, just as his breaths turned rapid through his nose hole.

She's turned-on. I want to touch her so badly. And yet, he was fucking stuck!

He'd always hated the fragments, but he resented them even more in this very moment. This female, this tempting little creature, was *teasing* him, despite her reservations, and he was limp. His cocks were pointed towards the ground, when he'd much rather them be pointing towards the hot heaven between her thighs.

"Do I really have to sing?" she asked, her brows furrowed and her eyes bowed. She tightened her lips. "What if I flash you my tits?"

She revealed them, and all his fingers twitched as another growl rumbled from him – although he didn't know if he did it aloud or in his head.

Dismayed, she hid them and lifted his head once more. He saw the whisper of a disgruntled expression.

"Come on, Nathair." She came closer, just to kiss his maw again. "It must be really bad today, huh?" She kissed down the side, following the bony seam of his mouth. "I'm feeling better, and I want to touch you. Don't you want that?"

I do. Absolutely he did. She was flitting around him like a fucking aroused fairy, and he was a freaking statue.

More than ever, Nathair fought. He battled as his entire consciousness seemed to tremor and shake, threatening to shatter and fall like glass panes. The fragments refused to let up, even when his sight blackened as she kissed at his neck again before travelling back up his jaw.

She came to the centre, pressing her lips right where she knew he liked it. Yet he could scent her arousal waning.

Linh pulled back, only to sigh again.

No! Don't you fucking dare sing. His vision was straightening, his body was beginning to respond. His heart was rapid with the strain, but he could feel himself winning. *Don't you dare put me to sleep.*

She opened her mouth, and a yell roared from within his skull.

Nathair darted forward, and she rolled back with a squeal at his lunge. Within seconds, he'd wrapped the back of her head in his left palm to stop it from knocking against his treasure while simultaneously lifting it. With his right elbow, he kept himself up so he didn't crush her beneath the power of his leap.

A groan fell as he licked across her lips. She immediately parted them to let him inside, and his entire body shuddered with aftershocks from his fragments. They clamoured inside him, shouting to clutch at him again, while he used all his might to stay focused on her.

Her slim arms slipped around his neck to keep him to her, and the warmth helped to soften him. *Fuck, Linh.* Nathair shuddered again. *She brought me out.* She'd really done it, and not even he could do that for himself.

He usually had to let the power of them wane first when they were that stifling. To let them play and have their moment before he was given a drop of unquiet peace.

Today, she'd battled his will with him, and he still felt muddled, like there were blobs of oil in his brain. He was hard, his cocks threatening to break from his tentacles, and his heart was beating so fast he thought the tendons holding it in place would snap.

His mind was not sound, and instincts bit at him with sharp fangs.

Before he knew it, he darted his right hand beneath her dress and was grasping a naked breast. Thankfully, she arched into his harsh knead rather than away from it. His palm weighed her soft mound, her nipple scraping along the crease, and he quickly reminded himself to sheath his claws before he attempted to do more.

Nathair didn't care what her reasons were – if she'd desired to touch him because she truly felt well, or if she was brave enough to try again. Perhaps she missed his constant presence and wished to show him just how much.

Whatever the case, his skull felt like it was trying to split in two as he attempted to stay present – here, with her and in this moment.

When Linh gave a soft moan, his palm slipped down her body. He didn't make it to his destination. Instead, his hand caught her dress as he placed it against the bottom of his nest when a voice barrelled into him. He pulled his snout away from her lovely lips to huff.

Fuck. Leave me alone! He was tired of this, of them. Hadn't he suffered enough for his mistake?

Linh stole his focus purposefully by licking, sucking, and kissing the side of his neck. His gills flared, and a pleased growl burst from him. He touched her once more.

Palming her stomach to make sure she understood his destination, he glided past her navel. He expected to feel material at her pelvis, but a thatch of hair greeted him, just as she rose her hips to quicken his apparent slow pace.

Underneath her dress, her entire body was bare. *Had she... always been intending for me to touch her today?* No wonder the scent of her arousal had been strong – there'd been no barrier.

Nathair glided into the wet lips of her pussy, and somehow her scent strengthened in his senses. He slammed two fingers inside her, and he was delighted when her loosened core easily accepted them. Her little moans whispered across his gills as he quickly pumped his digits in and out, trying to get her to be louder so she could quieten his mind.

There we go, little nightingale. Cry for me, he thought when she started milking his fingers. She'd fallen off the edge so swiftly for him, as if her body had been pleading for his touch.

Her nails dug into the backs of his shoulders, while her scent, her voice, her very presence grew stronger for him.

"N-Nathair," she croaked, her tone lax and thick, while she pulled back to give him a heavy-lidded gaze. "Can you go to your back?"

His shoulders twitched when he realised he was towering over her and had pinned her to the bottom of the nest. Refusing to part from her, Nathair took Linh with him as he moved to lie back. Her legs slipped across his treasure, making it clink and chime before he laid her across him.

Before he could do anything more, she started kissing her way down his torso. Nathair grabbed the back of her dress to see if she'd willingly slip out of it, and she ducked so he could toss it. The moment she was completely bare to him, he soaked in the lovely sight of her naked body upon his.

The crooks of her thighs slipped over his cocks, and he hissed out a breath of need. *Fuck. I'm so hard.* He'd been hoping she'd put one out of its misery and just mount it, but she sat behind them. Precum leaked from the tips of both.

"Inside," Nathair signed, his chest weighted with lustful need.

Both cocks jerked in opposite directions at just the thought of her gloving one with her wet heat.

He forced his hands to grip the ledge of his nest with a growl rumbling from his chest when she gave him a *defiant* glare.

She had a very horny, unwell, and agitated Mavka below her. Teasing him further was unwise. To stay in control, he tilted his head back so he could settle himself by looking away from her and wading through the thick mud in his mind.

Be calm for her. His fists bunched, cracking a branch of his nest.

The pads of her fingers *gently* pressed against the left cock, directing it, just as softness pressed against it. Unfamiliar with the sensation, but instantly jerking for it, he waited for Linh. *Be calm.* He couldn't do what he wanted with this female.

Perhaps one day he could be more demanding and forceful, but until then, he had to be a good Mavka.

Well, that was what he intended.

A snarl burst out of him when a strange warmth engulfed him, and one of his hands shot forward to grab the back of her head. He looked down in shock to find her lips one-third of the way down his purple cock. Her brown eyes sparkled up at him, hinting at mischief and playfulness.

Nathair took his hand away when the nagging desire to shove her head down until he'd breached her throat and forced her all the way to the base gnawed at him. Her mouth appeared to be filled to capacity, his cock thick against the features of her face.

She was a little human, he a big Mavka, and although his split dicks meant she could properly suck him, it didn't mean they'd ever be able to play with abandon. They were long, and the true power of his girth came from them nestled together.

So, Nathair just absorbed how nice she looked bobbing her head while her soft, warm, and wet mouth glided up and down. It was a snug fit; her teeth constantly scraped over the sides of him and her lips were stretched as far as they could, but he didn't mind. The roof of her mouth was textured, bumpy and ridged.

The important thing was that she was sucking him, while she fisted the other to give it attention as well. She didn't seem to mind his lubricant, since she greedily swallowed it along with any seed he produced.

Nathair parted his maw to pant at the vision of her before him. *Take it slow for me, little nightingale.* Linh, naked, sucking him, while her eyes flicked between his purple orbs and his cocks. *I want to savour this.* He flicked his tongue forward so he could greedily taste her arousal in the air. *Fuck. So lovely.*

She removed her mouth just to lather kisses along both, apparently wanting to show affection before she gulped the one she had yet to take in her mouth as far as she could. Nathair groaned and palmed the top of her head again.

He almost lost his fractured mind when she even licked up the middle of both, sucking on the head of each at different intervals. He watched her pink tongue dabble his purple cocks, while her lips sucked with hums, moulding to his hardness.

He wanted to ask her questions. Did she like the feel of him in her mouth, his taste, how he had two for her to play with? Instead, he was so fucking lost watching her that he could do nothing but jerk and twitch. His abdomen constantly dipped as bubbles of precum crawled up the lengths of his cocks.

One moment the left was closer to release, then it was the right, and his tail bunched and knotted in confusion.

Then she attempted to squeeze them together to lick and suck them – although poorly due to the size difference between them – at the same time. Her tongue swirled, drawing little patterns, circling one, then the other, then stroking in the middle.

She brought the left back into the heaven of her mouth, and Nathair's sight flashed with black.

"I'm about to come," he signed with shaking arms, his head tipping back as his spine arched downwards. She moved to the other cock, and Nathair gently, *gently,* guided her back to the left. "Swallow me, Linh."

When she slipped those lips up and down him, gaining speed, Nathair's entire body rippled. *Oh fuck. Nhn.* Tingles raced through him, just as the left swelled, with the right following directly behind it in reaction to the deep clutch of his groin.

The groan that fell from Nathair was accompanied by his maw parting and his venom-coated fangs dropping. He slipped lower inside his nest, which forced his sight forward to land on her, just as he released the first rope of seed – straight into her mouth.

She gulped it down when the second rope began to overflow through the seam of her lips, and his right cock began to release up his torso from her stroking it. The delay had him shuddering beneath her as he slid further down the nest wall. When the first cock only produced dribbles, she placed her mouth around the other to take what cum she could from it.

She'd taken full control of him, of them, and the sight was fucking killing him. He felt like he was moments from splintering.

Panting as he watched her *clean* his cocks once he was done violently spending, his body was hit with aftershocks. He'd always hoped she'd suck him, but this? Where she played with both at the same time, loving on them with licks and sucks as she gave little contented moans... it'd been perfect. The experience – the sight of her, feel of her, smell of her, the cute sounds of her – would forever be seared into his mind.

"You're so messy," she stated around his cocks with kisses. She wasn't wrong; much had overspilled from her lips, and he'd come all over his abdomen.

I'm still hard. Sure, slightly drained, but she kept playing with them, stopping them from softening after what she'd just done to him.

Nathair reached down and grabbed her round arse with both hands while slithering back up to sit somewhat upright.

When she was lined up above his cocks, he caressed his right hand up her body. He appreciated her hips, the narrow dip in of her waist, and all the soft skin that covered her. He grasped a breast, flicking her sensitive nipple, before palming up her throat until her head tilted back for him.

Dipping his head down, he followed his hand by licking at her throat while letting his cool, bony maw brush over her. She gifted him a shaking moan with her lips parting on a rasp. Then he brought his hand back down between them, so he could stroke her saturated clit, only to dab at the entrance to her warm, overflowing cunt.

He teased her and waited for her to answer the silent question. She tried sitting on two of his fingers, and he refused to let her.

"Please, Nathair. Inside me," she whispered against his

horn. "My pussy aches."

He lowered her while fisting his cocks together. He nudged them against her entrance to see if she would let him mount her with both – or one – he really didn't care which right then.

Linh sat back on them, and he let out a small groan at the pressure. Together, they tried to push them inside. Nathair knew by the tightness that greeted him that getting her to stretch around both in the first thrust wasn't going to work. He let one go, and she let out a loud cry when the left one bottomed out within her.

Fuck, hot. At least her mouth had warmed them in preparation so he didn't *squeal* this time.

Nathair continued to lick at her neck even when she tipped her head back, leaned back on straightened arms to arch her spine, and began *riding* him. He cupped a bouncing breast, and just let her release all the energy from earlier. Her moans were loud, and they tingled in his mind as she fucked herself.

He pulled her up and away so she could mount the other, wanting to get to that same state as before. The one where she'd made his groin twitch and convulse in confusion, unsure of which would release first. Nathair switched her constantly, and he was too dazed to know where the one not currently mounted was slipping. Linh rode each one with enthusiasm, unbothered that he kept pulling out of her so long as one of them shoved back in.

Nathair growled when her pussy walls snapped tight around him as she started to come. *Nnhn, she's perfect.*

The scent of her orgasm, combined with wet and hot liquid squelching out of her, had his tongue lazily drinking it from the air. Her melodic cry was mind-altering as it rung in his sensitive ears. He rocked as her tension had her jerking and missing her own thrust beats. Nathair stayed with her, refusing to remove his cock until she was done wringing herself around it.

The moment she was done, he made her mount the other so he could feel her scramble his brain by coming around it as well. Their movements were still slow, but he had no desire to rush this.

She seems insatiable today. And luckily for Linh, Nathair was *hungry* for her. She was still wearing the tiara, even though it was partially dislodged, and it was like he had a princess riding his cock like a wanton nymph.

That's it, little female. Fuck yourself as much as you need. He groaned against her neck when she clamped him with little spasms before loosening. *I'm all yours to use.*

Then he felt her hand push against the head of his cock nestled between her arse cheeks. He grunted when it lined up with the tight hole, only to hiss out from the groin-clenching spasm that blasted him when it went deeper.

Nathair parted from her so he could apologise and connected with her gaze. Her eyes flicked between his purple orbs as she bit her lip.

"Y-you said I can claim *all* of both of us, right?" she asked around airy breaths, never taking her stare from him. Her pink cheeks deepened.

Wait, she wants *to mount both like this?* he thought, his mind too muddled and weak to understand clearly.

"You did let me know you wanted this last time," she continued.

Did I? He could no longer sift through his mind to remember anything beyond what they were currently doing. He was so horny that his entire essence was obsessed with hers.

Seeing as he wasn't stopping her, she backed onto it more, and his left hand, still gripping her arse, pulled her cheeks apart. The other gently cupped her throat as he began to rock to the tightness that greeted him. His maw parted as he let out feverish huffs.

Her face twinged, as if in uncomfortable pain, and he instantly healed her. He'd take any aches for her so long as she sat that ass around his fucking cock. He barely felt the stings in his spine as she softened and took him deeper, and he continued to heal her even when the head popped through.

Ohhh, fuuuck, Nathair groaned, as his tail twisted and contorted.

The muscled ring of her was so tight it tried to crush him, while her soft pussy nursed the other. Beautiful heat greeted both his cocks, and yet it felt like his body was being split in two.

Holding her with both hands to keep her steady, he thrust up until he bottomed out in her pussy. But Nathair could feel he could go deeper within the tightness of her ass.

Cool, orange magic continued to swirl around them, and her little moans said he was doing everything right. She felt no pain, no uncomfortableness, and was able to just bounce on both his cocks freely.

From the front, he grabbed both her thighs and pushed her back while balling his tail behind her. She gasped as she fell, but he made sure to settle her weight in his palms as he spread her. Then, *finally*, Nathair saw all of this woman bare to him.

He'd glanced at her pussy last time, but now he took his fill of her pretty pink clit. He lifted her up and down his purple cocks. Although he struggled to see the one that had twisted beneath the other, he felt it.

Thighs wide, her knees bent, he could see her pussy was spread and greedily taking him. The entrance to her cunt looked overstretched as it clung to his purple cock, but he thought by now she may be able to swallow both inside it. Yet, even if he wanted to, Nathair couldn't pull away from her like this.

The conflicting differences, the textures, had him breaking apart beneath her. Her body was on show for him. She gripped his wrists to keep her torso steady as he worked her up and down his cocks.

Fuck. I've never seen anything as erotic as this. Not even the intimacy in his fragments could compare to seeing his own body being mounted this way.

Her breasts bounced and swayed, her long, loose hair along

with it. With her back tilted to a half-seated position against his tail wrappings, she looked down to watch how he used her body to fuck his own cocks. She moaned for him, and her insides spasmed and clenched.

She didn't fight him, and instead spread herself further apart as her feet bounced, toes clenching.

She looked naughty like this, and her eyes crossing on lewd moans had him snarling in triumph.

Nathair knew something with absolute certainty in that moment: *I love her.* He produced a pitiful moan as his cocks swelled hard. His sight blackened just as her face darted up to him with parted lips, and his head lolled to the side, too heavy to hold up right then. *I love her. I love this. I love the way she looks, smells, feels, and how she accepts all of me. I love how sweet she is to me, and how she sings when she comes for me.*

He wrapped the tip of his tail around one of her thighs so he could free up his right hand.

"Deeper," Nathair signed, unsure if he even spoke out loud along with it.

Fuck, I want deeper. He wanted it so much right then, he considered just taking it with how his clawed fingers tingled. Even when his mind had grown hazy with lust, he knew he wouldn't.

"Y-you can't go deeper, though," she answered, barely able to speak properly.

With an annoyed, growly groan, Nathair cut his palm with his middle finger and slapped it against the side of his nest. He opened his sight just as his orange light symbol glowed to life beside them.

Her eyes flicked to it, and it seemed to register in her mind.

"Deeper." Then, with a pathetic whine ripping his chest, he signed, *"Please."*

If he needed to beg, he fucking would. He'd plead, whimper, he'd grovel for it. Whatever would convince her to envelop him so completely he shattered.

"Will it hurt?"

He shook his head; he didn't believe so? At least, not enough that he couldn't heal her from it. He knew what the buzzing in his fingertips meant; he would need to lance her. He could sense in the back of his mind what he needed to do.

"Is it... permanent?" she asked, and Nathair paused the movements of their joining to stare at her through deep huffs.

I don't know, he thought. He didn't know if he could reverse such magic, or if... he'd even want to. She said she wanted to claim all of his body, and that was the only way to. Until she did, until she swallowed every inch of him, she'd claimed him in a sense, but only partially.

"Okay." Her eyes flicked to the magic symbol again. "Do it. I want all of you."

Nathair struck so fast she didn't even have a chance to react until he'd already embedded his claws into her abdomen. The devious, quiet chuckle that fell from him was excited and maddened. He released the pressure but not the steadiness of his left hand and tail, so she would *fall* down the lengths of his cocks.

"Oh!" she gasped, only to let out shuddering, quivering moans as they let gravity do the work.

Her body arched and dipped as she wiggled her way down. Her legs tried to shut, only to open wide, as her toes curled. His tongue fell forward to pant in feverish lust as he watched his cocks disappearing inch by inch into the sopping wet heat of her.

Linh's pussy changed for him as his cock pushed the boundary of it. When she was seated to the base, his tentacles snapped around her hips to keep her to him. He removed his claws, and the body-altering magic stopped her from bleeding on his exit, while allowing his puncture marks to remain.

He considered completely healing her in case she felt pain, but he *wanted* to scar her. Her body was perfect, not a single marking or scar upon her – except for *his* claws.

From now on, when she looked at her own body, she'd see what they'd both done to her.

He lifted her by the backs of her thighs while dipping his hips down, only to shunt hard inside her. He did it again, slamming into her as hard and deep as he could, and she remained soft and pliable for him. *I can do whatever I want now.*

He didn't have to take into consideration her human boundaries. She'd seated herself completely and wholly around a Mavka, and now became ripe for his rutting.

Nathair darted forward and swallowed Linh in his limbs. He coiled his tail around the little female to bring her into their nightly cuddle to ensure she, hopefully, felt safe. He tried not to be above her, although he couldn't help partially being so.

"Nathair?" she asked softly, as she wrapped her legs around his hips and her arms around what she could reach of his back.

Nathair buried his snout against the top of her hair, ignoring the half-dislodged tiara on it. With his arms wrapped around her and squeezing her in place, his purr and growl mixed together as he fucked into this human as fast, as hard, and as deep as he could.

All slowness fell away as he gave her body *everything* he'd been holding back.

Her answering and immediate scream was accompanied by her pussy and ass clamping around both his slamming cocks as she came. He cupped the back of her neck to support her head as he ruthlessly pumped through her orgasm.

That's right, little nightingale. Come for me as I fuck into you.

His chuckles were not of humour, but of his utterly blissful delight as he took this female in the way he'd been longing to. In a way that was so consuming for them both, that she clawed at his back with her little nails until she'd flaked off scales.

She continued to come as the hard and long lengths of his cocks hammered into her pussy through their combined pressure. He could feel himself moving inside her through their abdomens squished together, and knowing she was so utterly stuffed only made him be more vicious.

His entire body moved, his tail slithering and squirming around her in rapture. He soaked in her heat from all around, while her insides warmed his groin, and his very heart.

He didn't mean to give a menacing *hiss* against her hair, but his seed sacs clenched unbearably hard, and liquid shot up his cocks. They both swelled like they would burst.

Even as the deep pelvis clutch obliterated his groin, Nathair didn't soften any part of his thrusting as he ruined her insides for himself, as he came inside both her holes. He just quaked, twitched, and wriggled as he exploded heavy, thick ropes within her. Her pussy quickly overfilled, but her ass took every drop until it was by the force of his pumping that it leaked.

For once, he didn't cover them both in his possessive sexual scent, and instead gifted it all to her. She wouldn't be able to wash this away, and he hoped to give it to her constantly. To have her milk him nightly, hourly, whatever she wished.

Mine. I want her to be mine so badly. Now and forever. In this life, and in the next. Nathair wanted to give it all to this female, and be gifted with everything in return. To connect with her on this deep, pleasurable physical level so completely that it transcended all levels of their psyche, their spirit, their essences.

With a final thrust, he made sure his hips were slammed against her so he could be seated deep while he crashed back to reality.

Their hearts raced so fast he couldn't figure out whose beat belonged to who. Her breaths sounded strangled, his rough and broken. *Fuck. That felt amazing.* He groaned against her hair as a last – likely small – bubble of cum escaped him. *I cannot believe she took both for me.*

I love her. She was so brave and resilient, despite everything, despite her soft and sometimes meek personality. She was so good, and sweet, that if he hadn't experienced it firsthand, he never would have believed she could be this *naughty.*

Little nightingale... when will you gift me your soul?

She'd let him change her... Did that mean she would bond them? This could be permanent, and yet she'd agreed to it. That had to *mean* something.

I only intended to ask for this once she gave me her soul. But he'd been so damn lust-brained that he'd asked anyway. Nathair winced when he realised he may have made a mistake. *I should have done this while she was taking my cocks in her pussy. Hopefully it's possible to do it a second time if need be.*

Now that they'd both settled, he pulled back to cup the side of her flushed and sweat-dotted face. *I hope she is okay.* He lifted her head enough so that he could gaze down at her.

In the dark, her eyelids continued to flicker, but she didn't appear distressed. She remained lax in his arms, soft and docile, after he'd rutted her like a beast. He adored feeling her body pulse around his thrumming cocks.

Her features stiffened as her cores clamped around him momentarily. Her muscles stayed soft, though, even as she said, "Can you pull out now?"

He did so gently, while unfurling his tail to give her freedom should she need it. It looked as though he'd been correct. She hadn't minded their position, even though he was slightly above her, since she was in his familiar cuddle, which kept her feeling secure.

As he exited her, he noted that his cock within her pussy was saturated in their combined liquids, while the tight ring of her ass stole every bit of his cum and lubricant. She cleaned him by taking it and holding it all.

Sitting up, she straddled his tail with her hands upon his waist until he turned beneath her and lay straight.

"I feel okay," she said through a croaked and cracked voice, flashing him a warm smile. The relief of that flooded his veins. "Are you feeling better?"

Nathair didn't wish to respond to that question, as he doubted she'd like his answer.

His seed sacs felt much emptier, and his heart was light, but the fragments continued to skitter in his skull. Now that his body wasn't receiving intense pleasure, his mind was being pulled at its edges. Like fraying rope, he wondered how long he could hold on before the wiry stings of his consciousness disintegrated.

He nodded, though.

Her smile grew as she cupped his jaw and kissed his snout. "I'm so glad you're okay," she whispered against his skull. "I was really worried about you. I woke up wanting you, but you weren't in the nest with me."

"Again?" He signed the word with a deep chuckle, rubbing his cocks and tentacles against her round backside.

"No!" she squealed, her eyes gleaming with mirth as she pulled the tiara from her hair and dropped it to the coins below. "I think I'd like a shower. Can we go to the beach? I really feel like being in the sun with you today."

Nathair playfully sighed. "Sure. Beach it is. But you must take the lantern with you, just in case you need to return on your own."

If she cannot bring me to the forefront again, I do not want her outside with the Demons. He doubted he'd be able to protect her should they be attacked and his fragments were too strong. And, if she sang, she'd put him to sleep.

"I can just hum for you as we walk back, though." She rubbed against his snout, apparently wishing to dole an endless amount of affection on him today. "I can even hold your hand and guide you if need be, so long as you put your light magic on my clothes."

She would do that for me? He didn't imagine he'd be in any state to move well. The lethargy he'd been weighed down with before had ached his bones, but if she was willing to walk with him back to the main cave...

His heart swelled in tenderness for this sweet female.

She slipped off him, squeaking as seed leaked down her thighs in thick globs. She snagged her dress, and he was pleased she intended to wear it again. Then she climbed her way out of the nest, and he licked at his snout as she flashed him her dripping pussy from behind.

With his arms shaking, he propped himself up on the wall.

Just as Nathair began to slither out of his nest, wincing at the muddiness in his head, he paused. She'd stopped halfway to the exit of the main cave and was waiting for him to notice her.

With her bundled dress barely shielding her nudity, Linh held up her right hand.

With her pinkie straight, her middle and ring fingers curled down, and her thumb and index fingers straightened to make an 'L' shape, she pushed her palm towards him. Then she shook her hand.

Nathair tilted his head. *Is this a sign from her people?* He didn't know it, as it wasn't one he'd taught her.

"What does this mean?" he signed as he slipped from his nest towards her.

Her lips flattened as the edges curled. Tenderness, joy, and other emotions beamed in her features, making her eyes soft and warm. Linh let out the cutest giggle as she turned and ran off.

"Wait!" She didn't turn to see his hand gesture, and he chased after her until she went into the shadows of the tunnel. Nathair halted. He refused to follow, as he didn't want to violate her only place of privacy.

He turned his sight down to his own right hand. A streak of sunlight hit his palm as he made the same gesture, and his orbs shifted to dark yellow in curiosity. His sharp claws made it more menacing.

What does it mean?

TWENTY-NINE

Oh my gosh! Linh's mind reeled as she patted her flushed cheeks in disbelief. Crouching down in the water's spray at her washing area, she covered her mouth to hide her grin from *no one*. With the oil torch she always left in here giving her light, her gaze flickered over the dancing shadows.

Oh my gosh. He said he loves me!

Well... not *him*, not truly. Like always, his thoughts had leaked through, and he never seemed to realise – as if he was too distracted.

I thought he might... but I didn't want to just assume. He'd asked for her soul, but he'd never stated anything regarding his feelings.

He could want her soul for a bunch of reasons, some of them selfish, others fond. He could have been instinctually possessive, like a neanderthal bashing his chest going 'mine' at the first female he saw.

He was also a... Duskwalker, a *monster*. Love may have been too deep of an emotion.

He loves me. And it didn't feel *wrong*. She'd had someone else say that to her, and it'd made her skin crawl. It'd made her feel suffocated, like a set of chains around her throat.

But if this was Nathair's love... then it felt right. It felt obsessed in a way that wasn't cruel or controlling, but enlightening. It felt safe, like she was perfect – like he'd *said*

– and she could feel secure in that infatuation.

Her heart had responded to it immediately.

Little fuzzy balls had unfurled in her chest like butterflies – so light, fluffy, and beautiful. The warmth of it had swirled around in her bloodstream, making her want to do or give him whatever he wanted.

Even her sternum had grown hot, like her soul had been moments from fluttering out of her so he could take it.

As much as she truly thought she needed a shower, as she was covered in seed and a little tender, she'd needed a moment to digest all this. She didn't feel sick, quite the opposite. Her stomach felt gooey with lingering desire and her returned affections.

I love him too. She'd known at the quartz cave that she'd been falling for him, but she knew it for certain once she woke and wasn't radiating aches.

Aches she'd suddenly been missing and had hungered to have returned to her. Aches that stiffened her muscles and made her wince, but were the evidence of a well-pampered body.

I want to give him my soul. She wanted to be with Nathair. *Hopefully he'll let me visit my family and will help them with the bandits anyway.* Even if it meant Bragg's men were no longer an issue for Linh if she were to stay here with Nathair, she would still like to help the valleys. *He would. He says he doesn't want to help, but I know he will do the right thing.*

She smiled as she thought, *I want to tell him I love him too.*

She'd like to do it in the sun with the beach beside them. She'd like it to be special, and for her to get all her nervous jitters out first. To feel clean, and hope that he'd already be combing his claws through her hair when she offered her life to him. She wanted to be sitting on his tail, all wrapped up, knowing that would be her life from then on.

With an excited bounce to her steps, she stood to exit the water. She picked up her pink dress and thumbed the green leaf pattern. The bumpy texture made her smile, and she was glad she'd be wearing this today as she spoke with him.

Just as she went to put it over her head, a loud, boisterous roar made her jolt. Linh stumbled, catching her foot on the edge of a rock, and fell to her knees. She popped her head through the neckline and turned her head towards the darkness.

That sounded like Nathair. And it'd sounded... *distressed.*

Without thinking if it would be wise or not, Linh guided her hand down the wall to go to him. Although she wanted to sprint as fast as her heart was beating, her feet were never steady at the best of times.

She stumbled when she thought, *what if it's a Demon?*

Then again... a Demon would have come straight for her.

With her lips flat in determination, she went faster when whines, whimpers, and raspy hisses came from the muted light before her. She entered the main cave, and gasped so hard her lungs seized and her throat stuck together.

Reared back with a dipped torso, as if he was struggling to hold himself up, Nathair squirmed. He clawed at the sides and back of his neck. Then he dipped forward to grab the underside of his skull from behind, claws stabbing deep, and pulled with all his might like he wanted to rip his own head off!

His maw parted, and a chill instantly clutched at her bones. Gut-tightening dread knotted her insides.

"Please, don't," a woman cried from *him,* before she screamed. *"S-stop."*

Nathair's yells, as if his level of distress was so strong it broke through his silence, overshadowed the woman as he roared, "No! Make it stop! Not these memories. Not these thoughts!"

"Nathair!" Linh exclaimed when she noticed how much *blood* there was. Dark-purple liquid steamed down his humanoid torso in rivulets.

She was right. He truly was trying to remove his own head. *It's like the day on the beach.* Like Nathair was partially conscious, able to move and react rather than being in what she considered a half-sleeping trance.

"Please, calm down," she yelled, putting her hands up, but didn't dare touch something so large and dangerous.

His white orbs flared bright orange, and he shoved her away so hard that she fell onto her backside. "Stay *back!*" he roared, while dropping his fangs, and giving her a resounding *hiss*.

Heat drained from her features as she pushed up on straightened arms. *He's never pushed me before.* Then again, he's never done *this* before either.

His whines and whimpers made her heart squeeze.

Linh backed up but didn't back down. Instead, she used the only tool she had in her arsenal: her voice. She sang with all her might. Through sheer force of will and the desire to help him, she managed to keep her voice from shaking so it wouldn't ruin whatever power she had.

Even as he continued to writhe and scratch at his own neck, she didn't stop. Nathair clawed down his throat until he tore open his flesh all the way to his spine. His wounds gaped, revealing purple muscles.

Then, after a minute, he began to slow as a deep breath left his parted maw. He snapped it closed as he turned to her, to the sound of her voice. She expected him to dart around her in comfort, but he just fell to the side until his skull and one of his horns bashed against the stone with a horrible *thunk*.

"Linh," he rasped, reaching out a hand until it fell against the ground weakly.

She kept singing as she crawled her way to him. Linh knelt behind his head, and he shuddered as he rolled to his back to give his chest room to breathe. He struggled, each rise and fall accompanied by a wheezed whimper.

As carefully as she could, she lifted his weighty skull and propped it on her legs as tears of sympathy bubbled in her eyes. They fell directly onto his beautiful, bony face. She never stopped trying to lull him, yet he didn't fall asleep instantly like normal.

He appeared to be in too much pain, or perhaps his rapidly

heaving chest was too frantic. She placed her hand over his heart to feel it was fretful and so fast she feared it'd burst any second.

His gills on both sides were torn to shreds. If he tried to swim, she knew he'd suffocate. Blood saturated her favourite dress, but she didn't care; all she cared about was his wellbeing.

Nathair gained the strength to lift his right hand so he could rub a claw under her tear-filled eye. "Little nightingale..."

A distressed hiccup burst through her song as she grasped his hand to keep it to her cheek. She rubbed against his knuckles and claws, wishing she could talk to him. She wanted to tell him how sorry she was that he had to go through this, that she wished she had a way to help him more than what she was doing now. She wanted to tell him she loved him, cared for him, and wanted to be with him in hopes it would ease him through his pain.

"Don't cry for me," Nathair stated, his voice stronger in volume, as if the memories were gone, but his tone was weak and sluggish. "I will be fine."

Every time he swallowed, blood bubbled faster, and it was *harrowing* to watch.

He lowered his hand, despite her desire to hold on, so he could nudge against the corner of her lips. She didn't even know what song she was singing, or if it was just mumbled, pointless words.

"Thank you," he rasped.

As if he couldn't hold on any longer, the weight of his arm became too heavy for her to hold up. It slipped through her trembling grasp as his orbs blackened and he fell asleep for her.

Linh refused to stop singing. Like her body was in unison with her mind and heart, she didn't eat, didn't go to the bathroom, didn't do anything but this. She settled her tears to keep her strength, and only gave herself moments of rest by humming.

She knew he would eventually heal. After the fight with the bandits, he'd returned to her without a single wound. That didn't stop how pity swirled behind her sternum, aching for him and what he had to go through.

She hated that he'd been suffering through this for centuries.

Like the first time she'd done this, Nathair slept for hours. He didn't wake, even when the day morphed to night. The longer it dragged on, the more her eyes drooped. She longed to stay awake for him, but she found herself lying down around the top of his skull with her belly pressed to his horns. On her side, she stayed near his head so that if her singing softened, she'd be near his ear.

I'm so tired. A whole day and night had passed, and it wouldn't be long before the sun rose.

She closed her eyes and just focused on humming.

Something clasped her bare ankle, but she was so exhausted she barely registered it. Sleep had befallen her, and she kept waking just to sing, only to slip back under.

Linh screamed when she was tugged.

With eyes stark and wide, she gripped one of Nathair's horns when she was dragged across the ground. She held tight and braved looking at the Demon grabbing hold of her.

Its face was pointed and almost fishlike, with minute human qualities. She noticed an eel-type tail flopping around, so like Nathair's and yet so different.

"Shush!" she hissed, the Demon female in nature. "It sleeps! It's injured. Don't wake the Mavka."

Don't smell of fear! Linh told herself, choosing to remain as unafraid as humanly possible. She just clung to Nathair, hoping he'd wake to save her.

"Get off me!" Linh screamed, kicking her free leg to boot it in the face.

Red flickered in Nathair's orbs while a growl gurgled up his torn throat. It made his blood bubble through his maw, and even from his bony nose hole. It was a harrowing sound and sight, and she clenched her eyes as she looked away.

Claws dug into her calf as the Demon tried to obtain a better grip on her, and blood welled. The pain was small, the Demon's claws tiny, but Linh winced. She kicked harder and pulled on Nathair's horn to get away from it.

His maw parted, just as she whispered, "Please, Nathair. Help."

"Shut up, silly human," the eel-like Demon hissed. She darted forward to cover Linh's mouth. "His blood travels. More Demons come. Already fought for my prize."

It was then that Linh noted the gashes over its body, and the purple blood – like Nathair's – leaking from them. It covered her mouth to quieten her, while trying to pry her hands from his hooked horns.

Her own blood welled when her fingers were sliced, but she refused to let go.

Nathair moved like a flash of lightning. One minute she was clutching him, and the next, she belted out a scream when fangs lanced straight through the torso of the Demon and embedded into her thigh below it simultaneously. Ice-cold liquid burned her flesh as it spread deep into the muscle of her leg. He quickly removed his fangs to tackle the Demon, coiling around it like a snake trapping its prey.

A new Demon entered the main cave. Linh shuffled back while covering the punctures in her thigh. Nathair's fangs were so large that blood welled constantly from the deep wounds, and touching them made her whimper.

I need to get away from here. From the Demons and Nathair.

She eyed the water behind her.

He gave an ear-splitting roar with Demon blood coating his face. His orbs were red, his fins flared, and he looked *menacing*. He shuddered constantly, and his poor head tipped as if the muscles in his neck were ruined and unable to support it properly.

Using his hands to walk, his tail flicked side to side as he went into the tunnel to chase the scampering Demon.

But Linh knew, without a doubt, that her protector was currently not her friend.

He bit me in confusion. Well, the Demon's torso, but she'd been below it.

She dived into the water to minimise her blood scent. Holding onto the ledge, she splashed water onto the stone to reduce it even more. With that done, she started to swim to the other side of the lake, ignoring how cold the water was, how she was already shivering from blood loss. She'd never been more thankful that he'd taught her how to swim, otherwise she would have drowned.

She winced, only to cringe when her leg stopped responding. *The venom is spreading,* she thought, as her stomach muscles contracted. She was almost to the other side when her right arm began to grow lethargic.

Propping herself up enough that she could use her left arm and leg, the right side of her body became limp and useless. The second half of her quickly began to lock up as the paralysis spread faster now that it'd moved through her heart.

Managing to get out of the water until only her right foot was submerged, she focused on trying to breathe. Her lungs were tight, as if they, too, would turn to stone. Her breaths grew sharp, and she gasped for air.

The only light came from the torch on the other side of the cave and his magic circle still inside his nest. She stared at his magical glow when her head lolled. Screeches and roars reverberated up the tunnel while Nathair fought, only for silence to fall upon her.

For a long while, everything went quiet.

What's going to happen to me? Would she die? Lie here forever? She had no idea how his venom worked. *N-no. N-Nathair will heal me.*

Linh stopped being afraid when she couldn't even muster the strength for it. Her heart calmed to an eerily slow pace, and she worried it'd halt with how shallow her pulse was.

Her lids lowered as she tried to blink, but she never finished the movement. Her entire body went cold. *Shit.*

THIRTY

When Nathair heard the Demon, he'd hammered within his consciousness to break free. When he scented Linh's fear, everything pushed to the side to let his bloodthirsty rage charge forward.

His fragments quietened, as did his self, and he struck. The Demon, her, he wasn't quite sure.

The moment the Demon's blood filled his maw, and it wriggled against him like squirming prey, his focus became it. He ripped it apart and chased the second as it fled. Its scream of fear and scampering excited the most feral part of him, and his body ached for the hunt.

It escaped halfway down the tunnel before it ran into others. They all shrieked and screamed as he dived, coiling his limbs against each of them like a springing trap. Envenoming and consuming them had been swift.

He gained new claw marks, most situated over the length of his tail, but they did little to stop him. They only pushed him to be more violent and more aggressive, his veins flooding with the need to destroy. Then, once there was nothing but Demon blood infiltrating his senses, everything went quiet besides his own snarls and hisses echoing against the walls.

His rage slowly slipped away.

Nathair choked before he retched. With his shaking hands against the ground, he hacked, and each one broke his orbs until ethereal tears glittered around his skull. Human souls that had attached to the Demons' flesh, to their very essences, clogged in his throat as he tried to vomit them all up. They lingered in his gut, their white-hot flames burning his insides – despite Nathair not truly being able to feel them.

Get out of me! He wanted them out, to not have them attach themselves to him. To not curse him with more fragments when he already couldn't handle what gnawed at him.

Collapsing once he thought they may be all gone, he whined on his stomach. His lengthy body shivered and shuddered in the cold darkness, as wind from further down the tunnel brushed over him. *It hurts. Everything hurts.* His mind, and how it ached within his skull. His heart that had been racing too hard with all his extensive injuries. His limbs and scales that had been torn, battered, and bruised.

His nose was flooded with blood, much of it his own.

With orbs blue, and still crying, he snarled at a Demon that dared to come near. It skittered outside at his warning.

Linh, he whined.

He wanted to go to her. He wanted that little female like the pillar of salvation she was. He needed her near, to feel her stroking his skull while he dealt with the fact he ached. He craved her soft scent, the warmth of her skin bleeding into him, the way her pretty voice swirled around his throat and skull.

But he'd lost so much blood in the last few hours. He'd torn his own throat out until his spine had been exposed from the *inside.* All his strength had bled from him. All that remained to get him moving was the adrenaline of rage, which had withered away.

Then, Nathair fell asleep – on his own.

Blackness took him over totally. No Demons came; they would have alerted his lethargic, limp form.

Only when the wounds of his neck healed, a day finally fully passing, was he shoved into full alertness. His other injuries remained, punishing him with their stings. Sunshine glowed as it bounced off the exit tunnel to brighten a spot in the distance, and he assumed that was why nothing came to disturb his rest.

The blood in his nose disappeared when he healed, and his breaths and heart grew stronger. Weakness dissipated, leaving only worry and concern in its place.

Did we hurt her? Shit! Nathair spun, bracing his hands on the wall, before darting up the tunnel.

I haven't scented her blood. If she'd been terribly injured, the smell of it would have called to him. He would have hunted for her and awoken with the taste of her flesh within his maw.

It was all that gave him hope.

She did not follow. He wanted to believe it was because she was wise enough to stay away.

Yet the moment he broke into the main cave, he immediately knew something was wrong. Her lingering scent made it hard to pinpoint where she was. The sound of her was so quiet that it was covered by the constant trickling water.

He checked his nest to find her absent, and it was only when he searched the horizon of his home that he saw her. His heart nearly stopped at her pale form.

Unmoving, and silent like the dead, she lay on the other side of his underwater lake. He slipped inside it, only to breach the surface next to her and discover dried blood tracking down the rocks and into the water.

The whimper that broke from his chest was so hollow, his lungs almost collapsed under the brutal shudder of it. He thumbed next to the two puncture wounds on her right thigh, his heart breaking at the sight of them.

I'm so sorry, little nightingale, he whimpered, while scooping her into his arms when he made his way onto the thin ledge. He cradled the limp female to him, and alongside her weak heart and shallow breathing, she was as cold as ice.

Bumping the side of his snout against her chin, he took her wounds from her as his whimpers grew louder. He hoped she could hear them, and that she could feel when he grabbed her hand to circle it around his chest.

I'm sorry, Linh.

Because, no matter what he did, no matter how he tried, there was one thing he could not save her from: himself.

Healing her strengthened her heartbeat and breaths, but... Nathair was immune to his own venom. He could not envenom himself, and therefore, could not take this from her. She would not heal in a day.

Instead, every minute that passed, every hour, she would only grow weaker. His hunger was insatiable, and he could not ease it, not deepen it by stealing hers. He did not thirst, so he could not ease this for her. It wasn't possible to empty a well that was already barren.

Within a few days, unable to eat, unable to drink, she would naturally wither away.

This is why I could not kiss you when I had venom in my mouth. He didn't know what would happen if she ingested it, if it would matter or not, but he hadn't wanted to risk it.

I do not always bite.

Nathair only used his venom when he had many enemies to contend with. Swallowing paralysed bodies often immobilised him for a short period of time, so he preferred to excitedly rip apart his prey while they still kicked.

So, his fears of this, of envenoming her, had been small.

If she had given me her soul... Although morbid, he could have gently taken her life, and awaited for her to return to him in the same state as when he'd first taken it.

She would not be able to die permanently, forever tied to him. She would not grow old, or wither from sickness or hunger.

I would take it now to save you... but he worried that if he did, she would only return to him in this state. Then he would curse them both, and Nathair didn't have the will to survive in a life with a female that lay sleeping forever.

His whines never ceasing, he looked around his home.

He took in all the pieces she'd unwittingly left behind. Her bag nestled next to a dead campfire. Her seashells sitting on the ledge of his nest. Her purple dress and pants lying out to dry. Linh's scent clung to the earth and rock, and was strongest in his bed. The evidence of this woman being here was everywhere, and he knew he'd immediately evict himself once she was gone.

Turning his sight down to her, he brushed his forefinger against her soft cheek. *Why?*

Why did this have to happen? They were so close; he could feel it. She'd accepted him fully, had accepted his affection and touch. Why could his ill mind not have waited a little longer to break apart? Why did her gift of quiet have to come with such horrible consequences?

You are the heart that beats outside my chest.

And it was dying.

Not now, but she would. In a few days, this female's body would give up without sustenance.

He'd seen it before in many of his other victims. When he realised what he'd done when slipping out of a rage or fragment, he healed them and watched to see if they'd awaken from his venom. They never did, and he'd slit their throat and eat them to spare them of any pain their passing may cause.

To take their humanity and physical growth as a parting gift, only to spew up their soul.

I don't want to do that to her.

Hands trembling, his heart beat with agony from the loss already drowning him.

Staring down at her cold, dulled face, he hissed at her. *How dare you steal my heart, only to fucking die on me!*

He didn't even remember biting her! Only lancing the Demon before tackling it with its blood in his mouth. Flooding another creature with venom felt euphoric, so he wasn't even able to sit in the morbid triumph of feeling her warm flesh around his fangs.

Anger, spite, and hatred burned in his chest. At her, at himself, at how sickening his heartache felt. He'd chosen this female to be his damn bride, after years of telling himself he wasn't supposed to have one! He'd convinced himself that being alone was better, safer, quieter, only to fall for a pretty canary that would no longer *sing*.

I want you, he whimpered, nudging her with his skull in hopes of stirring her, unsure of what to do, how to fix this. *I want you within my tail coils at night. I want your warm body caressing me in your hold.* He wanted something to protect.

He knew of an answer, but unless Weldir was watching this very second, there was nothing Nathair could do to call him. His voice was lost, his ability to call his creator for aid non-existent. He was alone and had no one he could turn to. No one with magic who could undo his own.

He paused. *Her singing lulls me to sleep.* He leaned back to stare down at her beautiful face. *She's only partially human.* If she was part Anzúli, as were her ancestors, that meant... *There are more in her village.*

Could *they* aid him? The bigger question was: *would* they?

He soaked in her light breathing, the soft features of her face, the way she lay lifeless in his arms. *They will help her.* Not him, but this little human who was gentle, kind, and radiant. A female who constantly thought of her people's wellbeing – enough to plead for it from something as despicable as him.

Nathair slipped into the lake slowly, and carefully laid her on the surface. She didn't even tense up to the cold. When the water was to her neck, he tugged her low enough that it touched her lips.

His venom had left her body asleep, but her eyelids flickered in mild alertness. He covered her mouth and nose, pulling her under, only to bring her back to the surface. The moment she took some form of deeper breath, despite it still being rather shallow, he covered her mouth and nose again.

Nathair dived and bolted for his underwater tunnel.

Stopping halfway, he uncovered her face in an air pocket so she could breathe, then rubbed the side of her face and pushed damp hair from her blueish lips. The water in his lungs became stifling as he adjusted more slowly to breathing through his gills after healing her messed with his system. Once her breaths were strong, he dived again to head to the clearing of his pond, only stopping once more at another air pocket.

She will be okay.

She had to be. He could not take it otherwise.

THIRTY-ONE

As the mid-afternoon sun shone down on Nathair's back, he approached the western village of this northern mountain range. He did so slowly, making sure the people could see the female in his arms without interference.

There were no forests here, just meadows and hills rolling forever across the horizon. The river his pond was connected to rushed nearby. Grass swayed in the flower-filled wind, causing flurries of pollen, dust, and floating seeds to swirl around him.

He'd seen this village from a distance many times in the last few months, but he'd never approached the tall, wooden-stake wall that encompassed it.

At its base, surrounding the semi-circle village, were metal and wooden spikes sticking out from the ground, hoping to deter hungry predators. Small metal prongs had been hammered into the bottom sections of the stakes, acting as further deterrents for those who wished to climb.

The village itself pressed deeply up against a mountain wall. The stone had been carved smooth purposefully, likely to prevent Demons from climbing their way in from above. Smelted chains criss-crossed the village in an ingenious metal canopy, stopping anything that attempted to fly in from above from landing.

Being this deep in a mountain range, the humans had

figured out a way to truly keep monsters at bay. It wasn't foolproof, as he doubted anything would stop a rather large Demon, but everything they'd done would ensure there were fewer casualties.

He figured they had found a large iron or steel deposit to mine. That, or they traded with the other village to the east of here for it. Either way, one village had the metal, and the other the coal to produce the materials for *both* villages to survive in such harsh, Demon-infested conditions.

A horn blared as he slithered up an incline. It wasn't the first time he'd heard it, and he doubted it'd be the last.

When the ground levelled out, the village's wooden doors came into view. Archers, wearing fluffy brown animal-hide armour, nocked their arrows and pointed them at him.

Nathair halted and folded his tail underneath himself to 'sit' while he waited for them to decide on what to do. He did nothing as he let the sun warm him and the weak female in his arms. Linh's heart was steady, but her limpness continued to infuriate as well as dismay him.

She grows paler with every hour.

He doubted she'd eaten or drank anything before their intimacy. *The last time she'd ingested anything would have been before she went to sleep.* That was two nights ago. Her stomach grumbled, and her lips had produced a thick layer of sticky saliva.

Nathair cupped the side of her face as he held her in his cradle.

For a long while, no human dared to move. He could hear their chatter, their curious questions. Then a man, who was dressed in plain clothing, approached the top of the wall. Nathair met his gaze, and its familiarity to the weak female in his arms was unmistakable.

Even with the distance between them, he noticed the similar colour of their eyes. His skin was a light, fawny brown, his short hair black as night, and he had the same softness to his eyes. The biggest similarity was their nose and ears.

"Linh!" the man shouted, shoving the soldier out of the way as he scrambled to climb down some kind of ladder. "Tahlia. It's Linh!"

A ring of gasps sounded before chatter increased, and Nathair's vision clouded when their voices mixed with the ones in his mind.

"Open the gate," her father shouted. When nothing happened, his bellow was louder, grainier, and far more infuriated. "Open the fucking gate!"

A few grunts followed. Within minutes, a crank began to turn, chains clinked and clanked, and there was a *schluck* of sliding wood before it thudded against the ground. The large doors creaked as they parted, and her father instantly ran out.

Behind him, two men followed, wielding a sword and a battle axe, and both wore hide armour. Their garments were dark, as if they wished to give the appearance of shadows — which was wise when hunting Demons. It was best not to glimmer, as that could be an attractant even at night.

Nathair choked and was forced to halt his breath when her father approached. He reeked of fear, but none of it appeared to be for himself. Instead, her father braved coming closer to Nathair, as if the human could tell that he had no ill intention.

"Please," her father begged, holding out his arms. "My name is Kai. I'm her father, and the mayor of this town. Please. Please give me my daughter."

Nathair didn't.

Instead, he tilted his head towards the two men behind him, pointing their weapons up at his skull. Nathair gave a low, hissing growl for them to back the fuck up. Kai looked behind him, and the human male almost produced a growl himself.

"Get back, you idiots!" The lean man shoved one of their shoulders while pointing towards the village. He even gave Nathair his back — which was rather moronic. "It's brought her here. Obviously, it doesn't intend any harm."

"You'd be a fool to trust a monster," one of them stated with a chortle, while doing as he was told. They didn't go far, but they put space between him and them.

Kai turned to Nathair once more with his arms out. Nathair didn't give her to her father.

He didn't want to give her up. This was the female he'd chosen, and the idea of giving her back to humans filled him with pain. Each of his scales lifted in aversion. *What if she does not come back out to me?* He was putting his trust in them, in her, alongside a hope that she felt something deeply for him.

He had no promises from her.

She would, should, be safe here. If they were able to save her, she would not need him so long as the bandits didn't come for her. First, they would need to know she was here, and he figured her father and the villagers wouldn't allow her to be taken a second time.

Nathair's sight landed on the two soldiers. Were they some of the people or bandits? Were they safe or dangerous to her? With his lack of speech, he could not ask these questions. The choice was taken from him with each breath from her that seemed weaker than the last.

"Please," her father pleaded once more.

Nathair took in the way the male's eyes welled with unshed tears. He finally released the breath he'd been holding to find the smell of his fear had dissipated. However, the male's heart raced with anxiety, and it coursed within Nathair's mind.

"What's wrong with her?" Kai asked, taking in her limp state.

Nathair leaned forward and bared his fangs at the male. His features grew ashen, and the soldiers raised their weapons. But, with no hiss, and no attack from Nathair, Kai threw his hand out to ward them.

"Wait," he demanded.

He eyed Nathair suspiciously, his gaze slipping over his bony face and exposed fangs. It lingered there, on the liquid that dripped from them.

His features fell as realisation seemed to dawn. He turned

to one of the soldiers.

"Get me Tahlia and one of the Priestesses," he demanded, stepping back from Nathair.

He closed his maw with a nod, wanting to confirm the male's suspicions. A soldier quickly did as he was asked, while Kai remained with a guard. He and Nathair stared at each other for the entire duration.

"You're a Duskwalker," Kai stated matter-of-factly, and Nathair answered him with a nod. His dark brow rose at Nathair's confirmation. "You understand me, don't you?"

Once more, Nathair nodded. Nathair cupped the side of her face and rubbed back over her ear, trying to show that he cared for the female in his arms. Kai's lips flattened, and his slight beard growth poked his inward-curling lips.

Nathair held the female in one arm by squishing her to his chest to free up an arm. *She said her father knows sign language.* He gestured with one hand, "I did not mean to hurt her."

Kai's brown eyes widened. "You can talk!"

"Yes," he answered. "You will keep her safe? You are her father–"

Kai shook his head while his dark brows drew together tightly. "I'm sorry, but I don't know the language you're using." Then he brought his own hands up, and Nathair noticed two missing fingers on his left hand, and that his other was rather stiff. "Do you know Austlan?"

Nathair winced at that. *Shit. I taught her my signs, rather than learning hers.* Had he not been so stubborn, he may have been able to communicate with this male. He knew a few words, but nothing that would aid this situation.

Nathair shook his head in answer, and the male appeared to curse. The human closed his hands, pushed his index knuckles forward, and pointed them at the ground.

Nathair didn't know the gesture.

"Hey! What are you saying to him?" the soldier asked.

Nathair waved his right hand to the side, asking, "What?"

Realising Nathair couldn't understand it, Kai pursed his lips before eyeing him in an odd way. It didn't look distrustful, and more like he was trying to ponder a solution.

They were interrupted when two females approached. One wore dark robes that had purple symbols etched into every seam available, including the hood over her head. A mask situated over her face was painted half white from the nose down, with silver from the nose up. Black mesh covered her eyes and mouth holes.

The female next to her was a dark brunette, her skin a lighter brown. Her lips were pouty, full, and her eyes a molten hazel. She had a similar chin, cheek, and brow structure to Linh, but her gaze wasn't as soft as Linh's or Kai's. He could see she got her curves from her mother.

A tangy, sweet scent exploded into the clearing, all of it coming from the Anzúli. Nathair leaned towards her and bared his fangs.

"Watch it, Duskwalker," the Anzúli snapped out distrustfully, backing up a step.

Kai put his arms out to grab her forearm. "He's showing you what's wrong with Linh," he stated, pointing at Nathair's face. "I think he's trying to say he's envenomed her."

Nathair pointed at him and nodded.

She cupped the pointed chin of her mask. "I see. If it's anything like Demon venom..." She turned to Kai sharply. "You were right to call me here. The only ones that *may* be able to help her are us."

Kai's brown eyes fell on the other female. "Tahlia, you can't? What about our medicine?"

"No," Tahlia answered, and her sharp gaze softened as worry etched across her features. "Our medicine can't even help against snake or spider bites if they're fatal. We can only aid the symptoms and wait to see if the person can fight it."

Nathair finally relinquished the wounded female in his arms – straight to the Anzúli. *Only she can help.*

"My sweet baby," Tahlia cooed as she brushed the side of

Linh's face. She turned to Nathair slightly, and her eyes crinkled and bowed with wary gratitude. "Thank you for bringing her here."

The Anzúli tilted her mask up to Nathair. "Would you be willing to stay here until I return? I will need to *extract* some of your venom to help her."

Nathair shuddered at what they could possibly mean. *Whatever will aid Linh.* He gave a stern nod, willing to do anything to help his little nightingale so she would sing again.

They turned to take her away, and Nathair grabbed her father's arm.

"I want her back," Nathair signed, gripping the male hard.

"I'm sorry, but I don't understand," Kai responded, looking down at Nathair's grip but not trying to break away from it. "We'll look after her."

That wasn't good enough. Nathair let out a growl.

He pointed to Linh, then to himself. He pointed to his chest, to his very heart, to show what that female meant to him.

Kai turned to shake his head with a lack of understanding. Yet, he curled his index fingers again, and pointed his knuckles downwards at the ground. Once more, Nathair didn't know what it meant, and the language barrier between them was just too vast.

Nathair whimpered. *He doesn't understand what that female means to me.* And Nathair was watching her being rushed away, both females sprinting as if time was of the essence. His grasp on the male tightened, alongside his heart constricting.

"Let him go, Duskwalker," one of the soldiers demanded.

He stepped closer with his large axe, forcing Nathair to let go. If he stubbornly fought now, he would become enraged and terrorise the town and its occupants – one of them being his little female. *I must not act like a monster.*

Her father stepped back, but Nathair did have a question.

He grabbed the male's forearm once more to tug him closer. He let go only to wave his hands to the side and made his orbs turn dark yellow, hoping one would show he had a big fucking question mark.

The male furrowed his brows at him, his lips pursing in confusion.

Nathair then stuck up his pinkie finger, curled the next two downwards, and straightened his index and thumb so they made an L shape. He shook his hand towards the male.

What does this mean? Why had that little female currently being carted away giggled as she did the gesture towards him? He wanted to know its meaning, if it was important, if it would... help the situation.

Kai's features dropped as he looked down at Nathair's hand – even his lips parted, and his eyes widened.

"Come on. Let's go," the sword-wielding soldier commanded, grabbing Kai by the arm to drag him towards the town. "We need to keep you safe."

With a horrified expression, her father stumbled as he said, "Did she sign that at you?"

Nathair pointed at him and nodded, just as he needed to back up when the axe wielder stepped forward. His weapon glinted in the sun, while his yellow teeth flashed behind a bush of facial hair.

"No more talking, Duskwalker," he demanded, not showing an ounce of fear. "We'll keep the little lass safe. Now fuck off back to the forest where you belong."

The growling hiss that rattled from Nathair was deadly as he lowered himself to the male's height. His tanned features paled when Nathair parted his maw, bared his fangs, and gave him a menacing, venom-flicking hiss as his back fins flared. His orbs shone bright crimson.

Fucking make me.

"Callum, get inside," the sword wielder yelled, his lean yet tall frame walking next to Kai. "You'd be a dumbass to take on a Duskwalker by yourself."

Kai kept looking back at Nathair with his eyes stark. There was no fear in his scent, but he cupped his stubbled jaw as he took Nathair in from a distance.

The axe wielder, Callum, wrinkled one side of his nose before backing up a few steps. It appeared he didn't wish to give Nathair his overtly muscular back. The distrust in his gaze was unmistakable, as was his disgust.

"You're lucky you brought her back alive," Callum sneered, before grossly spitting on the ground. The action was lost on Nathair, as he didn't know what spitting meant in this context.

Nathair watched them enter the gates before they temporarily closed them. By the general lack of clacking and cluttering, he knew they hadn't locked them.

He lifted his sight to the large mountain backing the village. Just beyond the curve of the cliff wall, Nathair knew this mountain contained water. He'd followed it deep beneath the ocean's surface to discover much coral and reef wildlife attempted to live around it.

He then turned his head to the right, examining the grass and very few trees. It looked like the world suddenly fell away, when really the cliff wall became the beach. Just a little more east, and he could easily locate where the entrance to his home was.

He shifted his sight to the left, where the hills and mountain collided. The village was in a dangerous location, as the sun would only truly shine down upon it until a little after noon.

Behind him, up a large incline, sparse trees dotted here and there before the forest further south shielded everything.

Even now, Nathair could scent Demons on the wind, as if the mountain that partially protected them was filled to the brim with void monsters. Yet, the village still stood, strong and protected due to its chain canopy and other fortifications.

When humans choose to be, they are rather inventive.

Give them plenty of resources, and they'd make sure they'd survive, no matter how. But, as he once said to Linh, humans were selfish, greedy cretins.

Her home was safe from Demons but not from those who

wore the same face. *I've seen how vile humankind can be.* He'd tried to rip his own skull off in the face of it. *They call me a monster, yet bite and snarl at each other.*

'You'd be a fool to trust a monster.' Was he the fool or the monster in this scenario?

With a groan, he covered his bony brow as his orbs turned a darker orange than normal, only for them to shift to deep blue. *I don't trust them.* He didn't trust anyone. He'd just given what he cherished the most in the world... to the very creatures that had let her be harmed in the first place.

Watching Linh come out of her shell, going from a reserved and frightened pixie to one that rode him like a wanton little bunny, had taken weeks. *I don't want her inside the village.*

Nathair wanted her in the coils of his tail, where she was safest. Where the only thing that could harm her was him. Guilt clutched at his gut more than ever when he realised, despite this being the worst, it had not been the first time he'd hurt her.

Her arm. Her delicate neck. But should she remain unafraid, he truly didn't think he would ever hurt her again. She was wiser around him now; she knew how to manage him, *tame* him even.

If everything else left them the hell alone, he wanted to believe Linh was safe with him.

Or am I just telling myself that because I don't wish to let her go? Even after envenoming her, Nathair was... selfish enough to not care. So long as she returned to him, eyes bright and lips smiling, he would risk his venom with her again. *If she just gives me her soul...*

He could save her himself.

I want it. I want it more than I can bear.

The gates opening once more broke his spiral of thoughts. The robed Anzúli from before walked forward with a graceful saunter to greet him, with two new guards in tow. Once more, they wore hide armour, but one did have an additional steel or iron breastplate and helmet.

Under her arm, the Anzúli held a ceramic jar with a cloth lid and twine to keep it secure.

"Thank you for waiting," the Anzúli woman stated.

Nathair hated that he couldn't see her expression, and the only thing he had to gauge her on was her mild yet feminine voice.

"All you need to do is lance this with your fangs." She pushed the jar forward. "Try not to press too hard, as I'm assuming you are rather strong. Just enough to express your venom."

When the two males with weapons tried to crowd him as she approached, Nathair reared back with a growl bubbling in his throat. He didn't trust them, or her – or anyone, for that matter.

"For the love of the holy maiden, please stand back, sirs." The Anzúli female tsked as she shook her head, looking over her shoulder at them through her mask. Her black robes fluttered with the wind, revealing a blue dress beneath them.

From those I saw in Tenebris, they usually only wore white. Or was that only the lower level of their hierarchy?

"If it wished any harm, it would not have brought Linh here, nor would it be offering assistance." *It. She calls me an it.* When they stepped away to give him space, he could hear the roll in her eyes as she whispered, "Fools, the lot of them. They all share one singular idiotic brain."

She reached forward with the ceramic jar, and Nathair let her place it in the centre of his palm. He positioned the side of his finger next to its base, slipped it up and down, then waved his hand to the side.

"Are you wanting to know how high to fill it?" she asked, leaning her head to the side. He nodded in answer. Her tone was coy as she stated, "To the top."

To the top? He snorted a singular huff. *Doubtful they need that much.* They likely wanted to experiment with it since he was so willingly offering it.

Regardless, Nathair removed the cloth despite her earlier

instructions. Then he retracted his claws and parted his maw.

"I don't know whether or not I should thank you for bringing Linh back," she whispered with her head lowered. "It was wise, and I'm assuming it was due to you knowing you couldn't save her."

Indeed, he thought, as he extended his fangs.

He slid the point of one into the jar and pushed his fingers into the roof of his mouth just behind it. A squirt echoed within, and the stream didn't end until he fully emptied his venom sac. He shuddered in repulsion, before doing the same to the other, expressing his fang himself.

That was wildly unpleasant. There had been no warmth to give it a euphoric feeling, and it somehow felt dry.

"A Duskwalker asking for aid on behalf of a human, and *humans* ask *it* to stay," she muttered, before looking off to the side. "What has the world come to?"

He licked the inside of his maw to settle the feeling of his empty sacs, only to flick his tongue forward at the female in annoyance. *No one has asked me to stay.* If he recalled, the male from earlier told him to get lost. They would soon learn he had absolutely no intention of leaving until his nightingale was placed back into his arms.

He offered the female the ceramic jar, its venomous contents swishing within. She took it and bowed her head.

"Demons and Duskwalkers are no different. Whatever you crave from that woman, forget it." She backed up a step with the top of her hood showing. "But remain nonetheless."

Remain? She is asking me to stay? He wished she'd be more direct, as she was just being needlessly confusing.

She turned, giving him her back as she walked between the guards. Once more, the males tried to get him to leave.

Nathair merely coiled his tail around himself, showing he would be stubbornly immobile to their demands. He also used it to block out the sounds and scents of the humans within the village walls. His orbs shifted to blue at the loss of her, his heart burning with guilt, but his longing and worries were too deep to change his sight.

Minutes bled into hours, day shifting into cold night. Even when Demons crawled over him, but left him be as he was not disturbing them, he refused to unfurl himself.

Despite the fragments he fought to keep at bay, a constant thought remained.

My heart feels colder without her.

THIRTY-TWO

As the last of the light drizzle faded, the sun eventually peeked through a few gaps in the clouds. The warmth was minimal, but Nathair's wet form soaked it in nonetheless.

It's been two days, he grumbled, mulling over the time span.

Two days of no answers.

No one had come to visit him, nor to inform him of what had happened to Linh. He took solace in the silence, hoping it was a good thing, rather than being told something dreadful. That his little female had died, and instead of pining over her, he should be mourning.

My chest hurts. It radiated with an intense ache constantly.

His orbs shifted between two colours that sat like acid in his gut. Blue as he drowned in the well of his sadness, and dark orange as he lay in the ice of his guilt.

I wish I could be by her side.

Rather than being stuck outside of this fortified village, he would have... entered it if they permitted him. The echoing loneliness that had never bothered him before gnawed at his mind in the wake of her absence. He would subjugate himself to the humans' chattering, and how it would batter in his skull, if it meant he could curl her on top of his tail while she slept, got better, passed away...

He wanted to hold that female more than he wanted his next

breath. He needed to feel her warmth, while he took in greedy draws of her scent. He craved brushing the back of his fingers over her cheek, her soft brow, her jaw, or have his claws comb through the silky strands of her glossy hair. He longed to feel her slim curves moulding into the hardness of his body.

If she survives... I will rip my fangs out. They would return in a day, but until she gifted him her soul, he would remove them daily so as to not do this again. *If she dies because of me...*

He twisted, spinning in his coils. A snarl broke free, directed at himself.

How did I ever think I would be able to let the little female go? He promised her that she could leave him should she choose it, but that was no longer possible. He knew it, could feel it.

Like he had flooded her with venom, she had snuck her own within him. A sweet, enthralling, and tantalising venom that rippled his scales. Something that bled into his very veins and became necrotic now that she wasn't here to give him the sweet nectar of her entire essence as a form of antidote.

This wait is excruciating.

It persisted. Annoying him, making him itch with irritation. He'd already flaked off scales from the need to barrel his way through the gates and find her.

The gates clanked and clunked as they opened. *Fuck! Finally!*

He shoved just his snout through the coils of his lengthy limb and flicked his tongue forward to check the scents. He grunted. Two were unfamiliar, but the Anzúli's strong magic was undeniable.

It wasn't Linh. That's all that mattered to him.

Why has she not come to me? He shook his head as a whine threatened to break.

When the footsteps stopped just beyond him, Nathair slipped through the fold of his tail. He placed his hands on the ground and looked up at who approached him. The guards wisely stood back, whereas the Anzúli continued to approach.

"Well?" Nathair signed with one hand, hoping she'd just spill everything swiftly so she could either destroy him or finally remove the tempest in his chest.

"Linh is recovering," the female stated coldly, and the fucking breath that fell from him was like a balm to his being.

She's alive. Thank goodness!

"Where is she?" he asked, before placing both hands on the ground.

The Anzúli's mask followed his gestures, but she only tsked at him. Nathair tilted his head when he noticed her posture was much straighter, stern, and more defensive with him than a few days ago.

"You obviously care enough about her to have healed her," the Anzúli female bit out in a dark, snide tone. "If you hadn't, I don't think we would have been able to save her. Your venom is strong, and it was in her system for a long time. She hasn't woken, and her right leg still isn't responding properly, but we hope continued healing will save all her limbs."

Nathair leaned back and propped his torso upright so he could utilise both hands. "Give her to me. I will fix her."

If they removed the venom, then his ability to heal her would save her entire body. His magic was superior.

"Your venom is rather unique," she continued, reminding him that even if she could read sign language, he could not speak Austlan – only Nathair speak. "It doesn't fester in the organs, but is purely muscular. It completely cuts off the nerves and leaves your *victims* alive and aware. It's rather cruel."

Nathair gave a low, although dark, chuckle at that. *Do you think I asked to be formed this way? To have the ability to envenom?* It's not like he could choose what he became.

Neither had his mother.

She had no idea what she was doing when he was born. She fed him fish meat because it was easiest to capture. Weldir had informed him that Nathair, in his infant stage, had protected her by consuming a venomous serpent when it went to strike her. He, being indestructible, had been unaffected by its venom, and had shortly formed his skull and lost his two legs.

He'd started to become what he was now.

A Mavka, who was growing annoyed with this female's sudden hostility.

"Thank you for all you have done in helping her," the Anzúli stated, despite her tone holding not an ounce of gratitude. "Now that you know she is alive and recovering, I hope that means you will take your leave."

Nathair immediately parted his maw just enough to let his hiss be quiet and unnerving.

"We will not trade one monster for another," she bit out through obviously gritted teeth. "She has suffered enough, and if given the choice, I would rather she not endure more. Linh has always been kind-hearted. Her blissful ignorance of the cruelty of the world was something to be commended, and now that is lost."

He leaned forward to get an inch from her mask with a growl.

"Haven't you caused enough damage?" she shouted, seemingly unafraid of the way he menacingly towered over her. "First you... you..." She audibly swallowed, and looked behind her at the guards, only to shove her head forward. "You are more of a danger to her than anything else. You almost killed her. Is that not enough for you to put aside whatever deplorable need you have and let her live some kind of proper life?"

Nathair bared his fangs at her. *I made one mistake!* Okay, a few, but none as bad as this.

He pointed towards the village. *I have protected and cared for that female for almost an entire month. I have never truly hurt her in that time, never done anything she did not want.* A whimper threatened to crawl up his throat, but he shoved it down with all his willpower. *I can no longer breathe without her.*

I need her.

Although her voice chased away the fragments, this wasn't why he needed her. Even if she became as silent as he was, he would value and cherish Linh with all his might. From her hair all the way to her toes, he was enamoured by that female, that woman, that *human.*

No person nor creature would be able to steal his heart, not now that she'd forcibly shoved herself into it.

He did not ask her to do this. He did not even want her to. When she first came to his pond, he wanted her to leave! *She* climbed into his nest on her own. She took kisses from him, and showed him he could give them in his own bony way.

So, until his little nightingale came herself to tell him she did not want him, he was not leaving this fucking spot.

And then I will convince her otherwise.

THIRTY-THREE

Linh produced a small moan and let her head fall to the side. She turned to the right, keeping her leg straight with the other bent, so she could stop the ache crawling up her neck.

Couldn't they have turned me? Who just let someone lay on their back like a corpse for however long?

She opened her eyelids, only to squint them at the blaring light piercing her poor eyes.

Bright sunlight was broken up by small fluffy white clouds, and she followed one as she stared out of what had to be a private room in the hospital. Her lips thinned as she pondered, her disorientated mind still groggy from sleep as she examined the blue sky.

I can't believe he took me home.

Not only did he go against his own demands of not returning her to her village, but he'd been wise enough to do so when he couldn't save her. He'd thought outside the box, outside of his own wants and desires, and had done the right thing for her sake.

She was undoubtedly proud of him.

It was why she knew, while lying on a soft pillow and stupidly uncomfortable bed, that she truly loved him.

What's the bet he's waiting outside of the village for me to come to him? She snorted a quiet laugh, only to give the window a sad smile. *He's probably so worried.* Her smile died swiftly, and her eyes snapped open wide when another possibility infiltrated her thoughts. *Oh shit! What if he left because he hurt me?!*

Linh sat up so fast her vision swam. Her empty stomach immediately protested as anxiety clutched at her gut.

If Nathair left due to some silly, chivalrous notion that he no longer deserved her due to one measly accident, she'd kick his weird snake butt!

Before her vision cleared, gentle hands pushed against her shoulders. "You should lie back down," a young, feminine, and familiar voice stated. "You've only just woken up, and you refused to eat anything. I've been pouring nourishing potions down your throat for days."

Linh did as she was told, just as a white clay mask and hood came into view. Two red lines were painted from the top of the mask, down the eyes and then the cheeks. They curved inwards until each line came to the corners of the mask's lips and painted them. Linh shifted her position enough to be half-seated against the pillows.

Linh blinked at her. "Glenda?" she asked, guessing due to the anonymity of the masks the Priests and Priestesses wore.

Her light-brown hand pushed back a few strands of Linh's long fringe – the only part of her skin she could see. "Yeah, it's me. Your dear, old cousin."

Linh gave a small laugh at that. "Aren't I older than you?"

If memory served Linh correctly, Glenda was only eighteen, whereas she was twenty-one. Perhaps due to her age, she didn't act as cold and unfeeling as the other *Anzúli* Linh had briefly met.

Her great-aunt was the leader and often wore black robes to highlight her position. Linh didn't know her name, but Glenda had accidentally spilled her own when she shouldn't have.

"Yeah. I let the guards know you're awake. Hopefully they let your parents visit you," Glenda murmured, before touching her warm palm to Linh's cheek. "Your temperature is still low.

That Duskwalker's venom really did a number on you. Once we removed it, we had to put you into a coma due to your seizing."

What little humour she maintained was sucked right out of her. "How long have I been out?"

"Two full nights." Glenda pushed back the grey blanket and lifted the white hospital dress Linh wore. "How's your right leg? Can you wiggle your toes?"

Linh tried to, but they barely moved. "A little."

"Any soreness? Since we couldn't find any puncture wounds, we assumed it'd bitten you on this leg due to the lack of movement. Our magic really struggled to combat it. If it hadn't offered us some of its venom to make an antidote, we wouldn't have been able to save you. We think our magic did some harm, but we've been trying to fix that as well. The whole situation was unusual for us. There were no texts to help with Duskwalker venom, so we kind of had to... wing it."

Linh bent her knee. It was slow, but she had movement in it. "If I walk around, it'll help to make blood flow properly," Linh stated, gaining herself a tsk.

"You and your mother are always the worst patients. You think just because you work with herbs and medicine that you know everything." The disappointed and frustrated tone in Glenda's voice made Linh weakly grin.

"Someone has to annoy you," she playfully bit back.

"Someone has to annoy you," Glenda mimicked with a mock sneer. "I should put you back into a coma."

She's a little more bitchy than normal. Glenda didn't usually say things like this, not even playfully. Why did Linh get the feeling the woman had hardened in her absence?

"Are you okay?" Linh asked, her forced cheer fading. She sat up a little better so she didn't feel like a feeble child with a cold. "What's happened since I left?"

"Nothing," Glenda stated firmly. "Everything has been easier since you were taken. The bandits stationed here rotate once a week, but they tend to leave everyone alone. Your father finally came to an agreement with them, and we received some supplies, proper food, and even medicine."

Lowering her head to look down at her hands, Linh fidgeted with her fingers. She picked at the sides of her clean fingernails, then twisted and scratched at a finger when it suddenly felt itchy.

"I'm sorry," Glenda stated, her tone quieter and low. "That's likely something you don't want to hear."

With her eyes closed, Linh shone a dead smile at her. "That's not true at all. I'm thankful things got easier for everyone after I left."

"You and I both know that's a lie. Nothing should have been a cost for your freedom," Glenda bit out, sitting back in her wooden chair and sinking into the light. "But Bragg was right. The moment you were taken, your father lost much of his will to fight back in fear he'd hurt you."

"He did hurt me," Linh quietly muttered, looking at the wall her bed was pressed against.

The silence shared between them was heavy, clogging, and cruel. The unspoken statement was in the air, even if Linh didn't truly wish to utter what she'd suffered.

"I'm sorry. I know it must have–"

"Don't. Please don't," Linh rushed out, digging her nails into her arm. Tears instantly welled. "I want to forget."

"I guess we should just be thankful you're alive. That's all that matters?" Glenda asked, her question more a way to check if her response suited Linh.

She was sure it was awkward to talk about this. How could anyone give a suitable response when it could never change what happened?

"I'm alive, and I'm home." Linh was *home.*

So why did it feel weird being back in her village? Sure, it wasn't her bed, but she'd worked in the infirmary. She often helped her mother with tending to patients. The room she was in was situated on the top level for ultimate privacy and was one of the biggest and well cared for.

It should be comforting to be here. The sound of the villagers outside should be soothing, so why did their cheer or noises feel strange? She used to love waking up in the morning to bright sunshine, birds chirping, and lively people who were flourishing.

Instead, a swallowing pit of reality made its way into her heart. While Linh was suffering, at the exact same time, the world kept moving. People still laughed, embraced their friends or loved ones, and got to experience life in the ways she'd missed. They ate delicious food, slept in soft beds, and they may have done so at the same time she was weeping.

It felt like a cruel joke.

She dug her nails deeper. *I miss Nathair.*

She missed the quietness of his cave, and how his entire body blocked out everything except for his radiant heartbeat. She missed the abnormality of his life, his environment.

I wish I had woken up in his arms, she thought, as a singular tear slipped down her cheek. Hopefully with her head down, Glenda couldn't see.

The Priests and Priestess were always considered hard. People often thought they were emotionless with how they reacted to others.

Linh needed that now more than ever. If her serpent rock couldn't be here right now, she needed Glenda to at least be a hard pebble. Something that sat in her shoe and annoyed her, rather than embraced her with words that only trickled more pain into her heart.

Grunting beneath her mask awkwardly, Glenda folded her hands on her lap and stiffened her back. "There is already chatter that if you're taken again, the entire village will riot. They want you home, and the bandits are wary now that you're back. They've been acting out of sorts since."

Linh bit her lips so hard she feared she'd draw blood. "Have... have any of them left to go tell Bragg?"

She didn't want to admit it, but she was kind of... scared that she was home. She hadn't wanted to come back here without a solution.

I don't want to be taken again.

She also didn't want to be the cause of exactly what they were threatening: a riot. If a fight broke out and a thick blood scent fluttered into the air, many Demons would come. Two or so a night were relatively easy to fight off with all their fortifications, but a swarm would just be a death sentence for everyone she'd ever known and loved.

"No. We don't believe Bragg is aware," Glenda answered. "Any time one of them tried to leave, the Duskwalker hissed and growled until they went back inside the gate."

Her face shot up as hope bled into her veins. "He's still here?"

She'd been so worried about asking, but there just didn't seem to be a good time to insert her question until now.

"I don't know if that's a good thing or not," Glenda stated with a sigh behind her mask. "The leader of our guild tried to make it leave, but it's refused. I don't know how I feel about it either. It's selfish of me, I know, and I'm really sorry, but I'm glad it's stayed. I feel like the Duskwalker is the only thing keeping the bandits from leaving to tell Bragg you're here."

Linh's brows drew together so tightly they knotted her forehead. "She tried to make him leave?" Linh asked in disbelief. "Even after he brought me here with the intention of saving me? Why?"

She looked out the window as a dark pit swelled in her stomach. *I wanted to prove to him that he was wrong and my people would accept him.* Yet, they'd told him to leave when he'd done something selfless and noble, just for her sake.

"I think that's what makes this so hard," Glenda stated quietly, her mask tilting towards the window as well. "The bandits... if you were sick, I think they'd just abandon you as a lost cause."

Linh's heart clenched at the truth of those words. Bragg and his men wouldn't care for her wellbeing if she became too much of a liability.

"But the Duskwalker... it brought you here," Glenda continued. "Your father doesn't want to listen to us and refuses to let us talk to it again to make it leave."

"Stop calling him a fucking *it*," Linh bit out, her eyes narrowing at the sun. She turned her glare to Glenda. "Have a little more respect for someone who saved me."

Taken aback, a small gasp echoed beneath her mask and was accompanied by her head rearing back. Linh didn't think she'd ever sworn in front of another, except Nathair, so she wasn't surprised by Glenda's faceless reaction.

"I'm sorry," Glenda immediately offered. "How long has *he* had you? As far as we knew, you were still at the bandits' main camp."

So Bragg didn't tell dad that I'd run away, or probably died. Her lips tightened in annoyance. *I doubt he would have ever told him the truth, and just used my safety to keep up his manipulations, even with me missing.*

He really was a bastard.

Linh's features twinged, and for some reason, her pussy spasmed. She cupped her pelvis with a cringe.

"Almost a month?" Linh guessed, before giving a light moan as she keeled forward. Two seconds later, the pain dissipated.

"Here," Glenda offered, reaching for a cup on the side table. "You got your period yesterday. This tea should help with any cramps."

Linh drained it so fast she almost drowned. "Thanks."

I didn't even think about what would happen if I got my period with Nathair nearby. She figured he would have slithered off somewhere so he didn't fall into a bloodthirsty rage.

I kept forgetting how much danger I was really in. She still didn't care. Nathair was quick-witted, so she assumed he would have figured out a solution. She snorted a quiet laugh at herself. *I really do have too much faith in him.*

"We were relieved when you got it," Glenda stated, and

even Linh could hear the hint of a sad smile in it. "It would have been devastating going from one monster to another, only to end up pregnant."

Linh nearly choked. She patted her chest as she placed the cup down on the table. "What the hell are you talking about?"

"We cleaned and examined your body when you arrived," Glenda said, and once more, darkness entered her tone. Her voice became quieter. "We found trauma between your legs, as well as seed. It's why we wanted him to leave."

"Excuse me?" Linh whined, clenching her thighs together. She fisted the blanket in disbelief.

Trauma between my... Oh gods! *She's likely talking about his body-altering spell!* She understood this was a natural part of being in an infirmary, but the idea that someone went poking around her lady bits while she was unaware was concerning!

"He also placed some kind of spell on you. It took us a while to notice it, as it was deep beneath your skin." Glenda sighed as she shook her head. She lowered the volume of her voice even more. "I can only imagine what happened at the bandit camp, but to be forced upon by a monster would have been horrifying. I'm–"

Linh jumped forward, almost falling out of the bed, as she slapped both her hands over Glenda's masked mouth to shut her up.

"Stop," Linh pleaded. She eyed the door, worried someone would overhear. "Have you told anyone?"

Glenda shook her head. "No. We were waiting for you to wake up before we made any decisions. Due to you being an adult, it's not our place to speak on your behalf, or to inform anyone of private matters."

Thank goodness for that.

Leaning back to kneel on the bed with the blanket twisted around her legs, Linh placed a singular finger to her lips.

A coy, sheepish smile curled her mouth as shy mischief swirled in her gaze and heated her cheeks. "It was consensual."

Even if it was embarrassing, the last thing Linh wanted was for them to think Nathair was a cruel monster. His outsides may be different and scary, but he was truly a sweetheart.

I don't really care who knows I have feelings for him. She once thought she might, due to the oddity of their relationship, but telling Glenda of the perverted truth... she knew she didn't care. She adored that serpent Duskwalker with all her heart, and people would figure it out eventually when she told them all the truth.

He made her feel safe, cherished, and wanted. Not just for her body, but also her personality. He was sweet, funny, and weirdly charming.

Nathair was wonderful: scales, claws, fangs, and all.

Glenda took a moment to process what Linh had said. When it finally sunk in, the woman rushed to her feet, almost knocking over her chair in the process. Linh winced at its loud scrape.

"It was consensual?!" she whisper-shouted.

Linh reached out and grabbed her robes, yanking and pulling on them so she would sit. Her brows furrowed beseechingly until Glenda sat her bum down.

"Yes," Linh admitted, her cheeks flaring hotter. "I know it's probably strange to understand, but he's not a monster. He's really kind, and he... he made me feel better after everything. He took care of me and was really understanding and patient."

"You're joking," Glenda rasped out. "He's a Duskwalker, Linh!"

Linh rolled her eyes. "I don't think it's fair for you to judge. You would think with three eyes, you'd be better at seeing people for who they really are."

She cast Glenda's mask a hard stare.

"So, he told you." She cupped the chin of her mask and turned her face to the side. "How the hell did he know? Probably from eating a few of us, I guess." The woman shuddered. "And you still let him..."

Linh winced at that. She lowered her head to stare at her

hands sitting on her folded knees.

"I don't think he wants to hurt people. He explained that he couldn't help it in the past. They gain intelligence or something from eating people, and now that he has plenty of it... I don't think he wants to do that anymore." She picked at her nails again. "I don't want to judge him for the past. Not when he saved me from my present, and the hurdles I would have faced on my own if he hadn't come into my life."

"You do realise this may all be a delusion, right? Stockholm syndrome, finding security in wrong places to get over trauma. There are many terms and meanings for what you may be going through."

"No," Linh quietly, yet firmly, stated. "I don't want to think of it that way. He never kept me imprisoned. He told me to leave at first, and I chose to stay."

"Linh–"

"I know what I feel, okay?" Linh snapped out. "I know what feels right for me, even if everyone else will think it's wrong."

The wary suspicion in Glenda's voice was unmistakable as she asked, "Are you sure?"

"Yes." Linh's lips pursed, and she glanced up at Glenda's mask. "You're welcome to share my feelings with the others in your temple, but I ask that you let me tell my family and the villagers in my own time. I want to talk to Nathair first and introduce him properly."

Glenda folded her arms across her chest with a childish harrumph, showing her age, but it was weak. She wasn't truly upset, from what Linh could tell, and the Priestess quickly relaxed her posture.

"That's fine. Whatever you wish. I guess it's a good thing we were unable to remove the spell he put on you. We don't know what it was for, if it was some increased fertility magic or just ensuring the strength of your body for mating." Then she quietly muttered, "Why your ass, though? Are all male creatures weird?"

Oh my gosh, someone end me now! Linh threw her face into her hands, mortified they'd examined just what she and Nathair had done the other morning.

"Wait," she whispered, lowering her hands to her mouth. "You tried to remove the magic?"

She winced. *Why does that feel like a violation against my body?* Doing it had been her choice, and having the spell removed against her will, or even knowledge, felt like she'd almost betrayed Nathair somehow.

"I wish you hadn't assumed," Linh grumbled, only for a knock at the door to interrupt their conversation.

Glenda stood, and her robes fluttered as she walked to the door. Very little dust puffed into a flurry, the infirmary clean and tidy.

"Who's there?" Glenda asked through the door. Her tone was hesitant and unsure, and Linh figured someone had attempted to enter while she was unconscious.

She shuddered at what that meant.

"It's us," Tahlia, her mother, answered.

Glenda immediately opened the door. A girl, barely fifteen, almost pushed her to the ground as she ran inside.

"Linh!" May cried while tackling her to the bed.

With a choke, Linh let the girl wrap her slim arms around her neck and crush her beneath her body. She wrapped her arms around May's waist, and squeezed her with all her might, turning her face to her dark-brown hair to take her in.

"May, give your sister some room," Tahlia demanded as she entered, with her father stepping in behind her.

Glenda closed the door when a bandit, who looked as though he was standing guard, peeked inside. Linh shied away from his gaze, ignoring his presence. *I'm being kept here.*

She tightened her arms on May, who had started crying with girlish heaves. *They're keeping an eye on me.* Did that mean getting the chance to see Nathair was low?

She shook her head and opened her eyes when her mother's hand patted her hair. *No. I'll figure out a way to convince them to let me see him.*

Even if she had to lie and say she'd send him away, she wouldn't let them trap her in this village.

"We're so happy to see you're okay," her mother said, as she sat down in the chair her father brought closer.

Glenda stood by the door, giving them space, and allowed her chair to be occupied by Linh's father. May sat on the edge of the bed, refusing to leave her. She took Linh's hand, and her brows crinkled as she continued crying.

"Are you hungry?" Kai asked. He waved to a board he must have carried in that had a plate, a wide bowl, and cutlery on it. "I brought you some bún bò huế, since soup will be easiest to get down after not eating for a while."

It was also her favourite, and one of the few traditional Vietnamese meals her father knew how to make. He was a wonderful cook, and this was his way of showing how much he cared about her.

"Mum and I made you some orange sweets," May informed her, before she nibbled on her bottom lip. "I ate all the burnt ones."

Linh huffed a laugh and squeezed her sister's hand. "How can you be so bad at baking, May?" Her sister opened her mouth, likely with some childish reply, but Linh turned to the side table. "I'd like the soup, to be honest. My stomach doesn't feel too good."

The moment she turned her nose towards the beef broth, her mouth instantly watered. Her mother helped to bring the bowl over, and Linh dipped her spoon into it, swirling the fragrant soup.

"Wait," she rasped, lowering her head to investigate the bowl's contents. "Is that... are they rice noodles?" She looked up at her father. "How did you get rice? We haven't been able to get any supply for months."

There was only one town in the entire northern part of Austrális that could farm it. Due to needing a large amount of fresh, clean water, the eastern area closest to the Demonslayer stronghold, Hawthorne Keep, was the only place that could grow it. The town to the right of the mountains there was the most protected, since Demons needed to pass the stronghold to get to it – which the Demonslayers never allowed.

It was a large area with complete sanctuary, but was overpopulated now due to everyone travelling there for security. They blocked anyone from entering it without permits, and they traded rare foods for medicine, coal, metal ores, and basically anything else that wasn't food related.

Hawthorne Keep had already informed all nearby villages that they would protect it in order to feed the rest of the north, and even parts of the east. The south and west were forced to find other means, since travelling with certain perishables was idiotic.

Rice, however, could be long lasting if stored correctly. With them being in the mountains, they only put in requests for food that would last, not only during travel, but also in storage.

"Bragg is allowing us to trade again," her father stated, confirming what Glenda had told him.

"Yeah, but you're terrible at making noodles," she retorted with a laugh, trying to distract away from the darkening conversation. "Grandpa had to teach me how to make them for you."

He gave a fatherly, annoyed huff. His lips flattened, and his eyes narrowed at her. She flashed him a knowing smile.

"Eat it while it's hot," he demanded, before rubbing his recently shaved face. "All my children tease me."

"Give your father a break," her mother warned. "He's been pulling his hair out and picking at his face relentlessly since you've been gone. If he keeps going, he'll make himself bald."

"Sorry," she grumbled, casting her mother an apologetic expression. She picked up her chopsticks and began to eat.

Even though it had less chilli than normal, Linh was thankful for that when her stomach grew queasy. Still, she was happy to have something other than plums, berries, and fish.

She appreciated all Nathair had done to feed her, but nothing could beat a home-cooked meal.

Her shoulders turned inwards as she was gawked at by three sets of eyes. She hid away from their stares by letting her hair fall forward, and slurped away at the liquid more than anything else in the bowl. The beef was too heavy for her, the noodles too hard to grip with her shaky hands. She was just pleased the broth was flavourful and had plenty of coriander, lemongrass, and spring onion.

"Is no one going to talk about the elephant in the room?" her mother stated, eyeing her still-pouting father.

"Which one?" he asked, folding his arms as he leaned back. He placed his ankle on top of his opposing knee. "That she's here, or the fact that a Duskwalker now lingers outside our gates, waiting for her? How about the fact that a Duskwalker had her at all, when she was supposed to be in the main camp, and it looks as if she's been with it for a long time?"

Her shoulders continued to turn inward at every stern and straightforward word her father uttered.

"I ran," Linh admitted, no longer able to stomach another spoonful. "I'm sorry. I know I promised to wait, but I couldn't take it."

"Linh," Tahlia stated, cupping her cheek to make her lift her head. Her usual hard features softened exponentially as she brushed her thumb down the side of Linh's face. "Please don't apologise. We don't care how you got here, only that you got away and you're safe. We've been so worried and sorry for everything, and we were not far from enacting a plan to rescue you."

"David, Michael, and Sasha were going to sneak out and scout the camp to gather more information on how best to infiltrate it. We wanted as little bloodshed as possible, although we were all happy to kill every one of them."

Her people were talking about becoming killers... it was a depressing thought. They had once been so compassionate, only killing for survival, rather than in vengeance.

"Now you don't have to," Linh cut in, trying to give them a smile. "I'm hoping Nathair will help us. The Duskwalker, I mean. That's his name."

"Has he agreed to it?" Her father asked, tightening his folded arms. "The idea of trusting a... Duskwalker doesn't sit well with me. I also won't allow you to sacrifice yourself just for our sake. You've already done that once. If that's your reasoning, you can forget it – immediately."

"That's not–" A bash on the door cut her off.

"You've had your ten minutes," a guard shouted from the other side of it.

Kai stood and headed towards the door. Glenda bowed her head and stepped back to give him room to swing the door open. He came face to face with a sneering tall brute of a man.

"Listen here, you gigantic ogre," her father snapped up at his bearded face. "I will do what I want in my own village, and if that's visit my daughter in hospital, then you will shut up and let me and my family do so."

His dark-blond brows narrowed. "You agreed–"

"Yes, and Bragg agreed to take care of my daughter, and I found her half dead in the arms of a fucking monster. So, do kindly piss off." He slammed the door in the bandit's face, only to shove his back against it. His grin was of a man who was hopped up on adrenaline. "I think I made matters worse, no?"

Her mother shook her head before slapping her face in her hand in disbelief. Her sister, May, stood and prepared herself for what was likely to come next.

Linh slipped to the side of the bed and stood on shaky legs. She limped towards the door being bumped and shoved against with heavy slams. Her father was doing well to keep it shut, but he was sure to falter.

"You really do know how to cause trouble," Linh stated, and waved for him to move.

How did such an immature man become the mayor of our people? He'd always been like this. Stern when needed, reckless when he shouldn't be, and immature to make sure everyone fell in love with his goofy charm.

He shook his head, only to swallow when Linh glared at him. He rolled his eyes, stepped forward, then moved to the side, away from the direction of the door swinging open.

The bandit, with his fist raised in preparation, halted when he found Linh in front of him. He wouldn't dare touch Bragg's *property*, not if he valued his life. Her face was her shield.

"I spent most of my time eating," she explained, widening her eyes up at him in appeal. "I've missed my family and would really appreciate just a few more minutes."

"A few more minutes to come up with a scheme, no doubt," he sneered, lowering his fist as his lips disappeared when he pursed them.

His words only deepened her worries. She already figured they wouldn't just let her walk out of this room. Now she feared what they would do to her when she was able to, or *where* they would take her.

"I think you're forgetting who is really in charge here. What can we do?" she asked, raising her arms to gesture to herself. "Or are you that afraid of a sick woman and her family? Should I tell Bragg you couldn't even hold your wits while I was eating my first proper meal in a month?"

His blue eyes darted up to her sister cowering behind her mother, only to yank on the door to find her father behind it.

"Give me shit like that again, and I'll break the rest of your fingers."

Her father threw up his hands in surrender. "She gets her brains from her mother, and not me, obviously."

The bandit snorted a mild laugh. "Can say that again." His expression gentled, kind of, as he brought his gaze back to Linh. "You have five more minutes, and that's it."

She narrowed her eyes into a defiant glare. "That's not a lot of time."

He shrugged and lifted his chin nonchalantly. "Better make each one count then."

He backed up and slammed the door shut.

Linh turned to her family and had no idea how she was supposed to tell them everything in such a short period of time.

If I had known there was a timeframe, I would have eaten after they left. She let out a groan and Glenda caught her when her partially numb leg gave out. *All I can do is make sure they help me get to Nathair.*

Once she was with him, she would be safe.

THIRTY-FOUR

When the gates to the village opened, Nathair stuck his snout between the folds of his tail. He flicked his tongue forward, tasting who approached, and gave an irritated, yet quiet hiss.

More soldiers. But no Anzúli this time.

He made sure they weren't attempting to leave. Until his little female was returned to the security he offered her, no one was allowed to leave. Until she was utterly safe in his arms, every passing moment they courted their deaths by making him wait.

It had been a day since the Anzúli leader had approached him. He was growing more frustrated with every hour that went by, and no one had deigned to give him more information.

She was alive and recovering; that's all he knew.

The two soldiers approached him, leather creaking as their weapons thumped against their sides.

He retracted his head so he could pop out the top of his coil and face them.

He examined their dull expressions, both with cleanly shaved faces. Both wore a metal breastplate and hide armour, and appeared to be well composed. Their scents were new to him, as if they were drawing straws or daring each other to see who was courageous enough to face the 'Duskwalker.'

Nathair played nice – there was little other choice.

Are these two soldiers or bandits? Right now, everyone was suspicious to Nathair.

His orbs shifted red the closer they came until they were directly before him. He waited for them to speak.

"We've been advised by the mayor to ask you to leave," the one on the right stated, placing his hand on the pommel of his sword.

Nathair gave his usual response: a rolling, growling, low hiss.

"You won't let anyone leave to obtain supplies, and there are sick people here. You've been here for three days. At this point, we're going to start needing food."

Nathair gave a small chuckle and was purposeful with his sniffs. *I smell plenty of food coming from your town, human.* Lots of animals, and smokes with herbs on the wind.

Folding his arms across his broad humanoid chest, he settled back on his tail. Nathair tilted his head, waiting for a better excuse.

The other soldier shot his companion a ponderous look. "Look. We appreciate you bringing the lass here, but you're frightening everyone. The children are terrified, the women refuse to leave their homes. You won't let men leave to chop firewood, and you're essentially choking the village of necessities."

Nathair shrugged before pointing to the town.

"We won't give you the girl, Duskwalker," the man to the right firmly stated.

Just as he was about to growl in response, the left said, "She's asked for you to leave."

That immediately quietened him. *Linh asked for me to leave?*

Agitated, his gestures were jarred and sharp as he signed, "She's awake? Why did no one tell me?"

How long had he been sitting out here patiently while his female was awake?! It was concerning that she hadn't come out here, especially since it was likely she knew he was here...

waiting for her.

"Did you not hear us?" the one on the right asked, his tone growing deep with annoyance. "She's asked for you to leave. She doesn't want you here, doesn't need your help. She doesn't want to go back to whatever hovel it is you call a home."

Nathair raised his hands, but the left stated, "Now that she's safe and with her family, she wants to stay with them. It's ridiculous for you to keep waiting here for a woman who isn't interested in being your friend."

She's more than my friend. She would, hopefully, be his bride. But is that what she told them? That they were nothing but platonic companions, even after everything they'd achieved together? Even after all the ways he'd savoured the little female?

"She's scared you'll hurt her again. She almost died because of your venom." The one on the right tsked, only to fold his meaty arms across his chest. "You're a Duskwalker. To us, to her, you're no better than a Demon."

"What if you do it again and the occult can't save her?"

"Going with you will just end up being a death sentence for her, and she's not willing to risk it again. Let her be with her family."

"She has a little sister–"

They continued to talk over each other, speaking fast and low, making Nathair snap his skull one way and the other. He couldn't deny what they were saying.

I always knew there would be a possibility she may not want me once she was with her people. He'd known it when he brought her here, but he'd taken that risk purely to save her life. It was true she'd almost died because of him, but she would have to know that was an accident.

He had vague memories of that morning; he remembered enough.

The human males sped up their discourse, muttering loudly and then quietly, and the sound of their colliding voices clashed with those already swelling in his mind. He groaned and clutched the side of his skull, trying to keep them at bay.

He'd slipped into many fragments in her absence.

The removal of his sound barrier – his coils – only made the chatter from the village mingle inside his head. Many scents flittered through the air: a light tangle of fear, food, plants, and creatures. There was even blood, forcing him to drown his tongue in drool and breathe through his mouth to combat how it made his orbs brighten in their red hue.

It's dangerous for me to remain.

Yet Nathair produced a dark, possessive chuckle, and gave a universal hand gesture. One he'd seen his many fragments produce, no matter what land they came from.

He lifted his right hand, gave them his middle finger, and they both shut the fuck up. One's eyes even widened in surprise.

I'm not leaving until that female comes out here herself. Until then, these people could send out whatever messengers they wished, and they would get the same response.

The only creature he trusted was his little nightingale. Not her father, the Anzúli that tried to make him leave as well, and absolutely not these men. Whether their words were the truth or lies, he wouldn't follow anyone's orders.

They both pulled out their weapons, two swords that glinted in the muted lighting from the heavy clouds above.

"We told you to fucking leave!" the right one stated, foolishly coming forward to kick at his tail with the bottom of his boot. "She doesn't want you! Leave us be!"

He chuckled harder. It was the only thing keeping the rage at bay. It was the only thing stopping him from darting forward with his claws bared and rending these two in fucking half.

He released the tip of his tail and slipped it to the side. It caught the sides of their feet and sent them straight to their arses. As they were fighting to get up, Nathair reached down and grabbed the back collars of their metal-and-leather armour. They roared yells when he lifted them off the ground, their meaty legs dangling as they kicked, and he slithered towards the village gate.

He didn't dare get too close, but he threw both men towards the partially open gate. They rolled, thumping and clattering against the dirt. The one that slid across the dirt on his front almost had his feet touch the back of his head, while the other skidded on his side.

Nathair turned, giving them his back as he moved a safe distance away. He returned to his place of rest, and once more waited, wrapping his tail around himself tighter when the space felt emptier without his warm, soft female.

You are running out of time, Linh. Because Nathair was patient, but he wasn't *that* patient.

A hand slapping over Linh's mouth shoved her into alertness within seconds. Blinded by the darkness of night, Linh struggled just as a scream to her right cut short.

An oil lap being lit brightened the infirmary and revealed four men.

Her stark expression and wide eyes flicked to Glenda, who lay in the other bed. With a knife held to her throat, the wielder placed his index finger over his lips to quieten her.

"Be quiet, Priestess." He reached for the bottom of her mask to push it off. "I've always wanted to know what you guys look like under your masks."

With a hand still over her lips to stop her from crying out, Linh wiggled in a poor attempt to help. *Oh no. They'll see she's not human!*

When the mask was pulled away, Glenda had her eyes clamped shut, likely to hide whatever glow they had. A head cap was tied around her hair just above her brow, hiding her third eye from view.

Linh settled at the realisation that the Anzúli people were

wise enough to cover themselves even beneath their masks.

"I thought she'd be ugly, but she's actually rather cute," he stated, before one of his waiting companions grabbed his shoulder.

"Don't. They're not to be messed with," he stated, eyeing her warily. "Apparently they leave curses on people. Turn them into harbingers of bad omens. Best to do what we came here for."

The bandit with the knife to Glenda's throat sneered but nodded. He was given a long strip of cloth, and he shoved it between her teeth before they bound her wrists and ankles together. They tied her hands to the headrest of the bed.

Forcibly flipped to her stomach, Linh's heart raced when they shoved her arms behind her back.

"Please," she begged.

The bandit holding her down leaned over her. "Shut up." Her wrists burned when he knotted a strip of material too tight around them. "You knew Bragg would want you back when he heard of your return."

Huffing against the pillow, she shifted her face towards the window. Night was upon them.

"I-I can't leave. Not in the dark." Not at all! She didn't want to go back to Bragg.

Fearful tears instantly welled, and her throat thickened as she wept. Linh trembled and fought when he tried to pull her to her knees.

"This one over here thought telling us you're menstruating and sleeping in here would protect you, but you forget what we are, lass."

Another bandit gave a mocking laugh. "We may not be Demonslayers, but we're hunters of the night."

"Let the Demons come for us," the bandit across the room said as he rose away from Glenda. "Just more for us to kill."

Barefooted and in her white hospital gown, Linh was dragged off the bed until her hip hit the ground. They quickly yanked her to her feet.

"M-my people will riot." She was willing to say anything to stop them.

"They won't." One laughed, grabbing her by the arm to shove her against a different bandit. "They can threaten it all they like, but your father won't risk the women, children, and invalids of this village by bringing Demons upon them."

"How else do you think we take over other towns? Their fear of retaliation doesn't come from us, but monsters."

"The Duskwalker will come for me!" she shouted, just as cloth was shoved between her teeth and muffled her protests.

"That creature will leave when you don't show. It's already proven it won't enter the village, so it'll eventually get the point."

"We've already told the Duskwalker you don't want to see it again. And we'll keep doing so until it fucks off. We'll even make your father help us, if need be."

No, she mentally cried. *Please, Nathair. Please don't leave. Please don't let them take me.*

"Even if he does come to our camp, the pits will get him," one said with a chuckle. "We were surprised we weren't dragging your corpse off of spikes the night you left. You almost ran straight into one, you silly woman."

The blood drained from her face, and she was unsure if it was because she'd been close to falling to her death the night she escaped, or from fear that Nathair would fall into one.

She squealed as she was hoisted over one of their shoulders, and her hair fell around the sides of her head, blocking her vision. Linh kicked her legs in a futile attempt to escape.

"Are Johnathan and Daniel ready?" the one holding her asked.

"Yeah. They've already scouted and it's all clear."

They all gave a grunt of acknowledgement and swiftly moved out of the building. The early hour of the morning ensured no one had left their homes. The bandits travelled through the village in the darkest and most shielded alleys as possible, heading for the southwest region of the village.

This isn't the way to the front gate. Why go this way? There was only one exit to and from the village, and she'd been hoping Nathair would see and stop them from taking her.

She managed to look up and accidentally caught the gaze of a man running behind them. With her brows furrowed, she noted the way humour seemed to light up in his eyes.

"You didn't think we were going through the gate, did you?" he whispered. His following chuckle was cruel. "We always make our own escape routes out of towns."

Her heart doubled its frantic pace, and her struggles renewed in strength. Linh wiggled and squirmed, doing anything and everything to be put down.

"Just hold fucking still!" the bandit carrying her bit out, only to bounce her.

Her diaphragm came back down on his shoulder so hard she choked out a grunt. Pain made her eyes water even more, and bile rose to her throat at the intense hit. Linh coughed, gagging as her mouth drooled, only for her saliva to be soaked up by the rag quietening her. Her lungs seized, and she grew lightheaded.

A fifth man joined them. Her hazy eyes found his face, and he looked young and unsure.

"I don't see why we're doing this," he whispered, looking around as if he expected something to come along and stop them. "She's one woman. Is it really worth the risk?"

The man at the rear stepped closer so he could speak in a hushed tone. "Listen, lad, Bragg doesn't ask for much. He doesn't keep any coin, gives the best food to others, and takes care of us. All he wants is a woman and kids. I don't think it's much of an ask, considering he's been butchering Demons for others his whole life."

"Yeah, but she doesn't–" A choke grunted out of him when his throat was grabbed.

The troop carting her through the back end of the village moved on, while the two men stayed behind. She caught the first half of their conversation before the rest was lost to the distance between them.

"We're leaving tomorrow," the man grated down to the younger bandit. "We've had it with the villages in this area; they're people who have been hardened by the mountain Demons. Her father is the worst of them, and Bragg wants to take her with us. So, you can complain all you like, but you're either with us, or you're fucking dead. Pick one, because–"

When they reached the wall next to the mountain cliff, they halted. One of the wooden stakes protecting the village groaned and creaked as it tipped forward, and Linh realised they'd removed nails and bolts so it would move like a hinge. The gap was narrow. One bandit stepped through sideways, squeezing his thick body past before they tossed her into his arms. The rest followed behind.

Her breaths only grew stronger so she could suffocate on them. Anxiety clawed when she couldn't see the village gates from here; therefore, Nathair wouldn't spot their escape.

Skittering in the distance only made her aware that she was out in the open, with six guards, and bleeding between her legs like a piece of bait. She resumed her kicking as the village began to fade from view.

Oh gods. Someone help me!

THIRTY-FIVE

With a snarl, Nathair bashed on the town gate.

The day was late, and dusk shed its last light. Night crept over the horizon, proving another day had passed, and he was fucking done waiting.

Bring me that female, or I will obtain her. They should just be relieved that he was *knocking.*

When no one answered, he embedded his claws into the thick, rough timber with his maw parting. His scales puffed and vibrated as he let out a resounding hiss.

A shout echoed over the distance from within the walls. A warning that he, the Duskwalker, the *monster* – as they kept calling him – was attempting to get inside. Any minute now, and there would be soldiers above, aiming their arrows at him.

The moment they released one, he'd break through this measly barrier and hunt for her.

Linh! he shouted within his mind.

Four days of waiting was enough. He'd been patient. He'd been a good male. He let her heal, and rest, and be with her people. Now, he wanted her attention, her affection, a fucking cuddle if she was willing. He wanted kisses on the cool bone of his skull, and soft hands admiring his scales.

Fuck. He just wanted that female any way he could have her right now. Even just the sight of her in his lonely gaze would be welcome.

His gut twisted, yet it was his heart which felt greedy. He shook as he held back his annoyance and rage, his flesh itching with the loss of her essence that acted like a balm against his own. His fins raised and quivered as he tried not to let his guilt overcome him – he was beginning to fear they were right. That... this female no longer wanted him and was just waiting to release a breath of relief when he turned away.

A lung-seizing whine rattled his chest, and he placed his forehead and horns against the door. *Please. Please don't abandon me, not when I have just found you.* He didn't want the words from the soldiers to be true.

He bashed again with renewed anger, this time with a roar as his orbs reddened. *Come out here and face me!*

She incited desire. *She* was the one to instigate touch, and coaxed it from him until she'd envenomed him with her feminine wiles. She was the one who kissed him, pressed his cock to her pussy, fucking rode both his cocks until his mind almost blacked out in bliss.

I was patient. He let her lead, to show him what she wanted, so how dare she abandon him outside this wretched town when she'd woken up three days ago! Was he not deserving of a singular word? An explanation?

Another shout in the distance bombarded him, and Nathair bashed his forehead against the door this time.

So many voices. There are so many voices. Were they inside his mind or just beyond these walls? Was he about to slip into a fragment, or was he conscious with full clarity?

His insides squirmed when he didn't have the answer.

He'd not seen a blue sky this day, and the world had felt colder with the lack of sun. He'd been able to scent the petrichor of the approaching rain, yet it was slow to arrive. He hadn't wanted to be left in the dreaded, dreary cold by himself.

He choked, clutching his throat as he forced in a full breath, only to halt it at the perfume of fresh human blood in the air. It was light, but he heard screams now. Children, women, even men were wailing within the walls of this village.

Dark smoke lifted to the grey rain clouds.

Something is wrong. White entered his sight. *Linh...*

With one determined bash of his shoulder, Nathair broke the gate enough to cave it in. He shoved his clawed fingers into the gap he'd made, and pushed until the wooden slat locking the door cracked when he broke it in half. Within a second, he was able to shove the gate open with little strength, and the double doors bashed against the walls when they swung inwards.

Everything seemed calm until it suddenly wasn't.

Somewhere from the middle of the village, people ran to escape. A woman stumbled as she held her dress up with one hand, while holding the hand of a small youngling with the other. She tugged the youngling down an alleyway to escape the fight he could hear from deeper within.

I cannot breathe. He stilled his lungs. If there was a thick blood scent in the air, the humans wouldn't be running from each other, but him. *I won't be able to find her without my sense of smell.*

He'd been intending to find the centre of the village and lurk in it until it was safe to breathe. They should be used to his non-violent presence by now, and knew what he sought. They'd be fools not to realise what he craved.

Nathair risked it. He risked taking a small breath – and instantly regretted it. His orbs shifted red and the invisible hands of bloodlust massaged his brain, only for claws to tear at his empty stomach. Hunger blasted him at the thick blood scent.

So fresh. So tasty. So *tantalising.*

No! He shook his head and let out a wheeze. *No.* He backed up. He had to back up.

He didn't make it far in his retreat through the gaping entrance before a man dressed in a navy jacket ran towards him. His face was familiar, even if his blood-soaked hair looked messier than usual. His brown eyes locked onto Nathair, and they never left his skull as he sprinted.

Kai held his shoulder, and blood trickled down his arm.

Behind him, a soldier gave chase, until a random villager tackled the soldier from the side. They smashed against the ground and formed a writhing mass of battering limbs as they fought each other.

"Please," Kai pleaded, reaching out to Nathair as he passed through the gate to meet him. A dagger lodged to the hilt in his back glinted in the disappearing light. "Please, help us."

Nathair looked past him, wishing a certain pretty female would run to him for protection. She wasn't in the crowd of running humans who were beginning to dwindle out as they made it to the safety of their homes.

A soldier nocked an arrow and aimed it for Kai's back. With a hiss, Nathair caught it as he darted behind the man to protect him, only to toss the weapon. He spun around the male and shoved him down until Kai's back rested against his tail, now protecting him from all sides.

He grabbed the hilt of the dagger in the male's back, yanked it free, and grabbed his throat. Nathair healed him of his possibly fatal wound, and parted his maw to give a rattling, growly hiss. *Speak!*

"They took her," Kai stated up to him, his eyes wide and frantic. "Last night, they took Linh. They wouldn't let us see her, wouldn't let us speak with her. When we had enough this afternoon, we found the Priestess watching over her tied to her bed."

Nathair tightened his hand on Kai's throat. For a second, he considered pulverising it.

I gave her to you to protect! To keep safe! How dare you let her be taken?! He lifted his sight to the village, wondering when or how they snuck past him.

Nathair raised the claws of his free hand to strike in vengeance for their negligence. Her own father couldn't keep her safe – not just once, but twice. *Fucking useless!*

As he lowered his sight back to Kai's twisted expression, he took in the male's eyes. Their brown was remarkably similar to Linh's, and they lacked malice. They were gentle, and the gaze of someone who didn't want to be cruel. Kind, like hers. Pretty, even.

He faltered in his strike. *He's her father.*

She'd *hate* Nathair if he killed her parent. She'd grow to resent him, even if the male was part of the reason she was *gone.*

"This," Kai said, grabbing Nathair's free hand poised above him. He lowered two of Nathair's clawed fingers, only to do the same with his own hand.

It's the same gesture she gave me that day. The one she'd giggled at him.

"It means 'I love you,'" Kai stated, with his brows furrowed at Nathair's skull. "We didn't get a chance to speak about you for long, but she said you were safe. That we can trust you. I know my daughter. I know she wouldn't say this to just anyone."

For a moment, all his fear and worry eased. *She said she loves me?* Fuck, that warmed his heart so deeply it spread tenderness throughout his entire body. She even said it *to* him, just in the most insanely obscure way.

He was thankful he now knew how to say it, as he'd never needed those three words before. He'd been trying to figure out his own sign for it, so he could say it to her when he, she – they – were ready. Or, when he thought she would be ready to hear it.

He hadn't wanted to pressure her. It was the last thing he wanted to do. *I've been waiting for her to say it, so I could finally return it.*

"If you feel the same way, please save her." Kai grabbed Nathair's hand with both his own and pressed his forehead against the combined hold. "Bragg's men must have made their own route out of the village. They're dangerous, Nathair. We aren't a military town."

His head reared back, and he let the male's throat go. *She told them my name.*

"Please. You must go south, between the tallest mountain peaks."

Already planning to do just that, Nathair carefully lifted him out of his tail. He didn't waste any time as he shoved the male back towards the village. Using his arms as additional leverage for his slithering speed and agility, he headed towards the southern peaks of this mountain range. He knew where the male was talking of, as he'd snuck past it on his travels this far north.

Within a few hours, he'd have that female in his arms again.

His orbs reddened as venom flooded his maw. *I'll kill all of them for touching her.*

THIRTY-SIX

By the time they made it to the main bandit camp, the entire day had passed, night had come, and Linh's legs *ached*.

Barth, the bandit who carried her from the village, had put her bare feet on the ground. She'd been shoved the entire way, and they refused to stop. They never took into consideration that Linh was not made of muscle and didn't have the stamina of a horse.

At least they removed the mouth gag so she could breathe properly.

She'd tried not to be scared, but she'd jumped at every sound in the distance. They'd been attacked multiple times, all the Demons heading straight for her, and they lost a man in the constant brawls.

It worsened when night came. She'd been terrified of the dark, fretful about where they were taking her.

The first time she'd been forced to do this walk, she'd cried for her mum and dad. All she could picture now was the big, sweet serpent Duskwalker.

More than ever, she wanted him here to protect her, to soothe her anxious heart. She needed him to settle her constant tears and help rid her of the horrible memories that incessantly pervaded her thoughts. She needed his waterlily-and-moonflower scent to shroud her in a false sense of comfort, and for his cool body to dull the heat from her sprinting pulse.

As she was led through a particular path, the wooden walls she approached grew taller and more daunting with each step. Her face drained of heat, and ice shards frosted her veins. Yet sweat dotted her as a familiar sickening gut twist made her throat clog.

I never wanted to see this place again.

If someone gave her a torch, she'd burn it to the ground.

Linh fought when they took her through the entrance. Her strength came from utter fear, utter repulsion, and it flooded adrenaline straight into every muscle. Her heartbeat was so fast it thumped in her abdomen.

"No. Please," she begged, before a wall of muscle pushed her through the threshold.

Linh crashed to her hands and knees onto rocky dirt. When she fell to her hip, her long, loose hair swaying over her shoulder, she lost all her will. She would rather sit in the dirt than go any further forward.

A set of black boots stopped just beyond her hands. Then a set of leather-padded knees came into view as he crouched with one elbow rested on his knee.

A rough, meaty hand grabbed her chin, and Linh's face was shoved upwards into a man's. His green eyes were dark, like a poisonous plant, and they somehow came across as delighted in their narrowed glare.

Her lips parted on a silent cry as she was forced to take in his crooked nose, the strong brow and cheek bones, and lips which were partially hidden away by a short beard. His hair was such a light brown that it was almost blonde, and it was tied back in a low ponytail.

"Hey, sugar," Bragg greeted, his muscled shoulders stiffening beneath his stained cream tunic. "I'm glad the lads were able to get you here safe and sound."

"Yeah, but she fucking bitched the whole time," one of her escorts stated as he stepped around them.

Bragg reached down to grab the bottom of her white gown, and the tiny hairs on her body stood on end in worry.

"What kind of dress is this?" Bragg asked, refusing to let go of her face as he looked up at another bandit passing them. "And where's her shoes? She can't travel in this."

Folding his arms behind his head, Barth shrugged. "She was in the hospital. Not much else we could do."

Bragg tsked, and Linh's shoulders turned inwards when he returned his focus to her.

The warmth in his gaze didn't match his next words, even when he spoke them softly. "Run from me again, and I'll let the Demons have you." He stood and then dragged Linh to her feet by her upper arm. Bragg carted her towards the centre of the camp as he shouted, "Make sure you're all ready by first light. The others will meet us at our home base in a few weeks to make sure no one follows us."

Linh stumbled and tripped over her feet, especially as she used them to push off and away from him. Her gaze darted around the camp, and she noticed only a few tents were still erected. Items clattered as they packed their belongings and assisted with lowering fortifications they wished to take with them.

A few horses neighed and whinnied in the background, startled by the noises, whereas others just grunted.

Linh dropped to a crouch when she thought he was taking her to his tent, then screamed and kicked. Bragg dragged her across the ground, only to grab a tight fistful of her hair.

"Shut the fuck up," he sneered. "They already told me you're bleeding, and your screaming will only rile the Demons up even more. We plan to get out of here before your new protector even realises you're gone. Want him to find a dead woman?"

"He'll come for me!"

"I'd like to see him try," Bragg stated with a dry chuckle, hoisting her to her feet by her hair. "We're Demon killers, sugar. If we can't kill him, our iron will trap him for the Demons to take care of. Shit, even the three-metre pits might keep him down."

When he carted her in the opposite direction to his tent, her relief was short-lived. Copying the idea of her people, a central stake kept up a canopy of chains that stopped them from being attacked from above. A set of shackles hung from a curved hook, glinting in the firelight as he pulled her up a small hill.

Bragg secured her to the stake. Her toes barely skimmed the ground as she hung there with her arms stretched above her head.

"Since I can't fucking trust you just yet, why don't you *hang out* for a while? I've got shit to do before we leave."

Grabbing the chains, Linh lifted herself to swing and kick to get down. Her hair flung around her body, but she quickly stopped when Bragg gave her a mean glare.

"How'd you befriend a Duskwalker, anyway?" he asked, cupping his chin in thought. "Is that what killed three of my best trackers? I was upset when I thought your stupidity had gotten you eaten."

Linh said nothing and just huffed at him. *I can't reveal anything.* Her lips tightened, before the bottom one trembled. *He'll kill me if he finds out the truth.* He didn't want to be 'betrayed,' and would be infuriated if he learned Linh had been intimate with Nathair.

She'd known for a long while that Bragg didn't see any issue with how he treated her. Despite not being truly married, he called her his wife and treated her like she was property. No woman, unless they were unhinged, fearless, or just as deranged as the rest of these people, would choose this life willingly. Deals were made via unfair and forced trades, or women were stolen.

Her gaze slipped to a woman following a bandit, and the light had been lost in her eyes before Linh had even met her. Linh didn't even know her name, but the woman had accepted her wifely role because there was nothing she could do.

Bragg had just been waiting for Linh to break like her.

The idea that there would be a point where she just accepted this man was hollowing. It instantly made tears brim in her eyes, and her brows furrowed even further than they already were.

She wanted to throw all her hate in his face. She wanted to tell Bragg she loved Nathair, that he pleasured her, that he was better in any and every way possible she could think of. Instead, she bit back the small fire she had, only so she didn't increase her own suffering.

He will come. Nathair had to come.

The question was when, and what she'd be forced to endure until then. A tear slipped down her cheek, but she tried to settle her anxiety. She stifled the rest as she looked at Bragg through the strands of her hair that had fallen around her face.

"You know this is all your fault, don't you?" Bragg drawled, shaking his head. "All you had to do was stay put and be good, and I would've treated you well."

Linh was sure that was true. If she just obeyed, there would be no need for harshness. She wasn't willing to do that.

A few men stopped what they'd been doing to come watch their interaction. They always lingered when there was entertainment to be found.

"I don't think she'll stop trying to run, boss." One of the men snickered. "You picked a wildfire. Look at the way she's looking at you now."

What? With fear as she fucking trembled? If they thought it was a glare of hate, then they were poorly mistaken. Although she felt nothing but disgust and spite for the man before her, for all of them, she was too scared to register anything but her fear.

"I thought you kept all your promises," another shouted, which gained the attention of a few carting sacks of food they'd likely stolen.

"Yeah. Weren't you telling us all this morning what you would do once the lads brought her back?" The jeers were pointed and sharp, and they spelled out that Linh was in danger.

For a split second, Linh thought she saw a double glow of

red, like two lights, but they darted and faded within the blink of an eye. She searched the edges of the dark – the camp's torches only giving them enough muted light to see where they walked.

Bragg tsked, as he shot his men a sharp glare. "Damnit. I was hoping you all had forgotten."

Linh hadn't forgotten the threats of the past, and she swallowed thickly when he placed a hand on the hilt of his dagger.

"It's safer if she can walk on her own," Bragg argued.

"You're a bitch!" a man shouted from the left, and laughter erupted. "Look at her, she's as light as a sack of flour. Just cart her on your horse. It'll be fine."

From the back, an *uck* sounded from someone, followed by a thud. A few people checked behind them, but shrugged and turned forward to watch Bragg yank his dagger from its sheath.

"I did promise you that if you ran off again, I'd cut that little heel of yours." Bragg moved to stand behind her and knelt down. Linh kicked when he grabbed her left calf, but he held her still. "Don't worry, you'll still be able to walk – you'll just have a little limp."

Once more, she saw twin red glows and thought a person standing suddenly disappeared. She couldn't see properly as she searched for someone, anyone, to save her. She was given nothing but cruel gawks as a few chuckled.

Linh whimpered when she felt the cold steel pressing against her. "I won't run," she blurted. A complete and utter lie.

He snorted a humourless laugh. "Didn't really believe you the first time, and definitely don't believe you now." Then he shouted, "Someone get me a bandage."

When her Achilles tendon was sliced cleanly through, her foot became unresponsive, and Linh pelted out a scream.

A loud, deafening, ear-splitting roar answered her.

A monster with a long, continuous limb barrelled into the crowd of men with swiping claws. A white serpent skull dipped down like a wave as he dived, only for Nathair to rise when he'd killed two bandits in one go. He tackled another before the man had even gotten his bearings, and the Duskwalker's fangs lanced his chest as they crashed to the ground.

Linh didn't get the chance to be relieved to see him. She gasped and lifted her head back when a knife was pressed to her throat.

"How the *fuck* did it get here so fast?" Bragg whispered to himself. "What are the lads doing in the village? They were supposed to keep everyone distracted until we were gone."

Oh my god, he's here. Linh didn't care how he arrived so fast, and a relieved sob broke from her. *Nathair.*

The leather straps of Bragg's dagger hilt creaked in his white-knuckled grip as he bit out, "Shit! He's killing everyone."

"D-do you really think threatening me is going to help you?" she asked, her eyes never leaving Nathair as he shot through the camp like a cyclone of black scales.

Anything that moved became his target, unless a weapon hit him. Pain made him roar and bare his venomous fangs, and he lunged at his attacker with his claws at the ready. He didn't seem to care that he was forcing steel into his own body as a result, purely focused on destroying and eating the person wielding it. His snarls and hisses mingled with the roars and yells of men as some attacked and others fled momentarily to regroup.

Linh knew Bragg could see what she did: a slaughter.

They'd underestimated Nathair. They were stupid to think that a Duskwalker was anything like a Demon. Then again, Linh had thought them to be no different until she met one.

With how Nathair had briefly and sporadically described the rest of his kin... she knew that even compared to his own, he was different. He had to be the biggest, the longest, and perhaps even the deadliest.

"J-just let me go," Linh pleaded.

"You're my answer to getting out of this alive if he doesn't want to watch me slit your throat," Bragg bit through gritted teeth.

Why take me in the first place if I matter that little?! Then again, Linh would never understand the warped mind of an idiotic brute.

Linh's brows only furrowed when she knew the truth as she watched Nathair decimate the campsite. A tent was on fire from a knocked-over torch, and the thick smoke of it was black and disgusting. The wind suddenly picked up speed and had an icy chill to it, billowing leaves and forest debris around the carnage.

"We're both going to die," she whispered.

He's enraged. She watched as someone shoved their sword into his thick torso, while another cut their axe halfway through the last few feet of his tapered tail. *The lights I saw earlier, they were him trying to kill everyone without losing his senses.*

Her scream must have set him off, and now her protector didn't see her. She was just another body, another enemy – prey, food.

A droplet splattered against her cheek, and Linh lifted her face to the gathering rain. It'd been threatening them all day, and finally washed over them.

It's cold. She shivered and closed her eyes to it in welcome. *It's fine. I'd rather Nathair kill me than be the wife of a cruel man.*

She couldn't accept Bragg, but she could accept this.

Even if Nathair never learned of it, he saved her this night and was her salvation, despite the real possibility of it ending in tragedy.

At first, the rain was light, but it quickly grew in power. A roaring *shaa* landed over them like a blanket, somehow muting everything other than the constant fighting. Minutes passed, and she didn't have the heart to feel sorry for those who screamed. It was all deserved. They brought this upon themselves.

Everything went quiet.

With her hair wet and clinging to her face and neck, Linh finally looked down from the falling drops. Off to the side, in a collapsed tent, she watched Nathair tearing into a man. He tore a limb off, only to swallow it whole, before working on the next one. The moment he was done with the man, his tail curled under himself, and he crawled on his hands to a man bleeding out on the ground.

He made quick work of him, and only turned to those who made noise.

Linh took note of the many bodies. Most were injured, many looked unharmed but frozen as if paralysed. Many men had managed to run, abandoning the camp to save themselves after realising they weren't going to defeat him. At least ten lay envenomed, with many more either decapitated or dying from a fatal claw strike.

"Why isn't he coming over here?" Bragg whispered, lowering his dagger. "He's just... *eating* everyone."

She stiffened when Nathair, who had been slithering to another body, paused. His skull twitched, distracted by Bragg's voice, only to twist creepily in their direction. Red orbs seemed to zero in on her, and she swallowed at the menacing sight of them. Bragg didn't dare move, and she figured he was mostly hidden behind the stake.

For a moment, it felt like it was just her and this venomous serpent.

The blood washing from his face and open maw sprayed out when he let out deep huffs in the rain. Each one was clearer and clearer of red liquid, and she imagined with her unmoving, he was deeply disorientated.

She was another body among the many. Another victim.

He took away his stare to point his snout up towards the dark clouds. He reared back on his tail until he was upright, then greeted the rain with his palms flat and pointing upwards. His lethal claws were bared, yet he appeared to be welcoming the downpour like she had been earlier.

He became a stoic statue as his orbs blackened.

The water is cleansing him. The rain came down like heaven, and Linh bit her lips in sympathy when she thought, *Just look at him.*

He had so many gashes on his body that it was difficult to see where one ended and another began. Sputtering fires highlighted the purple blood washing off him in rivulets. Three arrows were embedded into his torso: two in his back and one in his side. Part of his tail was cut to the point it didn't sit right against the ground, and had a sharp, unnatural bend in it.

Nathair had fought fifty men, if not more. The camp wasn't small, and neither was Bragg's bandit army. She was aware that Nathair had eaten at least five men since the fighting had stopped.

His hip bones had disappeared, as well as two bottom ribs. He even looked... longer, bulkier, more frightful. Gosh, she wanted to hug him so badly. *Nathair...* Her tears gathered – her poor monster. *He came for me.*

Her precious Duskwalker looked like he was searching for salvation in the rain, and Linh opened her mouth to give it to him. To sing and lull him into tranquillity.

"Stay fucking quiet," Bragg rasped in her ear. He grabbed a fistful of her hair, ripping a cry from her before she could utter a single lyric.

Nathair's head fell to the side to look at them, and crimson orbs suddenly came to life.

Linh held back her squeal when he barrelled towards them in a slither of limbs. Bragg put the knife back to her throat, choosing to use her as a shield once more.

Don't be afraid, Linh pleaded with herself as she shut her eyes. She didn't want to go down screaming, especially if there was a potential that he may remember her doing so.

He'd come here to save her, only to be her demise. She worried Nathair would hate himself for harming her, but she just hoped he found a way to forgive himself. *M-maybe we can meet in his afterlife.*

What a horrible, saddening thought.

Silence met her. When nothing happened, not even a deep huff of breath, she braved peeking open her eyes. They flung wide when Nathair's snout was less than an inch from her nose, his red orbs seeming to stare into the very pit of her soul.

He parted his maw, and his lowered fangs rested against the floor of his mouth. A quiet, unnerving hiss shook from him, and it instantly had the tiny hairs on her body standing on end.

Her nipples budded despite the situation, and she found herself not holding even an ounce of fear. He wasn't striking her.

New tears bubbled, and her trembling lips parted.

Hey, Nathair.

Staring at the little female whose face was swollen with the evidence of constant tears, the rage that shook Nathair was brimming with quiet malice. Violence pumped into his muscles on every heartbeat, making his entire being swell with the desire to rip apart everyone who made Linh cry.

He also shuddered. *Fuck. My stomach hurts.*

The souls he'd eaten were burning him from the inside out and felt like they were trying to crawl up his throat. His mind told him to rid himself of them. Hunger gurgled and grumbled, rolling the hot sick in his stomach with a confusing ache.

He was a singular breath away from slipping back into a craze.

Although the blessed rain had cleansed his mouth and nose just enough to give him a break from it, it was the sprinkling cold which woke him from the worst of his murderous stupor.

This was not how he'd planned to rescue her, but it'd been a risk he'd taken all the same.

Nathair had stolen six humans before being noticed. He had

not clawed or bitten them, instead using a human means of killing. He'd snapped their weak and feeble necks. No blood to instigate his hunger, and no scream loud enough to alert anyone. He dragged their corpses into the dark.

He'd been hoping he could pick them off one by one in order to protect his little nightingale from himself. Unfortunately, her pain-filled scream dug its nails into his heart. Her blood had already been in the air, and it intensified, causing him to lash out as fury swept through him.

If it wasn't for the rain, I would have attacked her by now.

It did make her white dress nearly see-through. He was angered that anyone else was able to see the volume of her breasts and the cute nipples that dusted their peaks, the curve of her waist, and the vee of her pubic mound.

Not daring to breathe, his gaze slipped up to the male hiding behind her.

"Back up, Duskwalker, or I'll slit her throat," he demanded.

Go for it, Nathair thought darkly. *I'll just heal her wound and add it to the many of my own.*

The human wouldn't be able to kill Linh faster than the quick strike of his own hand touching her.

She gave him a wobbling smile. Her eyes saw into him, saw he was here, aware, and he adored her for seeing that despite his fleshless skull.

Nathair nodded his snout towards the male once, then twice. The movement was subtle, but Linh's shoulders went back despite her arms locked above her head. She nodded.

When he turned his skull towards the male fully, he opened his mouth to let the full strength of his hiss echo.

"Hum," Nathair signed at his own throat while he moved towards her attacker. The male of her tears, her nightmares, and pain. The one he'd been longing to slaughter from the very first moment he observed her parasite-infested soul.

"Stay back!" the male shouted.

What was his name again? Nathair was sure Linh had told him. *Bragg.* What a hideous name for a hideous male.

Linh hummed for him, and combined with the dullness from the voices of his rage, it gave him what he wanted. Or rather, he *hoped* it did.

Before Bragg could hurt her, he shoved the male to the left, away from her neck, and he stumbled to his arse from Nathair's strength. His puffed scales vibrated as his hiss grew lower and began to morph into a growl.

Bragg glared up at him, but didn't show an ounce of fear in his green eyes.

"I'm going to show you how it feels to be defiled," Nathair snarled over him.

If this human thought he'd fight fair, then he was about to learn that Nathair liked to give in to all his darkest impulses.

With his hand flat, claws ready and poised to slice deep, Nathair shot forward. He shoved his hand into the male's chest, and Bragg gasped in surprise. Nathair gave a grunt when the dagger's blade was shoved upwards through his neck.

The strangest sensation overcame him.

His orbs felt as though they'd rotated back into his skull when the tip of the blade penetrated his brain. Nathair seized, and yet the euphoria of the voices shutting the fuck up overcame him at the same time. He'd never had anything slice into him like this before and had no ability to stop it as he locked up and quivered.

It was short-lived, as was the quiet, when the male stupidly removed the weapon. Nathair's body compensated for his injury and gave him new ways to function, like what lay beneath his flesh wasn't truly formed, and was a messy blob of needless organs.

A stomach that had nothing beyond it as he absorbed all his food into his very being. A pulse that kept beating even when his heart had gone quiet. Lungs that could go still, only to restart seconds later. He was made of nothing, and yet had everything he needed to be a devastating creature upon the world.

Bragg gave a yell when he stabbed his dagger into

Nathair's throat again, but the blade tip came out just below the bottom of his skull.

Pulling back, Nathair took the male's soul as he gathered him up in his tail. Well, the part of his tail that wasn't ruined from the many attempts to sever his lithe weapon of destruction.

He brought the male into the air and slipped around Linh's feet until he circled the wooden pole she was tied to. He hung the male in front of her, and brought his arms forward from behind her to reveal Bragg's soul.

He tucked his snout into her hair until his nose hole was buried in those silky strands. He let out the breath that had been stinging his lungs, and braved taking in a new, singular one. The rain and her pretty aroma were just enough to dampen down the smell of blood pervading the air. Her hum was soothing, and he briefly darkened his orbs to savour it.

"Don't stop watching, no matter what happens," Nathair told her softly, hoping her humming meant she could hear him.

He didn't know what would happen, but he had a good guess from what Weldir had told him. It would be gruesome, but Nathair wanted her to remember this moment. To remember how this vile human died, so she could know he would never, *ever*, return to haunt her.

Bragg kicked as he shouted obscenities.

Nathair took his orange-and-red fully flaming soul and flipped it upside down. He hated that other than a few physical scars, his soul looked normal; Nathair wanted it to have the evidence of the cruelty that lingered in his heart.

He grabbed its little feet and pulled in opposite directions. It took Nathair a remarkable amount of power to do what he desired, but when it began, it was seamless. The male's arrogant roars turned into screams as he began to split in two, from the groin up. Nathair slowed the tearing of his soul and body, wanting to savour the way he wailed into the night.

Blood saturated his ripping leather breeches as he kicked his legs in a poor attempt to escape.

Only when Linh stopped humming to sob, the sight too much, did Nathair quicken the pace. He tore the male in half evenly down the middle and held the two parts of his soul in the palm of his hand. The flame blackened into charcoal, not even given the chance to turn white like the other humans who died, and both it and the physical male began to disintegrate.

Bragg's physical body withered like ash before it, too, disappeared, not leaving a single trace of him in this world, nor the next.

The male was no more.

Nathair looked up when the rain began to die down, and white flickered in his orbs. He'd been hoping it would linger, but it appeared its downpour was harsh, yet fleeting. It would return, but *when* was not a question he could answer.

Uncoiling from her stake, he brought himself in front of Linh once more. He made sure he was head height with her, with barely an inch parting them. He gave her a moment to decipher what he wanted.

When she didn't give it, he licked at his maw, and she let out a tired, tearful giggle.

She leaned forward and pressed her lips to the tip of his snout. Nathair healed her of her wounds as she did, giving a gift as she gave one. The cut on her ankle, the nick to her neck, and the bruising on her wrists transferred to his own body.

He'd needed this, to know that this female did hold affection for him. It made the next question he had for her less worrisome.

Reaching forward, Nathair pressed his hand into her chest. He tugged her soul out without needing to dive into her, and let it float between them as a question. She knew what he wanted, what he longed for.

He didn't have the time to pull her from her trappings. His lungs already ached to take a new breath, and with the rain disappearing, he knew death awaited her. The ground was wet, muddy, and saturated in blood and entrails. *She* was covered in it, and in her own.

She may be able to escape him if he let her down, but she was sure to run into the swarm of Demons that would soon be attracted to this area. She had three choices: face his hunger, face the Demons while she smelt delectable, or become his.

It wasn't a question of do this or else, but that there was no other path.

Linh sobbed as she kicked her foot forward. She tried to latch onto his side, brushing over his fish frills as she nodded.

"Please," she rasped. "Please take it. I want you to."

His heart swelled with elation, making all his wounds flare with agony, but he found it all the sweeter. He lunged and snapped his maw around her soul.

Nathair swallowed – and immediately choked. *Fuck. It's hot.* Hotter than any other he'd ever eaten. It was alive. Halfway down, his paranoia clung to his sternum, his stomach rejecting what he craved, and he almost threw it back up.

No! Go down! He turned his head up and used all his swallowing power.

It slid down. Heat met the coolness of his low body temperature, and it spread all throughout. He shuddered in the blissful euphoria of it, his reddened orbs flickering with black. He quaked as it reached his fingers and tail tip in a curling wave that chased his coolness away.

His hunger dissipated, and Nathair let out a relieved, panted groan.

The scents in the air no longer bothered him, didn't nag him into a craze. He approached his female, his *bride,* his little nightingale. When she hooked her feet around his waist, Nathair broke her shackles while being careful not to harm her wrists. Then he lifted her into his arms as she buried her face against the crook of his neck.

"I knew you'd come," she whispered.

He backed up to give himself room to spin until his tail had formed rings around them. He settled them into a cuddle by bringing them into a ball, blocking out the world and everything beyond just them.

"N-Nathair?"

I'm gravely injured, he thought, wondering if obtaining her soul healed him of his fragments and she could hear him.

She didn't respond.

It was disappointing that she still couldn't hear him, but Nathair shrugged. The voices did feel a little softer, though.

Since he'd bled out much of his strength, the will to move was weakened by the many wounds he had. Every twitch ached, and he shuddered around her.

She's cold. Why the fuck was she cold when he desperately needed her heat the most? It felt like ice had slipped into his vertebrae, and he had a fucking lot of them.

He grabbed the hem of her dress and pulled it up her body.

"Please," she whimpered. "Not now."

Nathair ignored her, since it was a pointless rejection. He had no intention of rutting her right now.

He removed her soaked gown and shoved the naked female against him. Then he nuzzled his snout into her throat, and forced her to wrap her limbs around his neck and waist. *I need warmth,* he thought with a shiver.

Brightness shone in the darkness.

He wanted to revel in what that meant – her soul had crested and hung between his hooked horns – but he couldn't. *Everything hurts.* He closed his orbs so he could focus on her.

Linh eventually softened in his embrace. Her nails dug into him, and she rubbed her cheek across his bony brow.

"I love you," she whispered against his skull.

He retracted an arm so he could do the sign she taught him. "I love you," he said with his right hand by pressing it against the small of her back.

Linh gave a sob that had a strange lightness to it. "Did my dad tell you what it means?"

Nathair answered with a nod.

Little female, I love you more than life itself.

She would never know just how much that meant to a creature who had been *dead* for most of his own.

My heart beats inside me once more. And it was growing warm.

THIRTY-SEVEN

Even before Nathair crested over the grassy hill, he could smell the devastation on the wind.

He paused and stared down at Linh nestled in the safe cradle of his arms.

There is blood and smoke, he thought. He didn't want her to have to witness it when she'd already suffered a terrifying night.

Not only had she been taken, but she'd been forced to face a Demon in human skin. Her protector had almost turned on her – would have, if things had gone even just slightly different. Yet, like she'd been waiting forever to be embraced in his coils, she'd found peace in the arms of a monster. One who would contend with all her enemies. One who would place this female on a pillar of worship and guard her ruthlessly for all time.

When he didn't move forward, Linh lifted her face up to him, and he had the deep urge to push back the loose hair swaying across her cheek.

Her brown eyes grew so light in the sun that they bordered on hazel and honey. They glittered with precious life. Her dark brows drew together in concern, somehow making her soft, gentle features look even sweeter. Her full, pink lips flattened, until the bottom one pouted forward in the adorable fashion she often displayed.

Nathair swallowed a groan at her face. *My bride is so beautiful.* The fact this female had chosen him in return boggled his mind.

It made little sense, and he didn't fucking *care.*

She was *his.* Every inch of her soft and tender body was his to touch, taste, and hold. Ever since she'd gifted Nathair her soul, his entire essence had locked into sensing hers. Her voice, her smell, her touch, and heat. Even her heartbeat was louder, constantly thrumming in his mind like a playful drum.

Even if she was insane to have chosen him, a Duskwalker, then that was luck on his part.

"Nathair?" she asked.

He leaned back and bundled his tail under him. He placed her round backside on him to free up one arm.

"We can go to my cave," he signed, before he cupped the side of her face.

Her lips tightened knowingly, and she turned her gaze in the direction of her village. "Is... is it bad?"

She gave him her attention so he could answer. "I am not sure."

When she only wrung her hands in response, Nathair knew what she wanted. He sighed, lifted her, and continued forward.

Black smoke rising into the air was visible before her village came into view. Two homes were on fire, and at least three others were nothing but charcoal foundations. The gates Nathair had damaged were completely broken off their hinges, and part of the chains above their village were caved in and broken. With his sensitive sight, he was able to see multiple claw marks and streaks of dried blood leading from the village.

"Oh my god," she cried, covering her face and burying it against his chest.

Unsure of how to comfort her through this, Nathair continued around the peak of this hill, descended it, and then he began to climb the incline to her village. Shouts grew louder, just as a new gate door was lifted. They were attempting to refortify before night fell – only for it to likely be attacked again. The sun was shining, but the moment its protective light disappeared, Demons would swarm upon them.

Without aid, these people would be picked off night by night until there was no one left or they abandoned it.

Linh trembled in his arms, and his orbs darkened in their orange hue. *I should have just come after her sooner.* If he'd entered the village despite his worries and uncertainty, he could have possibly prevented all this. He absolutely shouldn't have broken the gate, either.

He bumped the end of his snout against her forehead, and she peeked up at him. He shifted her in his arms so he could circle his chest in apology.

"I-it's not your fault," she rasped. "If it wasn't for me..."

The growl that barked out of him immediately quietened her. *It wasn't her fault.* She didn't ask for any of this, and likely would have tried to prevent it in any way possible.

When they finally rose onto the flat ridge of earth leading to the village, Nathair and Linh both flinched as a roar of cheers and clapping filled the area. She turned her face just in time to see her father, who had been directing the men fixing the new gate, almost trip over his own feet to race to them.

"Linh!" he yelled, one arm raised in the air as he waved.

"Dad!" she exclaimed back, wiggling in Nathair's arms to be put down.

She sprinted for him and forced the man to catch her when she leapt into his widespread arms. He picked her up and spun her before settling her onto her feet with his nose buried into her neck.

"I'm so glad you're safe." When Nathair came upon them, the male looked up at his skull through the strands of her hair and reached out to him. "Thank you. Thank you so much."

"The village..." she started, only to cut short when Kai pushed back to grab her shoulders.

"I told those idiots we'd riot if they took you again."

"Daaad," she whined. She gestured behind him. "But now

look at everything. How are you going to survive this?"

That indeed was an important question.

She cares about them a lot, Nathair thought, as he lifted his sight to the peak of the wall.

Linh had asked to come here today because she wanted to ease everyone about her safety. To say a temporary goodbye to her people, her friends, and even family. She'd chosen to come be with him in his home, a place that was comfortable for him.

He promised they'd visit, as he saw no issue with this. So long as she rested with him each night, and let him lavish as much affection as he wanted on her, he didn't mind visiting these humans.

They would die, whether that be now or in fifty years, and she would continue to live on – with him.

A few years was not a big ask in comparison.

"Don't worry about it, Linh," Kai stated with an unconvincing chuckle. "We're mountain people. We're sturdy like rock."

No. You're made of nothing but sand. Easy to claw into. Easy to slip through the hourglass of time.

"Come," Kai stated, reaching forward.

Nathair thought he was only grabbing Linh, but his clawed fingers were gripped by an unfamiliar touch. He looked down to observe Kai holding Nathair's hand with both of his, just as he pulled as if he wanted to drag his heavy body within the village.

"Everyone wants to thank you," Kai said up to his skull.

Linh's lips pouted in confusion at her father, only to laugh when Nathair remained unmoving. The male kicked at the ground, childishly pulling despite knowing it was futile.

Nathair hissed and retracted his arm when Kai grabbed his wrist and accidentally dug his fingertips into a deep wound.

"Be careful," Linh stated, placing her hand on top of her father's. "Nathair is really hurt."

I thought that would have been obvious, Nathair complained.

A day had not yet passed, and he was littered with gashes and many more puncture wounds. He'd been stabbed repeatedly in the chest, abdomen, and neck by either swords or daggers. Part of his throat was still gaping from a bandit who had shoved a dagger in and sliced sideways, not to mention what Bragg had done. His tail fared little better.

This time, Linh placed her hand in Nathair's so she could pull him between the gates.

"This is not a good idea," Nathair signed, shaking his head while remaining unmoving.

"My father speaks for our people, Nathair," Linh stated softly, supplying him with an inviting smile. "He wouldn't have offered for you to come inside if they did not want you to enter or didn't trust you."

Reluctantly, Nathair slowly slithered forward. He followed her pretty gaze as she walked backwards, his heart swelling when her smile deepened. He looked up at the wooden threshold, ducking beneath it.

His skull met many faces, all of them gawking.

A light tangle of fear entered the scents of many, but it was mostly mild. Their expressions appeared to be of awe more than anything negative.

Her mother stood off to the side, unarmed, but her face was pinched with exhaustion. A young female at her side went to run forward, but Tahlia grabbed her arm and tsked at her.

"Go slowly. Don't run at a predator."

Predator. That was how they saw him, yet both females approached. The younger one kept her eyes on Linh, a teary smile filling her features, while her mother's stern face looked up at Nathair.

The younger one tackled Linh with a loud cry, and they hugged each other.

Her mother bowed her head towards Nathair. "Thank you for saving our daughter."

A choked grunt punched out of him when the younger female tackled him and hugged his waist. She started rambling, showering him in gratitude as his orbs turned white just as the crowd before him fucking cheered again. He winced when it collided with his fragments.

He was uncomfortable with all this, and the young female was pressing against multiple wounds. Thankfully she quickly backed up under the direction of Linh, who once more spoke about his injuries.

"We want you to know that you are welcome to return here any time," Kai stated up at Nathair.

His heart constricted, and he grabbed Linh's forearm. He gently tugged her closer, showing them that he had no intention of leaving this female here. He did not save her for these people, but for himself, for her.

Kai placed his hands on his hips, tilted his head back, and let out a bellowing laugh.

"Yes, we figured as much," her mother said, eyeing her daughter cautiously. "After what we learned from Linh, and the, uh" – her mother coughed into her fist – "the Priestess, we know your feelings are not one-sided."

Linh's gaze grew bashful, and she turned to Nathair as if she wanted to hide her expression.

"Look, if you are who my daughter has fallen in love with, then so be it," Kai said, shining a grin up at Nathair. "Even if you are a little spooky."

The male grunted when he was smacked in the stomach by Tahlia. "The fact is, she's safe. That's all we care about."

Nathair's hold on Linh loosened when he absorbed their words. *They are accepting me?* He'd thought there would be outrage that he had bonded with their daughter and had no intention of letting her go. She was *his,* no matter what they thought or desired.

He did not expect their relationship to be welcomed so readily.

"See?" Linh said, casting him a coy, yet mischievous smile. She waved her hand at her family and then the rest of her people.

Sure, many faces looked appalled, but Nathair didn't mind. Her family were the ones who could whisper in her ear and cause a painful rift between them.

Nathair lifted his hands, but his fingers just twitched in front of his chest. He didn't know what to say, how to respond. He was completely at a loss for words.

He couldn't stop the way his orbs shifted to bright yellow, overcome with relief and joy that this wasn't as hard as he'd expected. No, instead, it was rather heartwarming to be accepted like this, especially as he knew what he looked like to them.

A faceless monster. A dark, venomous serpent. A menacing creature that brought death, destruction, and chaos wherever he went.

Someone who had found love in a fragile, delicate little female and was completely besotted by her. He was thankful they saw that and hoped they knew he would cherish Linh.

Her soul was his to protect, and he'd protect it fervently.

"However," Kai stated in a low murmur. "We don't really want her to leave."

All the relief that had just swirled within him rushed out in a gust. Nathair folded his arms across his chest and leaned back on his tail to show his annoyance.

"I'm sorry, but I've already agreed to go with him," Linh stated, and his chest puffed with pride.

"But he's of no danger to anyone, right?" Kai asked, his brows furrowing. "I don't see why you both have to leave."

A chuckle vibrated behind Nathair's sternum. "You just want something to protect you," he signed in indignation.

He bit out a growl when he realised only Linh would understand what he'd insinuated. His bride placed her hands on her hips and gave Nathair a disappointed glare.

"What did he say?" Kai asked, which caused her to narrow her eyes further.

"He said you're only asking for him to stay to protect everyone," she answered truthfully.

"Sure, the help would be appreciated, but we don't really need your aid." Kai sighed, shaking his head. "We plan to send an urgent message to the villages south of here. With the bandits gone, we only need to keep the Demons out for two or so nights. After that, we'd likely have competent soldiers helping us until we've managed to truly fix our fortifications."

That actually sounds like a very good idea. All of it made sense and would likely help them. They didn't need Nathair, so... why bother asking him to stay? What did they gain out of it? They didn't know what he could do, nor the magic he possessed, as not even Linh knew the full strength of his capabilities.

His sight fell on Linh, who still had her hands on her hips, and she was shooting her father a sour look now.

"I cannot stay with these people, Linh," he signed at her. "I tire of constant chatter, and there is much of it here."

When her father asked, Linh translated.

Tahlia scratched her neck as she blatantly pondered a solution. "If you don't mind lots of water, there is a cave just north of here. It's not far from our village and would be quieter."

"He's aquatic," Linh answered with a small laugh. "He has gills and breathes underwater."

"A water serpent," the younger female rasped. "That's so cool."

If she thinks that's cool, then she is easily impressed.

A small growl of irritation bubbled up his throat. "How far?"

"It's about five hundred metres from the northern wall of the village," Linh answered, as a big grin curled her lips.

He was faltering, and she knew it.

That is close. But it *should* be far enough away to bring him peace with her.

Nathair looked up, only to audibly sigh so they would all know he did it.

"Where is the centre of the village?" he signed roughly to

show his lingering annoyance, lowering his skull to Linh. She pointed towards the mountain. "Take me to it."

She explained what he wanted to her family. After sharing a few confused and uncertain looks, Kai nodded and led the way. As he did, Nathair slithered behind with his hand covering his snout.

This village is by no means small. It appeared to be at least three and a half kilometres in diameter, if not more. *It is even larger than the one to the east of these mountains.*

He looked up and hummed in thought. *Maybe it is possible? I doubt the other Mavka have tried.*

When they brought him to the centre of the village, Nathair headed north for what he guessed was six hundred metres. They followed him until he stopped at a random and unassuming home.

He turned to Linh, her family, and the growing crowd of people who had come to gawk at the monstrous Duskwalker slithering through their village.

"You wish to keep your daughter safe?" Nathair asked Kai, knowing Linh would translate for him. "Your people?"

"Of course," he answered, his brows furrowing as if Nathair had asked a stupid question.

"P-r-o-v-e it." He held both his hands out.

The male looked at his dark palms warily. When Nathair wiggled his fingers expectantly, the male eventually placed his own into them. Nathair found that rather courageous, especially since he hadn't told Kai what he'd do.

"Nathair?" Linh asked, and he merely lowered himself to lick at her cheek to let her know it would be okay.

Although what he was about to do was for her, she would not be the one he asked to participate in this gruesome bargain.

When Kai's palms touched his, Nathair shot his arms higher until he was near the male's elbows. He gripped his soft flesh, then sliced his claws into the male's forearms until he slit them open to his wrists.

Kai roared in pain, and many backed away in fear. But he

obtained what he wanted, blood – and *lots* of it. He heard Linh's shout in the background, but it quickly died.

When orange magic glowed upon the ground, Nathair let the man go and shoved his hands into the two crimson puddles. A hiss resonated from the back of his throat as he poured all his might into the spell and a dome began to form. It grew in width and diameter.

It slowed its forming, and Nathair knew it wasn't enough. A roar exploded from him. His fins lifted to their full lengths, his scales puffed and vibrated in aversion. His vision split as a wave of nauseating dizziness rolled through his body.

It felt like he was sucking out his own life force.

The dome doubled in size, growing wider and taller, as the blood against the ground sucked away into the magic. The more he took, the bigger it grew.

Cold pain lanced up his arms like a lightning bolt travelling through his veins. He halted when the agony became too much and his sight wobbled. The voices in his mind grew louder, and sickness rolled in his gut as he quaked in his fight to keep them at bay.

"Kai!" her mother shouted when the male, who had gone deathly pale, collapsed backwards.

Nathair dived forward and held his ankle to heal him of his wounds. He took them, but not without cost. *I've used too much magic.* He was too injured for this.

Belly down, he shuddered against the ground, as blood poured from his already aching arms. Any heat in Nathair's body dripped out of him, and he lay huffing through strangled breaths.

That fucking sucked.

"What is this?" Linh asked in both surprise and concern, her brows unsure if they wanted to rise or furrow.

He was sure she was angry at him, like the rest of her people were. They brought Kai to his feet, despite the male now being full of life, whereas Nathair suffered.

When he realised he'd ruined the tendons in his arms,

therefore making movement in his fingers minimal, he licked the inside of his maw in agitation. With what little strength he had, he wrote in the dirt with a single finger, "Protect."

"Oh! It's a protection ward, like what the other Duskwalker offers for a bride!" Linh exclaimed as she knelt next to his prone body.

Nathair felt tired and drained, but it was sure to fade soon. His body just needed to adjust to his new wounds, loss of blood, and whatever damage he'd done by pushing the boundary of the dome with his magic.

"You gave my people a protection ward," she whispered, biting at her bottom lip as her eyes glittered with appreciation.

He snapped his maw and pointed a claw at her.

She placed her fingertips against her sternum. "It's for me?"

Nathair nodded. *All I do is for you.* He managed to push up with his elbows, and Linh uselessly tried to help him rise.

Now that the humans understood what he'd done, why he had harmed her father and then healed him, they were no longer displeased. Surprisingly, a few ran forward to aid Linh so he could at least prop himself up on his own tail.

"Does this mean we can stay here?" The hope in her voice told him all he needed to know; he'd made the right decision.

With Nathair towering over Linh, he leaned forward to brush his snout against her cheek. *Yes, little nightingale.* He licked across her lips with his forked tongue, uncaring of who saw him kiss his bride. *Wherever you go, I will follow.*

THIRTY-EIGHT

Linh let out a quiet giggle when the big Duskwalker signed, "I don't want to do this."

He's been saying that since yesterday, she thought with humour.

"Too bad," she answered, kicking her feet with a squeal when he gave her a grouchy snarl. He tackled her, kind of, since she was already lying on the wraps of his tail. "You promised!"

Nathair gave a deep huff and blew it over her ear purposefully. "I am a Mavka, not a human. This entire thing is r-i-d-i-c-u-l-o-u-s." He'd picked a word he hadn't taught her just to emphasise it by spelling it out.

"But it's customary, and it's something I really would like to do," Linh answered as she lowered her head and looked up at him through her lashes. She batted them, while giving her most adorable, puppy-dog eyes she could muster.

She knew it'd worked when he cupped the left side of her head and groaned as he licked across her lips.

A smile lifted into her features while she looked around Nathair's cave. His magic light symbol brightened his nest, since it was too early for the sun to give its pinstripes of light.

I'm kind of sad we're leaving. She hoped it wasn't forever, as she'd love to visit the beach and the quartz cave in the future. This place held a lot of memories for her, and was witness to much of her healing. It was the place she'd fallen in love with him.

Nathair shifted his body in a way that he slipped out from underneath her, and she fell onto the remaining coins and jewels. A few Demons had come to take some 'shinies,' as he put it. Linh was just thankful the tiara had managed to slip under her bedding and hadn't been taken.

She picked it up and marvelled at the silver metal. *I was really hoping to wear this today.*

"Hurry up then," Nathair signed as he crawled his way out of the nest. "We must pack my treasures and your shells."

Cranky pants. She stuck her tongue out at his back. *Well, if he could wear pants, that is.* Tenderness did pang her heart when he took her shells into consideration.

Linh finally rose to her feet and helped pack in their comfortable silence.

Nathair had wanted to return home and be in a place that was familiar in order to heal and be unwell.

His human memories were quieter, and he didn't seem to be slipping into any long or lasting trances, but he still couldn't speak. He thought over time his mind might settle, but he didn't hold out any hope that it would be soon. Linh was fine with that, as she loved him how he was.

They set off to return to her village before the sun had finished rising. With him carrying her, they made it by mid-morning.

Linh raised her hand above her brow to shield her eyes as she took it in from a distance. His orange protection dome spanned it entirely, with a little wiggle room on the southern side for a small amount of expansion. On the right, there was a large gap between the village walls and the edge of the dome.

Nathair had made her father promise the village would never expand in the direction that would be their home. Her father had agreed in exchange for a bargain of sorts. One that Nathair had hesitated on, and was the reason he was being a sour danger-noodle this day.

As soon as they arrived, her little sister was one of the first to greet them.

"Come on!" May exclaimed. She pulled Linh's arm excitedly, as if she wished to drag her away – or dislocate the limb – which forced him to put her down. "You're both late. We were supposed to start getting ready an hour ago."

Her father approached Nathair and led him away. His skull and orange orbs never left her direction until buildings separated their view of each other.

Linh was taken home, and immediately shoved into a pre-made perfumed bath. She washed on her own, getting days, if not months, worth of grime off her body.

She barely had any time to soak before May bashed at the door. "I swear, you're so slow!"

The laugh that fell from Linh was accompanied by butterflies in her stomach and puffy dandelion seeds in her chest. *She's more excited than I am.*

In her own defence, knowing this entire event made Nathair frantic and uncomfortable kind of dampened it for her. She would make the most of it, as Linh wasn't only doing this for herself. It was both her parents' wishes to have this day, and considering she was choosing to live her life distantly with a Duskwalker, she wanted to appease them.

Her mother was there to assist Linh in putting on a bright-red dress that had belonged to her great-grandmother on her father's side. Her mother had worn it once, and her sister would likely – hopefully – wear it one day as well.

The neckline was lace and modest as it dipped into her generous cleavage. The sleeves were long but light, able to be worn in any season, while the skirts of it were layered and barely brushed the ground. Linh was a little taller than the women of her family, standing at a solid five-foot-five.

She dipped her toes into black slippers, opting for no heel, as she already had balance issues.

Her thick hair was parted into multiple sections. Down the front, she had two thin braids that framed the sides of her face before looping back under her earlobes until they were pinned behind her ears. They, and the rest of her hair, were then twisted into a spiral bun that sat low on the back of her head.

A silver comb with white flowers made from pearl was pushed into the top of the bun. The family heirloom was generations old.

Linh then placed the tiara on her head. It was her favourite piece of Nathair's treasures, and something she knew he would be delighted to see her wear in the sun. *Hopefully I can dazzle him into being joyous.*

Lastly, a very light amount of makeup was applied to her face: just some blush, eyeliner, and a red lipstick.

May grabbed her shoulders and finally spun her towards a mirror. Linh immediately burst out laughing, which only made her sister's gleeful expression fall.

"Why are you laughing?" she asked woefully.

"Don't worry about it," Linh answered, turning to her.

Because Nathair is right, this is ridiculous. She felt like an idiot wearing all this, but she also found it remarkably special at the same time. *I kind of feel like a princess.* The tiara didn't help.

Her sister's eyes flicked up to it sparkling on her head. "Where'd you even get that?" May asked, before licking at her lips with greedy brown eyes. "Can I have it once you're done with it?"

Linh's eyes crinkled at that, but it was her mother that answered. "For once, May, I don't think you'll be getting a hand-me-down."

"I bet you stole my favourite sweater again," Linh teased.

May lifted her gaze upwards. "It looks better on me anyway. Orange is more my colour than yours."

Not anymore, Linh thought, knowing she was going to be gazing into the colour for the rest of her, however long, life.

After a final check of her outfit, then her mother and sister fussing over their own, they left. Her father greeted them outside, wearing a red suit that matched her dress.

The man, incapable of being stoic, gave her the largest grin he could muster. He opened his arms towards all three women standing on their doorstep.

"Look at all my beautiful women. I am the luckiest man alive," he stated rumbustiously, waving in front of his face as if he was trying to fight back his emotions. "Linh, you look like a literal angel."

Holding one side of her skirts out, she couldn't help turning side to side for him. Her cheeks were warm from his compliment, despite being used to her father's flamboyant personality.

"How's Nathair?" Linh asked.

"He is rather surly, if I'm being honest. Does he usually hiss and snap his fangs?" He offered his elbow for Linh to take, and her mother and sister fell into a stroll behind them as they headed towards the village square. "For a moment there, I thought we would need to call the temple to bring us another antidote for his venom. He didn't like me touching between his horns."

A cold chill crept down her spine. *That's where my soul is.*

Oh yeah, her father absolutely went poking where he shouldn't have. Linh doubted Nathair would appreciate anyone being close to her soul, to what literally bonded them on a spiritual level, and he was likely very possessive about it. In the same way he was very possessive of her.

That unflappable obsessiveness made her stomach flutter.

All her musings disintegrated when she saw Nathair in the distance. Although he was supposed to keep his back to her, and had probably been told that, he turned the moment he scented her.

Her lips curled with humour, that she tried her best to hide, when he signed over the distance, "They put me in a fucking dress, Linh."

Leaning closer, her father whispered, "What did he say?"

"Don't worry about it," she whispered back, as her eyes crinkled with adoration towards Nathair.

A black suit shirt had been made to fit his size, but it was apparent they didn't know where to... *stop*. It was long, going past the length of his humanoid torso. It didn't help that he had no legs to put into pants. Beneath it, a white tunic stuck out from the collar, and already she could tell his ability to bend and twist had shifted it all wrong.

He looked messy, and she absolutely relished it.

By the tiny white petals all over his skull, in an eye socket, and even dotting his clothes, someone had put a flower crown on his head, which he'd ripped off. She was supposed to be wearing one as well, but she'd chosen not to in exchange for the tiara.

Her father was wearing one, as were her mother and sister, to highlight they were her immediate family.

No fanfare was made as she walked up an aisle of seated people, with many more standing off to the sides. She'd asked for silence, for Nathair's sake, and she appreciated everyone was giving it. All that could be heard was a dry cough here or there, the shifting of clothing, and the grind of a chair.

Well, besides her father's blubbering. Linh elbowed the crying man.

"I can't help it," he quietly wailed. "I've always wanted to walk you down the aisle on your wedding day, and I thought I'd lost my chance. It's a very special moment for a father." He gave a sniffle as he whispered, "My little girl is all grown up, and marrying some Duskwalker I barely know. It's all too much."

Linh rolled her eyes to the side. "You're the one who demanded this."

"I knooow, and it's so beautiful. I hope May's wedding is just as wonderful." He sniffled again. "But with more music."

When Linh was brought to Nathair's side, her father forced the Duskwalker to give him a handshake. Her mother and sister came to her side, whereas Nathair had no groomsmen. Her father had offered to fill that space so Nathair didn't feel alone, and had pouted to Linh when he'd been coldly rejected.

Kai placed his left hand on their combined hold. "Take care of my daughter for me," her father demanded with a firm handshake.

Nathair gave him an unnervingly quiet snarl. *Oops, you offended him, dad.*

Her father just chuckled and waved as he stepped away into the crowd to be a front-row spectator. The head Priestess began the ceremony – most of it in another language no one understood. They had their own gods that they asked for prosperity, health, and love from, even when being a wedding celebrant.

"I think you look lovely," Linh whispered as she brushed the back of her knuckles against Nathair's.

Her heart fluttered when the knuckle of his index finger brushed against hers in a way that showed he wanted to hold her hand. She bet he had his own compliment, and she let herself imagine what lay within his mind.

Perhaps... you are stunning, little nightingale? she thought as she smiled at the Priestess. *Yeah, that sounds like something he'd say.*

"You realise all of this is pointless?" Nathair signed, tilting his head at her. "This human bond is weak and barely a fraction of what it means for a Mavka to obtain their bride. We are bonded forever, Linh. In this life, and in the next."

"I know," she whispered.

"Then why are we doing this? I would rather go to our new home."

Linh gave a wary glance to the masked woman before them. They weren't supposed to talk during the ceremony, but the Priestess nodded in approval. Linh licked her lips nervously and cast her gaze to the crowd.

She kept her voice low as she said, "I know it's silly, but a lot was taken from me, my family, and my people. This is new for me, and something many girls dream about when they're little. As much as my father pushed for this, I think he did so on my behalf." Nathair's shoulders stiffened, and she gave him a sad, but reassuring smile; one that crinkled her eyes and made her head tip to the side. "Even if you don't understand it, I'm really happy I'm doing this with you, Nathair."

Nathair's head reared back a little, and his orange orbs darkened in their hue. He looked at the Priestess, as if he couldn't look at Linh under the weight of his own apparent guilt. This day was special for many humans, but she didn't blame him for not understanding the emotional weight of it.

He circled his chest. "Sorry." His skull tilted back towards her a little. "If this is what you want, then okay."

Seeming to come to a decision, he turned. He darted to her father, who gasped in surprise at his speed, before Nathair stole his flower crown. He placed it, lopsided, on his head before returning.

The Priestess eventually switched over to English so she could tell them to put their rings on. Nathair gave her one from his treasures – of course she'd picked it – and she gave him one that her village had helped make. Something that would handle being in the water and wouldn't erode if he took care of it.

Then they were allowed to give their vows.

Linh went first, and kept it simple. "I found you when I needed you most, and I've been so thankful ever since that day. Your embrace fills me with so much love, while your heart makes me feel so safe and nourished. You mean the absolute world to me. Thank you, Nathair, for choosing me."

Her damn father blubbered in the background, and she almost palmed her face in disbelief.

Then it was Nathair's turn.

When he lifted his hands, she noticed how steady they were. Instead of nervously shaking, he signed with confidence, as if he meant every word – which surprised her considering he likely made it up on the spot.

"I find comfort in your embrace, as much as you do mine, and I will cherish this life with you." His lithe fingers and strong hands slowed as if he wanted to highlight his next words, and his orbs shifted to bright pink. "You are the heart that beats outside of my chest, my little nightingale."

Then he made the gesture for 'I love you,' but extended his middle finger to cross it with his index finger, changing it to 'I love you very much.'

Tears welled in her eyes as her bottom lip trembled from the overwhelming love that crashed over her.

A small purr started. "Was that good?"

Linh leapt forward while nodding. She threw her arms around his thick, corded neck, and pressed her lips to the seam of his bony maw.

"I guess you may kiss each other now," the Priestess said, a small and deep chuckle falling from her.

"Oh, sorry," Linh rasped, pulling away with a flare of embarrassment.

Nathair cupped the back of her head, brought her closer, and shoved his forked tongue into her mouth. He let out a groan as his tongue brushed against hers.

A few people awkwardly clapped before a sea of applause roared. At the noise, Nathair reared back with a shudder, his head twitching in repulsion. He didn't bite at the crowd, and instead kept his attention on her by brushing her cheek with his thumb.

Thank you, Nathair.

She appreciated him finally accepting this, them, and just this day as a whole. Her heart felt lighter than ever, and she truly needed to have a proper wedding as a reminder that everything she'd suffered at least had a happy ending.

"Can we leave now?" Nathair asked.

Linh cupped the sides of his bony face so she could nuzzle her nose against his. "First, we must have festivities, and then we can excuse ourselves."

He grunted but accepted it with a nod. He lifted his skull in a direction behind her, before it tilted with his orbs flashing dark yellow in curiosity. When she began to turn around with a frown marring her features, he cupped her jaw.

For a few seconds, he didn't move.

"You said this day is important, yes?" When Linh nodded, he sighed. "Then turn and face someone. Do not bring too much attention to them, as it may cause distress to your people."

Why did that make a crawl of anxiety slip down her spine?

Linh turned as Nathair tilted his body in a different direction. It wasn't hard to guess who she needed to search for; two people stood in a shaded entrance of an alleyway.

One figure wore a dark-grey cloak which hid them entirely from their forehead down to their feet. The woman next to them wore a cloak made mostly of white feathers, with quite a number of them brown and kind of spotty. The hood was down, revealing dark-brown, loose curls, and a beautiful face that had stern features. Her skin was brown, but it was difficult to gain any other details in the shadows.

The woman lifted a hand to press a singular finger to her curling lips, then bowed her head in greeting.

"I don't understand," Linh said, turning to Nathair. "Who are they?"

He gave a small chuckle. "My mother and father, I think."

"What?!" she quietly rasped. She didn't even get to see his father under his cloak!

Then they were gone, as if they'd disappeared into thin air. She stepped forward, searching for them, only to be swarmed by her family, who were tired of waiting for food and festivities.

No, wait. She scanned the crowd, but couldn't find the woman in white bird feathers. *Where'd they go?*

She would have loved to greet them properly.

Did they come to watch the wedding? Linh couldn't help being disappointed that they'd left. *How did they even know about it?*

She spun to Nathair with her mouth open to voice her complaint. She shut it when she found him looking down at her with his orbs bright pink again, and her heart panged in tenderness.

It's okay. We'll meet them properly in the future.

They had plenty of time.

THIRTY-NINE

Finally, Nathair thought as dusk fell over them. Linh held his hand, guiding them north to what was to be their new home, while she gripped the handle of a lantern.

She'd changed out of her red wedding dress before they left, giving it back to her mother for safekeeping for her sister, and now wore a plain one that had no design on it. It was long with shoulder straps, and a shade of light lavender. He rather liked the colour of desire gently hugging her curves.

He'd ripped off that ridiculous 'groom' garment they'd dressed him in the first chance he'd gotten.

Nathair had not enjoyed any part of the events of today, except for how she grew all teary at his words in front of the Anzúli. It was gratifying that she'd kissed him so openly in front of the humans, proving to them, and him, that she wasn't ashamed to have him as her partner.

He'd hated being on display and gawked at while he 'bonded' himself to this female in her human customs. He also disliked feeling like an outsider as they all ate and chattered during the festivities, although her father had tried everything in his might to befriend Nathair. He was slowly coming around to the eccentric male, who had shared a rather heartfelt – although one-sided – conversation with him.

Nathair had also grown flustered and embarrassed with how she'd tried to make him dance with her. He had no legs, and propping himself up into a straightened position made him tower over her as she swayed her hips. He held her hands and remained still without complaint while she did her little performance.

I wish she'd just been honest with me at the start. If he'd known their 'wedding' had a deeper symbology than merely pacifying her family, he wouldn't have acted so irritable about it. Once she told him the truth, he suddenly wanted to gift her this day as well.

She is happy now, and that is all that matters.

He also couldn't believe his mother had come to witness, or that Weldir had been there in some kind of... physical form. He'd been hidden in shadow, making it impossible for even Nathair to see past the cloud of his magic.

Things to ponder at a later time.

Linh shone that genial smile as she pulled his hand, and Nathair observed his pretty bride.

"I have to tell you something," Linh said softly, yet he noted the coyness in it. Her cheeks pinkened as she slowed, and he tilted his head in question when she nibbled her lip. "I was wearing lipstick. It means there are kiss marks all over your skull."

Nathair covered the end of his snout in thought. *There are?* He liked the idea of this female leaving little possessive love marks all over the white expanse of his skull.

A small giggle fell from her when his orbs shifted pink. "I guess I'll give you more then."

I hope she gives them to me every day. He'd be more inclined to venture around the village just to show them off. To rub it in all the other males' faces that she'd given them to him by staining his skull in their evidence.

Dark green lifted into his orbs as a cunning chuckle bubbled in his chest.

After their short stroll, they reached the mouth of a cave.

Even though it reeked of Demons, he could tell they'd all been vacated – rather violently. *Did the villagers clear it for us?* He was thankful for that.

They entered, and he immediately removed the heavy bag of items he'd taken from his original cave. He plopped it on the ground as he absorbed *their* new home.

It wasn't very large, which immediately disheartened him.

Nathair was able to gauge its space rather accurately by the length of his tail, now that the villagers had measured him today – despite his annoyance with it. He didn't understand why they were so excited to do this, or why they'd shouted with glee that he was a 'whopping forty-five feet' from tail tip to the crown of his skull. Sure, he knew he'd grown quite a bit in length since coming back to life, and had thickened in terms of muscle and mass, but it felt strange being measured. He stood a little over eight feet when he straightened to tower over them.

In terms of width, he thought he could stretch his entire forty-five feet across the cave with very little wiggle room. The length of it was a little longer, perhaps sixty feet, with its height being around eleven.

A decent section near the left of the entrance was taken up by a pool of water that would only come up to his chest at normal standing height. There were two much smaller pools further in.

Two large mattresses had been sewn together and shoved against the right wall, as if the villagers wanted to give them a nice bed to lie on. There was no frame, which was wise, as his weight likely would have broken it. There was also a small side table next to it, and a dresser of drawers – likely for Linh. Lanterns had been bolted to the walls.

They are going out of their way to make sure we stay.

Since he'd been crowned the village protector, and they were trying everything they could to appease him, he was beginning to wonder if he could fuck with them. He'd find it rather hilarious if he made them kneel and worship him like a god. *Bow, little humans, or be eaten.*

However, Nathair knew the dangers of water, and

immediately dived into the larger pool. His entire body fit in rather nicely, and it was a little bigger than his abandoned nest.

His flesh quivered and rippled at the warmth that greeted him. He hadn't realised the water was heated, and it made him a little happier about their relocation.

I knew it, he growled when he found an opening that was large enough to fit the wide span of his shoulders. He shoved through the narrow tunnel and was surprised to find it was short.

He broke through to the other side and looked around in the darkness. It was remarkably similar to his old cave. A decent section of rock, although not as flat, gave land, whereas a good sixty percent was water.

No Demons were hidden away, but he dived once more to check there were no other entrances. There weren't.

There is an underground river nearby. He could feel the vibration of it against his sensitive scales and fins, even through metres, if not kilometres, of rock. He figured it connected to the waterfall that crashed into the ocean.

I'm surprised it's warm. In the darkness, and at the bottom of the rather deep lake, he cupped his bony jaw. His gills continuously flared as he thought. *So is the quartz cave, and I know that is nearby.* The quartz cave was northwest of his old pond, which meant... *Is it possibly below this mountain?*

The fact an underground river ran through the middle of the mountains here, and was heated, he wondered if there was a pocket of earthly heat. *The water here is agreeable,* but it was lukewarm, at best. Just a little warmer than him.

It reminded him of the quartz cave, and he knew he'd take Linh back there whenever he could. He wanted to return them back to a special place for their relationship – a place where they finally became one and she opened up to him. They would have many years to discover even more wonderful locations together.

"Nathair," Linh called, and he winced.

He'd let curiosity get the better of him and had abandoned

his bride in their new home. At least it was safe – that would be the excuse he gave if she were upset.

He pushed off and headed towards the narrow tunnel. From the light that greeted him on the other side, he could tell she'd lit a few of the hanging lanterns.

A set of legs from the knees down were already submerged, then a naked backside slipped in to sit on a boulder. She was joining him in the water, and he didn't know if he was disappointed he'd missed the show of her stripping, or relieved there lacked a barrier between them.

Then he absorbed that she'd so confidently, and comfortably, stripped in his lone presence, and was mollified by the knowledge.

Hello, naked female, he purred as he breached the water's surface directly in front of her.

She'd even removed the twist of her bun, leaving her hair loose except for the braids resting on both sides of her cheeks.

"Having fun?" she asked, her eyes crinkled with knowing humour. "I knew you'd like it."

Nathair rolled his head. "It's fine. Safe from Demons." His protective dome would make sure of that.

"Uh, huh," she hummed as if she knew better. Placing her straightened arms on his shoulders, she brushed one of her legs towards him in a way that parted her thighs. "You know... we're supposed to consummate our marriage now."

Her voice was sweet, as if she wanted to sing the words at him.

"I don't know what that means," he answered honestly. It wasn't something he'd heard or witnessed in his fragments. He did, however, come a little closer so he could nestle between her parted knees.

Her breasts, now just above the water, slipped against his scaled chest. Hardened nipples teased his sensitive skin as he pressed his abdomen to the apex of her thighs.

Leaning forward, Linh fluttered kisses to the front of his throat, narrowly missing the gills on the left side. "It means we're supposed to have sex."

Are we now? he thought with a humorous hum.

Nathair leaned back so he could get out of reach of her lips. "Are you aroused for me?" he asked, before pressing the backs of his claws against her cheek. He brushed a braid behind her ear, tucking it there while caressing the rounded top of it.

"Only a little," she admitted, biting down on her bottom lip. "But I'm sure you'll be able to take care of that."

She leaned forward while pulling, and he let himself be dragged closer. She kissed the centre of his maw, and Nathair instantly reciprocated. He moved his segmented jaw in a way that mimicked lips to greet hers before he found the opportunity to sink his tongue within her mouth.

She gave a rasp of enjoyment, and Nathair answered her with a light groan. He danced the back of his hand down her neck, her chest – only pausing there long enough to play with a nipple – before he went lower. When he glided over her hip bone, she tilted her pelvis for him, and her heart fluttered faster.

Nathair sheathed his claws before he delved between her lips and found her clit. He played with the sensitive bundle of nerves, and her legs spread wide as she moaned for him. He circled her clit with practiced pressure and waited for her hips to start greeting him with subtle rocks.

Only then did he go lower, dabbing his fingertips at the slick pool at her entrance. He speared her with two fingers swiftly, and her muscles locked as she squeaked. Nathair proceeded to pump them, pleased to find that their kissing and his touches had made her soft and ready.

He broke his mouth from hers so he could lash his tongue across her neck, and then brought himself lower to lick at one of her nipples. Clamping it between his jaw segments, he let her feel the pinch of it, before he soothed any sting with more of his tongue.

He pulled away and licked at his maw before tilting his snout downwards. *There is something I have always wanted to do.*

Without wasting any more time to obtain his prize, he removed his fingers and dipped below the water. While he waited for his lungs to fill with water and his breathing system to morph, Nathair wedged his shoulders below her thighs.

Beneath the surface, he lashed her clit with his tongue. Linh swiftly leaned back, parted her thighs, and gripped his horns – the only person he would allow to touch them.

Since her soul was made of essence, Nathair had already discovered it appeared to be safe despite being submerge within water. That just gave him freedom to be his aquatic self and play with his female like this.

A moan from her reverberated through the water as he took a breath through his gills. Just as he dabbed his tongue at her cute little hole, he choked at the sting that instantly clutched his lungs. He ignored it, thinking it was just the shift of breathing in new minerals in the water. The longer he tasted his aroused female, the more it felt like lava had entered the small nerves or special veins branching around his lungs and heart.

I can't breathe! Nathair had to breach the surface before he drowned. Placing a hand on the rock she sat upon, Nathair choked out pants as he forced his lungs to empty of water more rapidly than normal.

Linh sat up with widened, worried eyes. "Oh my gosh, are you okay?"

"No," he answered with shaking hands. "Whatever is on your skin is making the water t-o-x-i-c."

It'd tasted sour and sweet at the same time, and yet acidic.

Her eyelids fluttered. "Oh. I had a perfumed bath earlier."

"Please don't do that again," he pleaded, thankful the burning in his chest was dulling already. "If you join me in the water, what is on your skin will impact my breathing. Certain things are fine, like metals and salt."

"I'm sorry," she grumbled, lowering her gaze to his chest. All the rosiness of her growing arousal began to fade.

That is not what he wanted. Placing his hands beneath her thighs, Nathair lifted her and put her perfect arse on the edge of the rocky bank. He did so away from her seat, so he could have room to slide his head between her thighs.

"Is this okay?" he signed, as he licked at his maw while staring at her little cunt.

When she nodded, Nathair shoved his tongue inside her. The taste that instantly greeted him had him shuddering shoulders-deep in the water, then propping her knees up so he could widen her. Linh rested back on her elbows, but kept her gaze on his skull as he delved his tongue.

Even though he'd removed much of her arousal by fingering her, his orbs flashed to purple, and his cocks hardened rapidly in the water. He brought his tongue out just so he could twist his head and lash down her clit, then back up, wanting her to produce more slick. Only when he could scent it'd grown to be a little pool again did he shove his tongue back inside.

His tastebuds were more sensitive than other creatures, since he was able to sense things in the air with his tongue. It meant this female's naughty taste had his entire skull buzzing in reaction, and he flicked his flexible appendage in any way he could to make sure she produced more.

When he decided he didn't want to remove his tongue from the delicious well of her hot cunt, he reached his arm around her thigh. He pressed against her clit from above, and the sultry moan she gave him was lovely. With her head tilted back, her spine arched, and her breasts pointed towards the rocky ceiling, her lips parted on loud pants, and she looked stunning.

Her inner walls spasmed and quivered, just as she grew tight. Precum welled at the tips of his cocks from the intense swells when she came for him, and his ears tingled at her cry bouncing off the walls. Drool flooded his mouth in excitement at this female breaking apart and gifting him more of her taste.

I want inside her so badly. It'd been fucking *days* since he'd had this female wrapped around his cocks.

So much had happened, and he'd missed touching her, hearing her cries, experiencing all that was this sensual creature. He glided his hand away from her clit so he could palm her stomach and cup a breast, wanting to feel its softness rather than just remember it.

Instead of lifting to mount her, Nathair kept his head between her creamy thighs.

He considered fisting his throbbing cocks but decided against it. It was best he didn't bring himself to release – he didn't wish for his seed to linger in the water.

Even when Linh pushed on his head to get him away, Nathair latched himself to her. He wanted to make her come again, to have a sated female in his lap once he was done with her. To make her cry out in abandon until she couldn't give him another drop.

"Inside me, Nathair," she cried, pushing harder as she dipped an agonised gaze down to him. Brows furrowed, and lips bitten and kiss swollen, she panted, "I need you inside."

The whimper that broke from him hurt to produce. He shook his head. *I cannot.* He couldn't be inside her – not just yet, and doubtfully tonight.

Linh threw her head back when she let out a loud cry, right as her sweet pussy milked his tongue once more. Nathair groaned in satisfaction, taking what he could from her. His cocks brushed against the ground of the pool when he bucked his hips forward, desperate to sink them inside.

Once she stopped clamping him, he removed his tongue to lash at her clit to check if she needed more pleasure or not.

"Please," she whined. He let out a subtle growl and lowered his head once more. Linh quickly sat up to force him into letting her escape him, and she yanked a horn. "Why won't you have sex with me? You avoided being intimate last night too."

Damnit, Nathair bit within his mind.

He rose to lean around her on straightened arms, while wisely keeping his aching cocks submerged and away from the air.

He couldn't say he hadn't denied her last night, although he thought he'd been rather subtle about it. *She knows I can smell when she's turned-on.*

Having this female attempt to instigate sex by touching his back, scales, and chest until she'd slipped her hand dangerously close to his seam, had been a fucking battle. He'd shoved her against him, and just waited for her to go to sleep without letting her see he was awake and not in a fragment.

He hadn't liked lying to her in his own way, but he just didn't want to present a problem he didn't have the solution for. Apparently, he wasn't going to be given that grace.

"What's wrong?" she asked, cupping the sides of his jaw. "Nathair... I know it's not because of me; I know what your mind is like."

She had a rather intimate relationship with him and his lustful thoughts, despite his dislike of that.

"I told you that you are now a Phantom, and it comes with certain abilities," he signed.

Her lips puckered in thought. "Well, yeah. You explained all that to me yesterday."

"I have also made you compatible with me," he answered, dipping his head to the side to look down at her pussy. "This pussy is now mine. I claimed it, and you, when you gave your soul." Dark green entered his sight as he licked at his maw, and he brushed his fingertips over what he could touch of her folds. "You are no longer safe from my seed. You are now my b-r-e-e-d-a-b-l-e – breedable – bride."

"Oh," she rasped on parted lips.

"There is a spell to prevent it," he continued. "However, I do not know it."

Weldir had taught him much, as he'd seen many of his offspring perform many spells. He was a voyeur, one who watched to better learn and understand – even if he was uncomfortable with such knowledge.

Nathair's death had scarred his creator, even if he'd never

admitted it. Weldir liked to be prepared, and gave knowledge as much as he could to *all* his offspring through his female, the Witch Owl.

But this wasn't something Weldir knew how to do, only of its existence. Despite being a voyeur, even *he* turned away from watching his offspring mate.

"I am waiting until I cannot take it anymore," Nathair admitted, as his sight bled to purple once more. "I ache to be inside you, Linh, but I will figure it out on my own when I grow so desperate that I disregard my own cravings."

A sadness radiated around his heart, as he thought, *When the desire to breed you gives way to my need for you.*

Nathair didn't know if this was a Mavka longing, or just a deep one of his own, but he wanted to share in life with his bride. He wanted younglings, and to see this female grow them – the evidence of their union and how it continued.

"Why didn't you tell me?" Linh asked, and he didn't like the hurt in her voice.

"I already know how you feel about younglings," Nathair admitted. "You do not feel the same way."

Despite the heaviness of the conversation, his cocks continued to thrum in desire. Talk of knocking up this female was keeping him rock hard, and he was beginning to have thoughts of pumping into her anyway. Just the thought had him shivering in delight, and he'd just *adore* it if she would moan for him as he filled her with seed.

"I never said that." She frowned more deeply as her gaze bounced over his skull. "Why do you – Oh!" She gave a small laugh. "Nathair, I didn't really know you that well. We didn't have a relationship, and the idea of getting pregnant scared me for that reason."

"Are you saying–"

Before he could finish, Linh darted her hand into the water and cupped the head of a cock. Purple darkened in his sight, and he rose up to slam his hands against the ground next to her with a menacing *hiss*. Just the lightest damn touch from her nearly had him shoving her on one of his cocks.

He was pent up, needy, and he *hungered* to be inside his bride.

The laugh that fell from her sprinkled chaos around his heart, only for her to soothe it when she cupped his snout.

"My gosh, you can be rather beastly when you want to be." The open affection to his skull had Nathair gliding his claws into her hair, and his hips lifted higher out of the water. "I don't mind, you silly Duskwalker. You are my *husband*, and I your... bride? Wife? You can tell me later what you prefer."

"Bride," he instantly answered.

Fuck wife! You are the bride of a Mavka.

"I want you inside me, Nathair. I love you, trust you, and I don't mind what happens."

He wasn't going to argue with that. Actually, he wouldn't, not now that she'd given him permission to do whatever the fuck he wanted.

Leaning forward so he could bury his bony snout into her hair, he directed her head to the side so she could see his right hand. He licked her ear, panting over it, as he signed, "Can I put both my cocks inside you then?"

She gave a muffled moan as she nodded, only to belt out a squeal when he flipped Linh onto her back. He placed his hands on either side of her and lifted his hips until his cocks were no longer submerged.

Biting her lip, Linh looked down at them, but Nathair didn't waste a second. He twisted his hips until the end of one shaft nestled against her entrance and waited impatiently for her to look up at his skull.

With a light growl, he slammed his left cock inside her to the base in one quick thrust. Her back lifted off the ground as her hands fisted near her chest, her lips parted on an "Oh!" His insides instantly clamped up at the heavenly tight heat that greeted him. *Fuck, she feels so perfect.*

With most of his tail still in the water, and leaning over his bride, Nathair began to thrust.

That's it, little female, Nathair purred down at her. *Loosen up for me.* He removed his cock so he could shove the other one inside her, letting her snug core greet it in welcome.

When she tightened as though she was about to orgasm, he pulled out. Now that he was allowed to have his unrestricted fun with her, he didn't let her come – he didn't want Linh tiring too soon. Squeezing his cocks together to make them seem smaller, he nestled their combined heads against her pink entrance.

Nathair pushed *hard*. Seeing she wasn't going to take him with ease, when she winced as if it was beginning to hurt, he healed her. He'd take the pain of his own thrust, so long as she stretched this perfect cunt around both his cocks.

He looked down to watch himself mount his bride properly for the first time. The lips of her pussy flared as he began to sink in with a growl slipping from him. *Oh fuck, yes.* Heat greeted him, wetness kissed him, and he felt her slowly accommodating him.

The moment the rims of his cockheads popped inside, a quiet hiss resonated from him. *Hot. So hot and tight.* A ripple spreading out from his groin made his scales lift in waves up and down his body. He pumped back and forth, reaching further and further inside her, feeling her slowly accepting him with the help of his healing.

He was thankful he wouldn't need to attempt a second body-altering spell.

It was obvious her body couldn't handle this much girth, his size a bit too large and cumbersome for her human body, but she felt so damn good. Each inch he sunk inside pinched at his own cocks and tentacles, yet her accepting them both soothed him.

Linh had tightened beneath him, but her little moans were rapture. Her hips dipped back and forth, like she was trying to help him.

Barely a quarter of the way inside her, Nathair collapsed around her at the squeezing pleasure that threatened to break him. He wrapped his arms around her, and cupped the back of her head and kneaded her arse. *Perfect. She's so perfect.* His arms and hands shook as he held her, while constant groans fell from him the more he pumped. *Deeper. Take all of me, Linh.*

He panted against her hair, then nudged her in appreciation of finally being able to do this. To take this lovely female the way he'd always wanted to. *Mine. Little female, you are all mine.*

The further he penetrated her, the more he slipped up until the top of her head was just out of reach of his snout.

His cocks constantly swelled, thickening in enthusiasm and excitement. When their hips nestled up against each other's, his tentacles snapped around the crooks of her thighs, locking them together. With his chest tight in tenderness, his groin radiated in profound pleasure.

He stopped healing her so she could feel how full she was, hoping she would loosen even more now that he was completely buried. They were utterly connected, and he'd paused to let them both adjust.

Linh had her arms wrapped around his middle, her cute nails digging into him as she panted against his chest. Her thighs pillowed around his wide hips, and the balls of her feet pressed into his sides to keep him locked in. There was not a single space between their meshed bodies.

I'm... on top of her. And she wasn't fretting to get away.

A deep, desirous pant fell from him, and he gave her room to look up at him. Her pretty eyes sparkled with lust, while her face looked feverish.

Nathair glanced beyond her. Now that she'd swallowed him, clarity rained in his thoughts. Dark orange threatened to invade his purple sight when he realised he'd mounted her against the hard, uneven rock like a beast. He hadn't even left the pool properly, as most of his tail still lay within it.

He drifted his sight to the makeshift bed that suddenly looked too far away. It would be softer, and a better place to fuck his precious bride.

"You're so big," she whispered, and her pussy spasmed around his cocks. "I can feel your heartbeat inside me. I love it."

Unsure if she was just vocalising her thoughts, or trying to reassure him, any hope of moving them was stolen by her words.

You love both my cocks inside you, little nightingale? Nathair thought with a groan, drawing back his hips slowly. *You like me stretching you with two?* He shoved into the snug nestle of her cunt and watched as her head tipped back on a moan. *I'm going to fuck this pussy until I've flooded it with my seed.*

A husky pant escaped his parted maw. *I'm going to breed you, and watch you grow ripe with my youngling, Linh.* Dark green flickered in his sight from his thoughts, his desperate craving.

He lowered his body until he'd trapped her beneath him. Her head rested on the crook of his elbow and his hand gripped her shoulder to keep her secured in place for his rutting, while his other arm crossed down her back to grip her arse. His tail fins brushed against the insides of her thighs when he shunted his hips away, only to shove back in.

Dangerous excitement had his thrusts hitting harder, but he kept them slow so he could feel the way she was formed. So he could feel every inch of her drenched, textured, spasming cunt sucking on the lengths of his cocks. So she could experience each one of his tiny nodules popping in and out of her until he nuzzled the tips of his cocks against her cervix.

Pretty female, he groaned as he closed his sight to take in her warmth, her scents, the way her lungs sung the sweetest, lewd song for him. Her skin was so soft, her body docile and tender as he crushed it beneath his weight, and she hugged him closely.

He'd always wanted to hold her this way – to shield her as he fucked into her body. To be held deep within in return had his heart racing in adoration – only for it to stutter when her inner walls snapped tight around him.

She gave a scream as liquid squelched within her. *Fuck! She's squeezing me.* His hips picked up speed as she came around his cocks, milking them like she wanted to rob them of seed before he was ready to give it.

Nathair wanted to breed his little female, but he wanted to have lots of *fun* doing it.

She clawed at his back, tearing at his scales, and they lodged under her nails until she broke them off. His thrusts felt wetter with their combined fluids, her orgasm and his lubrication mingling to make a unique and perverted scent that was wholly theirs.

"Nathair," she called on a broken cry. "Don't stop. You feel so good."

A tremor wracked down his long spine until water flicked behind them from his tail. *Fuck, Linh.* He pulled her tighter against him as his seed sacs clenched hard and his dual cocks tried to separate inside her when he swelled in delight.

"You smell so nice, like waterlilies and moonflowers," she mindlessly rasped against his chest. She licked at his scales, kissed them, as if she wanted to suck on the taste of his flesh. "You're so strong, and I love the way your body feels against mine, how your scales scrape against my skin."

Her hips bucked back and forth, gyrating like she needed more friction. She didn't care where they were, or that they were on the hard ground. All she seemed to want was more.

She was fucking pulverising his heart and mind. *She feels like bliss.* Every part of her essence was washing over him.

And when her pussy smothered his cocks in a second clamp and held on, Nathair couldn't hold back this time. His tentacles squeezed her to him, giving her no chance to escape. His muscles lost all their strength as his seed sacs clenched repeatedly in unison, and his sight flickered open just so it could pulsate.

He came within his trembling bride, and each spurt was like

liquid bliss spilling from him. The pleasure clutched his groin, his flesh, his very bones, as he produced a quaking, euphoric groan. They came together, and it somehow broke his mind, shattering him so completely it went silent.

He needed more.

The moment her body released him, and his tentacles unlatched, Nathair slipped his cocks from her. He flipped her onto her knees and chest, fisted himself into one big cock, and slammed inside her to the hilt.

His tongue hung from his frantically panting maw as he leaned around her on straightened arms. Looking down, he forced his tentacles to curl back so he could have the freedom to watch as he rammed into her.

Mine, he growled, as he pulled back, only to double the strength of his next slam. She bounced, but his wrist pressing into the top of her shoulder kept her rooted for him. *Mine.* Her knees stayed parted, her back never stopped arching as she tilted her arse just right for his cocks.

Linh let him fuck her hard while she was on her knees, while he towered around her, like he pinned her there by the sheer force of his will. Her lips were parted wide, and she produced moan after moan that grew faster along with his increasing hip speed.

He watched as his earlier release slowly bubbled out of her and into the puddle they'd already made. *My female, my bride.*

She bent her elbow and gripped his wrist like she wanted to latch onto him. The backs of her thighs and arse grew red from his tail and hips constantly slapping against her. It didn't take her long to come for him, and that only elated him further, made him more ruthless with her fragile human body.

That's right, fucking scream for me! Fuck singing – he wanted her to belt out how thoroughly he was taking her body, making it his, pleasuring it. He wanted her so loud her whole village heard the way he made bliss dig its claws into her. *Is this what you wanted, Linh? Do you like having a Mavka inside you?*

Her clenched eyes never opened, but her cheek brushed against the rock when she nodded.

Nathair bent his back to lean down to her. He didn't slow his thrusts, instead quickening them, and her little cries never quietened.

"You are mine, little nightingale," he growled against her hair, realising she could probably hear him. "Mine to fuck, to fill, to breed however I please. Do you like that?"

She gave him a whimper in answer, and he took that as a deeply satisfying yes.

"Good," he rasped with a pant as his second orgasm neared. "I'm all yours, female. You can have me whenever you like. *Always.*"

"Please, Nathair," she rasped out.

"Just a little more," he pleaded, quickening his hips to race her, to reach his end before she could ask him to stop. "I'm so close. Just let me use your pretty pussy a little more."

I want to fill her again, make sure my seed is deep. Since he had two cocks, they didn't quite line up inside her properly. He wanted to flood her until he knew her little womb had taken as much as it could.

"You're so perfect. So beautiful, so lovely. Your cries, your scent, your warmth." A shiver rippled his scales, and he gave her an agonised whine. "Take all of me."

When his tentacles snapped around her thighs and hips despite his desire to hold them back, Nathair rocked into her as seed climbed up his shafts. His head tilted back and his fangs exposed themselves when the pleasure that clutched him was even more intense than before. The strangest longing to sink them into her and keep her still for his mating struck him when venom trickled against his tongue.

Linh... Nightingale... Nathair released a haunting roar as his body seized. She started milking him when she was already about to be gifted more of his seed. His hips shoved hard against her arse as he started to come within her, and his repeated swells were accompanied by her pulsating squeezes.

Everything felt tighter, like they both wanted to crush him, and his sight blurred. Nathair registered nothing but her scream, the wet heat of where they were joined, and the way his back had arched. He roared at the ceiling, at the world, as he quaked.

His huffs were loud when he flopped forward on his arms, and he had to utilise all his strength not to fall on top of her. With her face turned to the side, he noted how flushed and sweat-soaked she was, how her long, straight eyelashes fluttered as his seed continued to trickle from her. A few last drops splattered into the large puddle on the ground, growing and pressing against her spread knees.

Just when his left elbow was about to cave in, Nathair flicked his tail forward to quickly get it underneath him. Grabbing her thigh from below, and palming her chest, he lifted her as he fell back against the ball of his tail. Laying Linh's back against his front, he looped himself in a way that kept her spread while he was nestled inside her swollen pussy.

Nathair rested back and just let himself bask in this afterglow with his bride.

"Holy shit," Linh gasped out between quick pants. "What the hell, Nathair? I thought my pussy was going to explode."

She twisted slightly to look up at his skull, and he rumbled out a purring chuckle. He cupped her right breast, as well as between her thighs, looking over her shoulder so he could watch himself spread her lips to get a better peek at her.

It did explode, many times. It came and came for him, giving him little bursts of liquid that had tasted tantalising in the air. *Pretend all you like, female, but you loved it.*

"I know I did," she stated, and he reared his head back.

"You heard that?" he asked out loud, and she nodded.

My mind is still quiet. Like after she sang to him and he was given a small rest. It was likely temporary, as it always was.

Another dark chuckle came from him as he played with her clit. She gave soft moans, obviously sensitive, but didn't stop him.

With the way they were lying, he was able to see everything. His dark-grey fingers touching her, his purple dual cocks still nestled inside her stretched hole, and his pearly white seed saturating her entire slit.

"I think we're going to need a door for the youngling I'm going to put inside you," Nathair purred against her, dipping his fingertips into the seed bubbling where her entrance met the base of his cocks.

Her eyes widened as she jerked her head in the direction of the darkened outside world. "Oh god, a door!" she squealed. "My whole village probably heard your roar."

Mmm, good. Let them hear.

Her lips pouted, as if she'd heard that thought. "Nathair. Can you pull out now? It feels really hot."

He palmed her stomach and healed her instead. "Better?"

She nodded before flicking him a curious gaze. It was the least he could do, and he did really want to stay how they were.

He wanted to pet and worship his beautiful bride, who looked thoroughly fucked.

I cannot wait until she gives me younglings. I plan to make them all aquatic like me. Actually, Nathair planned to make them little versions of himself.

I will need to feed them lots of sea creatures, but make sure they eat a snake whole first. He gave a hum as he plucked a nipple. *Perhaps different horns, though, so I can tell them apart.*

He licked against the nape of her neck affectionately.

But... one will do for now. He'd take the breeding slow, as he didn't want to rush.

We have forever, and I plan to have an easy life with her. A life that is filled with love, pleasure, and hopefully lots of kisses.

His orbs flashed bright pink as she gave him her pretty gaze.

"Would you like that?" he asked out loud, knowing she heard his inner pondering.

EPILOGUE

5 weeks later

With a quiet hum, Linh held her Duskwalker's hand as they walked through Duneside, the eastern village.

They had been rather wary of letting him inside, even with the letter from her father she'd brought. Those who accompanied their travels vouched for him as well, but it was what Linh offered that truly made them open their gates.

Protection.

In exchange for food and special medicinal herbs they grew and coveted the seeds of, Nathair was willing to offer protection. Even though he could heal with magic, Linh had advocated against the use of it for her villagers when her father asked.

Her father was coming up with all sorts of ways to exploit her partner, and when Nathair healed Kai's wounds, the man started using his mind. Which, honestly, was a bad idea. Her father's schemes often got him into trouble, even if he had the best intentions.

She'd explained that it meant Nathair would be forced to bear everyone's wounds, and her father grew ashamed and apologised. He hadn't known.

But Nathair was willing to be a protector if it aided her people. *He's just doing it because he knows it keeps me happy.*

He shouldn't need to come to Duneside often, considering they were just as fortified as Ashpen Village. Her people were also offering them their chains, since they didn't need them due to Nathair's orange dome keeping the Demons away.

So long as Duneside wasn't infiltrated by monsters, Nathair wouldn't have to do much. Just come when called if they wished to safely expand, and perhaps watch over them when they farmed the tall seasonal crops that lay outside their protective walls. The open trade and expansion of resources would be beneficial for all, and perhaps they could make a new town between the two and expand the area.

The northern Demonslayer guild protected a safe haven. *With Nathair's help, maybe we can make our own.*

It was a dream, but one she loved.

Nathair's grip on her hand was tight, as he was uncomfortable with strangers staring at him, but he'd grown accustomed to the stares of humans. They often visited her village, since they kept being invited over, and Nathair allowed it. Actually, he seemed joyous at the thought over the last two weeks, practically patting her on the bum to make her walk faster.

He's so possessive. She placed her free hand on her rounded belly. *He's also a big show-off.* She had a funny feeling that was why he'd agreed to bring her all the way to this village today: more people to show what he'd done to her.

He was the world's most enthusiastic father-to-be, and he was very delighted to let everyone know he'd been between her thighs. Linh was rather nervous about the whole thing, considering she'd been pregnant for a little over three weeks and she felt like a bloated whale.

Her face had swelled, her feet too, and why did no one warn her about the wretched *back* pain?! She waddled, *waddled,* for pity's sake.

Apparently all the rigorous sex they'd had for two weeks leading up to the fertile days of her cycle had allowed him to truly flood her. *Twins? For my first pregnancy?* Nathair had been able to hear their little heartbeats and informed her of them – and anyone else who would listen to this news.

He often had the side of his skull pressed against her stomach, constantly listening to them as they grew. It was a sweet moment they shared in the privacy of their cave, and she loved seeing his orbs glow bright pink whenever they cuddled like this.

She'd been hoping they might be a mixture of them, but nope... apparently not. Nathair swore they would be featureless little Duskwalkers. *I hope they'll be cute.* She planned to put them in little dresses and outfits, no matter what they were.

She'd adore them regardless.

Nathair said he didn't want to have more children for a while, and the fact they were twins had her rather thankful. Being a new mother to two creatures she didn't really understand was going to be a hard battle.

He also said he wants to visit his brothers once we're used to them. It'd take at least a month to journey to them, and going beyond the mountains she'd never left, let alone to the Veil, was kind of frightening. As much as she trusted Nathair to keep them all safe, the idea of going to the Veil had her wanting to come up with excuses.

She always fell short when she knew how much it would mean to him.

Not long ago, he'd told her he didn't wish to endanger his brothers and their brides with his crazed presence. With her at his side, he'd expressed that he felt he had the strength to face them – as well as the reassurance of her voice and their bond snuffing his hunger.

He's done so much for me. It's the least I can do.

She'd go anywhere for him, just as he was doing so for her.

Linh nearly tripped when the tiniest pebble unsteadied her. *My feet are killing me today.* She hid her wince.

If Nathair knew she was in pain, he'd carry her like she was as fragile as glass. She wanted exercise, especially as he wouldn't have sex with her – to her dismay. She felt like she hadn't moved in a week.

"Are you okay?" she asked when they were almost at the gate.

Since they'd come to an agreement with the head of this village, they were leaving. She'd promised Nathair they wouldn't linger.

"I'm fine," he signed with his left hand. "I want to go home. These humans are making the fragments louder."

They were gossiping as they followed the freaky monster in their home. Everyone was nervous, despite the mayor explaining the details already. She couldn't blame them for wanting to come and stare, even if it was rude. She was ashamed to admit she would have done the same thing.

She hated that being around people made the voices harder for him to bear, only because she didn't like how much they bothered him. He always seemed exhausted afterwards.

When they reached the exit, Linh turned to Natasha, the mayor. A crowd formed a semi-circle around them.

"Thank you again for your hospitality," Linh stated, holding her hand out.

The tanned woman with blonde hair and a busty figure gave a deep laugh. She gripped the end of her baton weapon as she leaned forward at the offer of a handshake. The burly woman almost crushed Linh's daintier fingers.

"No problem, daughter of Tahlia. Your mother and I used to be good friends, and if she's chosen to trust this Duskwalker, so will we. We're thankful for your offer, and we look forward to having a stronger union between our villages." Then she swept a few loose strands of hair towards her low ponytail. "Lord knows we need some prosperity after what we've gone through."

Linh gave a small laugh in return, only to cringe when one of her kids kicked her in the damn bladder. *I hate it when they do that.*

"You can say that again," Linh answered with strain.

Natasha then gave her attention to Nathair. "Thank you again for ridding us of our bandit problem. Once the head was gone, the rest scampered away with their tails between their legs. We look forward to your protection."

"You are welcome," Nathair signed, in which Linh interpreted. "I am willing to do anything for my bride and our younglings."

As if he wished to highlight that, he cupped the side of her rounded belly and pulled her closer into his side.

Linh interpreted again. When she received an awkward cough from Natasha, her cheeks warmed. "Sorry. He's very proud."

"I bet," Natasha stated with a grunt. "You're a very beautiful woman. I bet he feels lucky."

Nathair's answering purr gave away how he felt exactly just that. His purr sputtered, only for a quiet hiss to rattle from him.

Like a bolt of lightning, he disappeared from her side.

A few screams came from the crowd when Nathair lifted a man by the throat and held him above his serpent skull. He gave the man a menacing snarl with his orbs crimson.

Linh's eyes widened when he was so irritated his fins flared to their ends. She had to admit, the back one flaring into over three feet in length was frightful.

"What the fuck?" Natasha yelled, turning to him as she removed her baton.

Linh put her arm out. "Don't," she warned.

She walked to the middle of the parted crowd to be at Nathair's side. She wouldn't ask him to stop, since she'd rather defend his actions as she looked up at the kicking brute.

Her lips pursed as she gave him a glare.

"Nathair is very particular. He doesn't mind people being offensive towards him, but he will not stand it if someone speaks badly of me."

"Brutus, you idiot," Natasha cursed, slamming her baton away. "You said something stupid again, didn't you? Of course the Duskwalker can hear your whispering!"

Now that his warning had been given, Nathair gently placed the man on his feet. He crumbled and looked as though he was moments from wetting himself.

Nathair turned to Linh and, with jarring movements, signed, "I want to leave. Now." He dipped his skull towards Natasha, and Linh noticed how much his fingers shook with controlled rage. "Before I change my mind about assisting these people."

Seeing she now had an infuriated Duskwalker, Linh ushered them out of the village before someone else could get under his scales.

She squealed in surprise when he suddenly picked her up. He darted into the forest, up a hill, and then down it, trying to put as much space between them and Duneside as fast as he could.

When they were far enough away that not even Nathair could hear the villagers, he halted. He balled his tail around them, settled them on top of his folds, and hugged her tightly. Burying his snout into the crook of her neck, he produced a quiet growl, which grew with each twisting nuzzle of his head.

She could tell the big guy was trying to pacify his own anger and was failing miserably.

"It was that bad, huh?" she cooed, petting his skull in hopes of soothing him.

Linh was aware some people called her a freak. Many couldn't swallow that she'd married a Duskwalker, and even less so that she'd physically mated with him. Some people from her village had left, stating they couldn't stand to live near such abhorrent behaviour.

They stated it was wrong, disgusting, and an affront to nature.

It hurt at first, but Nathair was always sweet and affectionate. He eased her heart by holding her like she was the most exquisite thing in the world. He made her feel special, and his love was intense.

It was enough to make her not mind their hatefulness when the love she received outweighed it. Plus, the important people in her life accepted it, and that's all that mattered.

Although Dad did get a bit pale when I told him I was pregnant. He'd been whining about grandkids since the moment she became an adult, and she rubbed that in his face when he'd behaved strangely about it. He admitted he thought part of her trauma meant that she'd chosen a partner she couldn't be physically compatible with, without knowing it was entirely the opposite.

Well, *had* been the opposite, until recently.

For the past week, Nathair wouldn't have sex with her, and she was starting to get really fucking mad at him over it.

Even if she managed to turn him on by giving him all the kisses and touches she knew he craved, the big Duskwalker wouldn't put his cocks in her. For some reason, being pregnant was making her body crazed for it, and the constant denial was crushing her heart and ego.

Linh was trying to be patient, but she missed being intimate with him.

"What did he say?" Linh asked out of curiosity, since Nathair was being needier than normal.

If he nuzzled her any harder, he'd start grinding her skin off.

"I don't wish to say," he signed, before palming the side of her stomach. He caressed it.

She could almost hear him thinking 'mine.'

"Just tell me, Nathair," she demanded, grabbing one of his horns so she could tug his head back.

He gave her a *bleurgh* noise with his maw parted, as he leaned back to stare down at her with reddened orbs. "Why do you want to know?" he signed with pointed movements, as if he couldn't understand her. "It is unpleasant."

Linh shrugged in answer, showing him she didn't really care what a stranger thought. He assessed her reaction, but he knew her better than anyone. Now that she was curious, she was stubborn enough to not let it lie.

He gave an annoyed huff, only to tilt his skull down to watch himself rub her side. Then he used both hands to sign, "He said you were a crazed woman whoring her pussy out for protection."

She stiffened at that. *Wow. That's really disgusting.* Was the idea of her loving Nathair that unbelievable that people would rather jump to such a horrible assumption?

Pursing her lips, she eyed Nathair's skull warily before her gaze slipped to his reddened orbs. She understood why he was angry, as she wasn't pleased either, but his reaction in Duneside wasn't beneficial.

I want people to see him, and Duskwalkers, the way I do.

Reaching up, she cupped the underside of his bony jaw and brought his head down to her level. She rubbed her cheek back and forth against his, hoping to soothe him.

"I know the things you overhear can be horrible, but you shouldn't worry about them, Nathair. Who cares what strangers think?"

She pulled back so she could drift her palm over his brow bone, down his temple, and brushed her thumb over his cheekbone. Linh gave him a warm and affectionate smile.

"All that matters is I think you're wonderful."

Despite how his body began to soften until she was carrying a small amount of his head weight, he blew an annoyed huff.

He retracted his head to sign, "But I don't like it when they are callous towards you."

"And I don't like that they say horrible things about you, but there's nothing we can do."

Nathair wiggled his head while licking at the inside of his mouth. Just the simple action, and she could read his thoughts. *'I could kill them.'* Or, at least, something of that nature.

Seeing this was a losing battle, Linh sighed. "How are the voices?"

"They are fine," he signed, until she lifted a brow. "They

are better now that we are away from the town."

Since obtaining her soul, Nathair hadn't receded into as many intense trances as before. He claimed that now they were bonded, all his senses seemed to focus on hers more. The loss of his hunger allowed her scent to be more soothing and her heartbeat more lulling – rather than both tingling at his gut.

Nathair was also more obsessed with her in almost every way.

She peeked up at her soul, which no longer bore a single palm print on it. It slept on its side with its knees to its chest and its hands clasped together under the cheek it was lying on. It was bright, appeared to be at peace, and she adored seeing the way it rested comfortably between his hooked ram horns.

"How are your feet?" he asked, obviously wanting to get away from the sensitive subject of his mind. He grabbed one of her calves and began kneading the tender muscle.

"A little sore, if I'm being honest." Then she crossed her arms and turned her head away with a false pout. "Doesn't help that *someone* won't have sex with me to make me feel better."

Nathair chuckled at that.

She knew why. Her womb had dropped to support their growing kids, and it made her smaller inside. Nathair was worried about hurting her and them, and would rather forgo sex.

"I still pleasure you," he argued, licking at his maw.

Her thighs clenched at that, only to immediately soften when he kneaded her other calf.

"Yeah, but licking and fingering me isn't the same and you know it," she grumbled, wishing her cheeks hadn't grown warm in memory of their nightly touches – in which she was the only one receiving.

I don't know how he holds back.

Nathair cupped the back of her head to keep her still, and dragged his tongue across her cheek. When he pulled back, his orbs were purple, and she had to resist the urge to bite her lip and tease him into getting her way.

His gestures were gentle and slow, as if he wanted his words to be taken lovingly. "Knowing that my bride feels adored and cared for makes me happy. You are carrying our younglings, not me, and I see how much it burdens you. I want you to feel appreciated."

Damnit. It was hard to stay mad at him when his feelings were so sweet and noble.

Just as she opened her mouth, he quickly cut her off. "Just know that you will have a very pent-up and horny Mavka. One that will be very excited to have you once more. You better be ready for me, little nightingale."

Linh let out a squeal when he dived for her. Wrapping his entire body around hers, he brought her into a protective hold that blocked out the late-afternoon sun. She giggled when his hand dived underneath her dress to cup the side of her belly, wanting to touch it directly as if he could feel the vibrations within through his palm.

"I think you should be more worried about how I will be! I'm going to punish you for making me wait," Linh stated around giggles. She wrapped her arms around his neck, thankful she was comfortable enough to feel this way about him, about intimacy, and their relationship.

In the darkness, she felt him open and close his maw mockingly, making the bones clack. Her smile grew when he cupped the side of her head and nuzzled her cheek with affection. Then he pulled back and bright-pink orbs shone down at her, making her heart flutter with tenderness.

He didn't even need to sign for her to know what he thought, what he was saying, and she knew he meant it with every part of his being. She adored seeing it glow while in this cuddle that allowed her to feel so secure and safe.

She kissed the side of his maw. "I love you, too, Nathair."

And I love that I'll have someone so attentive for the rest of my life. Someone who made her feel cherished in ways she never imagined, and made sure all her needs were met. Someone who had saved her when she was on the brink of drowning in fear, and made her love the skin she was in simply because it was a vessel for him to cherish her in every way possible.

Someone who was understanding on the days she wasn't okay, and never took it to heart when she lashed out without meaning to.

A Duskwalker who showed her it was okay to love a skull-headed serpent monster with all her heart.

Also by Opal Reyne

<u>DUSKWALKER BRIDES</u>
A Soul to Keep
A Soul to Heal
A Soul to Touch
A Soul to Guide
A Soul to Revive
A Soul to Steal
A Soul to Protect
A Soul to Embrace *(TBA 2024)*
(More titles coming soon)

<u>WITCH BOUND</u>
The WitchSlayer
The ShadowHunter
(More titles coming soon)

<u>Completed Series</u>

<u>A MM FAIRYTALE REIMAGINING</u>
Chased by the Fairy

<u>A PIRATE ROMANCE DUOLOGY</u>
Sea of Roses
Storms of Paine

~~THE ADEUS CHRONICLES~~
This series has been **unpublished** as of
20th of June 2022

If you would like to keep up to date with all the novels I will be publishing in the future, follow me on my social media platforms.

Facebook Page:
https://www.facebook.com/OpalReyne

Facebook Group:
https://www.facebook.com/groups/opals.nawty.book.realm

Instagram:
https://www.instagram.com/opalreyne

Twitter:
https://www.twitter.com/opalreyne

Discord:
https://discord.gg/opalites

TikTok:
@OpalReyneAuthor